Praise for

"This third book of the series does not disappoint! God's word is beautifully woven into the story and you are gently discipled as you drift through the lives of Suzanne, Jason, and the Somers family. Just when you think you know what is going to happen next, Rhine keeps you guessing, eagerly turning the pages to read more ...."

Michelle Reed

"Donna Rhine has a gift for writing stories that entertain and warm your heart, while teaching moral and Biblical principles. Her works may be fictional, but she has a 'real' relationship with the Lord, as evidenced in her everyday life and every book she writes."

Kathryn MacDonald

"A Heart Takes Flight is a compelling love story, showing God's amazing Grace and Mercy, a reminder that God will never leave us or forsake us. Though we don't always understand life's journey, keeping our faith and focus on Him, we can rest knowing God will bring us through. All of Donna's books have touched me in some way and this was no exception. A great read! I loved it!"

Kim Russell

Finding a great wholesome romance that keeps your attention is not easy, but *A Heart Takes Flight* is a rare delight ....

Donna's books are refreshing, inspiring, and uplifting. Her sweet and non-offensive presentation is a true reflection of her love for God, her husband, family, and others, crafted in a completely beautiful way ... one of my favorite authors.

Beth Henninger

A Heart Takes Flight

Donna Rhine

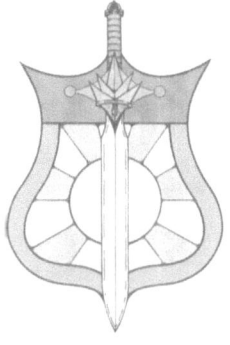

A Heart Takes Flight Donna Rhine

© 2011 Donna Rhine

Published by:
Armoury House Publishing
P.O. Box 60
Carleton, MI 48117 USA

http://www.ahpsite.com

ISBN-10: 0-615-48666-5
ISBN-13: 978-0-615-48666-6

Library of Congress Control Number: 2011908781

All scripture quotations, unless otherwise indicated, are taken from The King James Version of the Bible.

Author: Donna Rhine
Cover: Steve Rhine, James Dunayski, Chamira Jones
Editor: Rebecca Hayward, William Abbot, Kathryn MacDonald
First U.S. Edition 2011

Cataloging Data

Rhine, Donna, 1958-
  A heart takes flight/ by Donna Rhine. -- 1st U.S. ed.
      p. cm.
  ISBN-13: 978-0-615486-66-6 (pbk. : alk. paper)
  ISBN-10: 0-615486-66-5 (pbk. : alk. paper)
  1. Marriage--Fiction. 2. Runaway--Fiction. 3. Frontier and pioneer life--Michigan--Fiction. 4. Step Family--Fiction. 5. Domestic fiction. I. Title.

For current information about releases by Donna Rhine or other releases from Armoury House Publishing, visit the author's Web site: http://www.daisytales.com or http://www.ahpsite.com

Printed in the United States of America
tv1 05JUN20
cv1-2 02AUG11

Acknowledgments

*Let your light so shine before men, that they may
see your good works, and glorify your Father which is
in heaven.*

Matthew 5:16

The people who influence me the most and have a profound effect on the way I write are those who simply live out their faith before me. Although their imperfections, like mine, are present, their relationship with God cannot be denied. The fruit of His Spirit is evident, and they trust Him as their provider of all things in the spiritual and physical realm. The realization of how much God has used their influence for His glory and my good never ceases to amaze me. You know who you are. My heart rejoices over you.

To those who continue to pray for me, I am so thankful. No doubt, prayer changes everything.

To my husband Stephen—my dearest friend, God's favor was shining down on me the day we were joined in marriage—the love we share is a gift I will always treasure.

To Pastor Rocky Barra, thank you for allowing me to weave your life-giving messages into this book. Your input was, is, and always will be invaluable.

James Dunayski, thank you for sharing your illustration gifts, I continue to be blessed by your efforts. Chamira Jones, your finishing touches are amazing.

Joy Grzywacz, thanks for allowing me to use your image on this cover.

To My editors, Rebecca Hayward, William Abbot, and Kathryn MacDonald, thank you for all your input and hard work. Your expertise gave this novel the finishing touches it needed.

May God bless you abundantly for the many ways you have blessed me.

Love,

Donna Rhine

A Heart Takes Flight

A Heart Takes Flight   Donna Rhine

Contents

The Michigan Chronicles

The Michigan Chronicles are a collection of stories from the days of yesteryear. The adventures begin in the nineteenth century, with two families farming in a small pioneer community nestled along the Huron River. The site, now known as Ypsilanti, is where the old Indian trail crossed over the Huron River. Come travel to a place in time where life was simpler ....

He Loves Me!

Prologue

Ypsilanti, Michigan Territory

August 1834

T HE SOFT GLOW OF DAWN seeping through the windows guided her steps as Jayne Somers descended the creaky stairs and moved quietly through the house. Her hungry family would be waking soon. Eggs would need to be gathered, but first things first—a cup of tea was in order. As she entered the kitchen, her eyes filled with glee. Her middle daughter Suzanne was lying on her arms at the table, half asleep. "Full of vim and vigor this morning, are you, Suz?"

Suzanne's eyelids lifted just enough to peer up, but the illuminating smile on her mother's face could not be ignored. "You're up early and cheery to boot. Did I miss something?"

"I would have shared my wonderful news with you last night, but you were in bed when I came home."

"News?" Suzanne rubbed her weighted eyes and forced herself to sit up. Her mother was alight with pleasure, and while pleased to see her so happy, a dreadful feeling washed over her. Suzanne watched as her mother moved effortlessly about the room—as if in a dreamlike state.

Jayne, having no desire to rush the moment, added wood to the cookstove. After stoking the flames, she filled the kettle and put it over to boil before joining Suzanne at the table. Reaching for her daughter's hand, she gave it a squeeze and was near to bursting when she finally said, "Honey, Josiah Ordan asked me to marry him last night."

Too stunned to move let alone respond, she mulled over her mother's news. She shouldn't have been surprised. After all, she had witnessed the tender glances between her mother and Josiah for months now. Still, she had convinced herself that the attraction would pass. The thought of her marrying another man tied Suzanne's stomach up in knots. "He asked you to marry him?" she reaffirmed.

"Yes, and I've accepted."

Suzanne's face snarled up as her thoughts spilled out, "Please, tell me you're not serious!"

Jayne's spirit stumbled. She hadn't anticipated a negative response and needed a moment to collect her thoughts. In fact, several ticked clumsily by before her bewildered words broke the silence. "I've been seeing Josiah for months now. You know how dear he is to me." *Father, give me wisdom in this. She's more vulnerable than I had thought.*

Suzanne could see nothing beyond her own anguish. Her mother's announcement felt too much like a betrayal. Clenching the folds of her dress, she closed her eyes, desperate to shut all this out. Her father's memory was so precious to her. She loved her mother too, but this ...

Her mind was a mull of confusion! She wanted nothing more

than to go back to her room and pretend this conversation never happened, but her mother was waiting. What could she say?

The warmth of the morning sun on Suzanne's face distracted her for a moment, drawing her gaze to the window—the same window she had stood at time and time again washing dishes with her father after an evening meal, not so very long ago. His memory brought unbidden tears to her eyes that flowed down her cheeks in great abandon. She was torn, having no wish to hurt her mother, but how could she remain silent?

When Jayne came close and hugged her, Suzanne said, "I'm sorry, Mom. I wish ... I wish I could be happy for you, but I can't."

Jayne's heart ached for Suzanne as she sat beside her and met her tearful gaze. "Honey, Jesse, Lizzy, Jared, and Joseph have given us their blessing ... Louise has too for that matter. I really don't understand your hesitation."

Her defenses heightened. "Apparently, I'm the only one thinking this through. How can you even consider marriage? Daddy's memory ... if you go through with this, his memory will be tarnished forever."

Jayne questioned the wisdom in pressing her, but she had to try and help Suzanne understand. "Your father loved me. He wanted me to go on with my life—to find happiness in his absence. That's what I've done."

Suzanne's eyes lowered.

"Would you feel better if we sat down and discussed this as a family?"

"No! It would do no good. I can't believe you'd even consider marrying that man!"

Jayne was convinced that the only man her daughter would

deem acceptable would be her father, and that was not possible. Like her, Suzanne would have to come to accept the things she could not change and go on.

Suzanne wrapped her arms around her stomach, trying to dispel the storm brewing inside. As she did, her childhood flashed before her mind's eye. The joy and comfort of her father's love had been a welcoming presence in all of their lives. How could her mother ..?

"Honey, try to look at this from my prospective. I loved your father. I always will, but he's not here. I long for someone to share my life with—someone to hold—someone to laugh and cry with—someone to love." Seconds drifted by before she softly added, "So does Josiah. God understands our need for companionship. We both need someone to grow old with. Josiah and I are blessed to have each other."

Some blessing! To think, you almost had me convinced that God understands my grief. First He takes my father from me, and now this! Feels more like a curse, if you ask me!

An awkward hush fell over the room. Tears trickled down Jayne's face as she gently implored, "Pastor has agreed to marry us on Sunday after church. I hope you can lay your uncertainties aside and share in this special occasion with us."

With tears welling in her eyes, Suzanne stood to her feet, and ardently stated, "You marry the man if you must, Mom, but don't expect me to welcome him into my father's house."

Jayne's eyes narrowed in on her daughter. "Suzanne, your father would not have approved of your disrespect."

"And tell me, Mom, how would my father feel if he knew another man was sleeping in his bed, kissing his wife, and raising

4

his children?" Suzanne did not wait for a response. She flew up the stairs in a whirlwind of intense emotion.

He Loves Me!

Chapter One

Lies and Deception

Ypsilanti, Michigan Territory
Summer of 1834

"AMY POTTER, you had better be teasing!" Suzanne Somers declared, annoyed that her friend would make such an outlandish request.

"You clearly don't agree," Amy said to her testy younger companion, "but I've given this much thought. We'll be safer traveling as brother and sister ...." She paused, giving Suzanne a chance to concede. When she only stared, Amy gave her an earful, "We don't have time to squabble. The stage is leaving in less than an hour. I'm more than willing to take you with me, even pay your way, but you need to be reasonable about this." Seconds ticked by before she saucily added, "Really, Suz, haven't you read the papers? They're forever expounding on the dangers of women traveling without a proper escort."

Suzanne rolled her eyes. "Some proper escort I'd make.'

Amy's arms spread wide in a confident gesture. "As you are well aware, I'm the queen of drama. I would gladly accept the male role in this ongoing saga, but I could never pass for a man

7

with these curls." Amy reached around and slung her mass of bouncy ringlets over her shoulder for emphasis. "It'll be so much easier for you to hide your silky lengths beneath my father's cocked hat."

When Suzanne offered no response, Amy concluded, "So! Now that we have that settled, I'll be counting on you to play the part of my overprotective brother, Zanne."

Suzanne's eyes narrowed in on her friend. "Not a chance!"

Amy stomped her foot in frustration. "Why are you being so mulish?"

Suzanne wasted no time reminding her, "You forget too easily! My father insisted on my sister dressing like a boy several years back, and look at where it landed her."

Amy's dainty hand rose to her throat. "Horror of horror's! Elizabeth married a man she adores. How tragic!"

"That's beside the point. The choice was taken out of her hands, and you know it. Duplicity may seem like a good idea now, but lies and deception rarely bring anything but trouble." When Amy grew quiet and turned away, Suzanne waited, hoping she would change her mind.

Facing her friend, Amy's expressionless features gave nothing away. "Suzanne, you either want to get out of this town or you don't. If I remember correctly, you're the one who came to me. You went on and on about your desperate need. I would love to have you along, but I'm not willing to put you in harm's way. Your family would never forgive me if I did. Besides, you're the one running away, you're the one who should be hiding her identity, not me. If you don't mind, I'd rather not have your brothers breathing down my neck. Enough said. I'll not quibble with you further. The decision is yours. I will be leaving on the noon stage with or without you."

Suzanne's eyes lowered. "I can't bear the thought of that man living in my father's house. I have to leave." Brown lashes swept up. "But really, Amy, is it necessary to go to such extremes?'

Amy's head dipped ever so slightly. "I'm afraid it is."

While Suzanne was not enthralled with the idea of traveling as a man, what choice did she have? Beggars can't be choosers. "Are you sure your doctor friend won't mind training an extra nurse?" Speaking the words sent chills up Suzanne's spine. *What was she thinking? How can I be a nurse?*

"New York's a big city, Suz. If he does have an objection, we shouldn't have a problem finding you gainful employment."

Suzanne needed time to consider her response, but time was running out. "I suppose you're right." Edgy, but resigned, she grabbed the stack of clothes from Amy's arms and went to put them on. Rolling her discarded feminine apparel, she stuffed the outer remnants of her old life into her carpetbag and rejoined her friend in the parlor. Noticing Amy's pensive mood, Suzanne asked, "How long before the new owners move in?"

"They're already in Ypsilanti. As a courtesy to me they've been staying at Hawkins House. I told them I'd be leaving on the noon stage."

She understood Amy's mournful state. It wasn't easy saying goodbye to the past. Even so, she was convinced it was time to make her own way in this world. Her family might be angry with her for leaving without a word, but with that man moving in, she could not in good conscience remain.

In an attempt to lighten Amy's dampened spirit, she held out her hands and spun around, showing off her new look. "So what do you think of your brother Zanne?"

Amy laughed through her tears. "The clothes are a good start, Suz, but we need to do something about your perfect complexion ... and all that hair. You're too well kept for a sodbuster's son, My Dear." Leaning close, Amy took an exaggerated sniff. "You smell like a bouquet of flowers. That won't do!" She grabbed Suzanne's hand and pulled her into her father's old room. "Papa's bottle of manly scent should do the trick."

"Grand! I'm not sure I want to know what else you have in store for me."

Amy packed a bag of men's toiletries, extra clothes, and a few other effects that might come in handy from time to time. She handed the bag to Suzanne, admitting, "We'd best get moving, or we'll miss the stage."

After glancing at her reflection in the mirror one last time, Suzanne gathered her belongings and stepped out the door. Shivering, she pulled her coat snuggly around her. The air was cooler than it had been in days, and although the gleaming yellow sun kissing her face was a complete contradiction, she was thankful for it's radiating glow.

Determined to shake the odd feelings swirling inside, her gaze rose to the heavens. It was a perfectly lovely day to begin anew. Why should she allow uncertainty to ruin it? While she could have lost herself in the splendor of her surroundings, Amy's ramblings interrupted her wonder.

"Suzanne, there are a few things you need to be aware of if you don't want folks to detect your gender."

Since Suzanne had lived with three brothers, she found it

absurd to have Amy, an only child, coaching her on gentlemanly manners—but coach her she did. Amy went on and on about the way she should walk, talk, and laugh. She even threw in a few crude gestures, since she didn't want her brother coming across as goody-two-shoes. Best to keep things real.

For a while the distraction kept Suzanne's mind off her apprehensions. Unfortunately, the closer they came to their mode of transportation, the more anxious she grew. If someone were to recognize her and tell Jesse, she'd be in a heap of trouble. He wouldn't think twice about coming after her and dragging her back home. He wouldn't understand. She couldn't stay. Leaving was her only option.

If they were careful, the cash Amy had from the sale of her father's farm would be enough to hold them until they were settled in New York.

Amy was coming out of the ticket office, and Suzanne, thinking it was high time she stepped into her role as Zanne, threw their bags up to the man who was loading the stage's rooftop. When no one else offered to help, she slung the rest of the bags up as well. Although her muscles were screaming from overexertion, she finished the task and then offered Amy her arm. Suzanne put on quite a show for the other travelers. Confident she was not recognized, she gave Amy a hand up and followed her into the coach. The other travelers were all settled, so Suzanne and Amy took the last of the available seats.

They were well underway before Suzanne breathed a little easier and allowed herself to enjoy the adventure at hand. Her eyes scanned the other passengers, before she began the introductions. "My name is Zanne, and this is my sister Amy.

We're pleased to meet you folks."

Amy nodded in greeting.

"Likewise," the handsome gentleman sitting next to Amy offered. "I'm Doctor Jason Michaels."

Amy's brow rose. "You don't say! Zanne and I are on our way to New York. We've been offered positions training under Doctor Nelson." A jot of conscience for her half-truth pulled at Amy's heart, but not enough to silence her. "I'm looking forward to becoming a nurse under his patient tutelage and only time will tell if Zanne has what it takes to become a Doctor."

Suzanne, losing interest in Amy's endless chatter about the world of medicine, stared out the window. No sense even trying to get a word in edgewise. Amy was already knee deep in conversation with the good doctor. In truth, Suzanne didn't really mind, as she listened in. She couldn't help it. Doctor Michael's deep masculine voice held a gentle strength she found difficult to ignore. Often, she would catch herself hanging on his every word, though she gave no indication that she was doing so.

"Good nurses are hard to come by, Miss Potter. Doctor Nelson is a fortunate man to have two willing apprentices."

"Medicine has intrigued both myself and Zanne for years, but our father thought it wise for my brother to finish school before heading to the big city." Amy, noting the strange look Suzanne sent her way, wondered if something was amiss. She made a mental note to question her friend when they were alone.

The last profession Suzanne would choose to pursue was doctoring. Not even nursing appealed to her. But she would have to play along until something that better suited her came along. For reasons of self-preservation Suzanne had failed to inform

Amy that she typically swoons at the sight of blood. Why, a simple discussion on the life-giving fluid pumping through her veins was enough to make her loose a meal.

Amy continued flirting with the young doctor, discussing her latest findings in the field of medicine. While Suzanne found it quite rude that the other couple on the stage had not been properly introduced before Amy and Doctor Michaels entered into their own private exchange, she withheld her opinion. Unwilling to call their manners into question, she convinced herself to relax and enjoy the journey. She hadn't been away from home in years. Besides, there would be plenty of time for introductions before they reached Detroit.

She and Amy were planning to stay in Detroit for three days before journeying on to New York. Leaving Ypsilanti when they did offered Suzanne a measure of comfort. She did not doubt that Jesse would come after her when he found the letter she had left under his pillow. Amy's would be the first place he'd look. While she hated to worry her family needlessly after all they had been through, she could not stay.

The long trek to Detroit brought to the fore many wonderful memories. Her parents were originally from New York. As newlyweds, they had left their comfortable lives amongst family and friends to homestead in the wilds of this Michigan territory. For several years they made their home in Detroit. Hearing about the rich farmlands in the Huron Valley, they once again pulled up stakes and migrated to Ypsilanti. Suzanne, still young at the time, could recall the horrible condition of the Sauk Trail. They were constantly moving trees and debris that had fallen across their path. As if that were not enough, the mud was so deep it took all of their efforts to keep the wagons rolling through the sludge. The Old Chicago road was a huge improvement from the trail the Indians had carved out.

"Excuse me, Sir ... Sir ... Oh, Sir ..."

When still Suzanne did not answer the elderly woman speaking to her, Amy stuck an elbow in her side and drew a quick response. "What?" Suzanne, realizing how feminine her voice sounded, cleared her throat and lowered it an octave or two before adding, "I swan, Amy! What'd you do that for?"

Her friend scowled as she motioned toward the elderly woman. "Watch yourself, Zanne! The nice lady has been trying to get your attention for some time now."

"Sorry, Ma'am. Lost in thought, I suppose ...."

The lady snickered. "I understand. I often find myself doing the same. We haven't been formally introduced, but my name is Tilley O'Malley, and this here is my husband Jed."

Suzanne offered, "Pleased to make your acquaintance. Is there something you needed, Ma'am?"

Tilley hesitated for the space of several seconds. "Actually there is. My husband and I would consider it a fine Christian act if you could give us a hand when we arrive in the capital city."

"How can I be of service?"

"It'll be dusk by the time we reach the fair city and you being a strong young man and all, I wonder if you'd be willing to help us transfer our luggage to the hotel for the night."

Nothing like buttering me up! Suzanne, having helped load their heavy bags onto the stage, wondered if she'd be able to carry them any distance. But then again, how could she refuse this dear sweet woman. "My sister and I have our own bags to attend. As long as you're in no hurry, I'd be glad to help."

Relief registered on her face. "Musta had a good upbringing, I'm thinking. Takes a kind soul to raise such a fine young man." Mrs. O'Malley glanced Amy's way before adding, "Your sister's a friendly sort as well."

"Appreciate you saying so, Ma'am." Cognizant of the lie she had just told, Suzanne sloughed it off. She'd never see these people again, so what did it matter. They already thought her a man, what was one more falsehood. "My father was called to his eternal reward, but you are right, Mrs. O'Malley, he was the kindest of men. Made no bones about letting us know how much we were loved."

"It shows."

Suzanne glanced at Jed, wondering if she should speak to him, just to be sociable, but the way he stared off into space gave her a bad case of the willies.

Tilley must have noticed and said, "Don't fret about the mister, Zanne. He tends to give others a bit of a fright, but he's harmless. Had dropsy about six months back and hasn't said a word since. I'm thankful he's able to move about and tend to his own needs, but he's not much company. He's as silent as the dead."

If only the woman's explanation would have helped. "Oh, sure ..." Zanne said, trying to cover her unease. However, when she took another peek and shuttered, her cover was blown. Some things just couldn't be helped. Embarrassed by her inability to handle his abnormality, she slunk down in her seat, tilted her hat forward and closed her eyes. Wouldn't you know it? The ailing man's face haunted her until she fell asleep.

Suzanne awoke to Amy softly calling, "Zanne ... Zanne, wake-up. We're here."

"Already?" She tried to sit up but the terrible crick in her neck made movement difficult.

Doctor Michaels, noticing her predicament, offered his services.

At first Suzanne wasn't too sure about letting him touch her, but then Amy's insistence made it difficult to refuse. Setting aside her discomfiture, she allowed him access to her slender neck. After a few slight manipulations, she felt like a new woman and offered her heartfelt thanks.

The sounds of nightlife tickled Suzanne's ears as she stepped out into the muddy street of Detroit. As much as she'd love to appease her curiosity, thoughts of a hot meal, a warm bath, and stretching out on a comfy bed lured her toward the hotel. Amy had gone to check them in, while Suzanne took several trips back to the stage before she managed to drag the last of the elderly couple's bags in.

Doctor Michaels was chatting with Amy while Suzanne said her goodbyes to the O'Malley's. They were planning to catch the ferry to Chicago early the next morning.

Suzanne, feeling like the odd man out, walked over to her friend, took one last look at the tall handsome doctor and said, "Amy, I'm ordering a bath and heading up to the room. Doc, it was nice meeting you. Thanks for letting my sister chaw your ear off. You spared me having to entertain her the whole long way."

Amy slapped Suzanne's arm in a buoyant gesture. "Thanks a bunch, Zanne!"

Jason grinned at their playful bantering and interjected, "We were just talking about having dinner together. I'd be pleased if you would join us, Zanne."

She tossed him a restrained smile. "If you don't mind, I'll let the other folks in this establishment play chaperone tonight. Amy, if you'll order me the special and have it sent up to our room, I'd be much obliged."

"You're sure you won't join us?"

Suzanne shook her head in denial before her eyes narrowed in on the good doctor. "I'll be counting on you to send my sister up to bed at a decent hour."

Jason's crystal blue eyes twinkled with amusement. "Your lovely sister will arrive at your door by no later then ten, Zanne, with her impeccable reputation still intact."

"I'm counting on that."

Jason offered his hand.

Hesitating a moment too long, Suzanne offered hers, but as she suspected his nearly swallowed hers up. She was hoping he wouldn't notice. However, the look Jason sent her way told her he had.

"Not to worry, Zanne. My hands didn't grow much until after my sixteenth year." Zanne's sly grin peaked Jason's curiosity. He couldn't put his finger on it, but there was something odd about this young man.

"Glad to know there's still hope. Good night, Sir ... Amy I'll see you in just a bit." She nodded and Suzanne turned to leave. Escaping the young doctor's scrutiny brought her the greatest measure of relief.

❀ ❀ ❀

"So tell me, Zanne." Amy asked as she plopped down into one of the high-backed chairs.

"Suzanne!" she quickly corrected. "Don't call me that when we're alone."

Amy rolled her eyes. "If I don't call you Zanne when we're alone, I might forget myself when we're with others. Are you sure you want to chance our secret getting out?"

"I suppose not, but I'm tired of this sham already. We were both brought up to speak the truth above all things. Every time I tell a lie the next one comes easier. That can't be a good thing."

"All these lies are grating on my conscience, too, but we don't have a choice right now. Another week and we can put all this behind us. You'll see. Before you know it we'll be back to our old selves."

Suzanne was not convinced they would walk away unscathed. After all, sin did have consequences, but she had agreed to cooperate, and so she would. She could only hope that her father wasn't watching from heaven. If he were, his disappointment in her would be great.

"Come on, Zanne. You've been a slug-a-bed for days now. I'm bored. The least you can do is take me for a nice afternoon stroll through town. I'd like to see how the city has changed before we leave."

Suzanne walked to the window and stared out. "Just open your ears, Amy. You don't have to go out there to know how much the place has changed. Seems harmless enough during the day, but the night sounds make me wonder who could be lying in wait.

Like walking into a 'den of lions' if you ask me."

Amy sneered. "You're exaggerating. Couldn't be as bad as all that!"

"Give it another hour ... you'll see! You can just stand here at the window and watch the town come alive. If you ask me, it's hardly appropriate for two young women to be out wandering the streets alone."

"Zanne, you haven't been out of this room since we arrived two days ago. You don't really know, you're just assuming. Besides, Doctor Michaels told me our steamer *Walk-in-the-Water* arrived this morning. We'll begin our journey east day after tomorrow and all I've seen is the dinning room—and that, no thanks to you. If it wasn't for the kind Doctor Michaels, I'd have been dinning alone all this time."

"Nag! Nag! Nag!" Suzanne exclaimed. Knowing her friend spoke the truth did nothing to ease her mounding irritation. Without thought, she snarled, "Where's the good doctor now? Entertaining another young lady?"

Amy's mouth dropped open. "That's not fair and you know it. He's been the perfect gentleman. Jason lives and breathes his faith." Amy giggled as she recalled their last visit. "Truth is, he reminds me of a younger version of Jacob Woods."

"What?" Suzanne never would have guessed.

"It's true."

"I hope you had the good sense not to mention ... well, us ...."

"No, Suzanne. I told you before and nothing has changed. My lips were sealed on the matter."

"Good ... so where is he then?"

"Picking up the supplies for his new practice. He's planning to catch the stage on Saturday."

Suzanne's head lowered. "Perhaps I've misjudged him. Just seemed like a bit of a flirt the way he caters to you."

Amy's long lashes fluttered. "A bit jealous, are you?"

Rolling her eyes, Suzanne scowled, looking all too much like the young gent she was pretending to be.

"You've got no room to complain about my nagging, Suz. You've been in men's clothes so long you're starting to act like one. What happened to the spirited young woman I boarded the stage with in Ypsilanti?"

"Her spirit stayed back in Ypsilanti." For a long moment, Suzanne stared out the window. When she finally turned back to face her friend, tears were trickling down her cheeks. "Oh, Amy, I feel horrible about making my family worry. I keep expecting Jesse to walk around the next corner and haul me back with him. The truth of the matter is, I want him to. I'm so confused—so depressed. That's why I've stayed in our room. Instead of being glad to be rid of them, I miss them something fierce."

"Running away has its downfalls, but you'll see. Each day will get easier. By the time we get to New York you'll be happy you decided to leave. If you had stayed home, you'd be getting used to your new dad being around the house."

"He's not my dad! He never will be ...." Suzanne shuddered at the thought. Why did her mother not see her relationship with Josiah Ordan as she did—as a betrayal to her father's memory? Even the thought of her mother remarrying made her feel sick inside. Going home was not an option. "You're right, Amy. I have to let go of my past and get on with my life."

Suzanne, relieved by her new determination, sent Amy a

devious grin. "Give me a minute to change into my male role and we'll check out the sights."

"Good. I'm glad to hear it."

"Ya know, Amy, it's too bad your dad didn't have a weapon amongst his things. I'd feel safer walking the streets of Detroit and New York if I had one handy."

Amy's friend was too cautious in her estimation. After all, no one would bother a young man and his sister out for an afternoon stroll ....

He Loves Me!

Chapter Two

The Cost of Duplicity

*T*HE VIBRANT SUN shimmering through the window had illuminated Suzanne's room throughout the day, but the evening shadows were falling fast. After lighting the lard-oil lamp, Suzanne's transformation into Zanne progressed with ease. She wasn't sure if she had become more comfortable with her role—or if she was merely resigned to playing it? Although her britches were huge, a leather belt wrapped around her waist cinched them nicely.

Amy was sitting on the bed, her eyes never leaving Suzanne's reflection in the vanity mirror as she slicked back her hair and bound it with a piece of rawhide. After slipping her golden brown lengths inside her shirt, she settled the broad-brimmed hat on her head. Confident it sat at just the right angle to enhance the look she was going after, Suzanne winked at Amy's reflection in the mirror.

"Do I make a passable escort?"

Amy's wily grin said it all. "You'll do fine for a plow chaser's daughter playing the part of my protective brother." Amy could not deny it; Suzanne was a natural actor. Few would question her gender. Even the most renowned playwrights would be proud to have someone of her caliber acting on their stage. No doubt, if the illustrious Shakespeare were alive to partake of such a performance, he, too, would be impressed.

However, Amy thought, *Suzanne's choice of clothing for this particular performance should have been left up to me. Father's Sunday-go-to-meeting shirt and black vest would have been more appropriate. Even so, the plaid serviceable shirt and tan waistcoat would have to do.* If they were going to continue this charade in New York, she would have to be more mindful of Suzanne's attire. No sense giving folks cause for ogling.

As they stepped out of the hotel, Suzanne offered Amy her arm as they strolled down Woodward toward the river, basking in the iridescent glow of the setting sun. The sound of laughter coming from several buildings up the way called to them, but they were in no hurry. They had just cleared the entrance to a lively tavern when an intoxicated man came flying through the swinging doors.

"And stay out!" the irate man roared from within. "One would think you'd know better than to get me all fired up so early in the day! Ain't had my rations yet."

Thinking it wise, Suzanne led Amy to the opposite side of the street, but it wasn't much better. A vast array of music rang out from several establishments, apparently hoping to lure unsuspecting patrons.

The dank air from the river, though invigorating at first

chilled Amy to the bone. The thin shawl she had wrapped around her shoulders offered little warmth. She would have to be better prepared come morning or she'd freeze on the steamer. Shivering she admitted, "I don't know what I was thinking, I should have brought along my cloak."

"We haven't come very far. Want me to go back and get it?" Amy teased. "Feeling gallant tonight, are we, Zanne?"

"My concern is for your welfare alone, Sis."

Amy smiled. "Thanks anyway. I'll be fine."

Suzanne was impressed by her surroundings. "For a town that burned to the ground, they've recovered nicely."

"Ypsilanti sure does pale by comparison."

Suzanne glanced back to see how far they had come from the hotel. When she turned back, the courthouse had come into view. "I wonder if that strange judge is still around?

"Woodward?" Amy asked.

Suzanne nodded. "I've read several articles on the man. Of course, all of them were historical pieces, but they were interesting. It was kind of eerie the way Woodward and Governor Hull marched in with their group only days after the fire and took over like dictators. The rumors still circulating about Woodward do make you wonder."

Amy's brow furrowed. "Wonder what?"

"If a judge who keeps a glass of brandy handy while he's on the bench can ever be considered wise or fair?"

"Sounds a bit eccentric if you ask me."

Suzanne nodded in agreement, but they had come upon a dressmaker's shop and stopped to gawk at the new styles on display. Her eyes scanned Amy's attire and couldn't help but comment, "Either Ypsilanti is behind the times, or these frocks in the window are new styles sent straight from Paris, France."

"Could be! I kind of like the deep pink. If we could afford such an extravagance, which one would you choose?"

"Amy!" Suzanne exclaimed in feigned shock and then leaned a little closer, "I'm thinking the maroon would be nice on Suzanne, don't you?"

Another couple had stopped to look and seemed to be hanging on their every word. "Perhaps you're right." Amy said as she reached for her friend's arm and the two of them continued on their way.

They had been walking for some time when Amy heard a commotion and glanced up the way. "Must be a skirmish of some sort. Let's take a look!"

"I don't know. Maybe we should head back."

"And miss the excitement? Where's your grit, Zanne?"

Still reluctant, Suzanne admitted, "Must be twenty people or more in that gathering."

"Must be something worth hearing about!"

Although Amy's excitement was contagious, Suzanne insisted on them approaching with caution. However, when Amy's curiosity got the best of her, she started weaving her way through the crowd. Though the two of them were separated, Suzanne could still see her. Suzanne was trying to get the just of what the crowd was arguing about when a robust boy of about ten, maybe twelve, years stood on the boardwalk railing, yelling out as he pointed her way, "It wasn't me I tell ya! There's your man. He's the one who took your goods, Sir."

The proprietor's thunderous words carried over the clamor.

"That sod buster with the broad brim hat?"

"Yes, Sir ... that's your man, I swear!"

Suzanne turned around, needing to see who the boy was pointing to, but there was no one behind her. In an instant the tables turned and folks were staring as if she were the scum of the earth, and it was their job to free their town of vermin like her. *This can't be happening!*

Suzanne could hear Amy yelling in the background, but it was too late. By the time she reached Suzanne, she was being led away by the long arm of the law. The man yanking on her arm wouldn't listen and before she knew it they were entering the Sheriff's office.

This is crazy! Amy thought, as the sheriff told Suzanne to empty her pockets and place the rest of her belongings on his desk.

Amy, knowing desperate times called for desperate measures, raised her voice, "Sir, if you would just listen, I could tell you that my brother has never stolen a thing in his life. Zanne and I were just out for a stroll, enjoying your fair city, when we heard the commotion from a distance and went to see what was going on. That's all! My brother has done nothing to break the law, Sir. You have to release him."

"Afraid that's not possible, Little Lady." He then turned to his deputy and said, "Take him back to his cell, Jed."

When Suzanne was taken through a door to conditions unknown, Amy started to bellow. "You can't do this! My brother is innocent I tell you—innocent!"

"You present a convincing argument, Little Lady, but I'm afraid your brother doesn't have a prayer. We've had more than our share of hooligans in this town. The judge won't flinch at sending him away. He's made it known that if we're ever going to have a civilized city, precedence must be set or mayhem will break out. Young men who choose to go astray will be made an example of. No doubt in my mind, he'll spend the next year at the workhouse."

"He can't!" Her hands rose to her aching head. "Do you mean to tell me that even a lawyer doesn't have a prayer at getting him out?"

"If you could find one before tomorrow morning, it might help."

Pulling out her hanky, Amy blew her nose and dried her tears. This was no time for hysterics; Suzanne needed her. She had to think—fast!

"Do you know of any?"

"No, Ma'am."

He wasn't jesting when he said this was hopeless. "There has to be something I can do. We're on our way to New York to begin our training with Doctor Nelson. We're supposed to leave day after tomorrow. We have boarding passes for *Walk-in-the-Water*."

"I sympathize with ya, really I do. You heard all those accusing Zanne."

"Those folks are nothing more than a lynch mob! That boy was just looking for someone to shift the blame on. If you ask me, they had their culprit and let him go. Now an innocent young man is going to suffer for their false accusations." No longer able to restrain herself, Amy crumpled into a nearby chair and gave in to her emotional state.

The sheriff, desperate to get this blubbering female out of his chair, moved to open a drawer on the far wall. He had an idea. It might not work, but it would get this frantic young thing out of his office and give her something else to think about.

"Here it is!" The sheriff said, as he pulled a piece of paper out of the makeshift file. His mustache lifted on one side before glancing at Amy, but his features were otherwise unreadable. "There is one exception the judge has made on rare occasions."

Amy's eyelids flipped up. *A ray of hope is better than no hope.* "What exception?"

"Now don't get too excited, it's a one in a million chance."

Too late, Sheriff! "Just tell me."

"No need to do that when you can read about it just as easy after you leave."

The sheriff's large hand took a firm hand on Amy's arm and he tried to lead her to the door, but she would have none of it. "I am not leaving, Sir. Not until I've spoken with my brother."

He shook his head. "That won't be possible, Miss."

"I won't leave until I do."

He took a deep breath and let it out. "You're testing my patience."

She held up her hand and spread her fingers wide. "Five minutes. If you give me five minutes with him I won't bother you until I read this paper and accomplish what it says."

Now that's a deal! He wasn't convinced she would accomplish anything, her being a stranger in town and all. Still, if allowing her to see her brother would get this curly-headed female out of his hair, then so be it. That was all that mattered to him. "Five minutes. Not a second more."

"Agreed!"

This is highly unusual, Miss ... but, if seeing him will ease your mind, then leave your belongings on the desk and follow me."

Amy, pleased that the sheriff did not insist on searching her, did as she was told. He then led her through a locked door, down a narrow hall, and then through another door that led to three cells. The first one housed a scraggily occupant, apparently sleeping off his latest binge. As Amy listened to him snore, she wondered if Suzanne would rest at all tonight. Amy found her friend sitting against the back wall of her cell with her hands wrapped around her skinny legs and her face buried in her lap. She could only assume Suzanne didn't hear their approach.

The sheriff stuck a huge key in the lock, turned it, allowed Amy to enter, locked the door behind her, and walked away. She could only hope he wouldn't conveniently forget to let her out. "Zanne," Amy said as she knelt down beside her and placed a gentle hand on her shoulder.

"Amy!" Suzanne squealed, instantly snapping out of her stupor. "How did you get in here?"

"The sheriff let me in. We only have five minutes, so listen closely."

"Amy, I didn't do anything wrong. I can't go to a men's workhouse! I'll never be able to keep up this charade."

"I know .... The sheriff gave me this paper." Amy pulled it out and handed it to Suzanne.

She read it out loud. "I, Judge Woodward, will consider only one exception to my ruling that a mandatory sentence be handed down to thieves and scoundrels causing a ruckus within the boundaries of Detroit, requiring the law to interfere. Should a prominent citizen in good standing in this or another community be willing to take this young man on as an apprentice for no less than one year, I will reconsider my judgment.

"Amy, this is all well and good, but how is this going to help me? I don't know anyone in Detroit."

"I understand that, but the paper doesn't say that citizen has to live in the city."

"You're not being realistic. Who in their right mind is going to take a female on as an apprentice?"

"Why do they have to know you're a woman?"

"Are you suggesting I continue living this lie for another year?"

"If you don't, you haven't got a prayer."

Suzanne rubbed at her damp face, now raw from crying. "My father warned me ... over and over again, he said, tell one lie, you'll need three more to cover that one and they'll keep growing."

Amy could hear the sheriff returning, so she interrupted, saying, "You can't think about that right now. You have to tell me. If I can arrange this will you submit to his terms?"

"Terms?"

"Whatever you are asked to do, will you be cooperative and work hard?"

"Times up, Miss."

Amy moved toward the door. "I have to know, Zanne."

"I don't have a choice. Yes! As long as they don't ask me to do anything immoral, just get me out of here."

Amy nodded. "Try and get some sleep. I'll see you by no later than tomorrow morning."

"Try real hard, Amy!"

"I won't let you down."

As Suzanne lowered herself to the dank floor again, her eyes slid shut. This was such a mess. Even if Amy could find someone willing to take her on, how would she keep up this ruse for a year? The whole thing was too much—too much to endure.

Suzanne opened her eyes to catch another glimpse of her friend, but she was already gone. Suzanne was alone in this vermin infested hole—for how long? Hopefully Amy would be back to claim her this night. If not, she would be forced to stay here pending her moment in court, pleading her case before a judge who didn't give two hoots about the truth. She'd give anything to have Jesse walk around the corner. Somehow she knew he would not. How could he? He had no clue where she was.

What a fool I've been! You're real big and brave now aren't you, Suzanne. Your lies and deceit got you into this mess. Now it looks like you'll have to live the life of a boy for another year. Lord, I know I have no right to ask for Your help, but I'm desperate. If You get me out of this mess ...

Suzanne couldn't go on. She didn't have a leg to stand on with the Almighty. She could beg and plead for mercy, but she wasn't sure she still believed in all that stuff her parents taught her. She had tried serving God. Even committed her life to Him, but apparently it never took. If it had she wouldn't be in this mess. Her father served Him all the days of his life and what did it get him? Nothing! He was sent to an early grave and now her mother ... she couldn't even go there. If things had gone on as planned, Suzanne's mother was already married to *Josiah Ordan*.

Even if Suzanne did get out of this muddle, she couldn't go home. It just wouldn't work. She'd be miserable and everyone would be trying to help her rekindle her relationship with the Lord. As if God would want anything to do with her now!

In the midst of her anguish, she suddenly stopped and asked, knowing her friend was not there to answer. "Who in the world are you going to ask?"

Suzanne did not doubt that Amy's bubbly personality made it easy for her to make friends. In fact, Amy had told her about several new acquaintances. Suzanne had no way of knowing if any of them were businessmen. If they were, would they be willing to step out on a limb for a new friend, and her brother whom they had never met? Too bad Suzanne had spent so much time in her room moping instead of chaperoning her *sister*. She kept racking her brain, but eventually gave up trying to figure out whom Amy would ask. It would do no good. Even an educated guess would just be that, a guess. Surely this whole scheme was useless. Why would anyone come to her rescue?

Although Suzanne had no answers to the many questions running through her head, this she knew for sure: going along with Amy's plan would cost her plenty. How much before the year was up, she did not know. She hated to admit it, even to herself, but the cost of duplicity was high—higher than she could have ever imagined!

He Loves Me!

Chapter Three

Behind A Mask

"MISTER, PLEASE! You have to quit singing that horrible song. I have a terrible headache."

"Sher-iff's got some nerve ... stickin' an innocent back here with old Frank. Must-a did something aw-ful bad! You got a name ... Little Lady?"

Though his words were slurred, she understood every one. Stunned that an inebriated man could expose her gender after so few spoken words, Suzanne's mind reeled. How would this scam ever work? Surely there would be others who would know. Although it took her a moment to collect her thoughts, she chuckled tersely in an attempt to throw him off. "The name's Zanne. I tend to hit a few high notes now and again. Still a growing boy, ya know." *Lies upon lies!* her thoughts chided.

"I see ...."

"What do you see, Frank?" the sheriff asked as he came around the corner.

Suzanne held her breath wondering what Frank would say.

Fortunately, the old-toper only slapped at the air, rolled over in his bunk, and went back to sleep. Sighing with relief, Suzanne eagerly stood when the sheriff opened her cell.

"This must be your lucky day, Zanne."

"What do you mean?" She peered around him, half-expecting to see Amy, but he was alone. "Is my sister here?"

"No ... but someone else is here to claim you. Says he's contemplating taking you on as an apprentice, but he wants to talk to you before he'll sign anything."

As much as she hated to press him, her curiosity had peaked. "Do I know him?"

"I certainly hope so. You're going to sign an agreement that will practically make you his indentured servant for the year."

"His what?"

The sheriff gave her the evil eye. "You heard me right, Zanne. You'll work alongside of this man for one year and do as you're told or land yourself back in jail. Until he sends us a letter saying you've served your time without complaint, you're still in trouble with the law here in Detroit."

Without complaint! Why, of all things did you have to use Jesse's favorite phrase? She felt like a small child under the sheriff's uncompromising glare. "I don't see that you're giving me another option. Either way I'm paying for a crime I didn't commit."

"The crowd said you're guilty. It's your word against theirs. If you haven't figured it out yet, life's not always fair. I have to hear you say that you'll keep your end of the bargain, or the judge will have my hide."

"No need to worry about that."

"Good!" He led his prisioner back down the narrow hall and pointed to the door in front of him. "The gentleman is waiting for you in there. Come out to my desk when you're both ready to sign the necessary papers."

She lowered her head in resignation. "Yes, Sir ...."

If only she could open the door and find Jesse waiting for her inside. It was a farfetched dream, but if it weren't Jesse, she'd have to keep up this ruse for the next year. Considering the alternative, she took a deep breath for courage and pushed her way in. If she thought her head was aching before, it was booming when she found herself staring into the kind eyes of the young doctor who had been entertaining Amy. *Oh no! This can't be. He's a doctor. I can't work with a doctor!*

"You don't look relieved to see me, Zanne. Who, might I ask, were you expecting?"

Her mind was still in a bit of a conundrum when she reached the desk he was sitting at. "I'm sorry! It's just that ... well, I ... a ... suppose I was sort of expecting someone from my past."

"Your past? No one I need to worry about, I hope."

"No, Sir ...."

Jason knew he was staring, but he couldn't help it. The young man standing before him was about five-foot-six, but he had a bone structure inconsistent with ..."How old did you say you are, Zanne?"

Does it matter? her thoughts question, though she deemed it wise to be respectful, all things considered. "Sixteen, Doctor Michaels."

Jason let out a slow whistle, but didn't comment further—on Zanne's age anyhow. "I'm not sure how much Amy has told you about me, but I'm on my way to set up a temporary practice."

Suzanne nodded. She had no wish to come across as impertinent; even so, she had several things she would like to ask. If this interview were favorable, she would be living with this man for the next year. Peering up, she admitted, "I'm really not sure why you would come to my rescue, Doctor Michaels, but I am very thankful you have. The thought of spending a year in prison for a crime I did not commit has been most upsetting." Her uncertainties heightened when Doctor Michaels stood, leaned over the desk, and put a hand on her forehead.

"You look pale. Are you not well, Zanne?"

She forced herself to breathe when the kind doctor reclaimed his seat. "I'm not exactly myself ... I have a bit of a headache is all."

Jason was not surprised. He suspected Zanne was innocent of the charges. Being falsely incarcerated would be enough to give anyone a headache.

Desperate to get out of this place, Suzanne said, "My sister speaks very highly of you, Sir."

"She is a delightful young lady. Too bad she's not my type. It would be a wonderful asset being married to a woman who loves medicine as much as I do."

"I would imagine so ...." Suzanne sank down into the chair behind her, wishing she could close her eyes, open them again and find that she was back in her bedroom in Ypsilanti. Living with a new father would be a piece of cake compared to facing a year alone with a complete stranger. "You don't happen to know where my sister is, do you?"

Jason nodded. "I asked Amy to wait at the hotel."

"Oh!"

When worry creased Zanne's brow, Jason explained. "We have things to discuss that have nothing to do with her."

"I see ...." Suzanne's concerns mounted when seconds ticked by without an exchange of words. The silence was intimidating.

"I have to make a few things clear before I sign the papers and get you out of here."

Suzanne's head lowered. *Here we go ... not even out the door and already he's laying down the law. Since yielding to Doctor Michaels will be a slice of heaven compared to what the judge has planned for me, I'd better resign myself to the inevitable. Best to know up front what he expects.* "Yes, Sir ...."

"As I am sure you know, I'll be treating people from all walks of life in my practice and finding great joy in doing so. I need you to understand that it is God who I serve and must answer to for all I do and say. You will find me a fair man to work for; however, whether you agree with what I believe or not, my expectations will be the same. While you're living under my roof, you will conduct yourself in a manner that will not dishonor the Lord or the work He has called me to do. Are we in agreement?"

Grand! she thought as she stared at the man sitting across from her. *Amy's wishy-washy Christianity I can take, but this man wears his religion like a cloak—like my other family members—like my father did. I thought I left all that behind in Ypsilanti. Will I never escape this? So much for being in charge of my own life from now on!*

Fortunately, she was sensible enough to keep her disgruntled words to herself. Although this man was single-minded and godly, he was saving her from a year of hard labor in a workhouse for men. At the very least, she owed him respect and her assurance that she would do her part. "I can't promise perfection, but I will abide by your wishes, provided I know what they are."

"Even if you don't agree with me?"

"Yes ..."

Jason's smile was kind. "That's good enough for me. We can discuss this further when we get back to the hotel if you'd like."

Suzanne's face scrunched up. "But I'll be staying with Amy while we're here in Detroit ... won't I?" When Jason shook his head, Suzanne's eyes widened tenfold.

"Sorry, Zanne. The sheriff made it clear that you are to be with me until we leave Detroit. My original plan was to stay until Saturday. Considering the circumstances, I've decided we should catch the morning stage after escorting Amy to the harbor."

Something akin to shock and dismay registered on her face. "She's still going to New York?" *I can't believe she would abandon me at a time like this.*

"Well, yes. Doctor Nelson is expecting the two of you. Don't you think at least one of you should show up?"

"Oh ... I suppose ...."

"So we're in one accord?"

It was not without effort, but she answered with quiet resolve. "Yes, Sir ...."

"One more thing, Zanne, loose the Sir when you address me. I prefer to go by Jason or Doc. We are only seven years apart. I'm hopeful we'll become friends."

She gawked at the man, trying for the life of her to figure him out. The twinkle in his soft blue eyes told her he was amused, but she wasn't sure why. "Might take some time to get used to your ways, Doc."

"Not a problem. Like I said, I'm a patient man." When Jason stood, Suzanne followed him to the sheriff's desk, wondering as she did how she would manage to sleep a wink in this man's room.

The necessary papers were signed and Zanne was remanded to the good doctor's care with a firm warning, "Don't tempt fate, Zanne. Do what you're told or we'll hunt you down like a common thief."

Taken aback by the sheriff's threat, she wondered, *Has one false accusation really sent my reputation up in smoke?* If his stern expression were any indication, she'd have to say, *it had!*

Jason was giving her a chance to make something of herself, and that was more than the authorities in this town intended to do. She would not let him down—if she did, she'd only be hurting herself. "I'll give you no cause for concern, Sheriff ...."

Suzanne would have said more, but Jason had a firm hold on her elbow, as he moved swiftly out the door. His eyes, ever watchful, scanned the streets as they moved toward the hotel. She wondered if he suspected a confrontation. He was walking so fast, and his long-legged strides were no match for hers. She could not keep up. When her toe caught in a rut and she lost her footing, Jason caught her around the waist before she hit the ground, saving her from a nasty fall. She recovered nicely, but his comment left her feeling more than a little unsettled.

"I'll have to be sure you're eating heartier meals, Zanne. You'll never get your manly form if you don't."

Suzanne glanced up at the tall blonde gentleman beside her and grinned. "Runs in the family, Doc. Can't change the way God made us, you should know that better than me."

With a tilt of his head, Jason offered, "Can't hurt to try."

"True ... But no thanks!"

They were almost to the hotel before Jason's steps slowed. "How's the headache?"

"Still there ... nothing a hot bath and rest won't cure."

"And a full plate of hot food."

Suzanne shook her head. "I'm really not hungry ... just exhausted. This whole experience has thrown me for a loop."

"I can only imagine," Jason murmured as his steps slowed.

"Being punished when I haven't done anything wrong feels so different, Doc."

Jason patted Zanne's shoulder in a reassuring manner. "Many good men have suffered for things they didn't do. You're not the first, and you won't be the last. I'm not sure if you're aware of it, but Peter's first epistle addresses this very thing."

And I suppose you're going to tell me about it?

"Now mind you, this is my interpretation of the passage, not word for word, but Peter tells us there's no glory in being punished for your faults, even if you're patient about it. But, if you do what's right and suffer for it, yet you take the suffering patiently, this is acceptable with God. Endure this time, Zanne. Who knows? It could turn out to be a huge blessing in disguise for both of us. God knows I'll appreciate your help."

"I'm glad you feel that way," Suzanne offered, but she didn't think she would ever see this time of being an indentured servant as a blessing. Even so, she could appreciate knowing that Jason didn't see her as an imposition or worse yet, a criminal—guilty as charged.

Jason held the door open for his new assistant. An elderly gent, who had been among Zanne's crowd of accusers, glared when they passed by, but no one said a word as they moved beyond the desk, headed up the stairs, and knocked on Amy's door.

Amy's relief knew no bounds. On impulse she pulled her bedraggled friend into her arms. "Zanne, I'm so glad you're out of there."

"Me too."

Amy took a step back and really looked at her. "You're a bit smelly, so a bath needs to be ordered. Are you fine otherwise?"

"I will be."

Jason made a suggestion. "You and Amy need a few minutes to talk, so I'll head down and order your bath, Zanne." Stopping at the door, Jason added, "Gather your things. I'll meet you at my room in ten minutes."

"For my bath?" Suzanne's tone was incredulous. She couldn't help it.

Amy, noting the flush crawling up her friend's neck, said in a rush, "Would you mind if Zanne takes his bath in my room?"

"Amy, you know full well he's supposed to be with me."

"But, I can stay with him—can't I? We weren't expecting to be separated like this. We need more time to talk. Surely you can understand that?" Tears were clogging Amy's throat, making it difficult to go on.

"Don't start crying, Amy. I'm not an ogre. I understand, but you need to keep in mind that it's my reputation that's on the line here." Jason turned to his charge. "Have a good soak. As soon as you're done, I'll expect you to pack up and come to my room. No more excuses, Zanne. The hotel manager has been made aware of what happened. You can't be seen downstairs without me, or the papers we signed will be null and void."

"I'm not about to chance that happening."

"Good!" Jason said as he moved out the door.

Amy flopped down in one of the high back chairs and groaned, "Honestly, Suz, I thought he'd never leave."

Suzanne sat on the edge of the other chair and returned, "Ya, well try being in my shoes. Not only do I have to sleep in his room, the good doctor actually wanted me to bathe with him present!" Amy's smile turned to laughter, and then an all out fit of giggles broke out between them. In fact, tears were blinding both of them before they calmed. Perhaps it was relief—perhaps fear of what the future would hold—or perhaps a touch of both. Whatever had caused their outburst, it really did feel good to laugh again.

Unfortunately, time was not on their side. Suzanne had things she needed to ask her friend while she still could. "Amy, how am I ever going to survive a year—a whole year with *him*?"

"You'll be fine. At least you have an idea of what Jason's like. I've never even met Doctor Nelson."

"But I'm bound to him for a year. Unlike you, I can't walk away—even if we don't get along. If I do, he'll ship me off to that workhouse."

Amy's eyes welled up. "It's all my fault. If I didn't insist on you taking me for a walk, we'd both be heading to New York in the morning."

"Don't go blaming yourself. I could have said no."

"Ya! Well, maybe, if your friend wasn't so pushy."

"Laying blame won't change my circumstances, Amy. Let's just enjoy the time we have left."

Amy fidgeted with her hands. "Will you promise to write often, Suz?"

She shrugged. "You forget that I have no money for postage—or anything else for that matter."

Amy jumped up, rifled through her handbag and pulled out a few coins and bills that she handed to Suzanne. "This should hold you for a while. If you don't find a way to make some money, let me know. I'll see what I can do about sending more. I got you into this mess, I'll help in any way that I can."

"Thanks, Amy. I hate to ask, but there is one thing I'd like you to do for me."

"What's that?"

"If I write to my family, will you mail the letter somewhere along your way? I don't want them to be able to track me down, but letting them worry isn't fair either. I need time to sort all this out."

"I'm beginning to wonder if the Lord's trying to tell you something?"

Suzanne held her friend's gaze. "Don't you start preaching at me too, Amy. That friend of yours ..." Suzanne was about to say more, but when Amy grinned, she opted to keep her thoughts to herself.

"Just keep an open heart and mind, will yah, Suz?"

"I'll try," she offered feebly and then shrugged. "I've been thinking about my family. I'm not sure how much I should tell them. I could change my mind, but right now I can't bear the thought of them knowing all that has happened." Tears filled Suzanne's sky blue eyes. "Jesse would be so disappointed in me."

Amy's heart went out to her. "Suzanne, you know how much

your family loves you. And Jesse, he would move heaven and earth to help you if he could."

"Why did I leave?"

"You know why."

"Hardly compares to this mess ... I need to have things settled in my mind before I do anything rash. Maybe time does heal all wounds. Who knows?"

"There's no rush, Suz. Jason has already proven himself to be kind. I'm hoping he'll be fair as well."

"I'd be lying if I said I wasn't scared. Jason's a single man, and I am supposed to live under his roof. I can only imagine what the gossips back home would do with that news!"

Amy giggled, "Why, they'd have the two of you married so fast your heads would spin!"

"It's not funny, Amy. Jason really is stepping out on a limb for me. Sullying his name is the last thing I'd want to do."

"Just stick to the plan. If you play your role well, you shouldn't have any problems."

Someone knocked at the door, and Amy stood to answer it. A stream of errand boys trailed in with a large tub. After filling it with buckets of hot water, they handed Amy a bar of soap, a swatch of toweling, and a face cloth. They were gone as quickly as they had come.

The door had no more shut when Suzanne shed her masculine attire, stepped into the soothing fluid, and slid beneath its warm depths. After several seconds of head to toe revitalizing splendor, the need for a life-giving breath of air forced her to rise above the surface. Pushing her saturated lengths from her face, she savored her last few moments of freedom to be the woman she

was created to be. In just a short while she would be entering a new world—one that required her to hide behind a mask of deception for one full year. Could she keep up the ruse? Perhaps if she approached her confinement one day at a time, it would not seem so unbearably long. Lathering the small cloth provided, she scrubbed every inch of her crawling skin, unwilling to chance the smallest of vermin following her into her new life as Zanne Somers.

He Loves Me!

Chapter Four

New Beginnings

*J*ASON, HEARING A COMMOTION outside his room, laid the book he'd been reading aside and went to open the door. He found his new assistant overloaded with belongings and Amy standing behind her with two more small bags.

"Ah, there you are, Zanne. I was about to come and see what the hold up was. I'm starving! I hope the two of you won't mind taking in an early supper."

"Not at all," Suzanne affirmed. "Sorry about the delay. It was my fault entirely. The warm water felt so good, I couldn't drag myself out of the tub."

"So ... it was partly your fault all the tubs were still in use when I ordered one. I'll have to get my bath after supper. "

Oh, no! Suzanne mused. *This isn't starting out well at all.* Craning her neck around, she cast her wary eyes on her friend.

Although understanding Suzanne's unease, Amy knew her friend was going to have to take things in stride or she would never survive the year working alongside this gentle man. Offering a sympathetic shrug, she mouthed the word, "Sorry."

Jason took the largest bag from Zanne and reentered his room. Tossing it on the extra bed, he turned around to find his new assistant standing hesitantly just outside the door peering in. "Zanne, don't be shy. Come on in and make yourself at home."

His jovial tone did set her mind at ease, if only to degree. "Oh, sure ..."

While the warm flush of his new assistant confused the good doctor, he said not a word as they headed downstairs.

Suzanne was still trying to come to grips with her odd circumstances when the three of them were seated at a small table in the crowded dining room. The aroma of roast chicken filled the air, and if she wasn't mistaken, she had caught a whiff of baked cinnamon and apple as well. At any rate, she was more than ready to indulge her hunger pangs when Amy and Jason reached for her hands to offer thanks.

Although the meal was delicious, all else was a blur. Fortunately, Amy and Jason carried the conversation and didn't press her to enter in. Suzanne could remember the waitress setting a cup of tea in front of her with a large slice of apple pie, but she couldn't remember savoring a single sip or bite.

Before Suzanne had time to contemplate what she would face next, they were heading back upstairs. If only her thudding heart would ease—if only time would stand still. Jason, being the gentleman that he was, stepped into his room, so she and Amy could have a moment alone in the hall.

Amy, realizing how weary Suzanne was, wrapped her arms around her friend. "You need to get some rest. I'll see you in the morning."

Suzanne held on to her friend and whispered, "I'm not sure I can do this, Amy. I don't even know this man."

She murmured her reply, "Suz, you're going to be fine."

"I wish I could believe you."

Amy released her, stepped back, and gazed into her friend's glassy eyes. "Oh, Suz, please don't cry. I've been praying about this. God has His reasons for putting you and Jason together. I'm not sure what they are, but He does."

"Yeah ... to punish me for running away from home."

"I doubt that! I'm not always the best example, but I do know that God loves us more than anyone else ever could."

"You're only saying that because Pastor's been drumming it into our heads for years now."

"It's true .... I have a peace about this. I can't tell you what this year will bring, but I know Jason's a good man. You might even enjoy being with him."

"If only we could trade places. You're the one who gets along with him."

"When I'm not around, you'll get to know him better. To be honest, he reminds me a little of Jesse."

"Grand! Just what I need—another big brother!"

Amy giggled at the way Suzanne rolled her eyes. "It won't be as bad as you think, Suz. Now, get in there and go to sleep. Things always seem worse when we're exhausted."

"I suppose. Thanks for everything you did to get me out of jail."

"You're welcome. Sleep well, My Friend."

"I'll try ...." Suzanne knew the errand boys would be coming up the stairs with Jason's tub and water at any time. She had every intention of being under her bedcovers before he indulged. Taking a deep breath for courage, she stepped over the threshold and allowed her wary eyes to scan the small room.

Suzanne, so engrossed in her surroundings, started when Jason's voice broke the silence. She glanced his way.

"Come and have a seat beside me, Zanne."

Jason's Bible was open and he was leafing through a small journal. All appearances said he intended to put her back on the strait and narrow from the start. With reluctance, she sat on the settee as far away from him as she dared. He wasted no time filling her in on his thoughts.

"I'll see if I can pick you up a journal before we leave in the morning. I don't know about you, but I enjoy having all of my sermon notes in one place. Comes in handy for quick reference."

She nodded, wondering why he was telling her. When Jason pointed to a sermon outline on the open page, she nearly choked on the title. *You can run, but you can't hide.*

"Until we get settled in our new home in Saline—"

"Saline?" she repeated with emphasis. "Is that where we're going?"

"Yes. I thought I told you. Is there a problem?"

Of course there's a problem. That village is too close to my family! Swallowing past the lump now forming in her throat, she squeaked out, "No, Jason, no problem at all."

"You're not very convincing," he stated but then let it drop. "As I was saying, until we get settled in a new fellowship of believers, we'll be studying the sermons I have outlined in my journal. You can use my notes to study from and then we'll compare our findings."

Suzanne couldn't believe her ears. Her brow furrowed. "You expect me to read through all of those passages and your notes?"

"Yes, and come up with notes on your own interpretation."

If I wanted to be preached at, I could have stayed home. "I ... I thought I'd be working alongside you in your profession, not going to seminary!"

Jason chuckled. Firmly tapping the brim of Zanne's hat, Jason effectively covered his distorted expression. "Whining already and we haven't even reached our destination?"

Suzanne exposed her hidden gaze and peered up at her new superior. "Sorry, it's just, well, you know."

"I'm not sure I do. Care to elaborate?"

Unable to hold his inquisitive look, she buried her face in her hands and spoke through her fingers. "I never really enjoyed school. I did hope that part of my life was over."

"We should never stop seeking wisdom, Zanne."

"But wouldn't my time be better spent studying your medical journals?"

His head swayed slowly from side to side. "I'm more concerned about your soul than your knowledge of medicine."

Suzanne cringed. *What have I gotten myself into?* "Are you really a doctor, Jason?" Sarcasm oozed from her words, and while she braced herself for the worst, she was astounded by his calm.

"I am a doctor, but my relationship with the Lord comes before all else. Without His presence in my life, I am nothing."

"I see ...." Thinking she had better get some sleep before she said something she'd regret, Suzanne stood. "I'm really tired. Would you mind if I call it a night? I think you'll find me much more agreeable when I'm rested."

Jason reached out and touched Zanne's warm cheek. "You're flushed, are you sure you're not ill? Do I need to examine you?"

Wide eyed, she stood and backed up so quickly she nearly tripped over the small lamp table. Her defenses heightened and her words were harsher than intended. "You keep your hands to yourself, Doctor Michaels!"

"Relax, Zanne."

She took a quick breath, but could not let down her guard. "It's just, well, you know."

Jason threw him a baiting grin. "Don't tell me, let me guess. My new assistant is afraid of *doctors*?"

And I faint at the sight of blood! "How'd you know?"

"If you could see what I do, you'd know. Give yourself time. You'll find out soon enough that I'm not nearly as scary as I look."

"Your looks are fine—it's your profession that chills my bones. I've never liked doctors poking and prodding."

"Good to know. I'll keep my distance unless you give me cause for concern. You're my charge, Zanne. If you're ill, I'm going to take care of you, even if you protest."

"I'm not. Just tired." *Pretending you're someone you're not takes way more energy than I would have ever thought.*

"Go to bed. In case you're wondering, tomorrow we'll travel as far as the village of Ypsilanti. The hotel we're staying at is called Hawkins House."

Suzanne swallowed hard, trying not to panic. With the way her string of luck was running, she wouldn't be surprised to have Jesse show up, find her sleeping in this man's room and— *perish the thought!*

Before she moved toward her bed, she offered, "Thanks for

taking me on, Jason. I know you weren't planning to have a tag along. I really am grateful."

"You're, welcome."

Suzanne shed as few articles of clothing as possible before crawling beneath her bed covers. Surrendering her head to the pillow's downy softness brought her relief beyond measure. Closing her sore eyes, she managed to shut out her troubles and drifted off to sleep.

Suzanne fought back tears as she stood on the wharf with Jason watching Amy board *Walk-in-the-Water*. It wasn't as if they were the closest of friends, but Amy did know her true identity. For the next year, she would be known by all as Zanne Somers. Suzanne no longer existed. Amy had no more disappeared into the crowd on deck when Jason interrupted her thoughts.

"We need to go, Zanne. The stage will be leaving any minute."

They were the last to board, so as soon as they were settled, the driver took up the reins and maneuvered slowly through town.

As they rode away from Detroit, an odd sense of peace settled over Suzanne. She even began to wonder if Amy could be right. Was she meant to be with Jason? Perhaps in time she would have answers to the questions floating through her mixed up head. For now she would concentrate on paying her debt to society for a crime she had not committed. *No matter*, she thought, *Jason saved me from jail and deserves my cooperation. I'll do my best to serve him well.*

"Doc," Suzanne inquired, nearly an hour into their trip, "where are you from originally?"

"My older brother and his wife still run our family farm in Pennsylvania."

"What about your parents?"

Jason grew pensive and several minutes passed before he said, "My mother and little sister died in twenty-two when a cholera epidemic swept through our village. After several years, my father remarried a widow who had a daughter close to my age. My father and stepmother have since gone home to be with the Lord."

"I'm sorry for your loss."

Jason glanced at his assistant. "I miss them, but they had a very close relationship with God. They've gone to claim their eternal reward. In that, I rejoice with them."

She nodded. Ill-at-ease with the topic, she steered the conversation in another direction. "Do you mind my asking what brought you to Michigan?"

"An elderly doctor who practices in Ann Arbor wrote to one of his colleges in New York. With the territory being settled so quickly, there's a great need for doctors. I happened to be training under Doctor Taylor's friend at the time. He intends to retire in a couple of years and hopes I'll consider taking his place. After doing a little investigating, the village of Saline practically begged me to come there in the interim. In fact, the good people of Saline said a home would be ready and waiting for me when I arrived. All I have to do is find a housekeeper who likes to cook and we'll be all set."

Suzanne leaned against the carriage and stared out the window. She would gladly consent to keep house for him—even cook. Anything would be better than doctoring, but then she thought, another woman living with them could protect their reputations should her gender be exposed.

Fortunately, the stage rolled into Ypsilanti late that evening. She and Jason checked into the hotel, shared a quick meal, and were asleep and back on the road before the town came back to life.

Suzanne, though she longed to see her family, was relieved when they put that leg of the journey behind them. She needed time to adjust to her plight—time to think through what she should tell her loved ones.

As they passed through Ann Arbor, heavy rains began to fall. Suzanne was hoping the stage would continue on. Too many people in Ann Arbor could identify her, and if Jason were to insist on meeting Doctor Taylor, her sham would be uncovered. Doctor Taylor was not only an elder in the church she had attended, he and his wife were also dear family friends. Fortunately, the stage policy was to continue on, rain or shine.

They rolled into Saline at dusk to the patter of rain. As they disembarked, the fatigued travelers did their best to avoid the worst of the puddles as they headed toward the nearest establishment, a country store. Jason wasted no time filling the proprietor in on his arrival. It would seem they had come to the right place.

Suzanne, although apprehensive about living alone with Jason, was exhausted from their travels. Knowing they would need time to get settled in their new home before calling it a night, she tried to set her concerns aside.

"Welcome!" the gentleman behind the counter said. "I'm so glad you arrived safely. I trust the trip was uneventful?"

Jason smiled. "Quite peaceful. Thanks for asking."

"I'm Bill Chefan."

"Nice to meet you, Mr. Chefan."

"Sharon and I weren't expecting you for a few days, but as promised, your home is ready and waiting for you. We're so glad you decided to come to our village."

Suzanne was still standing by the door when Jason motioned for her to come near. "Mr. Chefan, I'd like you to meet my apprentice, Zanne Somers."

"Somers, hmm ... the name sounds familiar." Seconds had passed before he admitted, "I can't place it. Suppose it's a common enough name. Nice to meet you. Would you prefer to be called Zanne or Mr. Somers?"

"Zanne will suit me just fine. Glad to meet you." When Mr. Chefan looked behind him, as if he were expecting someone, she moved toward a glassed case filled with nick knacks and took a gander.

"Excuse me for a moment." Bill opened the door to the back room and called out, "Billy, come on out front, son. The new doctor has arrived. I need to show him and his assistant to their home."

A lanky boy with a crop of blonde hair walked into the outer room. Suzanne suspected he wasn't a day over eight, but he was taller than most his age. The twinkle in his eyes when he smiled, told Suzanne much about the young lad.

Billy nodded in greeting before looking at his father. "Take your time, Pa. I can handle the customers."

"I know you can, Son. If your mother comes by, tell her where I've gone. I'm sure some of the ladies will be glad to do some baking for their new doctor until he hires a housekeeper. Be sure the women know he has an assistant. We wouldn't want him going hungry." Bill sent Zanne a lighthearted wink. "Like you, Billy, he can afford to gain a pound or twenty."

Jason couldn't withhold a smile.

Suzanne took a daring step toward him and softly murmured, "That's enough out of you, Doc!"

Jason's head tilted. "Admit that you need to eat better and I'll let it drop."

She scowled. "Not on your life!"

"A bit feisty today, are we now? Perhaps you're coming down with something?"

She glared at the baiting man standing too near. "Keep your distance, Doctor Michaels, or you'll find out just how feisty I can be!"

Although he chuckled, he did let it drop. Their escort was coming toward them, and Jason had no desire to embarrass his new apprentice.

Bill stole his coat off the hook and said, "Let's head over to the livery and pick up my buck board."

Jason asked, "Is our place close to town, Mr. Chefan?"

"Call me Bill. Everyone else in town does. You're on the outskirts. We figured it would give you more privacy." Bill pulled a piece of paper out of his pocket and handed it to Jason. "There are a couple of widows in town vying for the position of house-keeper, but if you're asking me, I'd hire Gertrude. Her children are grown, and she's got a heart as big as the moon. She's also a wonderful cook. Sadie means well, but she's been known to spread a rumor or two. Besides, Johnny Tuttle's been after her to marry him. I've got an inkling she's sweet on him, too, so she might not stick around for long."

After picking up their belongings, Suzanne sat in the back of the wagon, waving at the inquisitive folks gawking as they rode through town.

"I'd like to meet Gertrude. Could you have her come by, say ... tomorrow morning around eight?"

"Be glad to. Knowing Gertrude she'll insist on bringing breakfast with her, so plan to sample her cooking."

"Sounds like a plan."

As they moved out of town, Bill took a sharp left down a narrow, unbeaten path. Passing through a grove of pines, they entered a clearing with a fair-sized home on it. Two wooden chairs sat on the covered porch, and the small barn off to the right would come in handy when Jason got around to purchasing horses.

"Well, what do you think, Doc?"

"Looks like home to me!"

Bill grinned. "Glad to hear it."

Jason was still taking in his surroundings when he said, "As soon as I find a couple of sound horses we'll be all set."

"Actually," Bill said, "the town purchased a gelding from a rancher west of Ann Arbor, but we didn't realize you had an assistant. The horse is in the barn."

"That's great! For now we can ride double."

Suzanne asked, "Does he have a name?"

Bill chuckled. "Suppose that would be helpful. The man who owned him called him Buck."

Jason commented, "That's a strange name for a horse."

"Wait till you see him run. He's as agile as any buck I've ever seen."

"Good to know." Bill pulled the buckboard up in front of the house, and the three of them tossed the bags onto the covered porch.

Jason didn't know who was more pleased with their new home, he or his new assistant. Jason motioned for Zanne to proceed and said, "Lead the way!"

"Sure you don't want to do the honors?"

"Nope!"

Suzanne lifted the latch on the door, stepped in, and for a few moments fumbled helplessly in the dark. The evening shadows had already fallen, and the small slice of moon gracing the heavens offered little to no illumination in this wooded haven.

Bill, being more familiar, moved out in front and said, 'Give me a minute, Zanne. I'll light a lantern."

"That would help," Suzanne affirmed.

"Sharon insisted on there being ample lighting in every room. I suppose she figured you might enjoy reading at night like she does .... There, that's much better."

Jason and Suzanne allowed their eyes to scan their new home, amazed to find it completely furnished and simply, but tastefully, decorated.

"I don't think my expectations were quite this high, Bill. The town folk have been very generous."

"We're thankful to have you here for as long as the two of you can stay."

"Well, we're grateful for the kind welcome. And, in case she asks, your wife is right. I do like to read at night. I'll have to remember to tell her how much I appreciate her thoughtfulness."

Jason waited until he caught his assistant's eye before adding, "The extra lights will come in handy when it comes time for our evening studies, won't it, Zanne."

"Can hardly wait to get started!"

Bill lightheartedly slapped Zanne on the back and he stumbled a bit. "Is that sarcasm I hear in your tone?"

Jason was quick to add, "He means no disrespect, Bill. Just a private joke between the two of us."

"I see. Didn't mean to be so rough, Zanne. Most boys your age are sturdier. Not to worry though, Gertrude will have you feeling stronger in no time."

Bill hadn't seen the way Zanne's eyes rolled, but Jason had, and he laughed out loud.

Bill asked, "Did I say something that struck you funny?"

"It was more Zanne's reaction to your comment. I've been giving him a hard time about his weight, too."

Bill slapped at the air. "Not to worry! Like I said, Gerty will have you fixed up in no time."

I can hardly wait!

Bill stayed long enough to give Jason and Zanne a guided tour and to assure them that his wife Sharon and the other women on the welcoming committee would be by with a bounty of food to hold them until Jason met with Gertrude in the morning.

Chapter Five

Gertrude

THE WONDERFUL AROMA of sizzling bacon tantalized Suzanne's senses, drawing her from the depths of slumber, but she could not bring herself to open her eyes. As hard as it was not to succumb to her rumbling stomach's demand for nourishment, she was still so tired. A quick peek at the blinding sun streaming in her bedroom window indicated morning truly had arrived, but she couldn't convince herself to rise. Sealing her lids against reality, she rolled over in her comfy new bed and buried herself within the warmth of her covers. Another hour, maybe two, and she'd be as good as new.

Unfortunately, Doctor Jason Michaels had other ideas. Without so much as a cursory knock, he barged into her room and stole the covers. If she hadn't stripped down to Amy's father's under drawers, the experience might not have been so unsettling. What would she do if he detected her womanly curves?

"Jason! Do you mind?"

The good doctor was on his way back out the door when he

glanced back and said, "Not a bit, but that girly screech has got to go. My patients won't take kindly to having a boy attending them instead of a young man."

What could she say? She wasn't a boy or a man.

"Get out of bed. And by the way, welcome to the wonderful world of doctoring. Gertrude has breakfast on the table, so get dressed and shove some food down your throat while I saddle the horse. Tandy Parker has apparently been waiting for us to arrive. She's in labor. First babies take awhile, so we'll head over to the Thompson's first. One of the twins fell and might need stitches."

Great! Curious, Suzanne looked up at him. "Do you even know where these people live?"

He chuckled. "We have a map to guide us, remember?" Jason's head tilted peculiarly. "After giving it a quick glance, I've come to the conclusion that the map could be our greatest challenge, so get a move on!"

"Yes, Boss ...." Fortunately Jason left, giving her the privacy she desperately treasured. Not only were her needs pressing in, she had personal items that had to be hidden, just in case their new housekeeper took a notion to snoop. Within minutes she was stumbling down the stairs in her stocking feet. Gertrude must have heard her coming because she greeted Suzanne with a kind smile when she appeared in the frame of the kitchen door.

"Mr. Somers ... how nice to finally meet you."

"Same here, Ma'am. Feel free to call me Zanne."

"Only if you'll call me Gerty."

"Be glad to. Pardon the interruption, Gerty. Don't mean to be rude ... I'll be right back."

Gerty nodded in understanding and took the time to dish up

a nice big helping for her charge. She had a plate sitting on the table when Suzanne came in the back door, washed her hands in the basin, and took the chair Gerty held out.

"Doctor Michaels and I have come to an agreement I can live with, so I'll be moving in this afternoon. You'd best eat your fill, Zanne. The way I hear it, you're leaving soon. Doc wants me to try and locate a milking cow or a goat. For now, black coffee or tea will have to do."

"Tea ... always tea, Gerty. And don't worry about having milk around for me. I quit drinking that nasty stuff years ago."

Gerty's expression revealed her concern. "You don't say?"

The way the woman scrutinized Suzanne put her on edge.

"But, how am I supposed to ..." she waved her hand at the air, adding, "never mind, I'll just have to find another way."

Suzanne knew Gerty was trying to figure out how she was going to fatten her up, but she kept her perceptive thoughts to herself. Out of habit, Suzanne bowed her head to pray before stealing a piece of bacon off her plate and taking a big bite. "This is really good, Gerty!"

"Thanks, I cured it myself. Amazing the difference a little honey will make."

"Amazing!" Suzanne agreed as she took another bite, savoring its flavor.

Gerty smiled. She did love to cook, and knowing folks enjoyed her efforts made them all the more worthwhile. "Go ahead and eat, while I pour your tea, Zanne."

"I should be offering to serve you." Suzanne glanced around the room, noting the changes. Gerty had already been working her fingers to the bone. "Looks as though Jason and I will need to make sure we're taking good care of you, too."

"I am here to serve, Honey." Gerty set a cup of tea down in front of Zanne, turned away, and started cleaning again.

Suzanne didn't miss what Gerty had called her or the odd smirk that tweaked her face. Suzanne would have to be careful. If she wasn't mistaken, Gerty sensed something was amiss. Unfortunately, she didn't have time to figure it out right now. Jason was calling from the back door.

"Gotta go, Zanne!"

She finished her tea, tied the laces on her bluchers, and smiled up at Gerty who had just dumped her half-eaten meal into a clean napkin. Gerty waited until Zanne stood before handing it to her. "Thanks! You're a lifesaver."

"You're welcome. See you when you return."

"Zanne," Jason said when she came out the door, "tell Gerty not to bother making supper. We'll be home late, if we make it home at all."

Suzanne grimaced at the thought of being away so long, but did as she was told. The minute she returned, Jason rode up alongside her.

"Give me your hand ... I'll pull you up."

How could she resist? "I'm awfully heavy! Are you sure you can manage?"

Jason harrumphed! "Give me your hand and quit with the nonsense. After a month or two of Gerty's cooking, we'll discuss your weight again. Until then, eat!"

"Gladly!" Zanne hummed contentedly as she savored every succulent bite. "I sure am glad you decided to hire Gerty. That woman can cook!"

"I'll agree with you there."

The trees along the path swayed with the warm breeze. Had the sky been overcast, she would have suspected that a storm was brewing, but that was not the case. "Can you tell me ahead of time what my responsibilities will be?"

"Does it matter?"

She shrugged. "Not sure."

"Most of the time I'll have to fill you in as we go. Doctoring isn't predictable. As long as you don't faint at the sight of blood, you'll do fine."

The silence lengthened. In fact, several minutes had past before Suzanne summoned the courage to admit, "I hope I won't disappoint you. I've never done this before, Doc."

"I'm not concerned."

She swallowed hard past the lump building in her throat. "Just so you keep in mind, Amy's the real nurse. I'm just a pitiful imitation."

"Not to worry. If you hit the floor, I'll take good care of you. Truth is, I've been told a time or two that I have a gift for doctoring."

As much as she appreciated Jason's playful manner, the thought of him examining her was enough to make her blood run cold. The repercussions of her secret being unveiled could be devastating. Why, he could have her thrown right back in jail. If that were to happen, surely the judge would throw away the key! "You just keep your hands to yourself, Doctor Michaels and we'll get along just fine."

Jason laughed at Zanne's lighthearted inflection. Even so, he also understood Zanne's fears and would do his best not to add to them.

All the talk of facing her aversion to blood was setting her on edge. She might have moved past her apprehensions if her stomach hadn't begun to churn—miserably.

"If this map is right," Jason said, "the farm should be just around this bend in the road."

Suzanne nodded, but her mind was elsewhere. "Jason?"

"Hmm?"

"I need ... no, I have to check on something in the woods ...." Suzanne slid off Buck while the horse was still moving and almost fell.

"Zanne!" Doc berated.

"Sorry ... just be a minute ...."

There was no mistaking the sounds coming out of the woods. The moment Zanne reappeared, he asked, "Are you all right?"

"Yes—and no."

He gave her a hand up. "Do I need to take you back home?"

"No ... if I'm squeamish, I'll have to get over it. I made you a promise. I'm going to do everything in my power to keep it."

"Suppose I can't ask for more than that."

As the map suggested, the cabin came into view around the next bend. Suzanne's heart leapt when three dark-haired stair-steps came running off the porch to greet them. She so loved children. They had a way of bringing out the best in her, and these little darlings were sure to brighten her day.

"Hello! Hello! He-wo!" they echoed. The oldest, a girl of about eight years, took their horse's reins and turned to her brother. "You know what Pa said, James. Take Doc in so he can

see to Carolina. As soon as you can, come back to the barn. We got chores that need tending. Carolyn, you stay with me."

Suzanne, captivated with Carolyn, listened as the small moppet took her sister's hand and inquired, "Ester, Doc not hurt my Lina?"

"Not any more than he has to, Lyn. You saw the way he smiled at us. Doc's a nice man. His friend looks nice, too."

"She not be scared?" Carolyn inquired further.

Suzanne, recalling a few of the times her father had comforted her throughout her life, realized that his willingness to pray with her, no matter how trivial the circumstance, is what had really brought her peace. As much as she would like to go on believing that God had abandoned her family when her father passed on, she was beginning to wonder if her thinking could be wrong. This child's need for comfort chiseled at the ice around her heart. Could she look beyond her own pain and comfort Carolyn as her father had her? Just as she was about to try, Jason reached for her arm.

"We'd best head in, Zanne."

Where the urge came from, Suzanne did not know, but she glanced back, calling out to Carolyn, "I'll pray with Carolina, Honey. God will help her."

Carolyn beamed up at Ester and announced with confidence, as she slid her small hand inside her sister's, "Lina not be scared, Ester! God be wiff her." Relieved, Carolyn moved with Ester into the barn.

Jason put his hand on his assistant's shoulder saying, "That was wonderful, Zanne. God used you to ease one little girl's fears;

let's see if you can look beyond your own and help me mend Carolina's flesh wound."

"If it's too awful, I'll see what I can do about comforting the child and leave the rest to you."

James led Jason and Suzanne into a cabin no bigger than their new parlor. Although diminutive in size, Mrs. Thompson had taken great care to give their home a welcoming appeal. The effect was in plain view before them.

Suzanne, recognizing the expression on the young boy's face, smiled when James scooted quickly out of the room, unnoticed by anyone but her. Apparently, she was not the only one leery of doctors.

A tall, bearded man nodded in greeting from where he sat in a rocking chair that was dwarfed by his large frame.

"I'm John Thompson, Doc. I'd stand up and shake your hand, but I just got Carolina settled down. I'm afraid she does better with her mama," he shrugged, and added, "but I suppose she'll have to make the best of it. My wife's over tending Tandy until you can get there. I saw no need to worry the women about this mishap—not when we have a new doctor who can tend to Carolina's wound."

"I'm sure they have enough on their plate with the baby coming. John, I'd like you to meet my assistant, Zanne."

"Welcome."

"Pleased to meet you." Suzanne nodded at the concerned papa, but her eyes were now glued on the frightened little wonder in his arms. Carolina was the spitting image of her sister Carolyn—identical twins. Suzanne took a chance and knelt down next to Carolina and offered a gentle smile. She could see the

blood seeping through the makeshift bandage on her chubby leg and knew the wound had to be severe. Focusing on the child, she asked, "Tell me, Carolina, do you like horses?"

Her eyes grew big as saucers, and her head bobbed up and down. "Papa gots Ed ...."

"He does? You know, Carolina, I told Carolyn that I'd pray for you while Doctor Michaels fixes your boo-boo. Did you know he's my friend?"

Carolina chanced a peek at the big doctor and shook her head in the negative. Her timid eyes transferred swiftly back to Suzanne.

"We rode Doc's horse over here, so ... if you'll be a big girl and let me hold you while Doc fixes your leg, maybe your pa will let me take you for a ride after we're all done."

Carolina peered up at her father, looking for confirmation.

"That will be fine, Carolina."

All hesitation washed away. She slid her little arms around Suzanne's neck and came to her willingly. John was shocked but pleased. She didn't normally take to strange men.

As promised, Suzanne prayed softly with the small child, while Doc tended her wound. Although the child tensed every time Doc came near and many tears were shed over the stitches she endured, Carolina clung to Suzanne, listening as she told her one silly story after another from her vast store of childhood memories.

When the bandages were secure, Doc tussled Carolina's hair and handed her a stick of hard candy.

Her wide eyes met his, "Sanks you!"

"You are welcome." Jason then glanced up at his assistant

and said, "Take the other children a piece of candy, and be sure you keep your promise. We'll need to be on our way, soon, but you hold to your promise and give Lina a ride on Buck."

Zanne took in her small charges delighted grin. "You ready, Lina?"

"Jep!"

Suzanne didn't miss John's expression or his comment as she moved away, "I'm not sure where you found your assistant, Doc, but you'd best hang on to that one. Zanne has a real gift with children."

"He does at that! Doc agreed as he watched the pair move out the door.

"So tell me, John, what can you tell me about the church situation here in Saline?"

"With folks spread out so far, worshiping together in the winter months can be difficult, but Crandall's have a large outbuilding with a fireplace. For now we've been meeting there."

"How many are attending?" Jason asked as he cleaned his instruments and repacked his bag.

"With children we've had as few as ten. In good weather we average between twenty and thirty."

"Wow! That is a good size group. Who does the preaching?"

"The circuit preacher comes every other week. On the off Sundays the elders take turns leading."

Jason pulled out his map. "Can you show me the Crandall's location on this?"

John chuckled when he got a good look at the rough map placed before him. His long fingers traced the road as he spoke, "Well, if you're heading over to check on Tandy, you'll take the

left fork in the road right here. The Crandall's are to the right."

"Sounds easy enough. I'll discuss it with Zanne, but unless something unforeseen comes up, we'll be there."

"Good! Thanks for all you've done for my daughter, Doc."

"You're welcome. I'll come by to take the stitches out in a few days. In the meantime, put a clean bandage on every day, and let her play. The movement will keep her leg from getting stiff and help the wound heal faster."

※ ※ ※

"I can't do this anymore; I'm too tired," Tandy Parker announced after her contraction passed.

The woman's pain was obviously unbearable. Suzanne had done everything in her power to make Tandy comfortable, but this was out of her control. A quick glance out the window told her it was nearly morning. Jason's furrowed brow exposed his concerns.

He had delivered enough babies to know that something was wrong. Tandy's contractions had been coming one right after the other for the past three hours. Sure, it was Tandy's first child, but she would not last long if her anguish didn't end soon. He had to do something—and quick!

Jason, sensing Zanne's unrest, sent him a piercing look, hoping he would buck up. He needed Zanne to be strong for their patient.

"Sit on the bed and hold her hands, Zanne. The cord must have this little one hemmed in."

Suzanne had watched a cow give birth. She knew what the cord was, but how Jason would go about unwinding it ... she shuddered at the thought. When Tandy's distressed cries pierced the silence, she squeezed Suzanne's hands so tightly they were numb, but Suzanne said not a word.

"That should do it, Tandy. I know you're tired, but if you'll give me one more good push ..."

When Tandy only lay there looking too exhausted to move, Suzanne was spurred into action. She sponged Tandy's forehead with the damp cloth and softly coaxed, "You can do this, Tandy, I know you can. Give us one more push. Your baby wants to come out and see his mama and papa."

A flicker of hope crossed the young mother's face. Where her strength came from, Suzanne did not know, but Tandy sat up and gave it all she had. Within minutes her torment was over.

Jason took the time to bathe the squalling infant before wrapping her in a soft blanket. With a huge grin on his face, Jason handed Tandy her precious baby girl.

Suzanne, thinking the whole experience too surreal, watched the new mother in wonder. The moment Tandy gazed at her daughter, all she had suffered seemed to dissipate. The elation on Tandy's face bespoke love—a love of the purest kind.

"Absolutely not! I won't hear of it, Doc!" Gerty insisted when Jason went to climb the stairs of his new home.

Confused by her bold statement, Jason turned back and asked, "What has you so riled, Gerty? I'm exhausted. I need to get to bed."

"I'll be agreeing with you there, but I've moved your things to the big room in the back of the house."

Jason scowled. "I told you that room was yours. I really don't mind being upstairs with Zanne."

"I appreciate your consideration, really I do, but a servant should not be taking the Master's room. I have made myself to home in the room across from your young charge."

Jason, too tired to fight with her, gave in to her insistence. "If you change your mind, Gerty, let me know."

"I won't be doing that ... no, Sir. Propriety demands it."

Jason had no idea what she meant by that, but some things were not worth squabbling over, least of all when you've been up all night.

Suzanne had just dozed off when a soft knock pulled her from the brink of slumber. "What now, Doc?"

"It's not Doc," Gerty informed her charge as she opened the door and gently scolded, "Tired or not, you have no business being disrespectful to your higher ups." The small candle in Gerty's hand illuminated her kind face.

"Not to worry, Gerty. I have the utmost respect for the man. I just don't like my sleep being disturbed. Never have."

"I'll be sure to keep that in mind. Sleep well. I'll be across the hall should you need me."

Confused, but too weary to ask questions, Suzanne offered a cursory nod. "Good rest, Gerty."

"Thank you, Sweet Child!" and she was gone.

Sweet Child? She wondered why Gerty would address her in such a manner, but was too exhausted to ponder it.

He Loves Me!

Chapter Six

Blasphemy

"YOU WANT ME TO GO TO CHURCH with you?" Suzanne's heart faltered. *But I don't want to go to church with you or anyone else, Jason. Part of the reason I left home was to get away from people like you.*

Zanne's bewildered look did not make sense. Jason thought this issue had already been settled. Although he wanted his assistant to come to church willingly, he had no intentions of backing down. Even so, he attempted to soften the blow. "Not necessarily with me. I don't care if you stand at the door, join me on a bench, or sit with a friend, but you will be in attendance unless I tell you otherwise."

Contemplating his words, she schemed, *That shouldn't be a problem, if I don't have to sit with you, you'll never know if I'm there or not.*

"Just keep in mind, we'll be comparing sermon notes and studying them together during the evenings we're home. Be sure you write down everything you'd like to discuss."

Suzanne snarled up her nose. "Discussing a sermon is hardly on my list of things I'd like to do, Doc."

Jason's big blue eyes narrowed. "Then I'd suggest you do some soul searching before Sunday."

"Fine!" she declared.

"Zanne!" he returned and then forced himself to calm. "While you live under my roof ..."

Her hand came up to stop him. She was wrong to challenge his authority over her. "I will do as you ask. I'm sorry, Jason. You just took me by surprise is all." As she spoke the words aloud, her thoughts challenged, *This really is a problem!*

She couldn't bring herself to look at him. Jason reminded her too much of Jesse when he spoke in that tone, and she so hated being ordered around. Needing a moment to collect her thoughts, she stood, set her plate on the washboard, and for a time stared out the open window. Perhaps knowing the choice was not hers to make irritated her more than anything. Frustrated or not, she would have to set her own feelings aside. They were irrelevant. When she turned back to face Jason, she sought clarification— just in case she misunderstood. "So ... you expect me to go to church ... and take notes on the sermon?"

"Yes, Zanne."

That means ... but how can I attend church as a man? Doing so would be blasphemy! She shook her head. "I don't know, Doc ...."

Jason's brow furrowed. "What don't you know?"

"Too much ...." She lowered her head. How could she tell him? *What am I going to do?*

"Zanne, I know you're struggling with everything that has

happened, but there is no need. God brought us together. I don't doubt that for a minute. The law put you under my care for a year. That means I'm responsible for your physical and spiritual well-being. Because I answer to God for what I do, I don't take my position lightly."

"I understand that, but there are things you don't know about me—things I can't tell you, not yet anyway."

Jason, noting Zanne's strained emotions, suggested, "Coming to know God is where true freedom lies. Don't run from Him, run to Him. He's waiting with open arms to help you through whatever you're struggling with."

"If only it was that easy."

"It is ...."

She took a deep breath and tried to explain. "I believe in God, Jason, really I do, but I'm not so sure I see things the way you do. I was hoping to have time to sort some things out before ..."

"Before what?"

"Before I become involved in another fellowship." Her father had loved God, had lived by His Word, and had even told her often that God loved her more than anyone else ever could. The way Suzanne envisioned God seemed so much more realistic than the way her father had described Him. She saw Him as a judge—one who sits on His throne, waiting for sinners like her to cross the line. Although she wasn't really sure where the line was, she had to be getting close with her latest antics. How could she press God further by going into a house of worship dressed as a man? She was already living a lie. God, her father said, was all-knowing. If that were true, how long would He allow her to go on without some form of retribution? *Was my brush with the law a warning? Is being tied to this man part of God's punishment?*

Jason watched Zanne's expression go from contemplative to fearful and wondered what he was thinking. Jason took a stab in the dark. "Amy said you've attended church for years. I don't understand your hesitance. You act as if my request is foreign."

"My family has always attended church, but God ... well, let's just say I've been questioning my faith since my father's death."

"God had His reasons for calling your father home, Zanne. Grief and loss are a part of life. We don't always understand why things happen as they do, but God's promises remain true. Just like your earthly father was there for you when you got hurt or needed a shoulder to cry on, our Heavenly Father has promised to be there for us. The difference is, He will never leave us or forsake us."

She could hardly think straight. "I'm trying to accept what I can't change, but it isn't easy."

"I understand that more than you know, but if you don't, bitterness will eat you alive. Concentrate on what you have left. It can change your whole perspective."

She faced him. "I have nothing left! Remember? The one consolation I did have was Amy, and now—now even she has been taken from me."

"Friends will come and go, Zanne, but God is the one constant we can depend on. He never changes."

Suzanne, staggered by his choice of words, stared at the good doctor. "You mean my sister ...."

"No, I don't .... I pressed Amy the day she asked me to take you on. I never saw the family resemblance. I was hoping you would tell me yourself." Jason shrugged, "I suppose your trust is something I'll have to earn."

"What else did she tell you?"

"Not much. She said the two of you went to school together. Something about your mother remarrying and you not wanting to hang around to see how it all panned out."

Her head lowered, "I couldn't ... the thought of my mother being with another man ..." tears flooded Suzanne's eyes, but she refused to let them fall. If she allowed herself to begin crying, she might never stop.

"Changes like that are rarely easy to accept.

"I'll agree with you there." She was afraid to ask, but she had to know. "Did Amy happen to tell you my real name?"

"No, said you'd tell me more when you were ready."

He had every right to demand answers, and yet he didn't press her. Awed by his selfless approach, she asked, "And you're fine with that?"

"I came close to turning her down because of it. When I prayed about it, I was at peace with taking you on. After seeing you in action yesterday, I no longer wonder why God brought us together."

Zanne smiled. It did her heart good to hear him admit that he needed her. "Give me time, Jason. Before the year's out, I'll come clean. Truth is, I wish I could tell you everything right now, but I can't .... I hope you'll be understanding when I finally do."

"Just remember that running from God and others won't help you settle things in your heart and mind. Ask yourself if what happened in Detroit could be God's way of trying to get your attention."

Zanne harrumphed, "I certainly hope not!" What she thought was entirely different. *Gracious! Can the man read my mind?*

"Don't be too sure. God loves you, Zanne, and He'll go to great lengths to expose your doubts for what they are—lies from the enemy. Experience has taught me that running only lengthens our agony."

Her brow furrowed. "You just don't understand. There's so much you don't know about me."

Jason lowered his head in contemplation. When he did peer up, the kindness emanating in his gaze told Suzanne much about the man before her. He genuinely cared. Why, she did not know, but the realization warmed her heart.

"We have a year together. I'm a good listener. When you're ready to talk, my door is open."

She could appreciate his concern but needed to reassure him, "I have good reason to feel the way I do about church—about God."

"I'm sure you think you do. I'll pray for you, but my expectations will remain the same. Be sure you're in church tomorrow morning at eleven, okay?" His tone was not harsh in any way. Even so, he was not giving her an option.

"You're the boss. I'm not so sure about the note-taking, though .... You may need to show me what you're looking for."

"That's not a problem. Tonight after supper we'll go over my notes from the last sermon I heard."

She snarled up her nose. "If we must ...."

Jason laughed out loud, slapped his knees, and stood to his feet. "You will survive the torture, Zanne. I'm heading out to the barn. Get your things unpacked and make yourself at home.

Gerty should be back with supplies in a bit. She'll need your help unloading, so listen for her."

"Yes, Sir ...."

Jason turned to leave and glanced back. "Zanne."

"Hmm?"

"Loose the *Sir*, will you? I told you, it makes me feel old."

Suzanne chuckled softly. "Sorry ... didn't even realize ..."

"I figured as much." Jason walked out the door with a renewed determination to pray for his assistant throughout the day.

While washing breakfast dishes, Suzanne devised a plan that should go off without a hitch, provided Jason didn't expect her to ride with him to church. If she remembered correctly, the farm they were meeting at was fairly close to home. After dumping the dirty water in the woods, she put the washbasin back on the work board and flew up the stairs to her room.

Removing her hat, she combed through her long hair letting it hang free while she worked. Unpacking her bag of feminine attire, she shook out her rumpled dress. It was a mess. Her skirt wasn't much better, but it would have to suffice. Although she'd feel better about wearing the skirt if she could press it, she wouldn't be able to manage that without someone catching her in the act. Perhaps hanging it in her armoire overnight would help. If all else failed, she could wear her long sweater over top.

Suzanne felt so dirty and grubby. As much as she would love to luxuriate in a nice hot bath with fragrant salts, a cold wash in the creek with a bar of soap would have to do—plausibly for the next year. If she hurried, she might be able to sneak out the back way unnoticed and return before Gerty.

After tucking the rest of her belongings away, she grabbed

her clean clothes and flounced down the stairs like she had on numerous occasions at home in Ypsilanti. As she reached the bottom, her heart stopped—and then sped out of control. Jason had come back in and was sitting at the table with a cup of coffee, grinning at her. The heat crawling up her neck was not a good thing. Her cheeks would soon be a bright shade of cherry.

"I'm glad to see you more at ease, but I wouldn't have guessed that you had so much hair under that hat, Zanne. I'm sure if you ask her real nice, Gerty will cut it before tomorrow."

"No thanks. I like it long." She pulled it back and stuck it in her shirt. "Amazing what you can hide inside your clothes." She turned to leave—couldn't wait for a response. If he insisted on her getting a haircut, she would just die. "Heading down to the creek to get cleaned up," she spouted, as she moved out the door. "Be back in a bit!"

"If you wait up, I'll head down there with you. I could use a good soak myself."

I don't think so! "Can't wait. Gotta be back in time for Gerty."

"Oh! Suppose you're right. No hurry, Zanne. I'll wait until Gerty gets here before I come down."

"Thanks!" and Suzanne was off.

❀ ❀ ❀

"I'm leaving for church, Zanne. You ready?" Jason asked as he came in the back door.

Her tentative gaze met his. "If you don't mind, I'd rather walk. Could use some time alone."

Jason eyes narrowed. His assistant was acting strange, but

he was trying to give him some rein. "Are you sure you can find the farm?"

"The Crandall's place is the one between here and the Parker's, right?"

"That's it. Be sure you give yourself ample time."

"Not a problem." Jason was heading for the door when she summoned the courage to say, "Don't bother looking for me, Doc." As she suspected, his expression was not favorable, so she reaffirmed, "You did say you don't care where I am as long as I can hear the message, didn't you?"

"Yes, but ..."

Suzanne held up her hand. "You don't need to remind me ... I'll take notes as promised."

"Good enough." Jason watched Zanne run up the stairs before he walked out the door. He had no reason to doubt that his assistant would be in attendance. For some reason Zanne's odd mood bothered him. Shaking off his unease, Jason headed for the barn to saddle Buck.

Suzanne couldn't believe her good fortune. Gerty had mentioned last night that from now on she would be spending the Lord's Day with her grown son's family who lived across town. On Sundays, Suzanne and Jason would have to fend for themselves. Since Gerty needed to be on her way right after breakfast and wouldn't return until that evening, Suzanne would have the time to make herself look both presentable and unrecognizable to Jason and the other inhabitants of the village of Saline.

Changing at home was risky. If the good doctor were to come back, Suzanne's cover would be blown, but she really had no other option. How could she resume her role as Suzanne without first inspecting her reflection in the mirror?

She smiled as realization dawned. This could turn out to be a blessing in disguise. On Sundays she would be free to be Suzanne Somers, if only for a few hours. Perhaps going to church wouldn't be so bad after all. Her spirit quickened as she began preparations. Donning her female unmentionables was only the tip of the iceberg. A flurry of fanciful memories came rushing in as she slipped her shift over her head and took a quick peek. Since the feminine garment was not a hand-me-down but made specifically for her, it hugged her every curve. Removing the leather tie from her hair, she brushed through her long lengths and for a change allowed it to hang free. Sticking her arms in her yellow ruffled blouse, she pulled it over her shoulders, buttoned it up, and immediately observed the way it set her features aglow. Why had she never noticed this before? Pulling her skirt up over her narrow hips, she tucked in her blouse, secured the waist, and strolled in circles about the small room. She loved the way the fabric swayed with every step—and then how it flared when she spun in delight. My, but it felt good to be herself, to smile and feel so carefree—so feminine. Too bad she couldn't go whole hog and smell like a woman, too. Best not to push her luck.

When her shoes were buttoned and her bonnet was tied in a nice bow, she tucked her manly apparel into her satchel. Slipping the handle over her shoulder, she picked up the Bible and notebook Jason had given her and took one last peek at her reflection before flouncing down the stairs. Suzanne, noting the mantel clock, realized that she would have to put a good foot under it. If she didn't hurry, she would be late. The last thing she wanted to do is draw attention to herself amongst her new neighbors.

The warm breeze tussled Suzanne's hair as she made her way through the dense woods that led to the Crandall's farm. Had she not taken so much time primping, she could have walked the beaten path. Fortunately, she didn't run across any creatures determined to keep her from her destination. The moment the farm came into view, she stuck her bag behind a tree and took a second to take note of her surroundings. It would never do to misplace her manly garb.

The Pastor was welcoming the small gathering of folks as Suzanne slipped in the side door. No one seemed to notice her late entrance, so she took a seat on the closest bench. When the congregation stood to sing a familiar hymn, she joined in.

> *There is a fountain filled with blood,*
> *Drawn from Emanuel's veins;*
> *And sinners plunged beneath that flood,*
> *Lose all their guilty stains:*
> *Lose all their guilty stains,*
> *Lose all their guilty stains;*
> *And sinners, plunged beneath that flood,*
> *Lose all their guilty stains.*[1]

The second stanza began, but Suzanne could not join in. She got all flustered when she realized that Jason was looking directly at her. As much as she wanted to turn away, she could not move. Did he recognize her? She thought not. His brow rose with interest, and then he nodded in greeting. Apparently, he was waiting for her to respond, so she returned the gesture. Thankfully he turned back to the young lady standing beside him and smiled

---

[1]   Cowper, William. *There Is A Fountain Filled With Blood.* 1771

tenderly. As soon as Jason rejoined the singing, Suzanne relaxed enough to glance around the room.

She counted twelve adults and seventeen children. Several of the adults were her mother's age, a few older. There were two young men who appeared unattached, and a rather shy young lady sitting with her parents who appeared interested in the available gents. Suzanne smiled, wondering which one of them had peeked the young woman's interest. As Suzanne took in the antics of all the small children, she shook her head, wondering how their parents would manage to keep them content during the sermon. Thankful that was not her problem, she set her Bible on the bench beside her and waited to see what would come next. The preacher stood at the makeshift pulpit, his smile kind as he looked out over his small congregation. She held her breath when his gaze fell on her, but she calmed when he bowed his head in prayer and then spoke to the group at large.

"As we turn in our Bibles to the book of Proverbs, I'd like you to take into consideration how much our attitude affects our approach to life. Read along with me in chapter fifteen and verse thirteen:

A merry heart maketh a cheerful countenance:
but by sorrow of the heart the spirit is broken.

"As much as all of us would like to avoid sorrow, it is inevitable that we'll face some form of sorrow during our lifetime. Those of us who have lost a loved one know how devastating that loss can be. But let me assure you, if you haven't realized this already, how we respond to grief is up to us. Grief is not just a state of mind—it's a process we must work through, and that process takes time.

Accepting what cannot be changed and focusing on what we have left is huge to our healing. We as individuals must take the first step by releasing our grief."

The more she listened, the more Suzanne began to wonder if this pastor and Pastor Williams in Ann Arbor had prepared their sermons together. The message was certainly familiar. But then she decided the common thread had to be the Word of God.

Her eyes scanned the meeting room. Folks were hanging on the pastor's every word. Amazingly enough, so were the children. Apparently, she was not the only one in the room struggling with this very issue.

"Have you ever stopped to think about how much our attitude can and will affect the outcome of an argument? Many of us know that the hurtful words often spoken in anger can plague us long after an argument is over. We have a choice to make when this happens. We can choose to forgive, or we can hang on to our anger and carry that hurt with us—sometimes for the rest of our lives. God's word says that we must forgive as Christ has forgiven us. Allow me to assure you that our attitude will make a huge difference in the kind of relationships we have with others.

"I'm sure some of you children can recall a time where you had to miss out on something you wanted to do, because you had chores that needed to be done. Think about how you felt when you began those chores. Were you upset, or did you approach them with a willing heart? Our attitude, as we begin our chores, will always affect the outcome.

"Sorrow and disappointment cannot be avoided, but how we respond to them is up to us.

"If you're like me, you'd like to believe that our attitude is automatically good, just because we're Christians. Unfortunately, that is not the case. Attitude is a choice."

Suzanne was scrambling, trying her best to catch every thought the man presented. She was shaking her hand, trying to let the blood flow through it, when she caught the end of her pencil on the bench. The lead broke. Her heart sunk. Now, what was she supposed to do? She had no choice but to just sit and listen.

"Skip down to verse fifteen with me.

> *All the days of the afflicted are evil:*
> *but he that is of a merry heart hath a continual*
> *feast.*

"Now turn to chapter seventeen verse twenty-two.

> *A merry heart doeth good like a medicine:*
> *but a broken spirit dries the bones.*

"The Scriptures are clear, wouldn't you say? We can choose joy in every circumstance, but I wonder—do you? Can you see how much our attitude affects every relationship we have, every trial we face, every obstacle that gets in our way, every fear we must overcome, every commitment we make, virtually every area of our life?

"We can't go back and undo the things we have done, but we can ask Christ to forgive us and go on. We can make better choices in the future.

"Paul could have lived with regret. He could have lived with bitterness. But he chose to live with a servant's heart—he chose to praise God in every circumstance. I encourage you to read Paul's epistle to the Philippians ...."

Suzanne had barely paused in her intent to capture everything the preacher was saying, but her mind was suddenly all in a whirl. She couldn't help it. If the preacher was right ... oh, what did it matter if he was right? There was nothing she could do about the way she left Ypsilanti—nothing she could say to make things right, not for a year anyway.

This is precisely why I hate coming to church. If I could just sit here and not be affected by the words spoken, I could walk away unscathed. Unfortunately, every service I've been to since my father's death has left me in a state of utter turmoil.

Suzanne would have to find a way to make Jason see that her being in church was all wrong. He was not a cruel man. Surely, he would understand.

Suzanne, needing to escape unnoticed, slipped out the door when the congregation stood to sing the last hymn. The whole experience reminded her of home. She needed time to collect her thoughts and change back into Zanne before facing Jason.

He Loves Me!

Chapter Seven

Attitude

"ZANNE!" Jason bellowed from the front door. When there was no response, he ran up the stairs and found his assistant sleeping. At first his anger flared. Had he missed church completely? However, recalling the message, he gave Zanne the benefit of the doubt and opened the notebook he had given him. Jason smiled. He felt like a snoop, but he was pleased with what he found. Zanne had been quite thorough—up to a point anyway. Closing the book, he moved to the bed and nudged his young friend.

"Zanne. Come on. We need to be on our way."

Suzanne couldn't bring herself to look at him. She didn't appreciate the way he just barged into her room without so much as a cursory knock. Even so, he did think her a boy. She would have to get over it. "Can't I just stay here this time? I'm tired, Jason."

"If you're sick and need doctoring, tell me. Otherwise, I'll expect you outside in five minutes."

Suzanne muttered with derision as she sat up on the side of the bed, "Must be nice being the biggest fish in the pond ...."

With raised eyebrows, Jason fixed his eyes on Zanne. "Excuse me?"

Suzanne was immediately contrite. "Didn't mean anything by it. Sorry ... suppose my attitude going into this needs a bit of work."

Jason chuckled softly. "So you were there. Good word, wouldn't you say?"

"Hardly!" *Irritating is more like it!*

Jason turned to leave, informing her as he thudded down the stairs, "Get a move on, Grumpy, and adjust that attitude while you're at it!"

Suzanne, knowing Jason had read her correctly, moved down the stairs with a skip in her steps, making a conscious effort to alter her mood. Jason was waiting on Buck when she came out the door.

"Where are we going?" Suzanne asked after taking the hand up he offered.

"We were invited to have dinner at the Crandall's. I don't know about you, but I'm starving. If you wouldn't have taken off the way you did, we'd probably be eating by now."

You're always starving! "You probably won't understand, but I'm just not ready to be social." She paused, contemplating how she could tell Jason what was plaguing her. But when the words rolled down her tongue, they came to a screeching halt. She opened her mouth to try again, but her thudding pulse made it difficult to think. In the end, she just blurted them out, "Jason, I don't expect you to understand, but I've given this considerable thought. I really think—for the time being, that is—it would be best for me to stay away from church."

Jason's head swayed back and forth.

She had to make him understand. "I can't go. Today I walked away feeling more frustrated and scrambled up inside than I was before I went. I need to stay away until I can get some things figured out in my heart and mind."

"Church is exactly where you need to be. Take it from someone who knows, feeling all scrambled up inside isn't necessarily a bad thing. You may not agree now, but in time you will. I'm afraid this topic is not open for debate. You can and you will be in church!"

"You're as bad as my brothers! Why must men always be so pigheaded?"

Jason chuckled. "You'd best watch what you say, Zanne. It's not wise to down grade your own gender."

Suzanne was silenced.

"So ... while you're revealing a small corner of your past, how many brothers do you have?"

"I'm not telling ... I wasn't supposed to say that much!"

"But you did, so come clean. How many?"

Suzanne slid off Buck and stayed behind Jason's mount, kicking at the long grass while she ambled along.

When Jason craned his neck around, she looked away. "You can't avoid me forever. Little by little the truth will seep out."

"Hopefully, by the time it does, this year will be over ...."

"If you try putting into practice what Pastor said, you might find yourself facing this time in a positive light. A year from now, you could be looking back and seeing all the ways God has helped you, instead of the negatives. The choice is yours. Peace and rest won't come until you quit resisting Him. He's for you, Zanne, not against you. Let Him love you through your storms."

"If you're going to preach at me, I'm going home, Jason."

"No, you're not!"

"Then bugger off!" she demanded with a stomp of her foot.

Unfortunately, his horse startled and reared up, dumping a surprised Jason on the ground. He didn't appear hurt, but she had no way of knowing how he would respond. She hadn't been around him long enough to know if he would retaliate.

When Jason stood to his feet and nonchalantly brushed off his jeans, the look he sent Zanne's way did not bode well. She thought about taking off after Buck, but the good doctor snagged her arm before she could get away and began tickling her. "Stop!"

Jason, satisfied that Zanne's downcast mood had been sufficiently altered, declared, "Now that's better, don't you agree?"

Suzanne lowered her head and Jason released her. As hard as she tried, she could not contain her amusement. "I suppose!" she said, as she stuck out her chin. "Laughter, I've been told by my brothers on numerous occasions, is good for the soul. Perhaps they were right!"

"No question about it. Something tells me I'd enjoy meeting these brothers of yours. Did you know they took that quote straight from Scripture?"

"No preaching!"

He held his hands up in resignation. "You were the one quoting Scripture, not me."

When she scowled, Jason latched onto both of her arms and pulled her close—too close for her comfort.

"As punishment for dumping me off my horse, Young Man, you will reveal one secret from your past."

Her eyes never left his as she shook her head in denial. She needed him to release her—now.

"A refusal is not acceptable. Extra chores for a week or tell me how many brothers."

"Are you sure your name is not Jesse ...?" Her hand flew to her mouth, as she turned away, but still he would not release her.

Jason chuckled. "Getting to know you should be easier than I thought! I'll assume Jesse's your oldest brother, since he's the one who irritates you the most."

"He only irritates me when he's ordering me around—like someone else I know ...."

"Get used to it! Care to tell me more?"

She wiggled out of his hold. "That's all you're getting out of me, Doctor Michaels!"

His eyebrows arched.

She held her breath wondering what he would say or do next.

"That works for me! I've got plenty of chores to keep you going for a solid week."

"That's blackmail!"

"You're the one running from your family—and from God. He put you in my care, Zanne. Tell me how many brothers, or pay the penalty."

She folded her arms, scowled, and started to walk away.

"Zanne!" Jason bellowed, thinking his assistant looked all too much like a spoiled female. However, Jason changed his mind when Zanne's brow knitted together, and he shot him a fiery glare. No female could look that fierce.

"I need time to think. I'll give you my decision on the way home."

"I can live with that."

"I'm glad you approve ...."

"Zanne?"

"What?"

"Do I need to tickle you again?"

Suzanne, unwilling to wait around to see if he would, took off running toward the Crandall's. When she realized he was not in hot pursuit, her steps slowed. The Crandalls didn't know her from Adam. She wasn't about to knock on their door without Jason present.

Jason saw Zanne leaning against a tree and asked as he approached, "Will you be all right?"

"I hope so. If I disappear, you'll know I've gone home."

"You're not going home, Zanne. These people are our friends. Besides, you know what I told you before we signed the papers."

She lowered her head. "I'll be the perfect gentleman, I promise."

Jason nodded, all to aware of what Zanne's words had cost him.

They were almost to the house when a portly gentleman with creamy white hair opened the door to greet them. I see you located your assistant, Doc. Welcome."

"Thanks for the invitation," Zanne offered.

"We're glad to have you."

As they entered the house, a flurry of activity was going on in the kitchen, so Suzanne headed that way. Several children were already seated at the table and the two gangly girls gawking at her couldn't be more than ten and twelve. A stocky boy of about fifteen was seated off to the right with a freckle-faced boy beside him who looked about five. The youngest, a girl of maybe two with a head full of blonde ringlets, was sitting between her older sisters, chewing on a piece of bread.

At the counter cutting bread stood the young woman who had been sitting next to Jason in church. Mr. Crandall promptly introduced her, "Zanne, I would like you to meet Emmaline. She's new to the area as well." Then he pulled a rotund woman into the crook of his arm and smiled as he kissed her brow. 'This here is my lovely wife, Celia."

Celia sent Suzanne a warm smile. "Welcome, Zanne. You too, Doctor Michaels. If you'd like to take a seat, the meal is ready to be served."

Suzanne was asked to sit beside Rachael, the older of the two girls, and Jason sat next to Emmaline. Surprise, surprise! The woman had wasted no time declaring her intent. The way she doted on the good doctor was more like a mother hen than a potential wife, but what did Suzanne care? She held no attraction for the man. Why shouldn't Emmaline have him?

Suzanne bowed her head while grace was being said and managed to be quite congenial for the rest of the meal. With Rachael's endless prattle, there was never a dull moment.

When the gentlemen were asked to retire to the sitting room so the ladies could tidy the kitchen, Suzanne tried to make her excuses and leave, but Jason sent her a look that startled her. She had no more resigned herself to more endless dribble, when Mr. Crandall's oldest son joined them and took the empty seat. A game table sat in the corner of the large room. Perhaps if she could interest him in a game of checkers, the day would not be a complete wash.

"Noel," his father suggested, "Doc's looking for a horse for Zanne. Why don't you take him out to the barn and see if he's interested in the gelding I bought off Bradbury last week."

Noel's brow rose. "Flash?"

Mr. Crandall nodded, the corners of his mouth curving up. "Yes, Son. He's spirited, but with a little work, he'll settle down."

"You sure a scrawny lad like Zanne can handle him?"

Suzanne's defenses rose. This sounded all too much like a challenge to her. "I've never been on a horse I couldn't handle, Noel."

Suzanne, wondering what Jason was thinking, glanced his way.

"See what you think, Zanne. Just don't let your pride get in the way. I need an assistant, not another patient."

She tried to contain her elation but couldn't quite pull it off. Walking over to where Jason sat, she leaned over and whispered in his ear, "You're sure we can afford this?"

Jason chuckled. "You let me worry about that."

Suzanne was elated—astounded would be more like it. Could this really be happening? Noel stood, and she gladly followed him out the door. They were almost to the barn when Suzanne asked, "Do you have a horse, Noel?"

"Sure. Kansas and I have been inseparable since my tenth birthday. By the way, Zanne ... didn't mean to come across so high and mighty in there. Flash can be headstrong, so don't let down your guard until you get to know him better."

"Appreciate the warning. Can I ask how old you are?"

Noel's chin lifted. "What do you think?"

"If I were a betting man ... I'd say you're fifteen."

Noel beamed. "That's quite a compliment. I know I'm big for my age, but I just turned thirteen in March."

"No wonder you think I'm scrawny for my age."

Noel led her down a row of stalls, stopping long enough to rub the faces of the horses as they passed. "My sister Rachel is only eleven, and she's already close to your height."

"How old is Danielle?"

"Nine."

"Wow! Guess I have some catching up to do. She's tall for nine, don't you think?"

Noel grimaced. "Sorry about the way they were gawking through dinner."

Suzanne grinned. "Not a problem. They were no worse than Emmaline was with Jason."

"She didn't waste any time claiming the good doctor, did she."

"Thought I was the only one who noticed." In awe of the massive barn filled with horses, she asked, "So tell me, Noel, why does your father have so many horses?"

Noel's eyes scanned the long rows of stalls. "The horses in here only scratch the surface. Most of them are out to pasture. We raise, train, trade, and sell them."

"My sister Elizabeth and her husband Kaleb raise horses, too, but on a much smaller scale."

"What's their last name? Could be my father knows them."

Suzanne simply said, "I doubt it. Which one is Flash?" She had no wish to come across as rude by avoiding his question, but she'd given away too much of her past already today.

When Noel walked toward a stall on the end and slid it open, Suzanne's heart did a flip. She couldn't believe her eyes. Flash was black with white markings much like Star's. Leaving her own horse behind in Ypsilanti was difficult, but she really had no choice.

"He's a fine animal."

Noel stuck a lead rope on Flash's halter and led him out. The way Flash skittered nervously about made her wonder if she were biting off more than she could chew. But then, she wouldn't know until she tried.

"You got a saddle and bridle I can borrow?"

"Sure. If you'll hang on to him, I'll get the tack he came with."

Suzanne's movements must have spooked the horse, because the minute she wrapped her hand around the rope, he back quickly away. The rope chewed up the flesh on her hand something fierce. "Whoa, boy ... easy now, Big Fella." Fortunately, her gentle words were a soothing balm. Within seconds she had regained control of the spirited mount.

The pain in her hand took her breath away, but right now her wounds were the least of her worries. If she couldn't ride Flash, Jason wouldn't even consider letting her have him—and she wanted him badly. The thought of owning such a lively mount thrilled her soul. She would do everything in her power to prove herself capable of handling him.

As Noel came back with the tack, he asked, "You sure you want to try this?"

"I have to ...."

Noel chuckled. "I recognize sheer determination when I see

it. We're alike in more ways than you know, Zanne."

"It's nice to be understood."

"If you get lost, look for the river and follow it upstream. The house can be seen from the banks."

"Thanks, Noel." Suzanne stuck her foot in the stirrup and before her leg was over the saddle, Flash was clearing the barn door. Good thing she wasn't wearing a dress. For a while she just let him run—let him blow off steam. And he ran like there was no tomorrow. In fact, they were about a mile away when she decided she'd better rein him in. Her surroundings were unfamiliar, but she wasn't lost. Leading Flash around a copse of trees slowed him to a degree, but she cut him too close and one of the branches snagged her. One second she was sitting atop her horse and the next she was dangling precariously from a tree limb. Other than a few scrapes and bruises, the only thing that was really hurt was her pride. Climbing down, she headed back toward the house.

Suzanne had been walking for what seemed like forever, when she heard a rider coming her way. It was Jason, and he was riding Flash. She glared at Flash when they neared as if he could read her mind. The ornery devil was behaving like a well-mannered gent for Jason. Irritated, she kicked at the grass, wondering what Jason would say.

"Lose something, Zanne?"

She sneered, offering a sideways grin. "We're a fine pair. Both of us thrown from the saddle in the same day."

"Are you all right?"

"Pride's wounded, but I'm fine otherwise."

Jason offered Zanne a hand up, cringing when he got a good look at the raw inflamed flesh on his assistant's hand. Instead of taking her hand, he reached for her arm and pulled her up."

"What happened?"

"It would seem that I'm not the only one with an attitude problem today. Flash here is a fine piece of horseflesh, but he's a bit skittish. Needs some work."

"If he's too much for you to handle, Zanne, don't be stubborn. There will be other horses that come along."

"I know ...." Suzanne wasn't sure why, but she felt a kinship to this particular beast already—or was it determination to master the ornery thing? She allowed the silence to hang between them, as she mulled over her decision. "Flash and I are alike in many ways, Doc. Would you give me the chance to try settling him down?"

Jason nodded. "Until he's more compliant though, I'd recommend you do your training inside the corral at home. We'll double-up on Buck until he's more agreeable."

Suzanne smiled. "Thanks."

"You're welcome. I know you'd like me to keep my distance, but I will be treating that hand of yours when we get home."

She snarled up her nose. "Small price to pay for such a fine horse."

Jason tried not to grin, but couldn't ward it off. "Be honest; a fast horse is what you mean, isn't it?"

"They named him right, that's for sure!"

Jason's assistant's youthful exuberance reminded him of a girl from his past. Since the comparison might not be well received, he kept his thoughts to himself.

Chapter Eight

Fellowship

"I'VE INVITED a guest for supper," Jason informed his housekeeper. "Would it be too much trouble to make something special?"

Gerty, standing at the counter making a small pot of vegetable soup, turned to face the young doctor. "Did you have something specific in mind?"

"The coop could use some thinning ... how about fried chicken with your special parsley potatoes and some of those green beans—you know, the ones with the butter-sauce."

"Sounds like a plan. How about a peach pie, or would you rather a cake for dessert?"

"Whatever you decide will be fine."

Suzanne, overhearing their conversation, laid the book aside she had been reading and asked, "Who's coming over, Jason?"

"Emmaline."

She rolled her eyes. "Should'a seen that one coming!"

Jason grimaced. "Now what's that supposed to mean?"

"Oh, never mind ...."

But he wasn't about to let it rest. "She's new in the community. I thought you'd enjoy having a chance to get to know her."

"Me! Why would I want to get to know her better? It's you she's after."

Jason shook his head. "Your off your rocker, Zanne. She's someone from my past who needed a fresh start. That's all!" When his assistant didn't appear convinced, he reiterated, "That's all!"

Friend my eye! "Whatever you say, Doc."

Jason, thinking Zanne was acting strange, stood and headed towards his room. His steps slowed long enough to overhear his assistant's conversation with their housekeeper.

"Gerty, Noel is expecting me this evening. As long as Doc doesn't put a kibosh on my plans, I'll be eating at the Crandall's tonight. You'll be here to chaperone, won't you?"

"Rest assured, Zanne, Doc's reputation will be intact when you return."

"Good!"

Jason stood in contemplation. Had Zanne's tone been rebellious, he would have told him straight up that he wasn't going anywhere, but that was not the case. He had made plans with a new friend, and that was a good thing. Now Jason could share a quiet evening with Emmaline and catch up on old news.

"Zanne," Gerty said, "I'm doing laundry today. Is there anything stashed in that room of yours that needs attention?"

Suzanne shook her head. "You have enough on your plate already, Gerty. I'll tend to my own laundry, but thanks for the offer."

Gerty smiled, thinking, *it is my job, Zanne, I really don't mind.*

"I'll be in the barn if you need help with anything."The pounding of hooves against the hard ground drew Suzanne's attention as she neared the barn. Young James Thompson was riding into the yard, his red swollen eyes telling Suzanne he'd been crying for some time. "James, what's wrong?"

"Mama's bad sick, Mr. Zanne. Papa said to get Doc in a hurry like."

"Maybe you should go in the house and sit for a spell?"

James shook his head. "Paw said no doodling!"

Suzanne patted the boy's hand. "You head back, then. We'll be right over."

Suzanne plowed through the front door, bellowing out as she did, "Doc, we've got an emergency at the Thompson's place!"

Within seconds Jason came out of his room, half dressed and spouting orders, "Saddle Buck while I grab my bag, Zanne. I won't be but a minute."

They were almost to the Thompson's home when Jason asked, "Who came by?"

"James. Mary must be in a bad way. He'd been crying his little eyes out."

Doc prayed silently as they rode up the path leading to the small home. He had learned early on in his training not to go into an uncertain situation without being prayed up. Hearts were involved when a life was at stake. "Father, give me wisdom," Doc whispered as he dismounted and moved up the steps.

James was standing at the door, apparently waiting for them.

He held the door open and reached for Doc's hand as he entered the Thompson's home.

Suzanne half-expected to find the children outside, but there was no one around. After seeing to their horse, she reverently entered the house and went to the back room. Although she had no way of knowing what was wrong with Mary, it didn't look good.

While Jason examined his patient, he asked, "John, other than a fever, what have her symptoms been?"

John swiped the tears from his eyes with the back of his hand. "She's been vomiting for several days. We didn't call you because she thought maybe she was expecting again. The last few hours the pain in her side has been something fierce. She's sleeping more now and seems calmer, but I'm not so sure that's a good thing. Her breathing has been labored for the last hour. I wasn't sure what to do."

Throughout his years of training, Jason had witnessed a few individuals with the same symptoms. Only on one occasion did the patient pull through. Unfortunately, this was one of the mysteries of medicine that had not yet been unveiled. Unlike the many plagues that sweep through communities, this ailment attacked individuals. Jason listened to his patient for a while. Mary's heart rhythms were so weak his faltered as well.

Jason looked up at his assistant, his expression sullen. "Zanne, I'd like you to take the children and go back to our place. Have Gerty fix them something to eat and try to keep them busy."

"I'd be glad to. If it's all right with you and John, I'll stop by the Crandall's on our way, ask them to pray, and let them know I won't be by this evening."

"That's for the best. No telling when I'll be back. If it gets late, put the girls in my bed and make James a bed on the couch."

Suzanne didn't have to ask, she knew. Outside of a miracle, Mary was on her way to her final resting place, but it made no sense to her. *Why, God? Why would you take this mother from all these precious children—from her husband?* As Suzanne led the children out of the house, she recalled her father's gentle reminder, *"It is not our place to question, Suzanne, but to trust. God sees the whole picture. He has a greater plan."*

Do You really, Lord? Was my father right? If only I could understand.

These children needed Suzanne to be strong right now. As much as she'd love to give into her whirling emotions and have a good cry, she set her feelings aside and concentrated on her mission. These precious children could be losing a parent and she knew exactly how they felt.

The day was warm, the breeze gentle, so Zanne encouraged the Thompson children to visit with Rachael on the porch, so she could speak with the Crandalls alone.

Suzanne was about to knock on the door when Rachel said, "Go on in, Zanne. Mom and Dad are in the kitchen having a cup of tea.

"Thanks. I won't be long." Suzanne, feeling all too much like an intruder, called out from the front door, "Mr. and Mrs. Crandall ...."

"Come on in, Zanne," Mr. Crandall said as he came to greet her. "Can you stay for tea? Celia just made a fresh pot."

"Thanks, but I can't right now. Doc wants me to take the Thompson children home and keep them busy. I just stopped by to let you and Celia know Mary is gravely ill."

"I'm sorry to hear that," Ralf said, "is there anything we can do?"

"I'm sure Doc would appreciate knowing others are praying."

Celia reassured him, "We will. Tell me, Zanne, is there anything else we can do for John and the children?"

"Not that I know of." Suzanne felt better just hearing them say they would pray. Her father, if he were here, would have reminded her that Mary was safest in the Lords hands. "Can you let Noel know I won't be by tonight?"

"Sure."

There was no doubt in Suzanne's mind; these kind folks would reach out to this young family in whatever way they could. Some people, she was learning, were just that way. They had a special gift for reaching out and showing folks that they care.

Suzanne was not at all surprised when Celia filled a basket with baked goods and handed it to her. After picking up a stack of oatmeal-raisin cookies, Celia followed Suzanne out of the house to greet the children.

Four sets of eyes glistened up at Celia as she handed them each a cookie, and she gladly accepted their heart-felt hugs.

"Come on, children," Zanne said to her small charges, "we'd best be on our way."

"Mr. Zanne," Ester inquired as they headed down the path toward Jason's house, "is Mama gonna leave us like Paw-paw did?"

Suzanne's heart sank. She had no wish to lie to this child, but neither was she prepared to tell her what she suspected in her heart. The tears standing in Ester's eyes were almost her undoing. Suzanne stooped down and drew Ester to her, just holding her for a time. "We're going to have to trust that God knows best, Ester. He loves your mama more than we ever could."

Suzanne's mother had said this same thing to her before her father's passing. Now to hear the words coming out of her own mouth made her wonder if she believed them, or was she merely repeating them because they once comforted her? When Ester lifted her head and smiled up at her, Suzanne was glad she had said them, whether she believed them or not.

"I see the house, Mr. Zanne," James said as he pointed up the way.

"We're close," Suzanne agreed, as she too glanced up the path. When she saw movement and a flash of white, she took a closer look. Sure enough, a skunk was ambling their way. Her heart did a jig. The children had noticed the skunk as well and stopped in their tracks. She drew them close and quietly instructed them to be perfectly still.

Throwing her walking stick to her right, she was hoping to deter the critter without giving it too much of a fright. Low and behold, her plan worked. Her nose curled up just thinking about the pungent stench those creatures expelled, as she and the children watched the teetering polecat scoot off into the woods.

Carolina's little hand came to her mouth, giggling when the danger was over. "Papa no like that smell ...."

"Me don't either, Lina," Carolyn added while rubbing her nose.

James rolled his eyes and shook his head. "No one does, you silly girls!"

"I'll agree with you there!" Suzanne affirmed as she latched on to the twin's hands, leading them up the steps and into the house. The five of them found Gerty in the kitchen slicing apples for the pies.

"Well, now, who do we have here, Zanne?" Gerty asked, her smile welcoming.

Instead of answering, Zanne looked down at them and asked, "Children, this is Miss Gerty. Would you like to introduce yourselves, or shall I?"

Ester immediately stepped forward. "I'm Ester."

"I'm James, Miss Gerty, do you remember me?"

Gerty nodded. "I sure do. Nice to see you again, James." Zanne appeared confused, so Gerty offered, "James and his father were in the country store the day I went for supplies. He helped me load the wagon and earned himself a bag of sweets." Gerty's eyes twinkled as she then turned to the girls. "Did he share his candy, Ladies?"

The three of them spoke in unison, "Yes, Ma'am!" The twins were licking their lips—a sure indication that the treats were savored.

"Zanne, if you and the children are going to be here for dinner, we'll need a few more chickens. Would you mind butchering them for me?"

Suzanne's heart faltered. But to her relief, James came to the rescue.

"I'd be happy to see to the chore, Mr. Zanne. Mama says chickens are my specialty. Are the ax and chopping block behind the coop?"

Suzanne looked to Gerty, who said, "Yes, James, they are."

The little tyke went immediately to see to the chore. Perhaps Suzanne should have followed him, but frankly, she didn't have the stomach for such things. Instead, she took the twins out to the barn to check on Flash.

※ ※ ※

Suzanne, hearing a rider coming up the path, peered out the barn door, staying just out of sight. Perhaps she was being rude, but Gerty had the children busy making cookies, and Suzanne had finally gathered a few minutes to herself. She had every intention of taking advantage of them.

When Emmaline came around the bend looking pretty as a picture and all decked out in a soft blue frock with an abundance of lacy frills, Suzanne snarled up her nose. She had forgotten Emmaline was coming. In no mood to entertain Jason's friend, she remained hidden, hoping Emmaline would head towards the house. For Suzanne, getting chummy with this woman was not high up on her list of things to do. Not right now, anyway. It wasn't that Suzanne disliked her, yet Emmaline did irritate her, and she wasn't sure why. When Gerty ushered Emmaline into the house, she breathed a sigh of relief. She went back to what she was doing.

After saddling Flash, Suzanne led him into the corral. She'd been working with him for several days, but still he fought her. The crazy horse seemed to have some sort of a grudge against her. Every chance he got he bucked her off. Between the scrapes and bruises, her flesh was a mess. At the rate things were going, breaking him could take months. Knowing Jason could control him with ease made her all the more determined. As she was coming to expect, she mounted, and after a few hesitant strides, he tossed her off again.

Unfortunately, she was still on the ground when she heard a low chuckle. Where he had come from she did not know, but the sound of Jason's voice interrupted her painful moans.

"Can you get up, or do you need my help, Zanne?"

Her guarded eyes met his. "I'll be fine. Just need a minute." She hesitated before asking, but she suddenly had to know, "Are you sure that beast has been gelded?"

Jason ignored his assistant's cherry complexion and went over to Flash, bent down to take a look, and confirmed, "Sure has!" I'm beginning to think this horse just doesn't like you, Zanne. Have you had enough? Are you ready to trade Flash for Buck?"

I'm convinced it's women he doesn't like, but I can't tell you that! "I suppose I shouldn't be so stubborn. Are you sure you can put up with his antics?"

"We'll do fine." Jason had no wish to make this harder on his friend. Admitting failure was never easy. Of course, Jason was enthralled with Flash; yet knowing Zanne shared his sentiment, he kept his feelings to himself.

Jason was heading back to the barn with Flash when he turned back to his assistant and asked, "Do you need doctoring?"

"No!" she exclaimed.

He grinned. "I was only asking. Calm down! Go ahead and get cleaned up. Gerty plans to have our meal on the table in about an hour."

"How's Mary?" Jason's eyes glassed over.

"She never regained consciousness. John's coming by to share our meal. He'll be taking the children back home after supper."

"Is there anything we can do?"

"The funeral is in the morning. This is going to be hard

on all of them. Whatever we can do to help ease their burden will be appreciated. Unfortunately, life stops for no one. John's got a farm to run if they're going to survive the coming winter. The brunt of the house work will fall on the children until other arrangements can be made."

Jason didn't say more. There was no need. Suzanne knew first hand that farmers rarely had the time to mourn proper like.

Suzanne evaded the kitchen by sneaking in the front door. In her stocking feet, she ran up the steps to retrieve the things she would need for a quick dip in the creek. Since she'd spent most of the last two hours being thrown into the dirt, she was filthy, and boy, was she sore. It was her hope that the cool water would take care of both.

Suzanne was gone longer than she intended, but her throbbing wounds had eased to a degree. There wouldn't be time to dilly-dally in the morning, so after a nice soak, she took the time to search for flowers. Although pleased with the lovely blooms she found, knowing their purpose brought tears to her eyes. The patches of forget-me-nots, Indian paintbrush, and blue-flag-iris made a nice bouquet. She also collected some chicory, daisies, and alfalfa for Gerty.

Suzanne put the funeral flowers in a bucket by the back door and took the steps two at a time. She slipped in the back door to find Gerty stirring her mouthwatering sauce and Emmaline slicing bread.

Gerty caught a glimpse of the lovely flowers and immediately looked to Emmaline, thinking they were for her. When Suzanne handed them to Gerty instead, Gerty was staggered by the gesture.

"A small thanks for all your efforts, Gerty."

"The way you and Doc enjoy my cooking is thanks enough, but I must admit, this is an unexpected pleasure. It's been years since anyone has brought me flowers." Setting her spoon aside, Gerty went to look for something to put them in.

Suzanne turned to greet their guest, "Emmaline."

"Nice to see you again, Zanne. Jason speaks very highly of you."

Suzanne nodded. "We work well together. Do you happen to know where the children are?"

"Jason has them in the parlor. He said something about telling them stories."

This news peaked Suzanne's interest, so she moved toward the parlor. John must have arrived while she was in the creek. The twins were snuggled in their father's lap with James and Ester standing beside him. Suzanne waited in the entrance until John had finished what he was saying to them. Since all four children had tears spilling down their cheeks, she assumed they were now aware of their mother's passing.

"Zanne," John somberly acknowledged as Zanne took a seat across from them, "thank you for helping with the children today. We'll miss her terribly, but Mary's suffering is over."

"I'm sorry for your loss," Suzanne offered.

A silence lingered, and so the room at large was very relieved when Emmaline called them to supper.

After everyone was seated around the long table, Emmaline glanced at John and offered, "You'll have to let us know what we can do to help, John. Gerty and I have discussed it with Doc.

We'll be by in the morning to make your family breakfast and help get the children bathed and dressed for service."

John glanced at Jason. "Are you sure you and Zanne can make do without Gerty?"

Jason nodded. "Zanne and I will manage just fine. Besides," he added as he sent his assistant a wily grin, "it's high time Zanne learned his way around this kitchen."

Suzanne's stubborn chin shot up in the air. "I'll wager I can cook circles around you, Doctor Jason Michaels!"

John mustered a half-hearted grin as he glanced at Jason. "Sounds like a challenge to me, Doc. Who knows, your protégé might just surprise you."

Suzanne was wondering what she had gotten herself into, when Jason's gaze narrowed in on her.

"In that case, as long as Gerty is in agreement, John, plan to have her help you out for the next month. That should give you ample time to adjust, and me enough time to take Zanne to task."

"A month, you say!" John affirmed. "That would certainly help me out. What do you say, Gerty?"

"I'd be glad to help in whatever way I can. Of course, I'd still have to stay the nights with Doc and Zanne."

Jason wondered why, but didn't question her.

Emmaline put in, "Gerty if you get too overwhelmed, you can always call on me to help."

"Then it sounds like a plan," Jason agreed.

Suzanne glanced around the table as her new friends took each other's hands. These people were not just guests; they shared a special bond because of all that had transpired. While John and his children were hurting because of their terrible loss, there was much to be said about folks joining in prayer, sharing a meal, and then taking their friendship one step further—helping the Thompsons through this difficult time of transition, somehow making their burden lighter, and somewhat easier to bear.

Chapter Nine

Treatment

*J*ASON RETRIEVED the medical supplies he would need and whispered a prayer as he made his way back out to the sitting room. His assistant had fallen asleep in the chair, but it was more than obvious to Jason that Zanne's wounds needed tending. He recognized the signs, and he was not about to ignore them.

Setting his bag on the end table beside his charge, Jason pulled a chair up close and nudged him, "Zanne ..."

Suzanne's arm came up to cover her face. "Oh, please! Go away, Jesse. I'm too tired to go ...."

Jason's soft chuckle seemed to lull her back to sleep. "I know you are, but I'm not your brother, Zanne. Your leg is still oozing blood, and I know from the way your sitting that your hip is killing you."

Suzanne's eyelids suddenly flipped up, and her face filled with alarm. "I'm fine—really I am. Sleep ... sleep, is all I need. Sleep will do wonders for aching bones." She tried so hard to stay awake, but she was drifting off again.

Jason's heart went out to his assistant, but he was not about to back down. "Zanne, remove your jeans so I can tend your wound! I'm not taking no for an answer this time."

Her droopy eyes widened tenfold. With great effort she pulled herself out of the chair and would have fallen if Jason hadn't been close by. "No!" she retorted, pushing him away. "I'll be fine."

Gerty, hearing a commotion, came to the sitting room. "Is every thing all right?"

Suzanne attempted to move away, but Jason reached for her arm and gently held her in place.

"Zanne needs doctoring, and he's being stubborn."

"I'm fine!"

But Gerty knew better. When she noted the bloodstains, she sternly admonished, "Take your britches off so Doc can take a look see."

Suzanne merely shook her head in denial.

"Quit with all the nonsense," Gerty added, "and take it like a man, Doc's only trying to help you."

Shocked that dear sweet Gerty would try and bully anyone, Suzanne turned to Jason. For a moment she only stared, but there was no denying his determination, it was steadfast. "If you're going to hurt me, I'll pass out. I'd best use the outhouse first."

"Go ahead. Can you make it alone?"

"Yes!"

When Zanne came in the back door, Jason was waiting for him. "Let's go upstairs to your room."

Finding no hope for her predicament, Suzanne did as she was told, albeit reluctantly.

While Jason did not doubt that every step brought his assistant pain, he said nothing as they moved slowly up the stairs.

When Suzanne ambled into her room, Gerty was lighting several lard oil lamps that she had gathered from around the house. It took a moment for her eyes to adjust to the brightness, but when they did, she realized that Gerty and Jason were staring—at her. Setting her discomfiture aside, she turned to Jason.

"Slide your jeans off, and we'll get this over with."

The thought of disrobing, even partially with him present did not set well, but she reminded herself that he was a doctor. And he only wanted to help. Unfortunately, this knowledge brought her little comfort. Resigning herself to the inevitable, Suzanne pulled her shirttail out and tugged her jeans off. Thankfully, her under drawers covered most of her. When she sat on the edge of the bed her hip joint caught, and she grimaced in pain.

"Zanne, go ahead and lie flat on your back, I want to try something. The doctor I trained under showed me a trick that should put your hips back in place."

"Is it going to hurt?" When he only shrugged, she admitted, "I'd rather know up front."

"I've been told by other patients that the manipulation gave them immediate relief."

She nodded. "Then go ahead."

Jason moved the leg in the oddest way before he asked, "How does it feel?"

"Better ... Thanks!"

"Good! One problem solved."

If only the gash in my leg could be fixed so easily.

Jason didn't wait for permission; he sat down on the bed beside her, took the scissors out of his bag, and started cutting up the leg of her drawers, stopping just above the wound. He would have berated his patient for letting this go so long without attention, but with Gerty present he had no wish to draw undue attention to his assistant's glassy eyes. "Have you taken a look at this, Zanne?"

"Yes and no. Every time I try, I feel woozy."

He understood. "I think you know what needs to be done."

She shrugged. "I suppose."

Gerty asked, "Do you have everything you need?"

"Everything but water, if I don't give him some laudanum, he'll pass out on me for sure." Jason sent his assistant a playful wink. "He already looks a bit green around the gills, don't you think, Gerty?"

Kindness emanated from the dear woman's eyes as she squeezed her charges hand and then turned to walk away. Gerty was almost to the door when she stopped to reassure their patient, "Don't think about what needs to be done, Zanne ... Doc will have you fixed up in no time."

If only she could. Suzanne rolled over on her side, needing a moment. Jason's intense stare was making her nervous. Although she did wonder what he was thinking, she didn't ask.

Why did I have to be so determined to break that

stubborn horse? As hard as she tried to ward them off her fears plagued her. It was childish, but she'd give anything to have her brother's strength to draw on right now. Like her father, Jesse had a way of comforting her as no one else could. Unfortunately, thoughts of her father and Jesse brought tears to her eyes.

Suzanne was relieved when Jason stood and moved to the washbasin. She could use a moment to pull herself together. Letting him see her in this vulnerable state was out of the question. He might expect tears from a woman, but not a young man. Minutes had passed before she gained a semblance of control, and by then, Gerty was walking back in.

As Suzanne watched Jason mix up a brew, she tried to make light of her circumstances. "Just hit me over the head, Doc. If you don't, Gerty will have to sit on me to keep me still."

"You'll be fine, Zanne. The drug should help take the edge off."

"I'm not convinced ... I hate needles and my tolerance for pain is close to zero."

Jason shook his head. "I beg to differ with you. I watched you get thrown from that horse over and over again. Your tolerance for pain is better than you think."

"I hope you're right. Otherwise, this whole experience could prove to be extremely humiliating."

"I'll be as gentle as I can, but that gash is deep. Do you know what you cut it on?"

"Not sure. Maybe I should go check the corral." She moved to get up, but Jason forestalled her.

"That can wait. Drink this."

Suzanne, terrified of what was yet to come, took the cup and drank every drop. She then turned her pleading eyes on Gerty. "You'll stay with me, won't you?"

Gerty smiled. "I will." In an attempt to get their patient's mind off what needed to be done, the kind woman's endless supply of stories flowed freely. In fact, she was halfway through her third tale when she realized that her charge had drifted off to sleep. Taking a clean hanky out of her sleeve, she dried the tears running down her patient's face and thanked the Lord for His mercy.

As Jason cleaned Zanne's leg, he noted how small the bones were and wondered if he should be concerned. *A young man's bone structure at sixteen should be much larger than this. Perhaps the other men in his family are small.*

Although stitching such a ragged wound was tedious work, he was pleased that Zanne was now unaware. He had just tied off the last of numerous stitches when blue eyes opened wide and met his. After a starry-eyed glance around the room, Zanne drifted off again.

Jason bandaged the wound. After propping Zanne's leg up with several pillows, he left his patient in Gerty's capable hands. Since she had to be at the Thompson's early the next morning, Jason offered to take the second watch.

The rooster crowed, slowly drawing Suzanne from her dream-like state. Sprinkles of lemon-colored light had set her room aglow, and the warm breeze coming from her open window only added to her delight. What a sight it was to behold!

A quick scan of the room brought Jason into view. His tall

muscular frame was scrunched in the small chair from Gerty's room, and his long legs were propped up on her bed. She wondered if he had been there all night and took a moment to really look at him. He was a handsome man—even with his blonde hair all askew. Like Jesse, he towered over her, and his soft blue eyes, often filled with compassion, had a way of easing her every care.

Thinking she had better get moving if she was going to be ready for the funeral, Suzanne tried to sit up, but the pain in her leg was too much. Her anguished cry, though muffled by her hand, woke the good doctor with a start.

Jason sat up and reached for his patient's arm. "Don't move, Zanne. You'll tear out all my handy-work."

"But we'll be late ...."

His brow knitted together. "You're not going anywhere, Young Man!"

Suzanne scowled. "I have to be there for the children, Jason. They won't understand if I'm not."

"Yes, they will. Your welfare is my first concern. I won't risk an infection setting in. Give it a couple of days, and then you can make it up to them."

The set of his jaw told her the subject was closed. "All right. I'll do as you say, but I have to go downstairs."

He was shaking his head.

"But I'll go crazy being up here all day."

"Oh, all right. I have a set of crutches in the barn. But you're only to use them to go to the outhouse, understood?"

She nodded, but a quick peek at Jason told her he was not finished.

"And you'll sit on the sofa with your leg up the entire time I'm gone!"

She peered up through squinted eyes. "Except when I need a cup of tea, yes."

Jason grinned as he moved toward his ornery friend. "Come on, I'll carry you downstairs on my back."

She scanned the room looking for her jeans, but they were nowhere to be found. "Where are my clothes? I need to get dressed."

"Nope!"

She scowled at the good doctor when he craned his neck around and glared. "Why not?"

"No stiff jeans until that leg heals some."

"That's preposterous! Indecent, if you ask me ..."

Jason's hand came up to forestall any further complaint. "My way or stay in bed!"

"Yes, Jesse ... whatever you say, Jesse ...!"

Jason shook his head as he helped his assistant to the edge of the bed. "You are a character."

"Sorry Doc, it can't be helped. Runs in the family ...."

Jason hoisted Zanne onto his back and said as he moved down the stairs, "One of these days ... one of these days I'm going to meet this family of yours."

"We'll see ...."

Chapter Ten

Caring Friends

$\mathscr{I}$N THE DAYS AND WEEKS that followed Suzanne's injury, her relationship with Jason grew deeper. His special care of her during her time of recovery made a huge impact on her. Although he often teased her about her skinny legs, if he suspected her scam, he had yet to acknowledge it. The way he reached out to her went above and beyond the call of duty but she often caught herself reaching out to him as well. They were becoming friends in the truest sense of the word. Although there were secrets Suzanne still couldn't tell him, if they continued to bond the way they were, anything was possible.

Every evening he was home, Jason would insist on going over their sermon notes together. At first Suzanne was so frustrated about having been stuck in the house that she barely gave him the time of day. When the change began in her heart she did not know; she just knew that it had. She was like a sponge—she couldn't get enough of God's Word. Even when Jason wasn't around, she was reading. The time they spent delving into new passages and uniting in prayer was affecting the way she felt about every aspect of her life. The peaceful transformation taking place in her heart and mind amazed her.

Suzanne had so many questions that were finally being answered. She was finding out her view of God in the past had been so wrong. The things her father had tried to teach her were finally making sense. The Bible expounded on those truths. Why could she not see them before now? God wasn't sitting on a throne waiting to punish her for her wrongs. In fact, He loved her so much that He sent His only Son to pay the penalty for her sins.

She was ready to find out how she, too, could know the same peace that seemed to flow so freely from Jason. When she finally summoned the courage to ask, he simplified things for her. She had to confess her sins to God and admit her need for a Savior. If she did, her new life in Christ would begin. This sounded too easy. There had to be more. At that time she wasn't prepared to press him further.

But ... last night, in the quietness of her room, she got down on her knees and did just that. She confessed every sin she could remember and even asked God to bring to remembrance the ones she was unaware of. As promised, God's peace flooded her soul. There was no doubt in her mind that her life would be different from this day forward.

When Suzanne awoke the next morning ready to tell the world about her new life in Christ, her thoughts cried out, *What was I waiting for? Why did I allow my stubborn pride to keep me from You for so long? Forgive me, Lord.*

She couldn't help but wonder, *Did You allow me to follow my own path so I could see the folly of it? I certainly botched things up, didn't I? Thank You for opening my eyes—for allowing me to see the error of my ways.*

Did God really have a plan and purpose just for her? Her father and Jason had said that He did. Although she had no idea what that purpose was, she felt certain she was now on the right track.

She was different—peaceful. A new desire was growing inside her—a desire to learn all she could—a desire to know her Lord & Savior more and more.

Her fears were dissipating. The pleasure she and Jason were finding in working toward common goals only added to her joy.

And then there was Emmaline. She had become an active part of both their lives. While Suzanne still saw her as a bit of a nuisance at times, Jason enjoyed having her around. Suzanne would just have to get used to her presence.

Gerty had been back for a few days now. The Thompson family, though still grieving their loss, had settled into somewhat of a routine. Several of the women from church were taking turns bringing them baked goods. Convinced that they were being well cared for, Gerty was at ease leaving them. She had missed the good doctor and his young charge.

After the dishes were tucked away, Gerty lumbered up the steps to tidy her room. A month of dust had settled in, so she saw to that first. Although her rugs could use a good beating, they would have to wait for another day.

Wanting to do something special for Zanne, Gerty gathered his dirty clothes to wash them. What she found hanging in the closet amongst Zanne's things gave her confirmation, but they also gave her cause for concern. Unsettled about confronting

Zanne, Gerty waited until Jason went to the barn.

"I don't want you to think I was snooping, Zanne, but you and Jason have been working so hard. I wanted to get your laundry done for you."

Suzanne, suspecting what was coming next, opted for nonchalance. "And you're wondering why I have female clothes amongst my things?"

"Well, yes, I am curious."

"It's simple, Gerty, one of Amy's bags got mixed up with mine, so I ended up with some of her things. I hung them up until I decide what to do with them." Guilt washed over Suzanne as she turned away. Lying was not nearly as easy as it used to be. Her conscience plagued her, but how to remedy the situation was still a mystery. She would have to commit it to prayer.

❀ ❀ ❀

"Excuse me!" Emmaline called out to the young woman who was practically running away from the meetinghouse. The young woman had done this for several weeks now, but today Emmaline was determined to speak with her and followed fast in her footsteps. She was either ignoring Emmaline's call, or her mind was otherwise engaged. She tried again. "Miss, oh, Miss!"

As much as Suzanne wanted to ignore the relentless woman, she suspected it was only a matter of time before she caught up with her.

Suzanne had noticed Jason ogling her in church over the last few weeks. Once he even had the gall to wink! What was he thinking? While it was not without effort, Suzanne had managed to avoid his flirtatious glances thus far. Had Emmaline caught him in the act? It would not be the first time a jealous woman set out to befriend the competition. Well, Emmaline had no reason to be jealous. Suzanne's relationship with Jason was strictly platonic—it always would be.

Although Suzanne cringed at the thought of facing the woman pursuing her, she had never shied away from a good intrigue before. Why start now? This could be fun. "I'm sorry, Ma'am, my mind was elsewhere. Were you calling me?"

"Yes. You've been coming to fellowship for weeks now and I have yet to meet you. My name is Emmaline. Since we're the only single adult *women* in the fellowship, I was hoping we could have dinner together. I'd love to sit and chat ... you know, get to know each other better?"

Suzanne pointed to Emmaline and then to herself, needing to be sure she understood her correctly. "Just the two of us?"

"Yes ..."

Hmm ... Suzanne thought. "That would be nice."

"I'm glad you agree. I have a small place in town. Isn't far, and the plump chicken I left roasting in the oven should be just about ready to feast on. We can chat while the trimmings finish cooking."

"Sounds wonderful, but I'll have to let the folks I'm staying with know I'll be eating out."

Nodding Emmaline said, "That's understandable. I live next to the country store ... can you find it on your own, or should I walk with you?"

"No ... ah ... I mean, that's all right. I've been by your place several times. And, in case you were wondering, my name is Suzanne."

Emmaline smiled. "My dearest friend from back home is a Suzanne, too. Come as soon as you can."

"I will." Suzanne smiled in return, and said, "Thanks for the invitation."

When Emmaline nodded, they went their separate ways.

Suzanne, after scribbling out a message for Jason, informing him that she would not be home, tied it to the leather strap by his saddle horn. Surely, he would find it. She had no way of knowing how he would feel about her not checking with him first, but Sundays were a day they fended for themselves. Pushing care aside, she quickly retrieved her bag of clothes. The congregation was joining in the last hymn, and she needed to get out of there before anyone else tried to stop her. Since it was one of her favorites, she joined them as she moved along.

> *Come, thou Fount of every blessing,*
> *tune my heart to sing thy grace;*
> *Streams of mercy, never ceasing,*
> *call for songs of loudest praise.*
> *Teach me some melodious sonnet,*
> *sung by flaming tongues above;*
> *Praise the mount! I'm fixed upon it,*
> *mount of God's unchanging love.*
>
> *Here I raise my Ebenezer;*
> *hither by thy help I'm come;*
> *And I hope by thy good pleasure,*
> *safely to arrive at home.*
> *Jesus sought me when a stranger,*
> *wandering from the fold of God:*
> *He to rescue me from danger,*
> *interposed his precious blood.*

O to grace how great a debtor,
daily I'm constrained to be;
Let that grace now like a fetter,
bind my wandering heart to thee.
Prone to wander, Lord, I feel it,
prone to leave the God I love;
Here's my heart, O take and seal it,
seal it for thy courts above.[1]

A subtle change was taking place in Suzanne's heart. The words to the song were reaching down into her soul and filling the hollow places with joy—joy that had been missing from her life for far too long.

Daddy, is God's mercy truly never ceasing as the songwriter says? So many times you reminded me that God loves me just the way I am. That drawing close to Him is the only way to find lasting peace and contentment in this life. Although I don't fully understand why God would love someone like me, I've read too many passages lately that say He does. How could I doubt God's Word—how could I have ever doubted you, Daddy?

Looking back over the last few months, she could see God's hand at work in her life. *You were the one who sent Jason to rescue me from that jail cell, didn't you, Lord? Thank you. Thank you for loving me, even when I mess up.* As she neared Emmaline's house, she began to wonder if Emmaline's friendship was also part of God's plan.

Suzanne had barely reached the top step, when the front door opened. Emmaline's gentle smile as she greeted her, was not that of a jealous female but that of a caring friend. She had apparently misjudged her. *Forgive me, Lord.*

---

1   Robinson, Robert. *Come, Thou Fount.* 1758

He Loves Me!

Chapter Eleven

Jesse

"JESSE?" Suzanne exclaimed, shocked to see her brother coming out of the livery in Saline. While she immediately regretted alerting him to her presence, it was too late for regrets as he headed her way. Suzanne's heart thudded faster with every step he took. She longed to see him. Even so, how would she explain her whereabouts? *What will he do? What should I say?*

Suzanne was the last person Jesse had expected to see on his way out of Saline, and his sister's expression told him she felt the same about him.

"Suzanne?" he questioned as he neared, lifting her chin to get a better look at her face. "What are you doing here? I thought you were in New York. And why are you dressed like that?"

Several onlookers had stopped to gawk. Jesse wasn't exactly quiet about his inquiry, and she had no wish to have tongues flapping, so she reached for her brother's arm, her eyes begging him to be silent while they walked toward the outskirts of the village. The respite gave her a moment to consider her words. She hadn't planned for this. Suzanne waited until they were out of sight of the town's people before allowing Jesse to hug her tightly. Her mind was going in every direction, but realizing her brother's love for her had not changed, warmed her heart. She savored the comfort she found in his arms—if only for a moment.

Suzanne, lifting her wary gaze to his, had guilt wash over her, as she stared into his big blue eyes. "Oh, Jesse. I'm sorry I didn't tell you where I was. I have good reasons. Something terrible has happened. I just couldn't ... I couldn't tell you." Her head lowered, but he cupped her chin and brought her eyes back to his.

"Suzanne, I'm your brother. I love you no matter what has happened."

"I know," she admitted as she crumpled to the ground in a heap.

"Suzanne, what is it?" His heart clenched. Her anguish was more than apparent, so when she didn't readily answer, he waited for her struggle to abate.

Summoning courage, she met his concerned look. "If I tell you everything, you have to promise not to tell anyone. If you need to check on me from time to time, I can understand, but I can't have the rest of the family coming around."

"Why not?" he questioned.

"You're going to have to trust me in this, I just can't ...."

His jaw tensed as he stooped down and took a firm hold on her arms. "Tell me what's going on, Suz, or I'll take you home right now."

Tears filled her eyes. She didn't doubt for a minute that he would, so somehow she had to make him understand. "It's a long story, Jesse."

He glanced around, lifted her to her feet and led her to a large stump so that they could sit together. "I've got all day."

"First tell me, how is everyone?"

"Worried sick about you!"

Filled with timidity, her eyes met his. "Did you find the letter?"

"Yes. I understand to a degree, but when has running from your problems ever solved them?"

"I had to, Jesse. I still feel like vomiting every time I think of Mom with that man."

His eyes narrowed in on her. "Watch what you say. If it wasn't for that kind man, I wouldn't have my wife or my children."

Her head lowered. "I'm sorry! I don't think it would have mattered who she wanted to marry. It would still feel like a betrayal of Dad."

"Her life is not yours to live. You have to let go of this and quit trying to control Mom. It's not your place. What she does is between her and the Lord. Josiah makes her happy. That doesn't change her love for all of us or for Dad. She has wonderful memories of Dad and she'll always cherish them, but Dad's not here. How would you feel if you told Mom you loved someone and she refused to accept him?"

She hadn't thought about it that way. "I suppose I'd feel betrayed."

"Exactly! Let go of your pride and come home, Suzanne."

Tears spilled slowly down her cheeks. "Oh, Jesse! I wish I could."

Perplexed, he asked, "I don't understand. Why can't you?"

She swiped her tears with the back of her hand. "That's what I need to tell you. Amy was convinced that we'd be safer traveling as brother and sister. As you can see, I'm the brother. We were out walking the night before we left Detroit and ended up in the wrong place at the wrong time. To make a long story short, I was falsely accused of theft. They've been having problems with young men in Detroit, so in these situations the judge issues a mandatory sentence at the work house for those charged—one year."

"But you're not a man. Is that how you got out of it?"

She shook her head. "No one knows I'm not a man except Amy, and she went on to New York."

His eyes widened. "So how did you get out? Why are you here?"

"The judge allows one exception."

"I'm almost afraid to ask."

"If Amy could find someone who would agree to take me on as an apprentice for the year, they would release me to that person."

He rubbed at his beard stubbled chin. "I take it she did."

Suzanne nodded. "A doctor was on our stage. He was only going to Detroit to pick up supplies and then coming back to Saline to set up his practice. You know how easily Amy makes friends. Jason agreed to take me on with a few stipulations."

Jesse's brow rose. "Care to elaborate?"

She rolled her eyes. *Do all men use that same phrase?* "I have to live under his roof." She held up her hand to stop him when he started to overreact. "Don't worry. He has a housekeeper who lives with us and shares the top floor with me. Besides, Doc still thinks I'm a scrawny lad of sixteen."

"Yeah! Until the first time you get injured, and he has to examine you."

She giggled. "I've made it quite clear that I don't like doctors poking and prodding on me."

He shook his head. "So am I going to meet this doctor?"

"Oh, no, Jesse, you can't. You just can't. I slipped one day and told him I have brothers. I even let the name Jesse escape. He knew with the way I talked that you had to be my oldest brother."

This news peeked Jesse's curiosity. "Why is that?"

She lowered her head and then slowly peered up. "He's been trying to get me to open up about my past. He even pressed the issue when I let my temper flair and startled his horse several days back." Her face scrunched. "Jason ended up on the ground. Let's just say he was none too happy."

"He'd better not be getting rough with you, Suzanne. How did he press you?"

"Don't worry. He would never do anything to purposefully hurt me. He gave me a choice: I could tell him how many brothers I have or face extra chores for a week!" Her tone lowered as she replied insipidly, "I asked him if he was sure his name wasn't Jesse ...."

"I see," he acknowledged, chuckling softly.

"It's not funny, Jess. You know what I'm like. I honestly don't know how I haven't spilled the beans about my gender yet." Her brother laughed out loud, and she relished the sound of it.

"You never have been very good at keeping secrets."

"Ya, well you should have seen the look on his face the day I forgot to alter my tone. I used the excuse that my voice is still changing, but I'm not sure he'll buy that line again.

"So how long before you can come home?"

She hesitated, leery of his reaction. "About nine or ten months.

His drawn cut whistle did not surprise her. "That's a long time .... I suppose I should be thankful you're alive."

Her eyes begged for understanding. "I really am sorry I made all of you worry. Do you think Mom will ever forgive me?"

"You know the answer to that already."

She nodded in understanding.

"So where were you heading?"

"Back home. If I don't show up soon, Jason will come looking for me."

Jesse stood and helped her to her feet. Reaching for Shadow's reigns he said, "Show me where you're staying, in case I need to contact you."

Wary of what he might do with this knowledge, she reaffirmed, "You won't blow my cover, will you?"

"Not unless I have reason to believe you're in harm's way." They walked for a while in silence, but Jesse, needing to remind her, said, "You know, Suz, God will never honor you living a lie. It just isn't right."

"I know .... I want to tell Jason, but I need time to pray about it."

Jesse grinned. "Pray about it! Am I hearing you right? If I remember correctly, you made it clear that you no longer believe in God."

Suzanne bumped into him. "Don't tease me, Jesse. Truth is, I wanted nothing more than to get away from God and all of you preaching at me. He got my attention when I ended up in jail. As if that whole experience weren't bad enough, He put me right back with a man who loves God as much as you. He even insists that I go to church and study with him."

"Is that so ...."

"Yes ... He's helping me to see things in a different light. I was so wrong, Jesse. I do need Christ. I tried to walk away, but it didn't take long to see that without Him, my life was completely without purpose. I just existed."

"Oh, Suzanne, that is good news."

"All this time I've been running—from what?"

"Each of us has to come to the place where we choose who we're going to serve. Unfortunately, in failing to choose God, we choose self. I suppose you've figured out where serving self gets you?"

"In big trouble!"

Jesse chuckled at his sister's wide-eyed expression. "You came to your senses, Suz. As long as you seek the Lord with all your heart, He will lead you."

"I'm not so good at doctoring, but God's using me to ease the minds of Jason's patients."

I want to meet this doctor someday, Sis."

She nodded. "You'd like him. In many ways Jason is like you and Dad."

"Good! Then I won't worry about you."

She grinned mischievously. "Worrying won't do you any good. Just pray for me."

"Every day."

"Gerty, our housekeeper is something else. I've wondered at times if she suspects that I'm a woman, but she hasn't come right out and asked."

Jesse chuckled as he ran his fingers down his sister's cheek. "Jason must be blind not to see how pretty you are."

Her arms stretched wide. "In this get up?"

Jesse cupped her chin and brought her gaze back to his. "Yes, Suz, even in that get up. You're too feminine to pass for a man."

"Then the whole town is blind!"

"Dad was right—people see what they want."

"Suppose so."

"Now tell me, Suz, if you had to, could you get home from here?"

She pointed east. "Sure! Ypsilanti is that way."

Jesse shook his head. He should have known better than to ask.

"Sort of ... if you need to come home, maybe you should take the stage." Jesse reached in his pocket and pulled out some coins. "Here, keep this in a safe place, just in case."

"Thanks." Suzanne hated goodbyes, but she really did need to be on her way. "I wish things were different, Jesse."

"I'd love to be taking you home." He pulled her into his arms. "I understand that you can't. Just knowing you're safe is a huge relief."

Her arms slid around her brother and hugged him tightly. "The farm is just around the bend. I need to go ... wish I could invite you in for supper, but Jason would ask too many questions."

"I'll be by to check on you often."

Suzanne stepped back. Her wide eyes, filled with alarm, met his. "You can't, Jesse!"

"I have to, Suz, you're my sister. I'll pray that you can tell Jason the truth soon, and that he'll understand."

Her head lowered. "Please don't insist that I tell him. If I do he might send me back to Detroit. I can't take that chance."

"Have some faith, Girl. God will lead you. When the time is right, tell him."

Suzanne nodded, knowing she should, but how could she? "You have to let me handle this my own way, Jesse."

"I'll only promise to try. What name are you going by?"

"Zanne Somers. It's the only thing about me that's not a complete lie."

Needing to see her smile, Jesse pulled her back into his arms, tickling her sides like he had so many times before.

"Jesse, stop!" she demanded.

He couldn't help it, he desperately needed to hear her laugh. After kissing her cheek, he released her. As hard as it was to let her go, he watched her disappear into the line of trees. Curiosity pressed him forward, however, and he followed her, staying just out of sight. Jesse watched Suzanne interacting with a tall blonde gentleman. After gently admonishing her for being late, he sent her into the house to eat her meal. *He's younger than I would have thought, but he's protective of my sister and that's a good thing.*

In the worst way, Jesse wanted to follow Jason into the barn, but instead he turned and walked away. He had made his sister a promise not to interfere. For now, he would pray. Fortunately, their time together was not a total waste. His heart was rejoicing. Suzanne was not only safe in the good doctor's home, Christ was now the Savior of her soul. He did not doubt that His Spirit would lead her. God's purposes for this time of separation were in full view before him. How could he be anything less than overjoyed?

"Zanne, you're awfully quiet tonight. Is something wrong?"

She and Jason had been going over his notes from last week's sermon. "I'm sorry ... I suppose I have other things creeping in. Can't concentrate."

"Care to share?"

For the space of several moments, she stared into the cold fireplace. How could she explain the awakenings taking place inside her? What should she say? Where could she begin? "The way I look at everything is changing since I surrendered my life to Christ."

"That's how it should be, Zanne. Old things are passed away and behold all things become new."

"True, but some of the things I've done in the past ... well, they're troubling me ... plaguing me would be more accurate."

Jason's brow furrowed. "You can't change what you've done, Zanne. Give your cares to the Lord. Remember, the enemy wants to use our past against us, but never forget that God is our redeemer. Forgiveness is yours because of what Christ accomplished on your behalf. With God's help, you can strive to do better in the future."

"I agree, but don't you think God wants us to make amends for the wrongs we've done?"

"Whenever possible."

"That's the problem. It's not possible." In the worst way she wanted to tell him everything, but how could she?

"Does this have something to do with the way you left your family?"

Her eyes welled up with tears. "Yes ..."

"You seemed fine this morning. Did something new come up?"

Wiping her tears with the back of her hand, she tried to pull herself together. Allowing herself to get all-emotional in front of Jason was completely unacceptable. Desperate to sort this out, she stood. "Something did happen, but I can't talk about it yet!"

She was making a hasty exit, when Jason asked, "Zanne, where are you going? "We've barely gotten started."

She stopped at the door and glanced back. "Would you mind if we put this off until tomorrow? I could use some time alone."

Jason shrugged. "As long as you don't make a habit of it."

"I have no intention of doing that, but ..."

"It's fine." Jason watched him go, knowing there was more to this than he was saying. With the way their relationship was changing, Jason was fairly confident his assistant would talk when he was ready.

Suzanne, needing to set her cares aside, drank in the warm air as she moved slowly away from the house. Loosening the bindings on her golden brown hair, she shook her head and allowed it to hang freely, reveling in the way the gentle breeze tossed it to and fro. Her gender, everything about who she really was down deep inside, longed to be exposed. Her femininity defined her. She had never realized what a gift it was to be a woman, until now—now that she was pressed to keep it hidden.

God, You know I'm struggling with living this lie. It's tearing me apart, and little wonder. Your word says to be anxious for nothing. To bring everything to You in prayer. I'm doing that now, Lord. If You want me to expose this façade, then give me a peace about doing so.

Suzanne took the time to pick some fragrant columbine and Indian paintbrush she found along the way. Her bouquet looked a bit sparse, so she filled it in with daisies and black-eyed susans before heading toward the water.

Bathing in the cool river had become her solace—her time alone with the Lord. One of the few times she could relax, unwind, and truly be who she was created to be.

Suzanne's spirit quickened as she took to the path that led to the moving waterway. This reprieve would avail her much. Shedding her masculine attire, she hung her things from a nearby bush and didn't so much as hesitate in walking into the water. Surrendering her body to the calming fluid, she glided across the water, dipping down at times to allow the clear liquid to rinse her hair. Retrieving the soap she had hidden away, she had barely finished scrubbing from head to foot when she heard someone coming down the path. Oh, no! This would never due.

Suzanne swam down river and hid in the first thicket she came to. Fortunately, the evening shadows had already fallen, availing her the coverage needed.

"Zanne!" Jason called out from the water's edge, "Hattie's having heart problems again. I'm heading over to her place."

Although she was relieved to learn that it was only Jason, she couldn't exactly go to him. Instead she offered, "I'll get dressed and come as soon as I'm done."

Jason waited to see if his assistant would appear. When he did not, he berated, "Zanne, we're both men. Why are you hiding? Come out of there."

Not on your life! "If you don't mind, I'll wait until you're gone."

Jason shook his head, but he did turn to leave. "Have it your way ... don't be long. If she's being ornery, I may need you to stay the night, so pack a bag."

"Not a problem." Suzanne breathed a huge sigh of relief when Jason's steps faded into the woods.

Chapter Twelve

Hattie

"NOW, HATTIE," Suzanne scolded her elderly patient, "do I need to fetch Doctor Michaels again? He won't approve of your being up and about with your heart racing the way it is. He left me with strict orders to see that you stay in bed."

"Oh fiddle sticks! I'll tell you what, Little Missy! I'll be good the day you decide to set aside this pretense and tell me your real name. And besides that, you need to get out of those manly clothes. A pretty young woman needs to show off her womanliness. You'll never catch a man if you don't start dressing like a lady."

"Hattie!" Suzanne was flabbergasted. Dumbfounded would be more like it.

"Oh, come on now, Zanne. You may have pulled the wool over Doc's eyes, but you don't fool me. I know you're young, but you are a woman. Admit it. It'll do you good, Sweet Pea!"

Suzanne didn't know what to say—or how to react. For the span of several seconds she just sat down on the bed beside her patient. Resigning herself to having been found out, she softly admitted, "Suzanne ...."

"Well, I'll be! Now that is nice. Should have known. I thought Zanne was a strange name from the start. You know, like it was missing something."

Suzanne's timid gaze met Hattie's. "You're the only one who knows, Hattie."

Her mind clicked. "You're the young girl who comes to meetin and sneaks out just before it's over, aren't you?"

"Yes ... Jason insists that I go, but how can I go as a man? It would be blasphemy. I'm surprised he hasn't asked me where I've been sitting. He knows I come because he insists on me taking notes."

A twinkle lit Hattie's green eyes. "Well, if that don't beat all! Doc left you here for the night, isn't that right?"

"Yes, Ma'am. He said he wouldn't be back to check on you till tomorrow."

"Good! There's an armoire in the other room. I have a full wardrobe of feminine things that are too small for me. They're barely worn. You go ahead and dig through them until you come up with something nice to put on. While you're here, I'd like you to tell old Hattie why you think it's necessary to dress like a man. In the meantime, I want you looking like a lady. You've been hiding in those things for so long, your actions are starting to fit the part."

Suzanne smiled. "I'd like that more than you know. I hate dressing like a boy. I just ... well, I got caught in a lie, and I don't know how to get out of it."

"Maybe that's why God brought us together, Sweet Pea. So I can help you."

Concern etched Suzanne's face. "But I'm supposed to be helping you, Hattie. Not the other way around."

"You are. I haven't had this much fun in years. Now skedaddle … and don't you come back until you're dressed like a lady clear down to your unmentionables."

"Hattie!"

"I'll be checking, so don't you try skimping on what goes under the dress."

Suzanne shook her head. "Yes, Ma'am."

Her heart was all a-flutter as she went to the spare room and slowly opened the door, awed by what she found inside. Lavishly decorated with cream lace and frills, the varying shades of plums and pinks scattered throughout enhanced the room's delicate appearance. As if all this was not enough, the scent of lilacs filled the air.

Suzanne couldn't help giggling, recalling Hattie's insistence. When her eyes fell on the skillfully carved armoire, she wondered what treasures she would find inside. Exploring its contents was like embarking on a treasure hunt. If she had gone to the store, she would not have found this many things to choose from. Hattie was right. The unmentionables she found did not appear worn, and someone had painstakingly embroidered them with a variety of wildflowers.

There were several dresses, lovely to be sure, but it was a rose-colored skirt and cream lace blouse that caught her fancy— the essence of femininity! Suzanne quickly peeled off her manly garb. Pulling the skirt over her hips, she held the fragrant lace blouse up to her face and drank in the aroma before slipping it on.

Hattie would be pleased. Everything fit perfectly. It was as if Hattie had the wardrobe tailor made just for Suzanne. She felt like the belle of the ball as she brushed out her hair and pulled it away from her face with the small pearl comb she found tucked in the top drawer. When all was in order, she swayed into Hattie's room, swirling nonsensically before her like a giddy child.

"My, but you look lovely, Suzanne!"

Suzanne went to her, sat down on the edge of the bed, and hugged her tightly. "I can't thank you enough, Hattie. You've made my day!"

When Hattie peered around her, as if someone else were in the room, Suzanne's heart faltered. Who could it be?

"Wouldn't you agree that my niece looks lovely, Doctor Michaels?"

Doc? Suzanne's eyes grew huge and her mind skittered to and fro. While she suspected he was truly present, the depth of his voice when he spoke still startled her.

"Wholeheartedly! Truth is, I'm glad I stopped back by, Hattie. I've been hoping to meet this remarkable young lady for several weeks now. She's made a habit of getting away before I've had the pleasure."

Suzanne had yet to turn. How could she? A red flush was crawling up her face and would not back down.

Hattie, noting her discomfort, tried to ease the way. "I'm afraid my young guest is embarrassed by her playful entrance, Doc."

"On the contrary, I found it quite entertaining, Suzanne. Grace and elegance is a rare gift."

Suzanne had never been worse off, but she was going to have to speak or make a hasty exit. Since she had a sneaking suspicion Hattie would never allow that, she offered, "You're too kind, I'm sure. Aunt Hattie and I do have a tendency to get carried away. Sorry you had to witness our nonsense." The warmth in her cheeks had eased, so when Suzanne heard Jason come near, she stood to her feet and spun slowly on her heal to face him.

Jason held out his hand palm up. As propriety demanded, she offered hers. He bowed and gently kissed it.

"Gallant, and a doctor to boot. Where did you find him, Aunt Hattie?"

She snickered. "He came all the way from Pennsylvania. They grow'em handsome out east, don't ya think, Sweet Pea?"

"Now, Auntie. You'd better behave or the kind doctor will ask me to leave. Too much excitement could be bad for your heart."

"She'll be fine, I'm sure," Jason said as he went to his patient's side. "Do either of you ladies know where my assistant disappeared to?"

Suzanne offered, "Zanne said he needed to see Emmaline about something. He should be back before too long."

Jason had barely finished checking Hattie's pulse and listening to her heart when she made a suggestion. "You two head out to the kitchen so you can get better acquainted. I need a nap, and all this noise is keeping me from it."

Jason knew it was a ploy, but who was he to interfere with her matchmaking games? Offering his arm to Suzanne, he led her toward the kitchen. "I went by Emmaline's on the way here and no one was home. I'm surprised Zanne and I didn't cross paths."

"Hmm ... maybe they went for a walk."

"I don't think so. The note on the door said she left earlier to take a meal to the Thompson family."

"Perhaps he had somewhere else to go?" She wondered when or if he would quit pressing her.

Doc moved to the window and glanced out. "I'll need to have a talk with that boy. I left him with strict orders."

Suzanne turned to fill the kettle, trying not to grin. "Don't be too hard on him, Doc. It isn't as if he left his patient unattended. I assure you, I am quite capable."

"I suppose you're right." Making himself at home, Jason retrieved a cup and poured himself some of Hattie's coffee, choking on his first sip. "I may have found the cause of Hattie's health problems. This coffee is strong enough to curl my hair."

"Then maybe you should have tea. For some reason I can't picture you with curls."

There was something familiar about the way Suzanne rolled her eyes, but Jason had no idea why. "Are you new in the area, Suzanne?"

"Yes and no. Visiting, you might say ...."

"Hmm ... with anyone I know?"

Suzanne turned to open the breadbox, pulled out a tin of cookies, and took the time to arrange them on a plate just so before answering. "No ... My other relatives live on the outskirts of the village. They keep to themselves." She was hoping this would be the end of his diligence. It was not.

"Do they have names?"

"Enough about me, Doctor Michaels. I'd like to hear what brought you to the village of Saline. Surely there were other more desirable positions available back home."

He chuckled. "You're not going to make getting to know you easy, are you, Suzanne?"

"A little mystery can be a good thing." *I am curious, though, what would Emmaline say about this friendly encounter?*

Jason held a chair out and motioned as he said, "If you'll take a seat, I'd be glad to tell you anything you'd like to know about me."

Anything? There were so many things she wanted to know and didn't hesitate to ask. As much as she enjoyed her extensive chat with Jason, the tables were turning, and she had already told him more lies than she should have. Besides, she suspected that if Zanne did not show up soon, he'd be in a world of trouble. The hour was getting late, when Jason stood and excused himself to go check on his patient.

Suzanne made a quick stop by the spare room to collect her manly garb and snuck out the back door.

When Jason returned and Suzanne was nowhere to be found, he stepped out the back door thinking she might have gone to the outhouse. While he didn't find his delightful new acquaintance, he did find his assistant stepping out of the crude structure.

"Zanne," Jason mildly berated, "where have you been?"

Suzanne hated having to lie to him, but what choice did she have? "I had a few things to discuss with Emmaline." She shrugged, adding, "I waited around for a while, but she didn't come back."

He nodded curtly, somewhat perplexed. "Suzanne was just here. Did you happen to see where she went?"

"She wanted me to tell you that she enjoyed your visit, but she had to get home."

Jason scowled as he questioned frantically, "And you let her leave alone? Which way did she go? It's getting dark. One of us should have escorted her home, Zanne."

The good doctor was overreacting, but she thought it best not to mention it. "You have a way with the ladies, Doctor Michaels. I'm curious, what would Emmaline say if she knew you were over here flirting with the competition?"

"I've told you before. Emmaline and I are friends. That is all!"

Right! "And I suppose Suzanne is a friend as well?"

His eyes lowered and he cleared his throat before saying, "She's an intriguing young woman."

"Intriguing?" Suzanne asked, following his every move. Unfortunately, his expression gave nothing away.

However, the words he muttered as he strutted back toward the house revealed much, "Truth is, I wouldn't mind getting to know her better in the near future."

For the longest moment, Suzanne just stood in the yard, dumbfounded by Jason's admission. As much as she'd like to chew on his words a while longer, she opted not to read anything into them. After all, there was nothing wrong with his desire to get to know her better—was there?

"Suzanne!" Hattie called out as Suzanne moved toward Hattie fully clothed in manly garb.

On his way out of Hattie's room, Jason craned his neck around, and listened to his assistant's response. "Suzanne had to leave, Hattie. It's me, Zanne," she said, as she knelt down beside Hattie's bed.

Hattie, still a bit groggy, winked at her friend. "She had to get home, did she?"

Suzanne would have scolded her for teasing her so, but Jason hadn't budged from his place at the door. "Yes, Ma'am, she did, so you're stuck with me, and you'd best behave."

"Don't have much choice. That doctor friend of yours must have slipped something into my tea. Can hardly keep my eyes open."

Suzanne caressed the dear woman's cheek and then reached for her hand. Hattie wasn't a small woman, but her bones were frail. "Don't fight it, Hattie. You sleep as long as you can and get well. If you need me, I'll be in that frilly room next door."

"I'm sure you'll suffer through, Zanne. Ruffled nightshirts are in the drawer. Help yourself. You know which one."

"You're such a tease, Hattie! Sleep well. You're in my prayers."

Hattie squeezed Suzanne's hand, and it wasn't long before she drifted off.

"Zanne," Jason said, his voice strained, "I need to speak with you in the kitchen before I leave."

Suzanne followed him, albeit reluctantly. Pouring herself a cup of tepid tea, she took a seat at the table. Jason sat down as well, but he only stared ... raising her apprehensions. Needing a distraction, she stole a cookie off the plate and nibbled on it.

"I'm curious. How do you know Hattie's niece, Suzanne?"

"Can't say that I know anyone here in Saline well. I met her walking home from church."

"Funny you would mention that. I never see you at church,

and yet the notes you take are very explicit. You are the one taking them, are you not?"

Wondering what brought this line of questioning on, she reminded him, "Yes! You told me I could sit anywhere I wanted to, remember?"

His brow wrinkled. "I did, didn't I?"

She nodded.

"Just think it's a bit strange that I never see you and Suzanne at the same time."

Her heart faltered. Was he on to her?

"Then today you've been acting mighty strange."

Before he had time to inquire further, she changed the subject—entirely! "I wasn't going to tell you, but ..." she hesitated. Looking up at Jason as she admitted, "I ran into my brother in town today."

This news took him aback. "Is that why you were late coming home?"

"Yes ... you don't know what he's like. He was determined to take me back with him until I explained my situation."

Jason stood to pour himself another cup of tea. "If you were my brother, I wouldn't have given you a choice."

She peered up, holding his narrowed gaze. "Jesse threatened to, but I told him what happened. For him that changed everything." *I want to tell him that I'm not Jesse's brother, Lord, but how can I?*

"So it was Jesse?"

"Yes. He wanted to meet you .... I made him promise that he'd honor my wishes and stay away for now."

Jason was confused. "Have I done something to make you

feel like your family wouldn't be welcome in our home?"

She shook her head. "No, Jason, but there are things about me you don't know—things I can't tell you yet."

"I wish I understood why ...."

She stood, walked toward the washbasin and began washing the dishes. His kindness was weakening her resolve. "In time I'll tell you ... I promise I will." The silence trailed on and on and on.

"Confession is good for the soul, Zanne. Until you lay every aspect of your life before God, you'll never be free. Only the truth will set you free ...."

"This truth could also put me back behind bars. I'm not ready to take that chance."

Jason scowled. After all they had been through together, he would have thought his assistant would have more faith in him. "Unless you took off without explanation, I'd never turn you in. You don't know me at all if you think for a second that I would, Zanne."

"Hearing you say so is comforting, but I need time, Jason. I have to work this though in my own way."

"I won't push you. When you're ready, I'm a good listener."

"I know. You've been there for me in so many ways."

Jason stood and walked to the window, staring out for a long moment before turning back to look at his assistant. "If Jesse comes back, I want to talk to him. I think it would do you some good to see your family over the Christmas holiday."

Surprised that he would even consider this, she held his gaze. "You'd allow me to go alone?"

"I'd have to talk to Jesse first. I am responsible for you. He needs to understand that he has to bring you back to finish out the year."

A crooked smile creased her face. "You don't have to worry about that. Jesse's a stickler when it comes to obeying the law."

"Good. Did your brother say when he'd be back?"

"No ... he just said often. I tried to convince him that you're a man of integrity, but I know Jesse. He won't just take my word for it. He'll have to see that for himself."

Jason's eyes narrowed in on his assistant, "When he comes I want to meet him. No excuses, Zanne, or I'll take you back to Ypsilanti, find him and introduce myself."

Her mouth dropped open. "Who told you I lived in Ypsilanti?"

"You just did, and besides, you and Amy got on the stage in Ypsilanti. Remember?"

"Oh! Guess I forgot about that."

Jason's eyes held a curious glint. "Truth is, I can hardly wait to see if you take after your brother."

She shook her head and rolled her eyes. "I don't .... He got all the brawn and me all the bones."

Jason laughed as he turned to leave, saying, "So I'm finally going to meet Jesse ...." He let the name hang as he strutted out the door.

Suzanne barred the front and back doors and then peeked in on Hattie one more time before she went off to her temporary room. She gladly shed her manly garb, donned the frilliest gown she could find in the armoire, and spun around merrily, thanking the Lord for his goodness. As she snuggled beneath the feathery soft bed coverings, she tried to recall a time where she had felt so cozy—she couldn't.

Earthly things could not buy lasting happiness. Suzanne knew that, but having Hattie's things about her at this moment was an extraordinary delight. She didn't think the Lord would mind her taking pleasure in her friend's generosity. After all, He was the one who brought Hattie into her life. She thanked the Lord for Hattie's giving heart that desperately needed His touch and for her willingness to share such pleasures with a friend.

Surrounded by frills—soft fragrant feminine frills—Suzanne drifted off in blissful splendor ....

He Loves Me!

Chapter Thirteen

The Effects of Sin

"YOU HAVE TO TELL HER, Jesse!" Olivia implored. "If this was one of our children who had run off, you'd be furious if someone kept her whereabouts from you."

"I know, Liv. I fully intend to tell her, but ..."

Her face flushed. "But nothing, Jesse Somers! You know all too well what procrastination can cost you. Find your mother and tell her now—or I will!" When Jesse's eyes narrowed in on her, Olivia suspected she had overstepped her bounds.

"If you weren't expecting, Mrs. Smarty Pants, we'd be heading down to the river right now!"

Olivia's head lowered, cognizant of his gaze boring down on her. Seconds ticked by before she reluctantly peered up. "Sorry, Jesse. Suppose I do tend to be a bit overzealous when I'm expecting." As she turned to walk out the back door she humbly murmured, "Still think Mom has a right to know. Suppose it's your place to tell her, not mine .... I won't interfere."

"Olivia, come back here, Honey ... come on. Don't run off."

He only wanted to make amends, she knew that, but her emotions were playing havoc with her mind; and besides, unbidden tears had begun to fall. As far as she was concerned, fleeing was her only option. She was almost to her garden when she heard the front door creak. Her husband was running towards her. Before she had time to react, Jesse's arms were about her, snuggling her close.

"Liv, I'll talk to her. Right now if it's that important to you!" When she offered no response, he turned her to face him. In her reluctance to look up, he noticed her damp cheeks. He just held her. "I'm sorry ... I didn't mean to upset you."

"I really don't know why I'm so emotional."

Jesse lifted Olivia's chin, kissing her tenderly. "You're with child, Liv. That explains everything."

Olivia caressed his cheek, her green eyes sparkling in the light of his gentleness.

"Honey, the sun's too hot for you to be tending your garden. Go back inside and relax while the twins are sleeping. I'll help you with the weeding after I talk to Mom."

Smiling, she pulled him close, indulging in several kisses more before inquiring, "How did I get so blessed?"

He sent her a lighthearted wink. "Oh, I don't know. Suppose it's in my blood to be chivalrous from time to time. Can't have my lady thinking I've forgotten how special she is to me." His crossed eyes made her giggle. Jesse had been her knight in shining armor in so many ways, but at the moment he was taunting her. Flipping his hat off his head he teased, "Gallant indeed!"

Her playful spirit did have a way of drawing him in. Scooping her into his arms, he swung her around, sobering under the intensity of her gaze. "Who would have thought?"

"Who would have thought what?"

"That it was possible to be so in love ..." he softly affirmed, as his lips met hers in a tender wave of passion.

After sending Olivia back in the house to rest, Jesse went to seek out his mother. Although he had a tendency to put off the inevitable, doing so had never given him the advantage. He suspected he would find his mother in her garden, and he was right. She was singing merrily as she tended her flourishing plants.

"Mom, I've never known anyone who enjoys this chore more than you."

Her eyes rose to meet his. "Probably never will, Jesse."

"Could be right!"

"This is a nice surprise. What brings you by so early in the day? If you're looking for Josiah and your brothers, they're in the barn."

"Truth is, I was looking for you. Would you mind taking a walk with your son?"

"I'd love to. Just give me a minute. I should let Louise know where I'll be."

Jesse waited for her in the yard, wondering how she would respond to his news—how it would affect her. Oh, she would be thrilled to know Suzanne was safe, he didn't doubt that, but would she be willing to wait nine months to see her daughter?"

❀ ❀ ❀

Jason, dressed in his Sunday go-to-meeting clothes, sat down at the table next to his assistant. After asking the blessing over the meal, he announced, "Emmaline invited us to have dinner with her after church, Zanne."

"Both of us?"

Jason's brow furrowed. "Yes! Is there a problem?"

None that I'd care to share! Instead of exposing her thoughts, she admitted, "Just surprised, is all. Noel and I had plans to go fishing ... suppose we could go another time."

A muscle twitched in Jason's neck and then he rubbed at his chin. Was he angry or thoughtful? When he spoke, she had her answer. "I'm sure Emmaline wouldn't mind if Noel joined us."

"Are you sure?"

He nodded in the affirmative, pleased to see that his assistant was receptive to his offer. "Then the two of you could go fishing afterwards."

"That'll work." Suzanne noticed the odd grin sweeping over his face and could not look away.

"I'm not sure if she'll come, but Emmaline is planning to invite our mystery woman."

"Our mystery woman?" she asked.

"You know ... Suzanne ... not sure what her last name is."

Suzanne choked on the tea going down her throat. How in the world was she supposed to pull this off? Since going to church dressed like a boy was not an option, she would have to avoid Emmaline—either that or turn her down.

Jason had been watching his assistant's expressions over the last few moments. They seemed to be ranging anywhere from worrisome to contemplative. His gaze narrowed. "Is there something going on between you and Suzanne that I should know about, Zanne? You're sending me mixed signals."

"No ... Why would you ask?" Opting for nonchalance, she took a big bite of ham and chewed slowly. She might have pulled it off had Jason looked away. Instead, he continued to stare, making her squirm. Did he know something was amiss?

"Oh, let me see ... perhaps because you're never around when she is. And ... every time I mention her name, you turn a deep shade of red."

His observations should not have surprised her. He was, after all, a doctor. "Merely a coincidence."

"I'm not so sure ...."

"Since we're talking about mixed signals, call me nosy, but I'm curious. How does Emmaline feel about your interest in Suzanne? I'm pretty sure Emmaline's sweet on you."

"She is not! We're just friends. Nothing wrong with that, is there?"

Suzanne stared for a long moment. "Suppose not," she conceded, but didn't believe it for even a quick second.

"So ... are you coming or not?"

"I'll see if Noel wants to join us and then meet you at Emmaline's."

Jason nodded in acquiescence.

Suzanne pointed at Jason's chin, her finger swirling around as she asked, "What's up with the odd patches of hair growth on your chin? Not a good look for a man going courting!"

He rubbed the offending growth. "It's the new look. Kind of like it myself.

Sure you're not jealous 'cause you can't grow one yourself?"

"Hardly," she stated as she snarled up her nose, adding

contemptuously, "Perhaps I'll do you a favor and shave it off while you're sleeping!"

Jason grinned, his eyes glistening with mischief. "Try it and I'll shave off your eyebrows."

A single glance his way told her much. Although his tone was taunting, his expression told her he just might do it. Best not to tempt fate. Feeling awkward for having mentioned it, she lowered her head and ate the rest of her meal in silence.

🌼 🌼 🌼

"Is Suzanne coming?" Jason inquired, as he and Emmaline walked toward her house, with Flash trailing behind.

The hopefulness in his voice put a twinkle in Emmaline's eyes. "What's this I'm hearing, Jason Michaels? Have you finally found a woman who has tweaked your interest?"

The tilt of his head and the lift of his brow told her she had guessed correctly. "Maybe I have and maybe I haven't!"

Emmaline moved just out of his reach and faced him boldly. "Jason's got a girlfriend! Jason's got a girlfriend!"

His face lit with glee as he darted towards Emmaline, wrapped his arms around her and tickled her unmercifully.

"Jason," she exclaimed, in the midst of childish laughter, "stop!"

"That depends, are you going to quit with the schoolgirl singsong and be nice?"

She was treading on dangerous ground, but she had to ask, "If you'll tell me the truth about the matter, I will be the soul of discretion."

He kissed her cheek. "I like her! But no more than I like you, satisfied?"

"It's a start. I suppose you don't know her well enough to say otherwise, but seeing that sparkle in your eyes definitely gives me hope. I'll commit it to prayer."

"Thanks! I would appreciate it. So what about you? Are you ready to meet all the available gents at the next barn dance?"

She bumped him good-humoredly. "You leave me be and take care of yourself, Jason. You've been a good friend, but if God has someone special for me, He will show me Himself. I won't need any help from you."

Jason pulled her into his arms for a hug, trying to reassure her, "He has a plan for both of us, Emmaline. We need to trust Him. Just keep in mind that while I am attracted to Suzanne, I'm not even close to thinking she's the one. Time will tell."

"Pray about it, Jason."

"You know I will."

Suzanne, standing perfectly still at the edge of the woods, had witnessed Jason and Emmaline's tender moments together. Even without hearing their spoken words, she no longer questioned their devotion to one another. In truth, the whole scene left her feeling terribly unsettled—confused. *I thought he liked me?* Unable to face them, she turned to flee.

The rustle of dry leaves, drew Jason's attention away from Emmaline and into the line of trees, but it was not the sounds that held him captive—it was the woman he had been longing to see. Mesmerized by her long flowing hair—a mixture of silky browns, highlighted by strands of gold. How could he miss the way it swayed in the breeze against the subtle backdrop of her pale orchid gown? "Where is she going?" he wondered out loud, wanting desperately for her to turn around and come near.

Emmaline, thinking Jason was acting strange, followed his gaze, but no one came into view. "Where is who going?"

"Suzanne was here. She's disappearing into the woods." He pointed up the way, "See, over there, she's weaving her way through the oaks."

"Go after her!" Emmaline insisted.

Her words were enough to snap Jason out of his stupor, and he moved quickly toward the mysterious woman whose presence was affecting him as no one else could.

The minute Suzanne realized Jason was following, her pace quickened. She hadn't gotten far before he had her in his grasp. She was pulling away, but why? When he turned her gently to face him, she did not look up. The tears spilling down her cheeks had him baffled. "Suzanne, I'm glad to see you, but why are you crying? Are you not pleased to see me? Is something wrong?"

She lied. "No ... it's just, well, I thought I could enjoy a quick visit. I've changed my mind. I'm afraid my emotions are getting the best of me."

"Have I done something to offend you?"

She assured him, "Not at all ..." She had to come up with a good excuse—or surely he would not let her leave. The real reason would never do. "You see my father is ill—he's not expected to live. I really should be with him." The words were true, several years back. It's just ... well ... they spilled out before she had time to consider whom she was talking to. *This man is a doctor!*

"If you'll take me to him, Suzanne, I'd be glad to see if I can help."

Her timid gaze rose. "I hope you won't take offense, Doc, but my father has refused further treatment. His heart is weak and he's ready to meet his Maker."

"I see. Well, can I at least walk you home?"

She shook her head. "I'll be fine. It's not far. Please tell Emmaline that I appreciate the invitation. Maybe we can do this another time when I'm feeling a bit more sociable."

Jason reached for her hand and gave it a squeeze. "Sounds like a plan. You just let us know when you're available." As she turned to leave, Jason called out to her. "Emmaline and I will be praying for your father."

She nodded, saying, "Thanks!" but thought, *No need. My dear father claimed his eternal reward a few years ago.*

Suzanne traipsed into the woods as quickly as she could. She hadn't gone far when a torrent of emotions transfused her body and soul. Thoughts of her deceased father made her miss him all the more. As if that were not enough, she had lied yet again to this man who had shown her nothing but kindness.

Falling to her knees, Suzanne gave way to a fresh rush of tears. Minutes passed before she calmed enough to consider what had just taken place. *What's wrong with me, Lord? Will I ever be able to accept what I cannot change and move forward? I've failed both You and Jason again. I was so sure I would not fall prey to this sin again and yet here I am confessing that very thing. Forgive me, Lord. I know I'm in the wrong. I have no excuse, but I feel so trapped. Show me what You want me to do. Help me to listen.*

When Suzanne opened her eyes, Jason's face came to mind. She would have to lay her agonizing circumstances aside and face him eventually. Best to just get this over with. He would be expecting his assistant at Emmaline's for dinner. *Perhaps facing them as Zanne will be easier to bear.* As tough as it was, she dried her tears, dutifully collected her bag, donned her manly garb, and headed back the way she had come.

How she would manage to sit through a meal with Jason and Emmaline flirting with one another, she did not know. Not only would she be forced to deny her own feelings for this man, she would have to accept that he had fallen for her friend. Fortunately, she had survived worse. *Why did life have to be so complicated, so heart wrenching, so unpredictable and cruel?*

Suzanne dragged herself up the steps leading to Emmaline's. The wall of dread creeping up her slender frame made her feel ill. As if she didn't have enough on her mind, her britches kept falling down. She took a moment to cinch up her belt. Not exactly the best place to do it, but better here on the steps than in front of Emmaline and Jason. As much as she'd like to turn and run all the way back to Ypsilanti, she refused to give in to her emotional state. She had a debt to pay and would do as promised, without complaint. Knocking ever so lightly, she prayed that Emmaline would not be the one to answer.

What in the world! Suzanne exclaimed, though only in her brain. Something was terribly wrong. Her pants were falling down again. *Well, I never!* When she heard the latch lift on the door, she panicked just a bit. Grabbing the back of her britches, she held on tight as she mustered a bogus smile.

"Zanne, welcome!"

Emmaline reached for Suzanne's free hand to pull her in, but she was quick to say, "I'll be back in a second, Emmaline. Need to use the outhouse!"

Emmaline's eyes never left Jason's assistant as he headed out back. What she saw—whew! A ruffled shift was hanging out of his—or was it her—jeans. Emmaline's thoughts were running in every direction. *A sight like this would certainly cause a stir among the women folk at a quilting bee. Since none of them will hear this from me, Zanne, Suzanne, or whatever your name is, your secret will be safe with me! My, but I surely would like to ask a question or two.* She thrilled at the thought. Thinking she should commit it to prayer, Emmaline waited at the door until Suzanne returned. After welcoming her guest, she acted as if nothing were out of the ordinary and inquired, "Is Noel coming, Zanne?"

"No ... his family made plans for him."

"I see. Then I hope you're hungry 'cause we have tons of food. Suzanne wasn't able to come either. Apparently, her father's not well."

"That's a shame. I was looking forward to chatting with her."

Emmaline winked. "Jason's really disappointed. But you'll help me cheer him up, won't you?"

In a bit of a conundrum over Emmaline's words and actions, Suzanne followed her into the kitchen and said, "Hi, Doc."

Although he nodded in greeting, his mood remained somber.

As Emmaline put food on the table she asked, "Are you going to mope all day, Jason Michaels?"

Suzanne, confused all the more, met Jason's gaze. "What's going on, Doc?"

"Nothing I won't get over. Come on Zanne. You mash the

potatoes for Emma while I slice the meat."

So it's Emma now is it? Although she couldn't put her finger on it, she had a sneaking suspicion she was missing something. Jason and Emmaline were acting strange.

The drippings from the tender roast smothered in onions made a succulent gravy, and the trimmings were not only plentiful, they were delicious as well. No doubt, Emmaline had a special gift. When she presented a chocolate layer cake for dessert, Suzanne was too full to eat a single bite. But after eying the slice placed in front of Jason, the temptation became too much to resist.

As the afternoon progressed, Suzanne could see clearly why Emmaline had captured Jason's affection. Her own heart was still in tatters, but she would get over it. Emmaline was a gem, and Jason was fortunate to have her in his life. So was she, for that matter.

After indulging in a second piece of cake, Suzanne needed to visit the little structure out back again. When she returned, Jason and Emmaline were seeing to the dishes. The animals still needed to be fed, and Jason's medical bag would have to be restocked, so Suzanne made her excuses, thanked Emmaline for her gracious hospitality, and was on her way.

Suzanne collected the shift she had stashed at Emmaline's before retrieving her bag. She then took to the beaten path. The walk would be long but pleasant. The afternoon sun had cooled considerably. Although she normally relished her quiet times alone, today, not so much, her thoughts plagued her. Could pastor's message be the cause?

Running away from home had definitely cost her more than

she was willing to pay, but was she really like Jonah? She wanted to think not. Jonah had deliberately disobeyed the Lord's direction. Is that what she was doing every time she put on this façade? Her father had said the story of Jonah was all about second chances.

Jonah's sin really did hurt him more than he was willing to say, and it affected those around him in such a big way. Is that what she was doing to her family and friends? Was her lie a slap in the face to their love? She prayed often that God would give her a second chance to make things right.

She wouldn't blame Jason if he stuck her on the first stage back to Detroit when he found out the truth. Isn't that what she deserved—to be punished for her sin? She highly suspected it was only a matter of time before the whole village found out. Then where would she be?

Lord, why has it taken me so long to fully comprehend the ramifications of my selfishness?

You want me to tell Jason. I can see that now, but how? I'm such a coward ....

He Loves Me!

Chapter Fourteen

Exposed

"SUZANNE." Jason said as she came out the back door, "Emmaline came by a while ago. She's been checking in on Hattie for me, and she's asking for you."

Suzanne smiled, recalling their last visit. Hattie had become so dear to her. "As soon as I hang my wash on the line, I'll head over."

"Check on her supply of digitalis. The only way I know if she's been struggling is if she uses them."

"She's not one to complain, is she?"

Jason shook his head, chuckling. "Only if I insist on her staying in bed."

"Can't say as I blame her." Jason was moving back toward the house when Suzanne reminded him, "When you head over to the Thompson's house, don't forget the cookies I made."

"I won't. I'll be a while yet. Gerty's busy adding other things to the basket."

Suzanne was not surprised. As soon as Jason was out of

sight, she rinsed her feminine attire that had been soaking in the sudsy water. After dumping the tubs, she ran up the steps to hang her unmentionables in her room and pack a bag.

※ ※ ※

Suzanne found Hattie sitting in her porch rocker when she arrived. "Well, well, well! Would you look at what the cat drug in?"

"Hattie!" Suzanne scolded, "that's not a very nice way to greet your guest."

Hattie shook her head. "You're not a guest ... you're family, Child. I thought you knew that?"

Suzanne dismounted, tied Buck to the post, climbed the three steps to the porch and kissed her feisty friend's cheek. "I missed you."

"That goes both ways, Honey. To what do I owe the pleasure of your company?"

"Do I need a reason to stop by?"

Hattie cackled with glee. "You don't, but knowing that doctor you're working with, he had a reason for sending you by."

Suzanne laughed knowingly and pulled the other rocker up next to Hattie.

For a time they simply rocked, listening to the birds carrying on with one another. However, when Hattie glanced over and noticed a single tear trailing down Suzanne's cheek, she had to ask, "What's troubling you, Sweet Pea?"

That Hattie would suspect something was amiss came as no surprise. The woman could read her as well as her own mother. "What makes you think something is troubling me?"

"Written all over your face! Besides, that tear on your cheek tells a story all its own."

Suzanne wiped the moisture from her face and sighed. She needed to talk to someone, but how could she bear her soul to this kind woman? Her heart was so frail.

"Quit fretting about me and my ailments, Honey, and get it off your shoulders."

Suzanne rocked back and forth contemplating her request. Hattie knew her biggest secret and had proven she could be trusted. "Are you sure you're up to hearing this? I might just shock you."

"Just tell me, Honey. Besides, you'll explode if you don't get it out."

Suzanne began by sharing how and why she left home. Although she half expected Hattie to comment—scold her— possibly even tell her how wrong she had been, Hattie did nothing of the sort. She just encouraged her to go on. So Suzanne did just that, telling Hattie the particulars surrounding her arrest and then explaining how she and Jason had ended up together. From there she barely missed a detail, including the night she had found Christ, her infatuation with the good doctor, and her brother's visit. She even told Hattie how desperately she wanted to go home and couldn't.

"Is that all of it?"

Suzanne nodded. "Do you hate me?" Tears were pooling in her eyes as she turned to her friend. Hattie's gentle smile warmed her deep inside.

"How could I do that, Sweet Pea? Love keeps no record of wrong, it doesn't rejoice in iniquity, but rejoices in the truth.

Have you told me the truth?"

"Yes, Ma'am, I have. I wish it wasn't my truth, but it is."

"You can't change what you've done, but there's nothing we can't take to the cross, you know that. Christ died to free us from the ties that keep us bound."

"But how can I get free of this? It plagues me. Keeps me tied up in knots."

Hattie reached for her hand and gave it a squeeze. "You can run but you can't hide from God, Honey. Expose that old devil for the liar that he is, then he has to flee. Let me guess. He has you convinced that if you tell Jason, he'll send you back to serve your time."

"How did you know?"

"I've been beating down that old devil for a few years longer than you, Child. Take it from someone who knows, he can only win if you let him. You know that perfect love casts out fear. Believe that you're forgiven, and Christ will set you free."

The tears welling in Suzanne's eyes spilled slowly down her face as she admitted, "I know God will forgive me, but I'm not so sure about Jason. I love him so much, Hattie. The man has shown me nothing but kindness and yet I sin against him every day."

"You have to tell him the truth. That's how you defeat the enemy. The truth sets you free."

"But I can't! I've tried!"

Suzanne's eyes flew up when she saw movement by the open window. Her heart felt as if it had dropped to her toes and was slowly creeping back up before she managed to say, "Jason?" The expression on his face told her all she needed to know. In a progressive panic, she ran for her horse, calling back to Hattie,

"I've got to go! Did you know?"

"Did I know what, Honey? Where are you going?" Hattie was so perplexed.

"Did you know Jason was listening from the window?"

"No ... but he has an open invitation to stop by any time. Must have come in the back door." Hattie tried to stop her, but Suzanne was gone by the time Jason came out of the house.

Hattie asked, "How long have you been here, Doc?"

"Long enough! I can't just let her go, Hattie. She thinks I'm in love with Emmaline. Zanne doesn't know the truth about Emma."

"Her name is Suzanne, Doc. Best you get that straight!"

"I thought it was strange that I never saw them together. How could I have been so blind?"

Hattie offered a crooked smile. "You know now, so what are you going to do about it?"

"My mind's all jumbled up. Pray that I can find her. She's hurting. I hope she won't do anything rash. I'm going back by the house. If she's not there, I'll have to leave town for a while. Please don't tell anyone what Suzanne said."

"Her secrets are safe with me. I love that girl like she was my own child."

"I'm glad to hear it. When I bring her back, she'll need a friend. Let the Chefans know I'll be back as soon as I can."

"Go! Bring our girl back home."

He winked. "I'll give it my all. Take care, Hattie. I filled your bottle of digitalis."

She nodded, and he was off.

❀ ❀ ❀

Suzanne's heart quickened as she ran up the stairs to her room and collected the supplies she would need for her journey. Thankfully, Gerty was off running errands; otherwise, the questions might never end.

Sliding the coins her brother gave her into her pocket, she moved to her bed. The bed covers would have to suffice for a bedroll. Securing them to her satchel, she shoved an extra set of clothes inside and flew down the stairs with the bag draped over her arm. After gathering an ample supply of food she ran out the door.

Jason could ride in at any minute. Although facing him sooner or later was inevitable, she preferred to put it off. She needed to think. Facing the wilds of Michigan alone would challenge her faith as nothing else ever had, but the great outdoors held so much more appeal than the alternative.

If only I was more like my brothers. They love a good adventure. Not me. The wilderness is not my cup of tea. I prefer living behind closed doors and sleeping on feather beds with ruffles and frills, like the one in the spare room at Hattie's.

Mounting Buck, she allowed her eyes to scan the farm one more time before she nudged him on. Although she would miss everyone, she had to go—for now anyway.

So much had transpired since she boarded the stage with Amy in Ypsilanti. *What was I thinking? Why did I agree to play the part of a boy?* Suzanne could hardly lay the blame for her predicament at anyone else's feet. She had made the choice. No one had forced her to do anything. No doubt her pastor was right. Her sin had taken her further than she wanted to go and had kept her longer than she wanted to stay.

Father God, I can't help thinking that if I had sought my brother's council in the first place, I'd still be home. I know I might regret leaving like this, but I need to make things right with my family before I try sorting this out with Jason. I'll come back to Saline with Jesse and face him ... I promise.

Suzanne was all too aware—good had come from her time away. How could she ever regret the friends she had made? *I found You in the midst of all of this too, Lord, and then there's Jason. Letting him go won't be easy, but I know I have to. Help me to move past this dreadful ache in my heart.*

Accepting what I cannot change has never been one of my strengths, but then You know that, don't You? Help me to lay my cares at Your feet ... to trust You implicitly ... and to follow Your lead above all else.

Suzanne, looking up at the soft grays of the afternoon sky, was drawn back to the present. Although it did look like rain, that was the least of her concerns at the moment. Finding her way home was a first priority.

If she stayed close to the Chicago Road, it would guide her. However, she needed to play it safe. A woman traveling alone could be at risk. Being dressed like a boy, that would help. Still, caution was necessary. Vagrants traveling these barren lands might wish her harm—if for nothing more than to confiscate a slice of bread. All things considered, she opted for the unbeaten path.

Ignoring her own trepidation over what lay within the forest, she rode in slowly. She needed the cover it would avail. If Jason were to follow ... well, she couldn't allow her mind to go there. Ypsilanti was a fair day's ride from Saline in the best of conditions. Jesse didn't have a whole lot of faith in her sense of direction. Even so, she refused to let her insecurities get the best of her.

Several hours had passed since the stage flew by. As tempting as it was to flag them down—or follow fast in their tracks, she suspected Buck would never make it. They had been traveling for hours and both of them needed rest and nourishment. As darkness crept in, she drew closer to the road while nibbling on a piece of dry bread and cheese, drinking sparingly from her canteen. Although the thought of stopping for the night went against every fiber of her being, she had little choice. She was exhausted, and Buck, well, he wasn't much better off.

When she came to a small clearing that was hidden from the road, she dismounted, hobbled Buck to a nearby tree, and removed his gear. He grazed contentedly while she spread out her blankets and prayed that the moon would offer ample light. A fire would only draw unwanted attention. In the morning she would have to stray from the beaten path. Buck needed water, and she had yet to come across so much as a narrow stream.

Before lying down, she found several dense sticks that she could use for weapons should any forest creatures choose to invade her space. Her insides quivered as she pulled the blankets up around her neck and allowed her heavy lids to fall. Unfortunately, her eyes opened of their own volition every time she heard the smallest sound. She was trembling from head to foot. What had she been thinking? Facing the wilds of Michigan alone was not better than the alternative? Even a jail cell would be more appealing than this.

As she lay there listening to the sounds of night, a squirrel scampered up a nearby tree and ran down the other side lickety-split, disappearing into the woods. Rabbits were plentiful, nibbling on greens long into the night. If she were the hunting type, she could have one roasting over an open fire. Although she relished the thought of filling her rumbling stomach with something warm and tasty, harming a sweet little bunny was incomprehensible.

A twig snapped, diverting her attention. It was only a white-tailed doe meandering into her camp. For a time Suzanne found her presence comforting, but Buck whinnied and the doe was gone. As time crept slowly by, Suzanne wondered if she would sleep at all. She couldn't decide which was worse: being exposed to the elements or having her façade exposed by Jason.

The bats swooping down from the trees offered no answers, but they were Suzanne's undoing. Unable to bear their presence, she pulled the blankets over her head, turned on her side and conversed with the Lord until she drifted off ....

He Loves Me!

Chapter Fifteen

An Unexpected Blessing

SUZANNE HAD BEEN WEAVING her way through the shadowy forest for nearly an hour before the gleaming yellow sun burst through the clouded abyss, sprinkling its warming rays through a shroud of trees. She smiled as her gaze rose to the heavens, thanking the Lord for His soothing presence. *Father, if You could just lead me to a moving stream, I'd be ever so grateful.* Not only was her canteen getting low, but Buck had also gone a full day without the life sustaining fluid. They both could use a bit of refreshing.

Not having laid eyes on the Chicago Road all morning, Suzanne wondered if she was still heading in the right direction, but refused to keep going back and forth to check. She had already pressed Buck harder than she should. Her first priority had to be water. Then she could find her way back to the beaten trail.

Ever watchful, she determined from the position of the sun that it was close to noon before she came across a small stream. Although it was hardly more than a foot wide, it was moving, so she drank her fill and allowed Buck to do the same. As she leaned down to refill her canteen, she heard a faint cry. It took some straining to make out the words. While she couldn't be sure, it sounded like a man calling for help.

Spooked, her mind filled with trepidation as she finished what she was doing. She was ready to hightail it out of there when she heard his pleading call again. Her skittish nature told her to mount her horse and never look back. Don't give it a second thought. If only she could ignore the still small voice pressing her to answer him.

Are you sure, Lord? Though it was not an audible voice, His answer was clear. Suzanne moved with caution, stopping to listen when his weakening cries resonated through the trees. She was heading in the right direction. When a horse snorted, alerting its owner of her presence, she stopped in her tracks. Spying a black mount, she saw the form of a man or woman lying on the ground. For a time she just stood there watching.

She needed to be sure this wasn't a trap. She had heard so many horrible stories of folks being tortured. Would she be next?

When the forest stilled and his pleading words resounded in her ears yet again, she set her cares aside and moved swiftly to him. A quick glance at his face told her she did not know this man, but why would she? A farmer's daughter didn't get out much. She scanned his body for injuries, her stomach wrenching when her eyes fell on his oddly twisted leg. "Mister, does anything else hurt?"

He nodded in the affirmative.

"Can you tell me where?"

His hand went to his mouth. "Thirsty ..." he managed, though his voice was still strained.

Suzanne went for her canteen, dampened his lips and drizzled small amounts of water into his mouth. Her heart went out to him. His leg was obviously broken. He had to be in excruciating pain. In truth, she was surprised that the man was conscious. Although she whispered a prayer for this debilitated stranger, she came to the conclusion that there was not much more she could do for him.

Although doctoring had become second nature to her, this was different. She had read Jason's medical journals—knew the procedures necessary to reset bones, but she had never witnessed them performed on an individual. For her to attempt such a feat could do this man more harm than good.

"Thank you for the water, Miss!"

Miss? She was dressed like a man ... how did he know? As hard as she tried to tamp it down, panic rose within her.

"I don't mean to pry, but is there a reason you're dressed like a boy, Suzanne?"

Too stunned to speak, she realized her mouth was hanging open and willed it to close. The injured man closed his eyes and whispered a prayer, of thanks, she thought, but she could only make out some of the words.

His eyes opened suddenly and the smile on his face was endearing. "How could I mistake a beautiful young woman like you for a boy?"

Her brow furrowed. "But how ... who are you that you would know my name, never mind my gender?"

"You have your mother's eyes, Child."

She took a closer look. The full beard altered his appearance, but that voice could only belong to one man. Her mind reeled as realization dawned. *Oh, no! Why did I have to be the one to find him? Surely You could have chosen someone else, Lord! It's not that I wish him harm, but ...* as much as she'd like to pretend she didn't recognize him, she had.

His face, now filled with concern, told her just how much he cared about her. The lie she had been living needed to end here. *Father, be my strength and guide.*

Understanding how awkward this must be for her, Josiah diverted her fretful thoughts by explaining what had happened. "I hit the tree when my horse reared up. I have some splinters in my back, but this bum leg is the real problem." His throat was going dry again so she offered him a few more sips from the canteen. "I've been trying to get up since it happened yesterday. I'm weak ..." he cleared his throat and added, "from lack of nourishment."

"And from your injuries," Suzanne said, and was about to get up when he reached for her hand. For the life of her she could not move, nor could she imagine what he might say. Reluctantly, she met his gaze.

"I never meant to hurt you, Suzanne. I didn't know how you felt. Can you ever forgive me?"

Quick tears filled her eyes. "Forgive you for what, Mr. Ordan, for loving my mom? I can hardly fault you for that. It's me who should be asking you for forgiveness, not the other way around. So many have been hurt by my selfishness. I really am sorry, Sir ...." As much as she wanted to say more, the words would not come. All that she had done was magnified in the light of this dear man's confession.

"You were trying to protect your father's memory. I only wish I had come to you earlier. I could have tried to help you understand. I love your mother with all of my heart, but that love will never erase the wonderful years I had with my first wife, Maryse. That's the amazing thing about love, Suzanne, it doesn't divide, it grows—like when a mother has a second child. She doesn't love the first one less to make room in her heart for the new child."

"I know that now, but I didn't when I left Ypsilanti. I was angry—hurt. Finding Christ has opened my heart and mind to so many things. I wish you and Mom only the best. For what it's worth, you are a welcome addition to my family. I would give anything to undo the pain I've caused. Mom needed you. I was so blind."

When his hand came up to caress her cheek, their eyes met. "Am I welcome enough for you to call me Josiah—or maybe even Pa, like Louise does?"

Her smile was warm. "Mom would like it if I called you Pa. It would show her that my heart really has changed towards you. Are you sure you don't mind? I haven't exactly been the most agreeable daughter."

He squeezed her hand. "We can't go back. We can only move forward."

She nodded, and stood to her feet. "Well, Pa, if we're going to get you home, we'd better see what we can do about fixing you up. She handed him her canteen so he could drink his fill. I have some cheese and bread in my bag. Do you want some before we set your leg?"

"Sure. Might make me sick, but I am hungry."

Suzanne slid Josiah's saddle off his horse and put it behind him to prop him up. After removing his shirt, he nibbled on the food while she worked at the splinters in his back. Thankfully, they were only on the surface. The weapons she had gathered the previous night would work well for a splint, but she needed something to secure them with. Since the shift she had in her bag had seen better days, she tore it into thick strips before taking a closer look at his leg.

"Pa, I think it's only fair to warn you ... I've read Doctor Michaels' books. I know what needs to be done, but I've never actually set a leg before. You decide. I might do you more harm than good, but I'm willing to try if you are." When he didn't readily respond, she added, "Either that or I could go for help."

He shook his head. "Jesse told me about your sense of direction." Josiah winked. "If you don't mind, I'd rather we stay together. Can't have my daughter roaming the countryside alone, now can I?" His silly face made her smile.

"Don't lay down too many rules just yet, Pa. I'll have to go back to Saline before long. Truth is, I was running from Doctor Michaels when I came across you."

He chuckled tersely. "Imagine that! I was on my way to check on you when this happened. Isn't it amazing the way God brings folks together to help each other out of tight spots?"

"That's how I ended up with Jason in the first place. I shouldn't have taken off the way I did, but he overheard a conversation I was having with a friend. Now he knows I'm a woman. I got scared ... I didn't even leave him a note." Her head lowered. "Wouldn't blame him if he sends me back to Detroit when I return."

"No sense brooding over it now. We can talk about it more when we get home."

For a long moment, she only stared. "Suppose I could use some fatherly advice."

He reached for her hands. "For now, Suzanne, we should commit your situation and my leg to prayer."

She nodded and together they bowed their heads.

"Father God, thank you for your goodness. You brought Suzanne across my path at Your appointed time. Her heart is troubled, but I can sense her longing to do what is right. We lift her circumstances up to You. Help her to look to You, the Source of all comfort. Give us wisdom in the days ahead. Anoint Suzanne's hands as she sets my leg, Lord. Give her the strength she needs and guide us safely home. We'll not fail to give you the praise and glory. Amen."

Josiah put on a brave front, but there was no way around it, the bone was not easy to set. She thanked the Lord for sweet mercy when Josiah passed out after the first tug and didn't wake up until the next morning.

She had just finished attaching the last of her blankets to the travois and tying it to Josiah's horse when he opened his eyes. He scanned the area before his eyes fell on her handiwork. "You've been busy, Suzanne."

She saw the twinkle in his eyes and giggled. "I know it looks strange, but we both know I'm not strong enough to get you in your saddle, and you certainly can't walk home, so ..." she shrugged, "this is what I came up with. I saw one several years back. If the Indians can transport their sick on one of these contraptions, so can I."

"I'm sure it will work just fine."

An irrepressible yawn caught her unawares. Rubbing at her weary eyes, she realized that the lack of sleep would make for a long day, but she was determined to have her stepfather home before nightfall. "The hatchet I found in your pack sure did come in handy."

"I'm glad. I never heard you. Were you up most of the night?"

"Not most of the night—all night."

She ignored the concern etched on his bearded face and finished gathering their belongings. "Are you ready?" When he nodded, she led his horse around the tree he was lying under, bringing the travois as close to him as possible.

"Your ingenuity is something else, Suzanne. Your father would have been proud of you."

Her head lowered in contemplation. She had so many regrets, so many things she would have done differently if she had them to do over again. She believed God had forgiven her. Her family, on the other hand, ... she wasn't so sure where she stood with them. "Dad would have liked this contraption, but there are so many foolish things I've done ...."

"Everyone does foolish things. You're trying to make amends and that's what matters. Trust me, most fathers would agree, they'd be blessed to have you for a daughter."

"Even you?" She held her breath, wondering what he would say.

"Especially me."

When tears filled her eyes, Josiah opened his arms wide and she went willingly into them. *How could I have been so wrong about him? This is one more lie I believed, now exposed in the light of Your love, isn't it, Lord. Daddy would have liked my new pa ... so do I. Thank you for allowing me to see Josiah as Mom does—as an unexpected blessing from You.*

He Loves Me!

Chapter Sixteen

Confrontation

*T*HE SUN HAD SET hours ago, but a thick slice of moon guided Suzanne as she led Buck toward the outskirts of Ypsilanti. Their journey had been slow and arduous. Josiah was in a great deal of pain, and while she wanted to get him home, some things couldn't be rushed. She was exhausted. Only knowing he would be more comfortable in his own bed kept her from making camp for the night.

The desire to see her mother and siblings was strong. Even so, Suzanne's reservations were many as she turned down the path that led to her family farm. She had no one to blame but herself for the awkward emotions filling her mind. Regardless, God was giving her the chance to make amends with her family, and she fully intended to do just that.

Her spirit lifted when she saw Star grazing in the coral outside the barn. She could hardly wait to get reacquainted. Allowing her eyes to scan the familiar surroundings brought tears to her eyes. How could she have walked away without a backward glance? *It really is good to be home, Lord.* Suzanne stopped in front of the house and dismounted. When she found her patient sleeping, she crept up the back steps and just stood there for a long moment. Facing those she had wronged would not be easy, but it was necessary. After taking a deep breath for courage, she raised her hand to knock, but the door swung open.

"Suzanne!" Jared exclaimed as he wrapped his arms around her and lifted her off the ground. He never gave her a chance to speak—he just pulled her into the house and announced to the rest of the family as they reached the parlor, "Look who I found prowling around outside!"

Overwhelmed by her daughter's appearance, Jayne burst into tears as she rushed toward her and hugged her tight. "Oh, Honey, I don't know what brought you back, but I'm so glad you're here."

Suzanne lost her composure when her mother tenderly kissed her cheeks. Joe and Louise were thrilled to see her as well, and suddenly her reasons for leaving paled in the light of their unconditional love.

Suzanne, desperate to get a handle on her emotions, looked at her sister and said, "Louise, would you be a dear and put some water over to boil."

"Sure!"

She then looked at her brothers and said, "Boys, I could use some help. On my way home, I happened upon our new Pa ...."

"You did?" Jayne asked, a dreadful feeling sweeping over her as she turned and hurried out the door. Her children followed fast in her footsteps.

When they neared Josiah and found him sleeping, they all

looked to Suzanne for answers.

Jared asked, "How did you find him?"

"Nothing short of a miracle, that's for sure. He broke his leg when he was thrown from his horse."

"Oh, no!" Jayne said, as tears flooded her eyes.

Suzanne wrapped her arm around her mother's shoulder. "I was able to set the leg, but traveling has been hard on him. We should get him inside."

Jared was gawking at the travois when he said, "Joe, did you take a good look at this contraption?" Meeting his sister's impish look, he asked, "Suz, did you make this?"

"Had to ... He couldn't ride, so this is what I came up with."

Joe offered, "We're impressed."

"Me too!" Josiah said as he opened his eyes and offered a sideways grin.

Jayne came up beside him and tenderly ran her fingers along his cheek. "What'd you do, Siah?"

"I'll be fine, Honey. Wasn't paying attention is all ... busted my leg, but my daughter found me and fixed me up just fine. Sure would like to sleep in my own bed, though. Hope you don't mind, Jayne, I might need you to dote on me for a few days."

Lovingly, she said, "I don't mind a bit. I've missed you."

Jared and Joe carried Josiah into the house and saw that he was settled in his bed.

"Mom," Louise asked as she came into the room with the basin of warm water, "where do you want this?"

"Right here on the table, Honey."

Louise hugged her pa and welcomed him back, before going for a towel and cloth so her mother could help him get cleaned up.

In truth, Louise needed to stay busy. He was not one to complain, but the pain etched on his face was difficult to bear, and she was determined not to cry.

Jayne stopped washing on her husband long enough to look up, and say, "Thanks for all you've done, Suz. We'll talk later, okay?"

"I'm not going anywhere. Jared, Joe and I have some catching up to do. They should be able to keep me entertained for awhile." The rascally grin Suzanne sent her brothers made Jayne smile as they took their leave.

Suzanne, grabbing her brothers' arms, asked as they moved out the back door, "Would you boys mind taking me swimming after we bed down the horses? Truth is, I haven't had a bath in days, and I feel as grubby as a worm."

Jared, sounding all too much like Jesse, informed her, "Kind of late for swimming, Suz."

A bit testy from lack of sleep, she declared, "Fine! If you won't take me, I'll go alone!"

Jared's eyes narrowed in on her as he questioned his brother, "She's a might too plucky for her own good, wouldn't you say, Joe? I'm thinking we'd best straighten her out."

"Couldn't agree with you more."

Suzanne did not doubt that they were toying with her. Even so, Jared's moves were too quick for her to avoid what happened next. He dipped down, tossed her over his shoulder, and they were almost to the river before she could quit laughing long enough to respond.

"Funny, Jar ... now put me down. We need to see to the

horses first. Besides, if I don't grab a bar of soap, swimming will do me little good."

Joe offered, "Not to worry, Sis, we have an ample supply down by the river."

"But the horses ..."

Jared's tone was unwavering, "They'll be fine until we get back."

She was giggling, begging him to put her down so she could walk, but he was not about to oblige. The second they reached the bank, Joe pulled off her bluchers and Jared threw her in. By the time she came up for air, their outer garments had been discarded and they were joining her in the water.

"What am I supposed to think about you two? We've been separated for months, and the first thing you do when we're back together is throw me in the river."

Joe put in, "We missed you, Suz. You know we love you, we're just making up for lost time."

"I do ... I feel the same way about you two. I really am sorry for the way I left. I was wrong to make you worry."

Jared thought she should know, "Josiah's been good for all of us. The day you took off, we saddled up and were heading out to try and find you, but Jesse stopped us. He wanted us to give you time to think things through. At first we were angry. Josiah was able to help us understand some of what you were going through."

"He's a good man. I can see that now, but then ... all I could see is that Mom was betraying Dad's memory by marrying again."

Jared reassured her, "Don't let this eat you up. You're home now. That's all that matters."

Suzanne nodded. After discarding her outer garments, she took the bar of soap Jared offered, and proceeded to scrub the trail dust from her skin.

"Hey, Suzanne," Joe put in, "you'll have to have Jared tell you about his latest flame."

"Oh?" her twinkling eyes fell on Jared. "Do I know her, Jar?"

Jared grabbed Joe's shoulder and dunked him a good one. "Joe's running off at the mouth is all. I took her to a barn dance, and he has us married already."

"Then tell me who she is."

"Her family bought Amy's father's farm."

Suzanne shook her head. "Her name, Jar ... does she have a name?"

He turned a nice shade of red. "Brianna, but don't make more of it than it is. We're only friends."

"Friendship is a good ..."

His stubborn look told Suzanne she was not going to get any more out of him, so she let it drop. They were heading back to the house dripping wet when Jesse came across the yard. He didn't so much as hesitate when he wrapped his arms around Suzanne and held her tightly.

"What brought you home so soon, Suz? I thought ..." When her head lowered, he lifted her chin, bringing her gaze to his. "We'll face it together. Just tell me."

"You won't like it."

"You let me be the judge of that."

She drew on his quiet strength. "Jason overheard a conversation I was having with one of our patients. He knows

I'm a woman. I shouldn't have, but I took off before he had a chance to stop me."

Jared and Joe were a bit confused since they had only heard bits and pieces of her circumstances. When her brothers started asking questions, they all took a seat on the porch, and she filled them in.

"So you're a criminal?" Jared asked.

"Yes & no .... I didn't do anything wrong. They just think I did."

"But you agreed to work with this doctor for a year as penance? Aren't you afraid he'll send you back to serve out your term for running off?" When tears filled Suzanne's eyes, Jesse pulled her close.

Her face was still buried in Jesse's chest when he led her inside the house. "Suzanne, run upstairs with Louise. Dry your tears and come down in a dress. It's high time you quit living the lie. Your clothes are as good a place as any to start."

"But, Jesse!'

"But Jesse, nothing! If I see you in anything but feminine attire for the next year, you'll answer to me, Young Lady. Do you hear me?"

Jesse was rarely firm with her, but when he was she took his words to heart. "A whole year?"

He nodded. "Unless I tell you otherwise."

Her shoulders slumped as she started to walk away, but was she ready to comply? When she looked back, her three brothers were staring her down. She didn't have a chance against all of them. Turning back toward the stairs, she simply offered a conciliatory, "Yes, Sir!" But it was what she mumbled to Louise on her way up the stairs that got a reaction out of her brother. "I've been gone for months, and what do they do the minute I get back? Boss me around!"

"Suzanne!" Jesse bellowed, bringing her gaze back to his. Fortunately, she had enough respect for him not to comment further.

Louise, feeling spry, leaned over and whispered softly in her ear, "Now that you're home maybe they'll lighten up on me."

Suzanne, knowing what her brothers were like, was quick to inform her, "I wouldn't get your hopes up too high. They came by their overprotective tendencies honestly. Daddy was just like them, or don't you remember?"

Suzanne and Louise prattled away, just like old times. As they entered her room, Suzanne allowed her eyes to roam. Everything looked and smelled the same as it did before she left home. When she realized her sister was staring, she tried to pull herself back to the present. "You should know, Louise, I'm not so sure how long I'll be able to stay."

Louise's smile faltered. "Suz, you can't leave me again. I missed you too much."

Suzanne shed her wet clothes and was standing in front of the mirror in a dry lacy shift brushing through her damp tangles when Jesse called from the foot of the stairs. "Louise, can you see what he's hollering about?"

"Sure." Louise jumped off the bed and snuck out the door. "She's not dressed yet, Jesse. What is it?"

"Tell her to hustle up. We have things to discuss before I head home."

"Give us a few minutes." Louise snagged her favorite skirt on the doorframe as she wiggled back through the small opening. Unhooking it, she stomped her foot. "Fiddle sticks!"

"What's wrong?"

Her round face snarled up. "Nothing I can't fix!"

Suzanne pulled her hair up, securing it with a decorative comb. "What'd Jesse want?"

"He needs to talk to you before he heads back home."

Suzanne and Jesse were moving toward the barn to bed the horses down when he asked, "How'd you find Josiah?"

"It had to be the Lord leading me to him. I was having trouble finding water, so I strayed from the beaten path. I eventually came across a moving stream. In fact, I was filling my canteen when I heard a man crying out in pain. Took me a while to find him. That beard kind of threw me. I didn't recognize him at first. He said he was on his way to check on me when he was thrown from his horse."

Jesse shook his head. "I wondered how long Mom would be able to stay away. Didn't think about Josiah going after you. He doesn't take his new position in this family lightly, Suz. He loves all of us as if we were his own."

"After you and I talked in the village, I spent some time praying about it. You helped me to see my actions for what they were—selfish. Wasn't easy to admit. I don't tell you often, but thanks for loving me enough to tell me when I'm wrong."

Jesse was taken aback. "Didn't think I'd ever hear you say that."

She reached for his hand and squeezed it tight. "With Daddy gone, I don't know what I would have done without you. You've been more than a brother, Jesse—like a father, too."

"I appreciate your saying so. Wasn't always sure if you resented my input or not."

She grinned mischievously. "Now I didn't say I always liked your input—I said I appreciated it. There is a difference, you know!"

"You still have some hard things to face up to, Suzanne."

"I know ...."

For a long moment he stared at her, contemplating his next words, "Are you done running?"

Her eyes lowered, but he wanted an answer. "Look at me, Suzanne."

Reluctantly, she obeyed. "Yes ..."

"Are you ready to make things right, both here and in Saline?"

Silence hung between them. As they entered the barn she admitted, "I'm willing to make things right, but that doesn't mean I'm not afraid of the outcome."

They were brushing down the horses when Jesse said, "Walking in obedience to the Lord is rarely easy, but that is where our peace lies .... You told me about the changes God is making in your life, but I have to ask, *who do you serve?*"

Confused, she peered up. The scant light from the lantern illuminated her brother's face. No doubt he had his reasons for asking. Suzanne responded, "The Lord."

"Then don't let people intimidate you. Fear of man will only rob you of your faith. If I know you, keeping your identity from Jason was your way of maintaining control. And if I'm not mistaken, you had it in the back of your mind that after you had served your term you could head home and no one would be the wiser."

"That's not true, Jesse. I always planned on telling him."

"Then why didn't you?" When she offered no response, he added, "Fear of what could happen kept you from doing what you should have done a long time ago. Am I right?" Jesse stopped her when she tried to turn away.

"Yes! You're right! Are you happy now?"

He shook his head. "Suzanne, when are you going to quit listening to the voices inside your head that lead you astray? They're lies from the pit of hell!"

"I'm well aware of that now, but how do I shut them up?"

"By standing in your God given authority. He tells us in His Word that the truth will set us free. He doesn't say blessed are the peacekeepers—He says, blessed are the peacemakers."

She was confused. "I don't see what the difference is."

"A peacekeeper avoids conflict, convinced that if he confronts an issue or makes waves, he lacks love or Christian character. A peacemaker confronts no matter what it will cost him. Your motivation has to be love for God and truth, Suz. That's the only way true peace can thrive. You either trust that God loves you, and no matter what happens He will be with you, or you don't." When she just stood there staring, he said, "Think about it while you bed down the horses. I'll be back in a few minutes with their water."

Jesse was walking out the door when she called out to him, tears streaming down her face, "I wanted to tell him, Jesse, but how could I? He'll never be able to forgive me for this." Wiping the tears from her eyes, she turned back to remove Buck's saddle. As she did, a familiar voice came softly to her ears.

"I have to forgive you. If I don't, my Heavenly Father won't forgive me, Suzanne."

She stood frozen in place. Butterflies filled her stomach. Jason was right behind her. Where did he come from? *How did he find me so soon? Oh, Lord, how can I face him?*

Before she could budge, his hands slid around her waist. She trembled in his hold, but somehow she summoned the courage to turn and look up. "Jason ..."

His expression held no malice, in fact, the tenderness that filled his eyes mystified her. Ever so slightly the corners of his mouth curved up. And then his fingertips ran tenderly down her warm cheek as he examined every curve of her beautiful face. "Suzanne ... I'm so glad this mystery has been solved. I've longed to see you—to be with you."

"You have?" she breathlessly questioned.

"Oh, yes ..."

As hard as she tried to ward them off, a fresh rush of tears spilled down her cheeks. Something deeper was going on here. Why did he have to be so gentle ... so kind?

Drawing her close, Jason enfolded her in his arms. For weeks he had wanted nothing more than to pursue a relationship with this mysterious young woman—only now to find out that she had been living under his roof for months!

In truth, he was not surprised to learn that Suzanne was not a man. Everything about her bespoke femininity—her features, her long brown silky lengths with golden strands running through them, her lack of facial hair, and how could he forget her slender frame? She had the whole village fooled except for dear, sweet

Hattie. And he called himself a doctor! Her ability to pull this one over on him was unfathomable.

Not wanting the moment to end, Jason savored her closeness—her softness. Having her near felt so right, but would he ever scale the wall of fear that divided them? The last thing he wanted was for her to feel vulnerable in his presence. He prayed that she would come to understand his budding love for her.

Zanne was my friend and brother in Christ—Suzanne was the woman I could only dream of someday making my wife, and now I find out that the two are one in the same! I'm both overwhelmed and overjoyed, Lord.

Although Jason would love to give in to his desire to kiss her sweet lips, they had much to discuss before he could ever consider more than a friendship between them. Besides, he hadn't asked for her hand—wasn't ready to. He had no right. The way she trembled in his arms made him wonder what she was thinking.

Jason cupped her chin in his hands and her tearful gaze met his. "Suzanne, please tell me that after all the time we've shared together, you know I could never do anything to bring you harm. Can't you see that sending you back to Detroit is not an option—no matter how this turns out?"

"I'm so sorry, Jason. I should have trusted you. If I were a man of my word ..."

"Suzanne ..!" he gently scolded.

She tried to make sense of the way he was looking at her. And why was he staring at her mouth? Did he intend to kiss her? Thinking she had to be misreading him, she put it out of her mind. After all, the man belonged to Emmaline.

However, when his finger ran slowly along her silky lips, the beat of her heart increased tenfold.

"Only the truth will pass through this lovely mouth of yours from this day forward. Are we agreed?"

I have a lovely mouth? Although she desperately wanted to know why he would say such a thing, she couldn't bring herself to ask.

Jason, retrieving a hanky from his pocket, tenderly dried her tears, confounding her all the more. When the hush trailed on, Suzanne realized he was waiting for a response. She tried to pull herself together. "Some habits are not easily broken. I was frightened. I should have stayed and faced you, but I couldn't."

"Forgive me for being so bold, but I'm puzzled. We've had numerous conversations, many of them concerning issues of the heart. Care to tell me why you couldn't talk to me about this?"

"I wanted to—but knowing you could send me back to Detroit if ... well, you know."

"But you know what fear can do to our faith. We've been studying passages on fear for weeks now. The only unconditional form of security we'll ever know is God's love. His perfect love casts out fear."

"I can see that now ... it's when I come face to face with my fears that I tend to waver. You know I hate confrontation of any kind. You may not realize it, Jason, but you can be very intimidating at times."

"Don't give anyone that power over you, not even me. God knows the last thing I want is for you to be afraid of me." He added coyly, "Especially now that I know who you really are ...."

She peered up at him. *What are you saying, Jason?* Closing

her eyes did little to calm the rapid beat of her heart.

"Suzanne, you serve the Lord, not me. I'm your friend. Can you tell me what you're so afraid of?"

He had proven repeatedly that he was worthy of trust, but this was different. How could she tell him this?

"Tell me ...."

"I want to trust you—really I do, but I'm so confused. Nothing makes sense anymore. The authority the courts gave you over me does frighten me ... at the same time, the thought of losing you troubles me more."

His brow furrowed. "Losing me? What would make you think you're going to lose me? If I have anything to say about it, we'll be together for as many years as the Lord allows."

Her timidity dissipated in the light of his bold statement But what was he saying—really? She might as well tell him the whole truth and get it over with. So what if she humiliated herself—completely! "I saw you with Emmaline, Jason. I know you have feelings for her. Truth is ..." Suzanne's words came to an abrupt halt when she saw movement out of the corner of her eye. Jesse was coming their way. *Phew! To think I was just about to spill my guts!*

"Jason, would you mind taking a look at my father-in-law? Suzanne was able to set his broken leg, but Mom just came out. He's in a great deal of pain."

"Be glad to. I'll need to fetch my bag from your house."

"Did that for you. It's on the porch." Jesse leaned toward his sister and spoke for her ears alone. "You may want to close your mouth, Suzanne."

As realization dawned, her anger flared, and she demanded

to know, "Jason Michaels! How long have you been here?"

He had the gall to wink. "Rode in yesterday morning. Probably passed you on the trail."

That's obvious! "Let me guess ... Mom and my brothers know you're here, too!"

He nodded. "I love your family already, Suzanne."

She groaned in frustration as she gave her brother a shove. "Jesse Somers, you're incorrigible. You knew Jason was here all along, and you didn't tell me?"

"I wasn't born yesterday, Sis. I've seen you in action enough to know you'll take flight when the going gets tough. Wasn't about to chance you leaving again. We figured it was best you didn't know Jason was here, until he was close enough to grab you."

"I should have known!" she gritted and then stormed off toward the house.

Jason grinned at Jesse before his gaze was drawn back to Suzanne's fleeing back. Long hair and skirts swished with each spirited step she took. *Even in her fiery mood she's charming and irresistible.* "Your little sister has spunk! Can't deny that ...."

Jesse stared at his new friend and smiled, wondering how long it would be before Jason was willing to confront what Jesse could clearly see in this young doctor's eyes—blossoming love.

Chapter Seventeen

Unspoken Devotion

*J*ASON STAYED WITH JAYNE until Josiah was resting comfortably. Their room was right off the kitchen, and since Jason was hoping to finish his conversation with Suzanne before calling it a night, he was pleased to find her there. For reasons he could only speculate on, Suzanne's siblings scattered as soon as he appeared. In truth, he found their actions somewhat comical.

If Suzanne realized they were alone, she gave no indication. However, when she lingered at the stove a bit to long with her back to him, he saw right through her façade. No doubt, she was highly aware.

Although the thought of leaving did pass through her mind, she held her ground. Her rumbling stomach needed to be pacified, or sleep would never come. She could feel the heat of Jason's eyes on her back. Since she was not ready to face him she simply proceeded with what she was doing. When the thick slice of ham she had in the frying pan was seared to perfection, she jabbed it with a fork and slapped it on a plate. Her mannerisms were anything but feminine as she reached for a muffin, filled a cup with tepid tea, and plunked down at the table, ignoring the fact that he was standing there staring. She bowed her head and prayed silently.

Unmoved, Jason took a seat across from the woman who of late consumed his thoughts. Apparently, she had no intentions of giving him the time of day, so when she lifted her fork to her mouth, he stole her plate.

She immediately stole it back. The evil glare she sent his way dared him to try taking it again.

"Aren't you going to share with your guest, Suzanne?"

"You were never my guest, and you're no longer a family guest either. Mom's rules, not mine. If you don't like them, take it up with her."

"Rules? Are you going to fill me in or leave me in the dark?"

She barely raised a single brow, never mind her eyes. "After the first meal you share with my family, you are no longer a guest. Outside of mealtime, you're on your own." She hummed contentedly as she took another big bite of ham and chewed slowly.

It was obvious she was rubbing it in, so he reached for her plate again, but this time he stopped abruptly. Her fork was raised as a weapon of war.

"Be that way! Didn't really want ham anyway." Jason stood, retrieved the last muffin, and poured himself a cup of coffee before rejoining his feisty assistant.

After taking his last bite of muffin, Jason licked his sticky fingers and leaned back in the chair, sighing contentedly. When she didn't so much as glance his way, he attempted to engage her in conversation. "You know, Suzanne, you were very close to exposing your thoughts when Jesse interrupted us in the barn. We're alone again, and I'm listening."

Oh, no! Her chewing ceased. While her body remained perfectly still, her brown lashes swept up, and sea blue eyes connected with his. Although she did her best to remain steadfast, the wall of defense she had erected was crumbling fast. As hard as she tried to shure it up, it was useless.

The emotions swirling inside her not only confused her, they terrified and thrilled her as well. Suzanne was vividly aware of her attraction for this man. Her heart fluttered. Warmth crept up her neck. And then her blood, the way it rushed through her veins confirmed it all. How could she deny such ardor? She had to get a grip, or she would never survive the next few moments, let alone nine more months at his side. Besides, she reminded herself, *how I feel about Jason matters naught! He belongs to Emmaline.*

With renewed determination, she stood and lowered her gaze. She refused to let those big blue eyes alter her plan. "I'm not sure I'm ready to expose my heart to a man who would rendezvous with my family in an attempt to take me unawares."

On that note, she proceeded to the counter to wash her dishes.

Jason swallowed the last of his coffee and followed in her footsteps with the intention of washing his own cup. As he stood gazing at her profile, he wondered why she insisted on this charade. It wasn't difficult to see that their feelings for each other were mutual. Since he had never courted anyone before, he wasn't certain if he should just ride out the storm or make his intentions known.

One thing he knew for sure: he loved being close to her. The scent of her freshly washed hair drew him closer still. In fact, he was basking in her floral fragrance when she turned abruptly and bumped his nose with her head.

The pain took his breath away. Quick tears flooded his eyes, and then his nose began to run. A second look at the fluid in his hand revealed all; his nose was not running but bleeding profusely.

"Jason! What in the world?" She reached for a towel and held it up to his nose. "I'm sorry. I didn't know ...." Then the reality of what had happened struck her, and she demanded to know, "Why were you standing so close?"

Suzanne, noticing that Jason looked a bit green around the gills, set her irritation aside, reached for his arm, and led him to the sitting room. After seeing him seated comfortably, she put the ottoman under his feet and went to retrieve a damp towel.

He felt like such a fool. Handling blood was almost an everyday occurrence for him, but the presence of his own changed everything. In truth, he felt like he was going to vomit or pass out. He tried not to think about it, even willed himself to calm, but then Suzanne started touching him—washing his face. He lost the ability to concentrate. When his mouth began to water, he lunged from his seat and ran out the door with Suzanne following fast in his steps.

She waited until his stomach emptied before handing him the damp rag. "Are you all right?"

He nodded as he covered his nose.

"Did I break it, Jason?"

She sounded so forlorn. How could he give her one more

thing to fret about? "I'm pretty sure the bleeding has stopped. It should be fine." He reached for her hand. "Come on, Suzanne. It's a beautiful night. We can sit on the porch and talk."

Talk? She glanced down at the large hand now enveloping hers. His simple gesture brought with it a turbulent gust of unfamiliar sensations traveling up her arm. My, but she needed to set her mind to rights. Allowing her emotions to run away with her would not help either one of them. He belonged to Emmaline.

Jason took a seat on the double swing and bade her to join him.

Distancing herself might have been wiser, but how could she deny him? Whenever those blue eyes met hers, she was a lost woman. Suzanne joined him, whispering a silent prayer as they swung slowly back and forth. Gazing off into the distance she contemplated what she should say to him. When nothing came, she remained silent.

"I've been thinking, Suzanne ... maybe if you put your manly garb back on and I go back to calling you Zanne, all this awkwardness between us will fritter away."

Her hand came up to cover her mouth and sweet giggles bubbled up. His perception amazed her. "It might, but you'll have to take that up with Jesse. I'm afraid he'd have a thing or two to say about it."

Jason ran the crook of his finger down her soft cheek, effectively bringing her eyes back to his. "Laying down the law already, is he?"

"Afraid so! If he sees me in men's clothes for the next year, I'm in big trouble."

Jason grinned. "Can't say as I blame him. Denying who God

created you to be isn't a good thing, Suz."

"How well I know."

"Always did think you were too pretty to be a boy."

Pensively, she scanned the yard, staring at a rabbit eating clover. "I never thought I'd be able to pull it off, you know ... with your being a doctor and all. In my own crazy, mixed-up mind, I wanted you to expose my secret ... just didn't know how to make you see me for who I really was."

"So many things make sense now: bathing alone, not letting Gerty do your laundry. And that day I thought you skipped church. I plowed into your room and threw the covers back. The curves I saw in those drawers ... whew! Took me days to shake that off."

Surprised by his admission, she asked, "You suspected way back then?"

He nodded. "Guess I did. I really should trust my instincts more."

Suzanne saw Jesse heading toward the barn and prayed that he would come and rescue her soon. It wasn't that she didn't enjoy Jason's presence, but she was tired and needed time to pray.

"Going to church as Suzanne. What was that all about?"

She squirmed just a bit, wondering if he would laugh. While she couldn't bear the thought of telling him, he did have a right to know. "Lying to you was bad enough. I convinced myself that God would strike me dead if I went into His house dressed like a man. Couldn't chance it. To me it was blasphemy. Little did I know, God was aware of my sin all along."

"We can't hide from Him, Suzanne. He knows everything

we've ever done and loves us anyway. There's no sin the blood of Christ can't cover."

"I know God forgives me, Jason ... but I wasn't so sure you would. I've wanted to tell you for so long. Knowing you forgive me means the world to me."

Jason reached for her hand and held on tight. "There's so much I want to discuss with you, but there's no rush. You're exhausted." He stood to his feet and pulled her up as well. "Get some rest."

She turned to leave but stopped at the door. Craning her neck around, she asked, "Do you have to go back in the morning?"

"No, Jesse and I talked earlier. He'd like us to stay for the week and sort things out together. Besides, it's important for you to have some time with your family."

Her gaze lowered and then rose. "I'm going back with you?" Tears flooded her eyes. The reality of what going back would entail hit her hard and fast.

"You're done running, Suzanne. You need to face those you've wronged and give them a chance to love the real you. If you're asking me, I think they'll be pleasantly surprised. I was ... still am for that matter."

She prayed he was right, but she did have her reservations.

"I'll see you in the morning. Sleep well, Suzanne."

"You, too ..." she countered before disappearing inside the house.

"Jesse!" Jason called out as he entered the barn. "Are you in here?" Jesse stuck his head out of a stall and motioned for Jason to join him. He rounded the corner, took one look at the struggling mare lying on the ground, and crouched down to access her condition. "How long has she been in labor?"

"Since last night. Something must be wrong. She should have delivered by now."

Jason rolled up his sleeve and had Jesse hold the horse's head while he proceeded to examine her. "The foal's leg is caught. If I can free it up, she should deliver."

Not ten minutes later, a slimy black colt presented itself. Only minutes had passed before the mare stood and welcomed her newborn colt. Jason didn't know how much time had lapsed, but the colt, determined to follow his mother's lead, made several attempts before he too gained his footing.

Jesse smiled up at his friend. "Thanks! I could have lost Genevieve. Olivia would have been devastated."

"Then I'm glad I could help." Looking down at his arms, he said, "Listen, Jesse, I'm a mess. Would you mind fetching me clean clothes so I can take a dip in the river?"

"Not a problem. Could stand a good soak myself after the day I've had."

Jason had been swimming for a while when Jesse joined him at the river. Jason was tired and ready to call it a night, but he wasn't sure how long it would be before he'd have Suzanne's brother to himself again, and there were things they needed to discuss.

Jesse, shedding his outer clothes, asked, "Is the water cold?"

Jason shrugged. "Not bad after the initial shock wears off."

"Then move aside." He took off running down the bank and jumped in, shouting as he came up for air. "Whew! Good thing I didn't stick my toes in first!"

"I wasn't sure how deep it was. Trust me, wading in was sheer torture."

Jesse chuckled and threw Jason a bar of soap that he caught with ease. Fortunately, the moon offered ample light on this particular night.

After scrubbing up Jason disappeared under the water. When he surfaced, his reserved expression drew Jesse's attention. "I have something I need to speak to you about. Truth of the matter is, I'm not sure if I should be talking to you or your father-in-law about this. Since no one is around, I'll start with you. Any chance you'd give me permission to court your sister?"

Jesse grinned and slid under the water without answering, leaving Jason in an uncomfortable state. When he came back up he had a question of his own. "Is my sister aware of your intentions?"

"I haven't said anything to her, if that's what you're asking. Thought I should talk to you first."

"So ... she doesn't know you're in love with her?"

Jason's wide-eyed look exposed his astonishment. "Now don't jump the gun, Jesse. I have feelings for her, sure, but love—that could be a bit of a stretch at this point. Besides, I'm not asking for her hand ... I'm only asking to court her. Not sure where it will lead."

"But you want to, don't you?"

Jason shook his head, surprised by Jesse's boldness and his insight. "Am I that transparent?"

"To me, you are. I'm just not convinced Suzanne sees what I do. Oh, I think she likes you just fine, but something's holding her back."

"I'm pretty sure I know what it is, but until I have your permission to proceed ..."

Jesse's protective guard came up. "If you don't mind sharing, I'd like to hear about it."

Jason slid under the water to get his hair out of his eyes. "That's understandable. A woman I knew in Pennsylvania came to live in Saline just after I arrived, but only a few people know we're connected from our past. Her name is Emmaline."

"Why the need for secrecy?"

"The poor girl has been living in my shadow for a long time and wanted to see if she could stand on her own in a new community. We both lost our parents at an early age, so I've been watching out for her. She's like a sister to me. I feel better having her close where I can keep an eye on her until she marries. Unfortunately, Suzanne got the wrong impression. She has it in her head that I'm courting Emmaline."

Jesse's brow rose. "And you think that's all that's keeping her at arm's length?"

He nodded. "Yes ... I really do."

Finger combing his hair, Jesse said, "I'll need time to pray about it before I give you my answer."

Jason grinned. "I'm in no hurry. We both need time to get to know each other without the deception hanging between us. It has been awkward, if you know what I mean?"

Jesse chuckled. "I can only imagine."

"I want to do this right. If and when we do agree to move forward, I know how important your blessing will be to Suzanne. She adores you, Jesse."

"She's been a handful since my father died, but I've learned the hard way that everyone deals with grief in their own way. She found Christ while she was with you. I don't doubt that you have her best interest at heart, but ... I'd want you to be sure she's ready for a commitment as permanent as marriage before you proceed. She may need time."

"I understand. But I need you to keep in mind that she'll be living under my roof for nine more months. Having Gerty living with us will help, but her reputation could be called into question when folks realize I'm living with a young woman who is not my relative—and a beautiful one at that."

"You're sure we can't get her out of this agreement?"

Jason shook his head. "If we try to alter things, I'm afraid they'll assume she's giving me problems and take her back. I have no idea what they'll do if they find out she's a woman."

"I don't like the deception, but I think this is one of those times where not telling all is best."

"From what I've heard about this judge, I'd have to agree."

"Let me talk to Olivia. We'll pray about it and discuss our thoughts with you soon. I don't doubt that you'd love my sister, Jason, but Suzanne's heart is at stake here, too. Until she's aware of your commitment to her, unspoken devotion is all you have. Your relationship is based on assumption—a wing and a prayer."

Jason's eyes slid shut as he prayed, *Your will, Father, not mine ....*

He Loves Me!

Chapter Eighteen

God's Timing

UZANNE'S WARY EYES stayed on the small window at the far end of her room as the rainstorm ensued. Turbulent winds whistled through the trees. Scattered lightening cracked open the darkened skies, and the unpredictable roar of thunder shattered what was left of her terribly frayed nerves. As thankful as she was to be safe in her room, the dreadful storm was robbing her of much needed sleep.

The morning sun had not yet risen when Suzanne descended the stairs. Apparently, her other family members were unaffected by the heavy rains pelting against the windowpanes. For a while she curled up on the sofa with a big afghan and tried to get comfy, but it was no use. She replaced the family heirloom and moved toward the kitchen to light the stove. Perhaps something warm would help to relax her. If nothing else, a cup of tea would warm her cold nose.

Jayne, hearing movement outside her room, wandered in to find Suzanne savoring a cup of tea.

The way her mother rubbed her eyes made Suzanne wonder, "Did I wake you up?"

"Wouldn't matter if you did. I'm glad for the time alone to talk." Jayne leaned down and kissed her daughter's cheek. "Is there enough tea in that pot for me to join you?"

"Plenty. How's my new pa doing? Is he resting?"

Jayne nodded. "Whatever Jason gave him put him out like a light. In fact, he's still sleeping."

"Good. I wish I could say I was doing the same."

Jayne grinned. "The storm keeping you up?"

"Yes ... I'm not sure if I'll ever get used to them."

"You will. Truth is, I never dealt with my own fear of storms until I realized how my fears were affecting you kids. I loved you too much to let you suffer because of my lack of faith."

"Lack of faith ..?"

"Yes, Honey .... Fear is the absence of faith. If we don't believe God is able to take care of us though our storms, whatever they may be, we'll succumb to our fears."

"I never really thought about it that way. Is that what Jason meant when he told me not to give up my God-given authority?"

Jayne nodded. "Basically ... we've not been given a spirit of fear but of power, love, and a sound mind."

Suzanne rolled her eyes. "If only I would have remembered that passage last night."

Jayne shrugged, "Maybe what happened last night has helped you to understand what we just talked about."

"Hmm ... could be." Her mother's words made so much sense.

"Tell me, Suz, did Jason mention how long he'd be staying?"

"A week ...."

Jayne's eyes glassed over. "You have to go back with him, don't you?"

Suzanne went to her mother and offered a heartwarming hug. "It's only nine more months, Mom. I'm not that far away. You can visit, and Jason already said I can come home for Christmas."

Jayne dried her tears and did her level best to pull herself together. "That would be nice. Don't take me wrong. I'm grateful for all Jason has done. Not many young men would go cut of their way to help a stranger."

"I know."

Hearing strain in Suzanne's voice, Jayne sat up, held her daughter's face in her hands and really looked at her. "Oh, Honey, what is it? What has you so distraught?"

If only she could tell her the real problem. Instead she offered, "Jason's been wonderful. The thought of facing everyone as a woman has me a bit frazzled, but I will survive."

"Suppose I didn't really think about all that. It'll be hard at first, but putting this season of your life behind you will be healing, too."

"I'm so sorry for everything I've done, Mom. Can you ever forgive me?"

"No question about it." Jayne grew quiet and took a sip of her tea. Holding her daughter's curious look, she admitted, "Jesse told me you found Jesus through all of this. I'm so happy for you. He has a way of changing the way we look at everything, doesn't He?"

"You've been telling me that for years, but I didn't understand what you meant. Now I do."

"Take His hand and let Him lead you through the days

ahead. Those who are not willing to forgive have yet to find what we have. Don't hold it against them. Pray for them. Love them as Christ commands."

Suzanne picked up her cup and emptied it. "Looking back, I really don't know how I could have walked away from all that I had. Amy made it all possible, but I can't lay the blame at her feet. I took the steps. She didn't force me to do anything. When Jesse saw me in the village, he helped me to see how selfish my actions have been. It isn't my place to tell you how to live your life. For what it's worth, I'm glad you married Josiah. You make each other happy, and that is a blessing!"

"I thought about telling him I couldn't go through with it, but then I realized that remaining single wouldn't help you to get over Daddy's death. I needed to move forward. I had to go on with my life. Allowing you to control me wouldn't have helped either of us. I would have been lonely, and you ... well, who knows?"

A yawn caught Suzanne unawares. "Could prove to be a long day."

"Honey, you're exhausted. The storm has settled. Go back upstairs and get some sleep."

"I'd love to, but you know as well as I do the boys won't let me sleep."

Jayne winked. "You just leave them to me. They've handled their chores this long without you, another day won't kill them."

"If you're sure ...."

Jayne tapped her daughter's leg. "Go on 'n get before anyone else wakes up!"

Suzanne shared a smile with her mother before moving quietly up the stairs, shedding her robe, and sliding beneath her covers. Her weary body quickly succumbed to slumber ....

* * *

Before helping Josiah to his feet, Jason gave him a quick demonstration on using the pair of crutches Jesse found in the barn. Although Jason would have liked him to stay in bed for a few more days, he understood Josiah's desire to spend time with Suzanne before they would have to leave. Jason and Jayne were following Josiah out of the room when Jason asked her, 'You don't happen to know where Suzanne is, do you?"

"I sent her back up to bed hours ago. The storm had her up most of the night."

"I see ... Jesse said he'd ride with me into Ann Arbor."

"In the rain?" the concern in Jayne's voice made him smile. "We'll be fine. I told Doctor Taylor I'd come to see him when I came to town. I'd rather not wait till the last minute."

Surprised, she asked, "You know Doctor Taylor?"

"In a round about way through the physician who trained me. Jesse mentioned that the Whites would be joining us tomorrow. I don't want to miss visiting with them. I'm not sure what Suzanne's plans were for the day. Will you tell her I have something I need to discuss with her when I return?"

Hearing tenderness in his voice, Jayne turned to face him. "Sounds important. Anything you want me to tell her?"

"Nothing that won't wait ...." Turning back to his patient, he said, "Mr. Ordan, I'm hoping you'll be fine, but if the movement proves to be too much, don't push yourself. I left some pain medicine on your nightstand. Just mix it into some water and drink it. Be sure you rest often and elevate that leg as much as possible."

"I will."

Jayne asked, "Any special requests for supper?"

He grinned. "I'm sure whatever you make will be wonderful."

Wanting to do something special for him, she pressed him a bit further. "Do you have a favorite dessert, Jason?"

His face brightened. "Did I see Louise shelling pecans?"

"Sure did. Are you in the mood for a nice pie?"

"Haven't had one in ages. Does sound good, but don't put yourself out."

Jayne grinned as she reached out and squeezed his hand. "It'll do my heart good to make you some pecan pie, Jason."

Her kind spirit warmed his heart as he turned to leave, amazed by the special bond Suzanne's family shared. That they so readily welcomed him into their hearts and lives was an unexpected blessing.

Jason's visit with Doctor Taylor was not only encouraging, it was productive as well. Although they both had concerns about the plans they had discussed in letters, Jason walked away from Doctor Taylor's office with most of them alleviated.

While in town, Jesse introduced Jason to Pastor Williams and several of his friends in the community. After meeting the Grants and making a few purchases at the general store, the two had dinner with Sheriff Kane before heading back to Ypsilanti.

The quiet ride home gave Jason time to consider how he should approach Suzanne about his growing love for her. Unfortunately, the more he thought about it, the more unsettled he became. Was he really prepared to have this conversation with her? As much as he would like to have things out in the open, not knowing how she would respond left him feeling vulnerable.

Jason couldn't help speculating. *Is this how Suzanne felt when she didn't know if I would send her back to Detroit? No wonder her uncertainties kept her from exposing her gender.* He wasn't trying to make excuses for her, but his own reservations certainly helped him to understand what Suzanne had been experiencing. He could see how easily someone could fall into such a trap.

After spending time in prayer, Jason gave his doubts to the Lord. At peace with moving forward, the only problem remaining was how he would get Suzanne alone long enough to tell her. In a family this size, doing so would not be an easy task.

Jesse told him on the way to Ann Arbor that he had talked to Olivia and their parents about him courting Suzanne. He had their blessing to proceed; however, they made a few suggestions that he would heed when he and Suzanne returned to Saline. For now, he needed to tell her of his changing heart—of his desire to court her and see where their friendship would lead.

As Jason and Jesse took to the path that led to the Huron, Jason's heart quickened. The thought of spending a nice quiet evening with Suzanne sounded wonderful to him, but would she agree? Their last few conversations had been awkward at best. Tonight, he convinced himself everything would change.

After tending to their animals, Jesse headed home to see his family, and Jason went looking for Suzanne.

Leaping up the back steps, Jason drank in the wonderful aroma drawing him in. Jayne must have heard him come in because she came out of her room to greet him.

"Did everything go well in Ann Arbor?"

"Quite well, actually ...." Jason could see that she was curious and wanted to press him, but she did not. In truth, he was thankful for her restraint. He wasn't prepared to say more. Much would depend on Suzanne and how she responded to his admission. "How is Mr. Ordan feeling?"

"We're friends, Jason. You can call us by our given names."

Jason nodded.

"Siah is doing well. He was hoping to visit with Suzanne before he went back to bed, but she hasn't come down yet."

"From the night?" He was astounded.

"She was extremely tired. She needs the rest ...."

Concerned swept over him, "Do you think she's ill? Should I check on her?"

Jayne grinned. She was all too aware of the young doctor's interest in her daughter. "I checked on her myself. I assure you, she is quite well."

"I'm glad." Feeling a trifle odd for being so obvious, he said, "Perhaps I'll see if the boys need any help in the barn. If it's all right with you, I'd like to speak to Suzanne when she wakes up."

"That's fine. I can't imagine she'll sleep through the night, but one can never tell."

He nodded and turned to leave, praying for patience in the matter as he headed toward the barn. Jason was afraid that if he didn't talk to her soon, he'd be the one up all night tonight. Reminding himself to be anxious for nothing, he busied himself for hours with Jared on the farm.

All, except Suzanne, enjoyed supper immensely. To Jason's

disappointment, she slept right through it. When he stopped by the house again before calling it a night, and still there was no sign of her, he was ready to insist that he be allowed to check in on her. Only knowing how ludicrous he would sound kept him from doing so. *It's amazing,* he thought, *how Suzanne, without even trying, brings out the best and worst in me!*

Since God's timing was always best, Jason set aside his longing and enjoyed a splendid evening with Jesse and the twins. Olivia, exhausted as well, had gone off to bed early.

"Well, well, well!" Jesse exclaimed, as Suzanne descended the stairs after breakfast the next morning. "Would you look at who decided to grace us with her presence?"

Suzanne's mouth curved up. "A woman needs her beauty rest, Jesse."

"Feel better?"

Suzanne nodded, as she scanned the room. She found Jason sitting in the parlor with the rest of her family watching Maryse and George play on the floor with an array of toys Jared and Joe had made them. For a time, Suzanne just stood and watched them, amused by their antics. They were so precious ....

Feeling like a ragamuffin in the worn brown skirt and cream blouse she had thrown on before descending the stairs, Suzanne thought about running back up to change. If it were only her family, she wouldn't have given it a second thought, but Jason's presence changed everything. Her tattered things were hardly what she'd call acceptable attire for special gathering. Then again, perhaps it was best that Jason realize right off that the dresses she wore in Saline were her Sunday best.

Olivia, noting her sister-in-law's odd state, hugged her and whispered, "Good to see you, Suzanne. I've missed you." When Suzanne only stared, she asked, "Are you all right?"

"I'm fine ... I've missed you, too." Her hands splayed across Olivia's rounding tummy. "When, Olivia?"

"Doc seems to think October or November."

"That soon?"

Olivia grinned knowingly. "I'm much smaller this time, aren't I?"

Suzanne giggled. "You read me too well. Pray that Jason will let me come home for Christmas. Little ones grow too fast. If I have to wait until summer to see the baby, I'll miss too much."

Both women's eyes fell back on Maryse and George—the proof in full view before them. They had grown so much in the few months Suzanne had been away.

Olivia admitted, "Hard to believe the twins are two already."

Suzanne's needs were pressing in when she looked back at her sister-in-law. "I know what you mean. I need to run out side. Want to join me in the kitchen for a cup of tea, while I make myself some breakfast?"

Since Suzanne had never heard his approach, she was taken aback when a strong male voice entered their conversation. She turned to find Jason standing directly behind her.

"I'm planning for us to come for Christmas, if your family will have me, Suzanne."

Her eyes glassed over as she met his soft blue gaze. "I don't think that will be a problem."

"You haven't eaten a normal meal in days. If you'd like, I'll fry you up some eggs."

His offer surprised Olivia but not Suzanne. In Saline, they were always taking care of each other. "Thanks, Jason, but if you have something else you'd rather do, I can manage."

Jason shook his head knowing that if he was ever going to find a moment alone with Suzanne, he might have to be somewhat aggressive about it. "Making your breakfast would be my pleasure."

A tinge of worry tweaked Suzanne's playful mind. She turned to Olivia and asked, "Will you keep an eye on him until I come back? He's pretty good at frying eggs, but he tends to burn almost everything else."

"Hey! Watch it there ...", Jason put in as Olivia countered with, "Be thankful he cooks eggs—Jesse won't even try. He willingly admits defeat and leaves it at that."

Suzanne stuck her feet into her brother's bluchers and ran out the back door, while Olivia and Jason collected the ingredients they would need from the cold cellar.

"When you live on your own as much as I have, Olivia, you try to make things out of desperation. Suzanne hasn't been willing to taste many of my concoctions, but I find them quite tasty."

Olivia grinned. "I think I saw some leftover hotcake batter on the counter. They'll help to fill her up."

Jason admitted, "As long as her mother has an abundance of Indian Syrup."

Olivia laughed out loud. "Then you're aware of her sugar obsession."

Suzanne's meal was coming together nicely when Olivia turned to the young doctor and asked, "Tell me, Jason, is it odd knowing she's a woman, when you've thought of her as a boy for so long?"

He chuckled softly as he flipped the eggs. "Odd ... that would be an under statement! What's even harder to swallow is knowing how attracted I was to her before knowing Zanne and Suzanne were one in the same."

"Jesse told me about your conversation. We'll be praying for you."

"Thanks ... Suzanne sleeping through yesterday was a bit frustrating at first, but you and I know it was no coincidence. God was giving me time to pray and really think things through."

"Did you come to any conclusions?"

"No ... I've come up with a plan of sorts, but it's not written in stone."

"Glad to hear it. His timing is everything. Look at how God brought Jesse and me together in what could have been the darkest season of my life."

"He gave you a husband and a family just when you thought all was lost."

"And I have Papa back in my life, too." Olivia rubbed her tummy, adding, "And ... Jesse and I have been blessed with children of our own."

"Maybe someday ..." Jason said, as his thoughts trailed off.

Olivia flipped the last pancake onto Suzanne's plate and turned to Jason as she said, "He has good things in store for you, too. Wait on Him ...."

His smile reaffirmed his words, "I fully intend to ...."

Chapter Nineteen

Forgiven

A THICK FOG HUNG OVER THE TRAIL still muddied from the rains that had fallen the previous day. The clouded expanse refused passage through its dreary haze to even the most persistent sunrays. As if the skies alone were not cause enough for gloom, Suzanne's tears had not ceased, even though they'd been riding for well over an hour. Jason was torn. He longed to say something, hold her, touch her, somehow comfort her, but he held himself at bay. She might not welcome his forwardness. For that he only had himself to blame. Over and over again Jesse encouraged him to tell Suzanne of his growing love for her. However, it never failed that every time he tried, the words would not come, or someone would interrupt their discussion. Now they were heading back to Saline without anything resolved between them.

Oh, sure, Jason was pleased to have her to himself again, but little good it was doing him. The repeated separation from her family was difficult enough, but then there were the people she must face when they arrived in the village. She had to be wondering if they would forgive her deceitfulness. If only she would speak to him! Perhaps if he told her he'd be with her every step of the way, maybe then she would be comforted.

"Suzanne, would you like to stop and have some dinner?"

She shook her head, nudged Buck into a canter, and rode on ahead. Her heart was in so much turmoil, she didn't know what to say or do. Although she desperately wanted to take off running and never stop, she refused to give in to the urge. She had to right this wrong. Being bound by a lie and running from difficult situations had to be a thing of her past. The town folk had shown her nothing but kindness up till now. She had no reason to doubt their willingness to forgive. Even so, the thought of facing them was disconcerting, and then there was Jason. Could she set her feelings for him aside and be at ease in his presence for nine more months? Her spirit was all in a dither when she finally began to pray.

Father, You know my heart. I long to make this right, so why am I struggling? I hated having to leave my family. I will miss them, Lord, but am I more afraid of being alone—of facing the days ahead without their support? Help me to lean on You, the source of all comfort. Forgive me, Lord, for the way I've been treating Jason. He's been more than a friend to me through all of this. Help me to love him as a brother in Christ. Thank you for Your unfailing love and for guiding my thoughts and words in the days ahead.

Drying her tears with the back of her hand, Suzanne slowed, allowing Jason to catch up with her. When he did, she reached for his hand and squeezed it. "I'm sorry I haven't been much company, Jason. I'm better now. I did pack us a nice meal if you'd like to stop. Might do us both some good."

He smiled, his eyes brimming with compassion. "I know the perfect spot. It's only about five minutes away."

"Sounds wonderful!" Suzanne agreed and held her hand out, motioning for him to take the lead. Before long Jason led them into a cul-de-sac lined with trees, with a small stream running through it. "What do you think?"

She slid off Buck and glanced around. "It's perfect." She handed Jason Buck's reins and said, "If you'll excuse me, I have needs to take care of."

He nodded, saw to the horses, and headed in the opposite direction of his assistant. When he returned, she was spreading a blanket on a patch of high ground.

"How far do you think we've come, Jason?"

He glanced up at the sun. "No more than five miles, if that."

She snarled up her nose. "Jesse said its thirteen miles or more from our farm. We still have a long way to go."

"If you're too tired, we could stop for the night."

Staring off in the distance, she admitted, "Jesse would have a fit if he knew I was even thinking about it, but all this crying sure does make for sore eyes. Can we decide later?"

"Sure ... need me to help with anything?"

She reached in the bag and pulled out two wooden tankards. "I brought along some strong sweet tea. If you fill these most of the way with water, we can add some and drink it cold."

"Sounds good." While Suzanne was busy setting up their picnic, Jason took the time to put out a few snares. If they did decide to stop for the evening, he'd like to have a filling meal ready to cook.

Suzanne hearing his approach, looked up. "What were you doing, Jason?"

"Planning ahead."

Her face snarled up. "You're not going to tell me?"

"No need. Jesse warned me about your aversion to certain things."

His expression told her asking for clarification would be unwise. "I'll have to trust you, I suppose."

During their stay in Ypsilanti she had been making a conscious effort to let go of the façade she had been living for so long and just be the woman God created her to be. Unfortunately, this was not an easy task. Some habits were harder to break then others. The way she plopped down on the blanket in a most unladylike fashion was just such a time. Although she caught herself and even recovered nicely, Jason had been watching her. The slight curve of his mouth told her much, and the flush creeping up her neck was the result.

Jason, noting but refraining from commenting on her cherry complexion, took a seat beside her, covered her hand with his, bowed his head, and prayed over the meal. They ate in silence, but the dragging silence became more disquieting as time ticked by. When they could no longer tolerate the awkward hush, they spoke in unison, making it impossible to understand what the other was saying.

Laughter bubbled up—joyful, gut-wrenching laughter that eased their anxious hearts as nothing else could have.

"So tell me, Jason, what were you about to say?"

He shook his head, insisting, "Ladies first ...."

She nodded. "As you wish. I was merely wondering if Gerty would be home when we arrive."

Jason's brow furrowed. "I hope so. If not, you'll have to stay with Emmaline until she comes back."

Suzanne did not agree and told him as much with a quick shake of her head.

"Why not?" he insisted on knowing. "I won't put your reputation on the line."

"I can appreciate your concern, Jason, but I miss Hattie. I love staying with her, and besides, I could use a bit of her grandmotherly advice."

"She does enjoy having you with her. Suppose that would be fine ...."

She was about to tell him she really wasn't asking, when she recalled Jesse's scolding before they left home. While her fear of Jason sending her back to Detroit was no longer an issue, he was responsible for her. As awkward as it was, she would have to deal with it. Jesse made it quite clear that there would be no more running off. If she had a problem with Jason, she needed to talk to him. As her guardian, she needed to obey him. What was it about that word that always rubbed her the wrong way?

Fortunately, Jason never made her feel beneath him. In truth, their relationship was much like hers and Jesse's. Although she might like it to be different, she couldn't allow her mind to go there. He belonged to Emmaline ....

Nine more months, Lord, and the torture will be over. Then I can go back home and put all this behind me.

Realizing that her mind was wandering, and that Jason

was waiting for a response, she looked up at him and said, "I'm glad you approve ...." But her thoughts trailed off again and she started to giggle, recalling the last time she stayed the night with Hattie. They always had such fun, even when Hattie wasn't feeling well. Jason had a curious expression on his face, but instead of explaining why she was giggling, she stood and dashed off.

"Where are you going? And what's so funny?"

She held her tankard up to show him. "I need more water for tea."

"But we both know that's not why you were laughing!"

She had been found out. "Thoughts of Hattie—she always makes me laugh."

Suzanne was halfway to the creek when Jason suddenly remembered the traps. Scrambling to his feet, he ran towards her and grabbed the tankard. "I'll get that for you ...."

She looked at him strangely.

"Wouldn't want you to get your boots wet."

Lifting the hem of her skirt, she said, "If I had them on, it might be a concern."

Jason glanced back at the blanket and sitting neatly beside the bag were her boots, and her socks were sticking out of them. "When did you take them off?"

"While you were setting the traps."

His mouth dropped open. "You knew all along what I was doing?"

She nodded and rolled her eyes, mocking him. "Really, Jason! I wasn't born yesterday! Have you forgotten that I have three brothers?"

She watched with caution as he slid his fingers through his

flaxen hair ... but it wasn't until his big blue eyes narrowed in on her that she suspected trouble and backed away. Better to be safe than sorry. When he took a daring step toward her, her apprehensions heightened. What had she been thinking? Why did she taunt him?

Suzanne knew the split second it was too late for regrets and took off running. She ran for all she was worth, swung around a big tree, and managed to stay just out of his reach—but only for a time.

"Jason, stop!" she begged as he wrapped his arms around her and tickled her sides.

"Why should I?"

"Because!" she squirmed, as she squealed outloud.

Jason joined in her laughter, squeezed her tight, and innocently kissed her warm cheek. Their playfulness ended abruptly when she turned, and her timid eyes met his. No doubt in Jason's mind, *she cares*, but this was not the place to address such things. "You'd best get the supplies put away so we can be on our way. I'll check the traps."

She wanted more tea, but perhaps it wasn't wise to drink too much. Reaching for the tankard, she headed back to the blanket to pack their gear. Everything was secured to the mounts and still Jason hadn't come out of the woods, so she went to the stream to wash her feet. She had picked up a splinter when she was running barefooted, and it was starting to hurt. She needed to get it out. Taking a seat on a fallen log, she was picking at the skin around the splinter when Jason suddenly appeared with two gutted victims. Sickened by the sight, she lowered her eyes and went back to what she was doing. The cover of the trees made it difficult to see.

"Don't mess with that!" Jason insisted, as he came and stood over her. "I'll put supper away and get my bag."

"No need ... I'll be fine." She reached for her sock and was about to put it on, when his oversized hand cupped her chin and lifted her gaze to his.

"I'm going to take care of it now, Suzanne."

She would have protested further, but his stern look did not invite defiance. Instead she said, "Always the doctor, aren't you."

"Yes, Ma'am."

She stood and followed him back to the horses—limping the whole way. All of her poking and prodding must have done more harm than good.

Jason spread the blanket back out and sat down. Patting the spot beside him, he said, "Suzanne, lay on your stomach and give me your foot."

She denied his request with a shake of her head, but was unable to hold his uncompromising glare.

"Please tell me you're not going to make me hold you down?"

Testing him would not be wise, but neither could she convince herself to lie down. She compromised. Sitting next to him, she offered the offending appendage.

Jason's head swayed in disbelief. When he went to work on the unwelcome object, she breathed a little easier, thankful to be spared the indignity. Unfortunately, her relief was short lived.

"Suzanne ... I'm sorry you're uncomfortable with my suggestion, but I can't see the sliver at this angle."

"Maybe we should wait until we get home!"

"Enough of this nonsense! Roll over and give me your foot."
She offered no response, so he added, "This needs to come out."

Again, silence.

"Turn over, Suzanne. We need to get this done before the
sun goes down."

The man was exaggerating. The sun had barely begun its
descent. It would not set for hours. But, knowing they needed to
be on their way, she did as she was told. Mortified as she was, she
might survive this humiliation if the strange sensations swirling
inside her would ease.

Jason worked at the sliver for some time before cleansing
the wound, covering it with ointment and a clean bandage, and
finally allowing her to sit up. "I got part of it, but it's deep." He
handed her a sock and said, "Put this on and I'll help you get
on Buck. If we give the skin around the wound time to soften, it
should come out easily tomorrow."

Grand! she thought, *something else to look forward to!*

When he stood, she asked, "Jason, will you hand me
my boot?"

Without answering, he swiped it off the ground and went to
tie it onto his saddle.

"Jason!" she berated, but it did no good.

The unwavering look he sent her way affirmed his words,
"No boot until after the splinter is out."

What? "You wouldn't do this if you still thought I was Zanne!"

"Zanne wouldn't have been running around barefooted.
Remember, he had to disguise his gender, and those feet are
too feminine."

The folding of her arms in resignation did little to soothe

her irritation. She hated being bullied by anyone, least of all him. "You may be the biggest toad in the puddle, Doctor Michaels, but how am I supposed to see to my needs without the boot?" When he offered no response, she added, "We're out in the middle of nowhere!"

He strode toward her with an air of superiority, setting her on edge. "You'd better watch yourself, Young Lady. This big toad may have a big heart, but I'll drag you through the mud if you get too feisty."

She could only imagine what he meant by that, because she couldn't summon the courage to ask! When he reached down and plucked her off the ground, she wasn't too sure what would happen next. If only her fluttering stomach would ease!

Without another word, Jason carried her into the woods and helped her stand behind an aged tree. Fortunately, the trunk was wide enough to offer the privacy she would need.

"Can you handle this on your own?"

Her eyelids flipped up. "I'll manage, but thanks for the offer."

"Call when you finish—or if you change your mind and need help."

Jason gave no indication that his intentions were anything less than honorable, but then she should have known that. While he had been treating her strangely since their first meeting in Ypsilanti, she understood. This was awkward for both of them.

Jason could hear her hopping out of the woods and met her part way. "You should have called me, Suzanne."

"Couldn't!"

"More like wouldn't!"

"When you grow up in a family the size of mine, you learn to be tenacious, Jason."

"Where I come from it's called stubborn pride!" He swung her up into his arms and held her gaze for what seemed like an eternity. "It's just the two of us now, Suzanne. Please let me take care of you ...."

His tender words set her heart to thumping, and his closeness made it difficult to breathe. *Oh, no!* her thoughts exclaimed. A warm flush was crawling up her neck. No doubt about it, her face would be next.

Why did this man insist on confusing her? Did he know the way her heart took flight when he was near? *Of course not you flibbertigibbet! The man is obligated to you for the next nine months. Besides, he belongs to Emmaline!*

They had reached her horse, but he just stood there waiting—*oh, for an answer.* If only she could remember what the question was?

"Will you?"

Will I what? Merciful heaven! With a single nod, she agreed— *to what?* She was pretty sure it had something to do with his care of her. When he placed her on Buck, she released the breath she had been holding.

Dazed by all that had just transpired, Suzanne took up the reins and nudged Buck forward. When Jason came up alongside her, she was pleasantly surprised. He didn't pressure her in any way. Instead, they shared stories from their past and even reminisced about their time with her family. Seeing Jason light up when he spoke of her siblings and parents, filled her with joy. He really did enjoy getting to know them. For some reason she was more at ease knowing they had this connection in common.

Jason and Suzanne agreed when they stopped for their evening meal that they should press on. Although they would be exhausted when they arrived, sleeping in their own beds would make their efforts so worthwhile.

The evening shadows had fallen hours ago. Although the skies were clear and the moon had cast a soft glow, the sounds of night set her on edge. Raccoons were out in full force, drifting in and out of sight. Knowing opossums with their rat-like features would be out as well made her think twice before looking up. The one she had already spied hanging from a tree branch had given her a dreadful fright. Wolves howled off in the distance. Fortunately, none had come close thus far. The flapping of wings—a long screech—and then a tussle close by was her undoing. She whispered, "Did you hear that?" Her wide eyes met his.

Jason's smile was tender. "Only a hawk or owl going after his supper."

"Are we almost home? I'm so tired, and it's creepy out here."

"You should have said something earlier. I would have let you ride with me." He pointed up the path. "The puffs of smoke you see up the way are coming from our chimney."

She breathed a huge sigh of relief. "Gerty must be home."

"Good thing ... it'll save us a trip into town."

"Sure is, I'm not sure how much further I could have gone. I'm ready to drop."

"Suzanne," Jason said as he lifted her from her horse and carried her up the steps and into the house. "Should I stay with you while you talk to Gerty?"

She smiled and touched his beard-stubbled cheek. "I appreciate your concern, but I'll be fine. I've been wondering for a while if she was already on to me. You go ahead and see to the animals. I'm not the only one who's tired."

He set her in the chair by the fireplace. "I can hear Gerty scuffling around upstairs. She should be down soon, but either way you stay put until I return."

She rolled her eyes. "Yes, Jesse! Whatever you say, Jesse!"

He tweaked the tip of her nose. "You'd better be good, Young Lady, or else!"

She knew he was teasing and asked as he moved toward the door, "Or else what?" She really did want to know, but he only shook his head as he walked out the door.

Suzanne's attention was quickly diverted when their housekeeper came down the stairs stared at her with the oddest look on her face. "Hi, Gerty. It's me. Jason said I had to stay put, so will you come and sit with me for a spell? I'm afraid I have a confession to make."

Uncertain, Gerty took the seat across from her. "Do I know you, Miss? I mean, you look like Zanne, but ..."

"Like Zanne's sister, maybe?"

"No, you're Zanne. But I'm not sure that's your name."

Suzanne's eyelids slid shut for a second or two. This was harder than she thought. "My given name is Suzanne Joy Somers." She waited, expecting a rebuke or something, but instead Gerty's eyes danced with glee.

"I was right! And look at you ... you're beautiful, Suzanne."

She heard Jason coming back in the door. Even so, she had to ask, "Have you known all along?"

"Yes, Honey. That's why I insisted on moving upstairs with you. Wasn't my place to pry. I figured you had your reasons for pulling the wool over Doc's eyes. Just didn't want your reputation to be in tatters when you finally came clean."

"You're a gem, Gerty. Maybe tomorrow we can share a cup

of tea, and I'll explain everything. Doesn't make what I did right, but it might help you to understand why."

"So are you going to stay on as Doc's apprentice?"

"If my new friends don't send me away. Can you forgive me?"

The older woman came and hunkered down beside Suzanne, hugging her tightly. "No question about it, Honey. I'm just glad the charade is over. I had a terrible time keeping a lid on your secret."

"I just hope the rest of the folks in the village will be as understanding."

"All we can do is confess our sins! Whether folks forgive us or not is between them and the Lord."

"Amen!" Jason reaffirmed as he moved toward them. "We've had a long day of travel, Gerty. Suzanne has a good-sized splinter in her foot that I need to dig out tomorrow. If I carry her upstairs, will you help her get settled?"

"Be glad to, Doc. Welcome back."

"It's good to be home."

Gerty smiled at Suzanne and then looked up at Jason as she said, "I've been watching out for this young lady for some time now."

"I'm not sure why you didn't tell me, but I do appreciate your care of her."

Gerty's eyes, so filled with love, met Suzanne's. "Always a pleasure to look out for a friend, even if she's unaware."

Seeing God's love displayed through her friends warmed Suzanne in ways nothing else could have.

Chapter Twenty

The Rescue

"JASON!" Suzanne bellowed from the entrance to the barn, but there was no response. As she turned to leave, he stepped out of the stall he was mucking—pitchfork in hand.

"What's wrong?"

"Noel came by. The Crandall's horse barn is ablaze! They need our help!"

"I'll go. You stay here with Gerty. I'll saddle my horse while you grab my bag. And Suzanne ... gather all the buckets you can find."

She was not oblivious to what he was doing, and it irritated her profusely. "I'm going with you, Jason. They need all the help they can get."

He looked up, his brow furrowing into a scowl. "I don't have time to argue with you ... go!"

Although she did as she was told, her dander had already risen. That he was trying to protect her was all well and good, but this was no time to be chivalrous. When Jason rode up to the back door, she was prepared to take him to task. Thinking she might get further with honey than vinegar, she peered up and smiled moderately as she handed him the buckets and his bag. He was securing them to the saddle when she asked, "Please let me go, Jason?" When he offered no response, she added, "Flash will let us ride double."

How could he resist the chance to have her so close? With a conciliatory nod, he offered her a hand up. "Come on ...."

Sticking her foot in the stirrup, she was ready to swing her leg over the back, but he pulled her onto his lap instead. "What are you doing, Jason? You're not thinking clearly. What will the town folk think?"

"You're as stubborn as a mule! I need you up here so I can set some ground rules before we arrive."

"You wouldn't be doing this if you still thought I was Zanne!"

"Well, you're not Zanne ... and you never were! Besides, I promised Jesse I would do everything I could to keep you safe, and I fully intend to keep that promise."

Her eyes lowered. He was right, but knowing did not make her feel any better. "I won't do anything rash. I promise ...."

"You'll keep your distance from the fire?" When she offered no response, he stopped Flash and demanded compliance. "Walk back home or agree."

"Fine!"

"Fine isn't good enough."

Her shoulders slumped. "Alright! I'll do as you say. Just hurry." She did wonder what their friends would think when they saw her riding on Jason's lap, but she couldn't worry about that right now.

John Thompson ran their way as they approached the Crandall's place. Anxious to get back to work, he quickly filled them in. "Doc ... Suzanne ... the fire's under control, but we could use your help locating James and the Crandall boy."

Jason asked, "Which one?"

"Kenneth."

Suzanne asked, "Were they playing together?"

John nodded in the affirmative. "We can't be sure, but we have reason to believe they're the ones who started the fire. I caught them smoking the other day. Crandall and I tanned their bottoms, but apparently, it didn't do much good."

She slid off Flash and was running toward the river when Jason called out, "Suzanne! Where are you going?"

Craning her neck around, she said, "I'll be back." She had a sneaking suspicion she knew where the boys were hiding out. Though a long shot, Noel had shown her a fort the three boys were building a while back. She had promised Noel she'd keep the location a secret, so she needed to go alone. If she remembered correctly, the fort wasn't too far off the main trail.

She had been walking along the river's edge for a good stretch when she began paying closer attention to the landmarks Noel had pointed out. The rough structure was hidden well and could easily be missed.

The river's banks were stretched to the max from the heavy rains they'd had over the last few weeks. The current was moving at a fast clip. Recalling her promise to Jason, she kept her distance from the water's edge. It would be too easy to slip on the muddied bank and fall in. A startled grouse flew up in her face, scaring the wits out of her. With caution, she kept moving.

Her dress was soaked to her knees, and her feet were sloshing in her boots before the fort came into view — about twenty-feet away from where she now stood. Remaining perfectly still, she listened. Several minutes passed before she heard a small voice. Sounded like James. She moved in slowly.

The second the boy's heard her approach, they took off running in the opposite direction. She followed fast in their path, calling out, "James, Kenny, it's me, Zanne." Their steps did not slow. In fact, when they glanced back, they ran all the faster. She wondered why, but not for long. Looking down at her own attire, she giggled so hard she could hardly contain her glee. How could she have forgotten her female attire? So much for the trust they once shared.

When the boys stopped suddenly, their expressions frantic, she looked beyond them. A rider was coming toward them. The boys were hemmed in. It was Jason, but where did he come from? Trapped, James and Kenny started wading into the river.

"Boys," Jason bellowed, "come out of there! That current is too strong."

They must have deemed the river safer than the alternative because they paid him little heed, as they moved into deeper water.

Suzanne, seeing that Jason's words were not convincing them, started wading out to them. "Boys," she calmly implored, "your fathers are worried sick about you. Don't make things worse than they already are."

James had turned and was heading out of the water by the time Suzanne reached him. When Kenny tried to turn back, the current threw him off balance, taking him downstream.

Terrified for his friend, James hollered, "He can't swim, Doc!"

But it was Suzanne who dove into the river first.

Jason, ready to jump in after her, changed his mind. She had a good hold on Kenny in no time, but when she couldn't regain her footing, the two were heading downstream.

Scooping James up, Jason ran to where he left Flash. Securing the boy in front of him, Flash's hooves pounded the damp soil as Jason called out, trying to get Suzanne's attention. She glanced his way several times before disappearing around a bend. He and James had been riding for what seemed like miles before he spotted her again. She was trying her best to keep Kenny's face out of the water, but driven by fear, he fought her every attempt. As Jason rounded the next turn he realized the current was slowing. Moving as far ahead of them as he dared, he could see that Suzanne was floundering. Something had to be done—and fast!

"God, help me—help her! I can't lose her now."

As Jason reached the next clearing, he came upon a man and his son who had apparently been fishing. The man was trying his best to throw Suzanne a rope. After several tries, she latched on, and he tied the other end around a nearby tree.

Jason, wondering if Suzanne's strength would hold when the rope jerked, worked his way down the rope to meet her. She collapsed in his arms, and the men worked together to pull the two of them out of the river. Kenny sat up immediately. Exhausted Suzanne rolled over onto her side and closed her eyes. Jason checked her pulse and breathed a sigh of relief. She would be fine.

Jason nodded to the stranger, "Thanks for your help. I hate

to think of what might have happened if you weren't here."

The man held out his hand, and said, "I'm Ray Scott, and this here is my son, Travis."

"Don't recall seeing you around. Are you from the area?"

James looked up at Jason and admitted, "Travis and I are in school together, Doctor Michaels."

Ray grinned. "So you're the new doctor I've been hearing so much about."

Jason nodded. "I hope they're good things."

"Every last one of them."

"I'd love to stay and talk, but I'd best get Suzanne and the boys back home."

Suzanne forced herself to sit up, but it took every ounce of strength she had not to lean on Jason.

Ray met her weary gaze. "Aren't many single women around these parts. Perhaps you'll save me a dance at the next social, Miss."

She didn't have the strength to speak, but she did nod. This man was instrumental in saving her life. She owed him her thanks at the very least.

Jason, feeling her tremble, said, "We'd best be on our way." Jason lifted Suzanne off the ground and set her on Flash. She didn't look stable enough to ride alone, so he mounted behind her. Ray handed her Kenny and then put James behind Doc and the weary bunch rode in silence toward the Crandall's home.

Jason's warm body did nothing to stop Suzanne's shaking. He needed to get her home, or surely she would be ill.

John Thompson and Ralf Crandall were rushing towards them as the group moved into the clearing. John and Ralf reached for their sons while Jason quickly recounted their misadventure. His first concern was for the woman in his arms.

Ralf suggested, "You're welcome to bring her into the house. Celia will tend to her."

"Thanks, Ralf, but the way she's shivering, she could have a fever coming on. Gerty will take care of her at my place."

"We'll pray, Doc."

Celia came out of the house with a blanket and wrapped it around Suzanne.

Jason thanked her kindly and was off.

"I helped her into a warm gown," Gerty informed Jason as they stood together at Suzanne's bedside. "Poor thing ... she was so exhausted; she couldn't keep her eyes open. If only she'd quit shivering."

After Jason added an extra quilt to her bed coverings, and still her trembling had not eased, he admitted, "The sleep will help ... but we need to get her closer to the hearth so her hair will dry."

Gerty agreed and stayed with Suzanne while Jason went to stoke the flames and add logs to the fire. She was close at hand when he came back. Bundled as she was, Suzanne's teeth continued to chatter. Her eyes peeped open as he wrapped another quilt around her, but she said nothing when he carried her downstairs and sat in the chair closest to the fire with her in his arms.

Gerty pulled a small stool close to where Suzanne's head now rested on the arm of the chair and brushed through her damp tangles. That task finished, she headed back to the kitchen. Having butchered a chicken earlier, she began preparations for a pot of soup.

Emmaline, hearing through the grapevine about Suzanne's condition, rode over to offer assistance. When she walked in and saw Suzanne's limp frame in Jason's arms, her heart faltered. *Oh, please, God, let my friend be all right!*

The tenderness in Jason's eyes as he glanced down at Suzanne told Emmaline just how hard he had fallen for this woman. In truth, she was thrilled. Jason needed someone. Not knowing how Suzanne felt about him, Emmaline would continue to pray. As much as she wanted to tell Jason her wonderful news, she would talk to him about it another day. He had enough on his mind right now.

The dinner hour was approaching, and still his patient slept on as he and Emmaline sipped at coffee and talked quietly.

"Jason, I have plans for dinner tonight. Would it be all right if I stop by in a few days to see how she is?"

"You know you're always welcome, Emma. Plan to come for dinner. I'm sure Suzanne will be better by then and glad to see you."

Emmaline smiled. "Sounds like a plan."

Jason meant to tell Emmaline how nice she looked in her new yellow gown, but she was gone before he had the chance.

Having Suzanne in his arms proved to be a bit of a distraction. As much as he hated to put her down, he had chores that needed tending. Running his fingers through her silky lengths, Jason kissed her forehead. Her trembling had ceased, and there was no sign of fever, so he carried her back up to bed.

Gerty, having followed Jason, took care to settle her in. They were back downstairs before Gerty said, "I'll keep checking on her and let you know if I have any concerns."

"She's warm now and sleeping peacefully. I'm hopeful the danger is over."

Gerty nodded. "We'll keep her bathed in prayer."

"Thank you. I don't tell you often enough how much I appreciate everything you do."

"Goes both ways, Doc. You and that slender beauty upstairs are family to me."

He nodded in agreement. "Family!"

❀ ❀ ❀

Jason climbed the stairs with Gerty again that evening. He had to check on his patient before he called it a night. Sitting next to her on the bed, he ran his fingers along her face. When that did not make her stir, he nudged her gently. "Suzanne, come on sleepy head. I need you to wake up, so you can go back to sleep."

"No, Jesse, please ..." She rolled over and added, "I'll do it in the morning ... I'm still sleepy ...."

Jason grinned and noticed Gerty's hand at her mouth, trying to suppress laughter.

"Do you want a damp cloth?"

He shook his head. "No ... she's fine."

"Who is Jesse?" Gerty asked as they walked out into the hall.

"Her oldest brother."

"I see. Had one of them myself. Understand her annoyance."

Jason rolled his eyes and turned to leave. "See you in the morning, Gerty."

"Suzanne!" Jason called from where he stood on the porch. She was coming out of the barn with her horse already saddled. "You're not well enough to be out and about."

"I'm fine. I won't be gone long, I promise." Her eyes lowered in irritation—he was shaking his head, no.

"I know what you are doing, Suzanne. We have a guest coming over who is expecting you to be here. You can check on Hattie after she leaves."

Suzanne spun around and was heading back to the barn when she offered her disgruntled words, "But I want to go now ...!"

Jason took a seat on the porch swing, his gaze following his moody apprentice until she disappeared inside the barn. He'd like to tell her to straighten up, that she was acting like a spoiled brat—but he had a pretty good idea what was bothering her. The blame lay solely at his feet. He still had not taken Jesse's advice and exposed his changing heart. Now both of them were paying for it. His decision to hold off telling Suzanne until they were back in Ypsilanti over the holiday might not be wise.

After returning Buck to his stall, Suzanne strode past Jason on her way into the house—ignoring his solemn glare. If Jesse were here, he would be disappointed, but she couldn't help it. Although Jason wouldn't say, she knew it was Emmaline who was coming for dinner. Didn't he understand how hard it was for her to see them together?

"Where is Suzanne, Gerty?" Jason asked, as he and Emmaline came into the house.

"Upstairs."

"Pouting no doubt!" Jason said, as he moved toward the stairs.

Gerty turned to Emmaline and asked, "How are you, Honey?"

"I'm good. I hope you're planing to join us for dinner. I have some wonderful news to share."

"I am. If you'll help me get the food on the table, we can eat."

Jason called from the base of the stairs, "Suzanne, our guest has arrived."

Suzanne sighed in disgruntalment. Her attitude left a bit to be desired, she knew that, but how could she go on pretending she was fine when she wasn't? As she came down to greet Emmaline, she tried to shake off her frustrations. "I'm glad you could join us, Emmaline."

When Emmaline hugged Suzanne, she noticed immediately that her gesture was one-sided. "You look so much better. When I was here the other day, you were out like a light."

Suzanne glanced at Jason and then back at Emmaline. "I didn't even know you were here?"

Emmaline smiled. "Jason and I had a cup of coffee, and visited for some time, but you never did wake up. You were sound asleep on his lap the whole time."

Emmaline's admission troubled Suzanne. Glaring up at Jason, she asked, "You were holding me without my knowledge?"

"Yes, Suzanne. You were shivering uncontrollably. Gerty and I were trying to get your hair dry and warm you up. Between my body heat and the fire, it took a couple of hours, but you finally quit shaking." Jason breathed a little easier when her mouth curved up and soft giggles bubbled up.

"I've been told I'm a sound sleeper ... hope I wasn't too much of a bother."

Jason grinned. "Sound you say ... that, My Dear, would be putting it lightly. Now about you being a bother ... that's another story ...." Looking up, she didn't miss the way his eyes twinkled with mischief.

"Don't tease me, Jason ...."

Before he could answer, Gerty appeared in the frame of the parlor door and said, "Dinner is on the table."

After Jason asked the blessing, the four of them shared a quiet meal.

Although the tension had eased to a degree, Suzanne was anxious to be on her way. When a reasonable amount of time had lapsed, she stood with her plate in hand and said, "I hate to eat and run, but I have somewhere I need to be."

"Suzanne ..." Jason gently chided.

"What?"

My, this is awkward. "You're being rude and you know it ...."

When she turned to leave, he reached for her arm and her irritation rose. "Jason, I stayed for dinner. Isn't that what you wanted?"

"Sit down, please."

"Fine!" she declared as she plopped down in the seat she had just vacated. "I really don't see what the big deal is. Emmaline, tell him you didn't come to see me. Honestly, Jason! She's your girlfriend. I would think you'd want to be alone with her. You haven't been alone in over a week!"

Jason's frustration rose and he stood to his feet. "That is quite enough!"

But Emmaline stood as well and went to Suzanne. Reaching for her friend's hand, Emmaline captured Jason's fiery look. "It's past time to tell her, Jason. You're not being fair and you know it."

Surprised by Emmaline's words but still leery of both of them, Suzanne asked, "Tell me what?"

"Since Jason's lips are sealed, perhaps my news will shed a bit of light on this uncomfortable moment. John Thompson has asked me to marry him, and I said yes."

Jason, still in a prickly mood, retorted, "Emmaline, aren't you forgetting something?"

"No ... not really! John has tried to speak to you on numerous occasions, but you've been unavailable."

He took a deep breath and forced himself to calm. "I'm available now."

She smiled. "Good! Because he should be here in about an hour."

Suzanne must have misunderstood. "But Emmaline, how can you marry John? I thought you were in love with Jason."

Emmaline shook her head. "I love Jason, but I'm not in love with him."

Scowling, Suzanne asked, "Why not?"

"He's my brother, silly!"

"What?"

Noting Suzanne's confusion she clarified, "we're not related by blood, but he is my brother, nonetheless."

"But I saw you two. He was tickling you ... he kissed your cheek."

Emmaline's eyes danced with glee. "You were spying on us?"

Suzanne's brow furrowed. "Well, yes ... I couldn't help it."

Emmaline grinned from ear to ear, barely holding back laughter. "If you must know, he tickled me because I was teasing him."

"Oh! About what?"

Emmaline glanced at her brother and with a lighthearted smirk asked, "Are you going to tell her or shall I?"

The heat in the room must have raised several notches because Jason was suddenly sweating profusely. And, the three women at the table were staring at him—waiting.

His mind whirled as his eyes fell on Suzanne. If only she could read his mind. He needed desperately to be rescued, but how could she rescue him when she didn't know he was drowning? *She doesn't even know how I feel about her.* At a loss for words and needing two less sets of eyes, Jason captured Suzanne's hand and led her out the door.

Chapter Twenty-one

A Wing and a Prayer

"A WING AND A PRAYER ..." Jason whispered, more as a reminder to himself than anything. Suzanne, the woman whose hand he could not bring himself to release, she seemed completely unaware of his fondness for her—or was she? Her silence made him wonder could her mind be reeling, too. When she did not reclaim her hand, he was encouraged. Was she at ease with his touch or merely unaware?

Suzanne, uncomfortable being under Jason's watchful eye, became suddenly interested in the wild lilies blooming along the path they were following. Her thoughts questioned, *What on earth did he mean by that? And why does his touch make my skin tingle?* If only she could make sense of his words—his touch—and all that they implied. Seeking clarification, she asked, "What were you saying?" She noted the odd twitch of his cheek and the unusual expression on his face.

Jason took a deep breath and blew it out. His restless heart thudding to the beat of an unfamiliar drum, he willed himself to calm. Giving into uncertainty would avail him naught. *Anxious for nothing!*

"Jesse ... Jesse was kind enough to inform me that until I make you aware of my commitment to you, unspoken devotion is all I have. A wing and a prayer, if you will."

"Commitment? You're confusing me, Doctor Michaels. What are you trying to say?"

So we're back to Doctor Michaels, are we? Lord help me! Why am I struggling to share my heart? Giving Suzanne his undivided attention, he began, "That I care about you. That I'd like to know you better."

Well that certainly makes things clearer! "I'm practically indentured to you for the next nine months. I'm sure we'll know each other quite well before you send me home."

"That's not what I'm talking about, Suzanne. I'm ...."

She waited for the space of several seconds. His actions were so strange, and now he seemed distracted, but why? She pressed him, "You're what, Jason?"

He hated to cut this short, but he couldn't think straight right now. He pointed back toward the house. "Can we talk later? I don't want to rush this conversation and John is here."

She stomped her foot like a spoiled adolescent, irritated that he would put her off—yet again.

His blue eyes met her fiery gaze. "Suzanne! What has gotten into you?"

She whined. "I won't be here later. I'm going to stay with Hattie for a few days." *Maybe for the next nine months if you keep ignoring me!*

While his scowl revealed his displeasure, his mind was on

more than the woman before him. In fact, he didn't so much as look her way when he said, "Suzanne, I'm not sure what's going on in that head of yours. You're my assistant. I need you checking with me before making overnight plans."

She rolled her eyes. "I really don't see what the big deal is. If you need me, you know where I am." Finally, she had regained his attention. But she cringed when his long finger came out and tapped the tip of her nose. She hated being treated like a child— even if she was acting like one.

"You can stay the night, but I'll expect you home before dinner tomorrow."

"Tomorrow?" she droned. "But you know what Hattie's like. We have too much catching up to do."

"That may be, but we're getting behind in our chores. You're needed here."

She read him too well. "That's just an excuse and you know it, Jason Michaels! Something has been stewing in that mind of yours for the last week. What aren't you telling me?"

His complexion turned a nice shade of cherry. *I can speak so freely with my patients and friends, so why do I get all flustered when I'm with you, Suzanne Somers?*

He was ignoring her again. "Fine!" she stated as she turned to leave.

But he reached for her arm and gently pulled her around to face him. "You know I hate that word ...."

"Exactly why I used it!"

"Suzanne ..."

All in a tizzy, she yanked her arm out of his hold and folded it into her other one. "What?"

Although he found her expression adorable, it would not be wise to tell her so. "I'm curious? What do you think Jesse would say if he heard you fighting me like this?"

She lowered her head, peering up without lifting her chin. *Are you going to bring him up every time we come to an impasse?* Recalling her promise to Jesse, she swallowed the retort that hung on the tip of her tongue and instead said, "I'm sorry. I don't know why I'm so agitated."

He captured her face in his hands and smiled tenderly. Her clear attempt to amend her ways pleased him. "You didn't answer my question."

"I don't need Jesse to tell me that my attitude stinks."

"Our attitude can change the outcome of our circumstances, Suz ... even turn our problems into blessings. How we respond to others is a choice."

You're quite the preacher, Doctor Michaels! "I'm all too aware of that ... I'm working on it, but facing you as a woman is so ..." her hands flitted aimlessly about, "awkward! You're not the same man you were before you found out."

He grinned. "You, My Dear, have no room to talk. You never were a man. Don't get me wrong, I'm glad you're a woman, but you try swallowing what I am. As a doctor I should have been aware of your scam from the start. Trust me when I say that this is awkward for both of us!"

"I suppose ...."

He winked. "My scrambled brain is still trying to sort all this out. I'm sorry if I'm confusing you more."

She nodded. "I guess we both have things to sort out."

"I meant it when I said I want to get to know the real you, Suzanne."

Do you really?

The warmth of his gaze made her heart soar, but she willed it to calm. She refused to allow her emotions to get the best of her. Her brother was right. Her hopes were based on assumption. Jason gave no indication that there would ever be more than friendship between them. All she had was a wing and a prayer. Then again, God was still God—and He would move mountains if she and Jason were meant for each other.

"I would like that. Especially now that I know you're unattached."

Jason's features brightened. "Is that why you didn't want to stay for dinner?"

"Well, yes. Of course! But now I'm even more confused." She shrugged. "Not sure what to think. A night with Hattie will do me some good. If nothing else, it will give me time to pray."

"We both need time to pray. I don't mean to be pushy but we'll never get to know each other if we don't make plans to spend time together. If Gerty packs us some food, will you go picnicking with me tomorrow?"

A single eyebrow lifted. "I suppose I wouldn't have a choice if you insisted."

He grinned, and his head dipped. "Then I insist."

The curve of her mouth exclaimed her pleasure. "Since you need me back so early, do you mind if I leave now?"

"But you haven't even packed a bag."

She giggled as she peered up at him. "Hattie likes me to make use of the clothing she has tucked away in the drawers and armoire in her spare room. Makes her happy, and makes me feel special that she's willing to share her pretty things."

Jason chuckled—he couldn't help it. "The way you danced into her room the first time I saw you at Hattie's was exactly what her weary heart needed. She lights up when you're around. I have to say, it did my heart good to see the two of you interacting."

She nodded, knowing how much she enjoyed having Hattie in her life.

Jason reached out and rubbed her arms. "Have fun .... If I am called out, I'll leave you a note on the secretary so you'll know where I am."

"Send someone for me, if you need me."

"I will." Jason laughed out loud when she twirled in circles the way she had that day at Hattie's. However, it was the coy look she sent his way just before she disappeared inside the barn that brought with it an onrush of emotions he could not define.

❧ ❧ ❧

"Hattie!" What are you doing out here on the porch? The damp air can't be good for you."

Hattie, who had been catnapping, opened her eyes and grinned from ear to ear. "Suzanne, stop your fussing. Truth be told, I've been waiting for you. I had a feeling you'd be stopping by."

"How'd you know we were back?"

"Didn't say I knew anything. Just had a hunch is all."

Suzanne slid off Buck and leapt up the steps to where her dear friend sat. Stooping down, she kissed Hattie's wrinkled cheek and reached for her feeble hands. "I missed you, Hattie.

Sorry I left in such a hurry."

"Did Jason find you, Honey?"

Suzanne rolled her eyes, taunting her. But she could not hide the uncertainty lurking there.

"Honey, what is it?"

"Nothing and everything. It's just, well, I wasn't expecting him to come up behind me in my family's barn the way he did."

"You went home?"

She nodded. "I had to. Talking to my brother always helps."

Concern swept over Hattie. "What did Jason have to say about your leaving without permission?"

"I'll share the whole story with you later, but I'll tell you this: Jason arrived a day and a half before I did. Needless to say, he was quite chummy with my family by then. When I found out, I was angry. I'm better now."

"Did he mention anything about Emmaline?"

Suzanne let go of Hattie's hands and pulled the other chair up close. "Not much, but Emmaline came by for dinner. John is at the house right now asking Jason for Emmaline's hand."

Hattie smiled. "I know."

Suzanne sucked in a screeching breath. "What? You little stinker! How long have you known?"

"A couple of weeks now. She's been taking special care of those children since Gertrude went back to your place. Her reputation would have been at stake if she cared for them in John's home, so when he goes out to work the fields, she collects the children, and they spend their days with her. They've been by several times to visit. Little Ester loves to cook, so they keep me well supplied in sweets and such."

Suzanne scowled, just a bit. "And you never bothered to tell me."

"Wasn't my place."

"I just don't understand why Jason didn't tell me she's his sister?"

Hattie straightened her apron and sat up straighter. "That was Emmaline's doing, so don't hold it against him. She wanted to see if she could stand on her own in the village instead of always walking in her brother's shadow."

Suzanne's head lowered. "I suppose I should be more understanding."

"Don't you worry yourself about anything. Tell me, Sweet Pea, did Jason fill you in on anything else I should know?"

Her eyes narrowed in on her friend. "Hattie! What else do you know that you're not telling me?"

Hattie squirmed, and hemmed and hawed. As much as she wanted to spill the beans, she refrained from telling Suzanne a single thing. She only made a suggestion, "Neil came by with a pitcher of milk. I sure could use some hot chocolate. Will you help me fix it?"

"I will, but you should know, I'm onto you. You're keeping something from me—I can feel it."

Suzanne helped her friend up, and together they moved into the house. In fact, they were walking into the kitchen when Hattie admitted, "If I could tell you, I would, Suzanne. It's just not my place."

"I figured as much. Jason said I'm to be home tomorrow before noon. He wants to talk, so we're going on a picnic. Now you've got my curiosity peaked. Should I be worried?"

"Anxious for nothing. You know where our peace comes from. Talk to God about it."

Suzanne grinned. "I did that all the way here."

"Keep at it."

"You know I will."

Hattie reached up and fingered the delicate lace on Suzanne's collar. "Sure is nice to see you in a dress."

Suzanne smiled as she broke off a piece of chocolate and put it in the pan with the warming milk. Adding sugar, she said, "I know you love me in spite of everything, but I can't help but wonder if others will be so forgiving."

Hattie reached for the biggest mugs she had. "God's Word says that we're to confess our sins, and He's faithful and just to forgive them. We're not responsible for how others respond, Honey; that's between them and the Lord."

"I suppose you're right."

"I know I'm right." Hattie pointed to a shelf behind Suzanne. "I have some cookies in that red tin from Sharon Chefan."

"Mmm! What kind are they?"

"Does it matter?"

Suzanne giggled. "Not to me. Everything that woman makes is scrumptious."

Hattie poured the hot cocoa into mugs, set them on the table, and took a seat across from her friend who was licking rosy lips in anticipation of what she'd find inside the tin. Hattie was not surprised when Suzanne lifted the lid and peeked in. Sighing extensively, they both hummed their way through several of Sharon's tasty delights, while they spoke of their time apart. Suzanne and Hattie were still lounging around swapping tales when someone knocked at the door.

"Who could it be, Hattie?" The rap came again.

She shrugged. "Not sure. You'd better take a peek out the window before you lift the bar."

"It's Emmaline!" Suzanne exclaimed as she swung open the door and invited her in.

So excited she could hardly stand still, Emmaline said, "Oh, girls. I hope you don't mind. I just had to stop. If I don't tell someone—show someone—I'll never sleep tonight."

Hattie inquired, "So tell us child!"

"He said yes ... I mean ... Jason ... Jason said yes!"

Hattie did her best to restrain a smile. "What did he say yes to, Emma?"

Emmaline held out her hand to show them her new ring. "John ... he told John he could marry me!"

Suzanne reached for Emmaline and hugged her tightly. That Emmaline was obviously in love with the man surprised her. How could she have missed the attraction before now? "I'm so happy for you, Emma. Have you decided when?"

Emmaline stood back, wondering what they would say, but there was no time for uncertainty. "Jason had a fit when we told him we wanted to marry tomorrow, but we were able to make him see that it makes no sense to wait. John needs me, and I need him and the children."

Hattie cut in, "Well, child, if you intend to marry the man tomorrow, we have things to get ready."

"Tomorrow, Suzanne! I'm going to be his wife tomorrow morning."

Emmaline's happiness was contagious.

"Then we'll need to get up early and gather a bouquet."

"That would be nice." Emmaline agreed.

"And for a wedding gift, Jason and I will keep the children for a week."

"A week? Oh, I don't know. John might not part with them for that long."

Suzanne swatted at the air. "We won't give him a choice. Besides, he'll need the time to dote on his new wife."

Emmaline's brow rose. "Now that idea I like."

Hattie put in, "Have you thought about what you're going to wear?"

Emmaline's head swayed from side to side. Thoughtful, she glanced down at her ring finger. "I suppose I could wear my soft green suit."

"No! No! No! That will never do," Hattie insisted as she tried to stand up but couldn't get her bones to moving. "Girls, if you can help me, I think I have just the thing."

Emmaline and Suzanne were more than happy to oblige. Their enthusiasm mounted as they followed Hattie into the spare room. They could hardly wait to see what she would unveil.

Hattie lifted the lid on the chest at the foot of the bed, pushed a few things aside and smiled. "Oh, Good! It's still here. She pulled a box out of the chest and handed it to Emmaline, saying, "Now, Girls, you have to promise not to laugh if I tell you the story behind this dress."

Emmaline and Suzanne spoke in unison, "We wouldn't dream of it!" and the three of them laughed out loud.

"Several years after my Edward passed, a kindly gentleman came to town. We met at church and it wasn't long before he started calling on me, bringing me flowers and such. I was so sure he would ask me to marry him that I bought this dress when

I was visiting a friend in Detroit. Oh, I knew my assumption was only based on a wing and a prayer, but I was still devastated when he up and left town without a single word. I couldn't bring myself to tell anyone about my misfortune before now." Hattie, glancing at Emmaline, said, "If you'd like to try it on, I'd be glad to see to the alterations while you girls fix dinner."

Emmaline lifted the lid and fingered the feminine creation. What she could see of the gown was lovely. "As long as you're sure, Hattie. John wanted me to have a special dress for our wedding, but as you know, funds are scarce. Our children's needs have to come first."

Hattie winked. "It'll do my heart good to see you make use of it."

The gown Emmaline pulled out of the box was simple but elegant and delicately trimmed with a fine tatted lace. She couldn't have been more thrilled with Hattie's treasure. Then, when she held it up and realized that it was just her size and a perfect length, she spun happily around.

Emmaline's exuberance made Hattie's day.

Suzanne, on the other hand, having grown pensive when Hattie used the same phrase her brother had with Jason, mechanically helped Emmaline with the silk creation. She could only wonder what Jesse and Jason were discussing that would require him to use such a phrase? Tomorrow she would have a few questions for her doctor friend.

In the meantime, Emmaline needed Suzanne to share in her joy. So setting her concerns aside, Suzanne finished buttoning Emmaline's gown. The three women spent the rest of the evening laughing and carrying on as girlfriends do, while preparing the bride for her groom.

Chapter Twenty-two

Wedding Bells

THE THREE THOMPSON GIRLS stood before Suzanne, pretty as a picture in the new dresses Emmaline had made them several weeks back. Their boots, though worn, were all freshly polished, and Suzanne had taken extra care to see that their hair was combed and tied back with ribbons. As Suzanne stooped down in front of them, she caressed their rosy cheeks and said, "Just wait until Papa sees how nice his girls look on his special day."

Carolina, a bit confused about all the goings-on, peered up and asked, "We got perdy like Miss Emma. We marry Papa too, Miss Su ...?"

"Not Exactly, Carolina. You'll always be Papa's special girls, but today he's going to marry Miss Emma so she can be your mama."

Ester, still unsure of whether she wanted a new mama, remained silent, scowling just a tad, but Carolyn was quick to put in, "Our odder mama go ta heaben. Miss Emma not go ta heaben? She gonna stay so Papa not be sad?"

Suzanne's heart ached for them. All three of the girls had tears standing in their eyes, and Suzanne was close to joining them. As much as she wanted to tell them that God would never let that happen, she had to be honest. "There are no guarantees in this life, Honey. But Emma will stay as long as God allows. We have to trust that He knows best." She drew the three little dollies into her arms, and after squeezing them tight, she dried their tears and said, "We need to get our smiles back before Papa sees our tears. Would you like to go with me to gather a bouquet for your new mama before the preacher gets here?"

Ester pulled a frayed blue ribbon out of her pocket and said, "Aunt Hattie said Miss Emma needs something blue. I brung my hair ribbon so we could tie it around the bouquet."

Suzanne smiled as she took the worn ribbon out of the child's outstretched hand. In her own little way Ester was trying to accept what she could not change. Suzanne knew all too well how difficult this kind of change could be to accept. "Your Mama would have been proud of you for sharing with Miss Emma, Ester." The child beamed in the light of her words, so Suzanne took a chance and added, "I'm sure your new mama will love the ribbon."

"Good," Ester said, relieved that all was settled. She tucked her hand in Suzanne's and led her out the door with the twins following fast in their footsteps. By the time they had a nice bouquet ready for the bride, the wagon with all the men was pulling into the yard. The girls snuck in the back door unnoticed and ran up the stairs to where Gerty had the bride hidden away so that she could help her with finishing touches.

Suzanne took a quick peek at her own reflection, wondering as she did what Jason would think of the raspberry gown she had borrowed from Hattie's collection. The delicately crocheted ivory trim offered a feminine touch, and the fitted bodice, revealing her womanly curves, set off the full skirt. Without thought for those who might be watching, she spun around, her heart so full of glee. The girls noticed and gladly joined in her elation.

Hearing a knock, the room full of giggly girls grew silent. Without opening the door, Suzanne asked, "Are you ready for us?"

Jason replied, "Ready and waiting."

"We'll be down in a minute. Now go away, or you'll ruin the surprise."

But Emmaline was quick to put in, "He can't, Suzanne. He's giving me away."

Suzanne's hand came quickly to her mouth. "Oh, that's right!" she acknowledged, as she slowly opened the door. "Sorry, Doc!"

Jason's face brightened as she met his tender gaze. As if his smile were not enough to make her heart do flips, he reached for her hand, kissed it, and then insisted on her turning around so he could get a closer look. She could not have been more pleased when he did the same with each of his new nieces-to-be, making them feel quite special. By the time he took his sister's hand, there were tears standing in Suzanne's eyes. Like her father and Jesse, Jason had a gift for making the women in his life feel treasured.

Suzanne, Emmaline's maid-of-honor, sent the children down first, enjoying the ooo's and ahh's before she followed. From the moment Suzanne entered the small room, her eyes never left John. She loved nothing more than to see a groom's face when he first laid eyes on his bride. As she suspected, his expression made her heart sing.

This man had lost so much. The life of a farmer stopped for no one. There had been no time to grieve his loss. His children needed a mother to care for them, and God had been gracious to him for the second time. He not only gave his children a mother, John was gaining a wife who loved him. There was no doubt in Suzanne's mind; John loved Emmaline as well.

The pastor asked, "Who gives this woman to be married to this man?"

Jason responded with a smile, "I do ...."

At that moment, James, thinking there had to be bells ringing or it wasn't a wedding at all, pulled out a couple of cowbells he had hidden in a nearby basket and rang them just as his father took his bride's hand.

Needless to say, John was not at all pleased with the distraction, and noting that several of their guests in attendance were in agreement, took one look at his son's features, and his own softened. It was obvious James had the best of intentions. "James ..." his father gently admonished.

The small boy's gaze lowered. "Sorry, Papa."

Emmaline's eyes glassed over when John left her side and hunkered down in front of James, offering his gentle response. "You need to give me the bells for now, son. Cow bells are a bit loud for inside the house, but I promise you can ring them as loud as you'd like to outside after the celebration is over."

James wrapped his arms around John's neck and whispered, "Thank you, Papa."

"That's my little man." John stood and gladly reclaimed his

bride's hands so the ceremony could proceed.

Jason, while he found his sister lovely in her ivory gown, was irrepressibly drawn to the woman in the raspberry creation. When he moved to Suzanne's side, he reached for her hand and squeezed it, whispering, "They look so happy, don't they?"

Suzanne nodded.

Perhaps he should have let go of her hand, but he held on tight. A quick scan of the room told him others had noticed. Even so, he ignored their inquisitive glances and relished the moment.

Suzanne held Jason's gaze. She was so confused. Had they not been in this crowded room, she would have questioned his actions. When he did not release her hand, she chose not to make a scene but turned her gaze on the couple standing in front.

Cognizant of Jason's warm hand covering hers, she could not resist looking back at him when John kissed his bride The big blue eyes that met hers sent trickling shivers up her spine, revealing the smallest measure of his changing heart. Having no wish to fall prey to wagging tongues like her sister Elizabeth had, she reclaimed her hand as soon as the nuptials were over.

Gerty and several of the other women in the church had gone out of their way to prepare a special meal for the celebration. With so many helping hands, the meal was served, and the dishes were all washed and tucked away before the musicians took their places.

The dancing had barely begun when Suzanne looked up and saw Ray, the man who had helped to rescue her from the river, coming toward her.

"If I remember correctly, you promised me a dance, Suzanne. I must admit you look lovely today." When she only stared, he asked, "Do you remember anything from that day?"

She did, but she had never thought it would come to pass. Did this man even know the bride or groom? Where had he come from? Suzanne looked frantically for Jason, hoping he would come to her rescue, but he was nowhere to be found. When Ray held out his hand, she had no choice but to take it.

The fast paced jig drew to a close. While Ray was a handsome man, and light on his feet, she had no desire to encourage his affections. Unfortunately, he had other ideas. He did not release her. Oh, she could insist, but she had no wish to be rude. However, when the fiddlers picked up their bows, her worst fears were realized. A slow waltz would be next.

Ray smiled when she stood as far away from him as possible. "I don't bite, Miss Suzanne."

She cringed when his strong arms drew her closer, and he leaned to whisper in her ear, "If I didn't know better, I'd think you were leery of me."

She blushed at being found out.

"Perhaps you'll be more at ease after a few more songs."

She shook her head. "I have other obligations, Mr. Scott. I'm afraid this will be our last."

"Then smile a little. Have some fun. My son is watching, hoping I'll make a good impression."

Suzanne's eyes met his. "I'm not sure what you're getting at, Mr. Scott."

He nodded. "Now mind you, I'd like to know you better before I declare my intentions, but if my son has anything to say about it, we'll be standing in front of a preacher before the month is out."

"Mr. Scott!"

He held his hand up. "Don't go getting yourself all upset. The boy misses his mama is all. He's always trying to match me up. Since the day we met, he hasn't let me forget how pretty you are."

"I'm flattered, Mr. Scott, really I am, but I'm not looking for a husband."

His smile was tender. "You're wise to give yourself time. I thank you for the dance, Miss Suzanne. Any chance you'd do me a favor?"

Her brow knitted together. "That all depends on what it is."

"Will you dance with Travis? You would certainly make his day."

She grinned. "I'll see to it right away."

"Thanks ..."

Jason had been watching Suzanne interact with Ray from a distance. While he suspected she was only fulfilling her promise, the odd emotions swirling inside of him put him on his guard. Had he already declared his intent, he would have reason to steal her away, but as things stood, she was open game.

Determined to put an end to his misery, Jason made a beeline toward Suzanne, fully prepared to whisk her into his arms and keep her close for the rest of the evening. If only Ralf Crandall hadn't stepped in front of him and asked her to dance.

Where is your wife? Jason found himself wondering, but he knew that wasn't fair. These people were their friends. They only wanted to show Suzanne that she was forgiven for her deception—that they cared about her and wanted her to feel accepted in this community.

If only his thoughts would have remained so pure ....

The evening was drawing to a close, and, like a well-planned conspiracy, one man after another had vied for Suzanne's attention. Little wonder, her special gift for igniting joy in the hearts of others was infectious.

"Jason," Emmaline informed her brother as she moved toward him, grinning from ear to ear, "Suzanne will think you've lost interest if you don't get out there and ask her to dance."

His scowl was fierce. "Where have you been? I've been trying all night!"

She giggled. "I know. I'm just giving you a hard time."

"Thanks a bunch, Sis! Forgive me for saying so, but if something doesn't change here quickly, your wedding celebration could go down in history as being one of the most frustrating evenings of my life."

"Can't have that! The power to alter history is in your reach, Jason, so get to it!"

"I fully intend to. Did you need something, Emma?"

She nodded. "John and I would like to leave after this last song. Are you sure you're up to keeping the children for the week?"

Jason had never taken care of one child, never mind four. He had many reservations, but Suzanne did not. She was elated with the prospect. "We'll be fine. Gerty will lend a hand if need be. The time alone will be good for you and John. Enjoy yourselves. Motherhood will overwhelm you soon enough."

She could have told him otherwise, but she had a feeling he wouldn't have heard a thing she said. His attention was elsewhere. Emmaline couldn't help but smile at her brother's determined look.

Jason's eyes followed Suzanne's every move. Though he did

not see Noel, who was dancing with her now as competition, there were others .... He knew the exact moment Ray started toward Suzanne, and his brain screamed out, *enough is enough!* Throwing caution to the wind, he bellowed her name from across the room, "Suzanne!" effectively staking his claim. His tone was more boisterous than he intended, but at the moment only claiming her for this dance mattered. When the music suddenly stopped and all eyes turned toward him, he offered, "Sorry!" but his steps never slowed until he acquired Suzanne's hand.

He suspected that the way everyone stared would put Suzanne on edge, so he informed them—as Suzanne's flush deepened, "Didn't mean to interrupt ... I couldn't risk having this beautiful woman stolen away from me again. I've been trying to dance with her all night."

The crowd erupted in laughter.

Suzanne, on the other hand, stood frozen in place, stunned by Jason's bold words. What would their friends think?

But their guests said not a word and went back to dancing before Jason really had a chance to look at the woman before him. In an attempt to soothe her enflamed cheeks, he leaned close and spoke for her ears alone, "I'm sorry if I embarrassed you, Suzanne. It's just, well ..."

All she wanted to do was to dance and forget that he had just declared her beautiful in front of most of the inhabitants of Saline. "I'll get over it, Jason."

His warm hand wrapped around hers. Unprepared for the effect his touch would have on her, she lost all sense of reality when he drew her close, much closer than necessary for this particular waltz.

If she could breathe easier, she might have asked him why, but she was suddenly caught up in the moment. Although her shimmering eyes met his from time to time, she could not hold his gaze. The warmth they exposed held a longing that matched her own. Even so, she could not allow her mind to go there. Not yet! What if she, like Hattie with her gentleman friend, read him wrong?

"We missed our picnic, and now we won't be alone for another week, Suz."

His use of her family's nickname brought a smile to her lips. "The children ..."

"Yes ..."

For a long moment they were content to sway with the rhythmic movements keeping them in one another's arms.

"Jason, I wish you would just tell me what has been on your mind."

"Some things can't be rushed, Suzanne."

Their tender moment ended when her irritation peaked. "Fine!"

He squeezed her tighter. "Suzanne ... that word is not my favorite, and you know it."

She was quick to inform him, "Since friendship is all you have in mind, perhaps I should consider more seriously the offer of marriage I received tonight?"

His movements stopped, and he glared at the woman in his arms. "Who asked you to marry him?"

"That is not your concern ... unless you care to ..."

"Suzanne?" Emmaline asked as she came up behind her.

"Emmaline ..." Just when she had Jason Michaels exactly where she wanted him!

The song had come to an end, and folks were already collecting their belongings and saying their farewells.

"John is bringing the wagon around. The twins are inside with Gerty, and they're asking for you, Suzanne."

Suzanne glanced back at Jason before she said to her friend, "I'll head in. You and John enjoy your week."

Emmaline kissed Suzanne's cheek, wondering the whole time what she had interrupted. The expression on her brother's face was not one of pleasure, but consternation, and Suzanne's face held a hint of smug delight. She would have questioned them further, but her new husband was sweeping her into his arms, and the kiss he bestowed upon her overshadowed all else.

While the sound of cowbells and children calling their farewells rang out into the moonlit night, Emmaline only had eyes for John. For the week, all of her cares must be left behind.

He Loves Me!

Chapter Twenty-three

Little Ones

$\mathcal{A}$ CHILD CRYING OUT in the night drew Suzanne from the safety of her chamber into the outer corridor of the castle. Not even the rumbling of thunder could dispel the heart wrenching sobs resounding in her ears.

Where could the child be? Suzanne wondered as she continued her search of the massive structure. Hours passed. No nook or cranny had been left unturned. Still the child was nowhere to be found. "Where are you?" Suzanne kept calling as she passed through the long halls with no definitive answer. Exhausted from her valiant efforts, she collapsed in a heap at the top of the great staircase. Closing her eyes for nary a second—maybe two—her weary body succumbed to exhaustion and before she could catch herself, she was falling ... falling ... falling .... Just as she was about to hit the stone floor, the lord of the castle, in all his masculine splendor came out of nowhere, rescuing her from certain death.

As she opened her eyes she found him a wondrous sight to

behold. But, her heart faltered. She was no longer in his arms—how dreadful! Disoriented, her starry gaze scanned the room, stopping again on the tall handsome man standing in the frame of the door. Something about him ... his strong male voice sounded so familiar.

"Suzanne!" He called for the third time.

"Jason ...? Is that you ...?"

He chuckled softly. "Yes ... who else would it be?"

Oh ... perhaps the lord of the castle? Thinking it best not to voice her thoughts, she asked, "Is something wrong?"

"Carolina is missing her papa something fierce. I've tried everything, but she's inconsolable."

Suzanne sat up and rubbed her sleepy eyes, realizing that while the child crying was a reality, the castle existed only in the hidden recesses of her mind. "I'll be right down, Jason."

Suzanne descended the stairs, following the sounds of the crying child. The soft glow of the candlelit scene unfolding as she entered the parlor was touching. James, Ester, and Carolyn were fast asleep on the makeshift tick, but Carolina was clinging desperately to her new uncle, saying over and over again in between sobs, "I need ... Papa."

Jason sat patiently rocking the small wonder, humming a familiar lullaby.

As much as she hated to interrupt, she could see that Jason was right. The child was inconsolable. Suzanne met Jason's tender gaze as she knelt down beside him and spoke softly to the child in his arms, "Carolina, will you settle for Miss Suzanne?"

Carolina practically dove into her arms, instantly calming. Jason was quick to offer his chair, but there was really no need.

Suzanne took a quick turn around the room as the exhausted child collapsed in her arms. After tucking Carolina in next to her sister, Suzanne was heading back up stairs when Jason stopped her.

"Do I have a wart on my nose or something equally terrifying, Suz?"

She couldn't restrain her smile. "No. That's just the way little ones are. Tomorrow night it could be only you she wants. There really is no rhyme or reason to their whims."

"I was getting ready to hitch up the team and take her home. Thanks for your help."

"I'm the one who offered to keep them. Would you like to trade rooms for the week?"

"No ... I really don't mind. There's nothing like having those little arms about my neck."

Suzanne couldn't have agreed more. "Wake me if you run into any problems."

He chuckled lightly.

"What are you laughing about, Doctor Michaels?"

"I'm thinking a cold rag might be in order if there is a next time."

She smiled. "Sorry! You know I'm a sound sleeper—especially when I'm dreaming."

"Dreaming, you say ... care to share?"

Her mouth curved up as she shook her head. "I'm thinking not."

"Why? The creative mind is an amazing gift, Suz. I would love to hear what goes on inside that lovely head of yours."

"A fine mix of truth and fiction, *Lord* Jason. Thanks, but no thanks. This one is staying locked up where it's safe. Besides, I've heard that if you tell your dreams they won't come true."

"Silly wives' tales ...."

"Wives' tale or not, this one would make your head swell, and I can't chance that."

Hmm ... now his curiosity really was peaked.

"Sleep well, Jason."

"Sweet dreams!"

Jason listened to Suzanne's soft giggles as she moved back up to her room, quite pleased with this new insight. Though her admission offered only a small clue that was somewhat undefined, it did expose a portion of Suzanne's heart and mind. He was encouraged. *If she's dreaming about me, there's hope ... possibly more than a wing and a prayer, wouldn't you say, Lord?*

"One, two, three, four, five, six ... fifty! Ready or not, here I come," James called out to his sisters, as he anxiously began his search.

Suzanne was working on supper and could hear the twins tittering from their hiding place under the back steps. She peeked out the window. They were well hidden, but they obviously didn't realize their voices were going to give them away.

Suzanne could see James from where she stood on her tip-toes looking out the window. Even though he was honing in on the girls, they kept on talking, tickling Suzanne to no end. She knew the exact moment the girls were discovered, because they screamed and so did she—for different reasons, of course.

"Jason!" she berated as she turned and swatted the tall man standing behind her with the great big smile. "Where did you come from?" He wasn't talking, but she had no trouble figuring it out. He had been spying on her, snuck up, and poked her sides at the exact moment the girls were found out. His oh-so-innocent look brought forth a dreadful scowl.

"What?"

"You know what, Jason Michaels!"

"All I know is that Gerty sent me in to get her basket. Couldn't resist giving you a bit of fright."

She rolled her eyes. "Try harder next time."

"Maybe I will, and ... maybe I won't!"

Feeling perhaps a tad too ornery for her own good, Suzanne turned back to the work table, scooped up a tankard of rinse water and flung it at him. If only she had thought this through! The moment Jason's eyes narrowed in on her, she knew she was in big trouble.

"No!" she squealed when he dipped down and lifted her off the floor. "Jason Michaels, you put me down!" But her demand was ignored.

He maneuvered out the back door, down the steps, and then strutted into the yard with her hanging securely over his right shoulder.

James, more interested in the goings-on with Uncle Jason and Miss Suzanne than in playing hide-and-go-seek, asked, "Where are you going, Uncle Jason. Can I go too?"

"Sure, why not?" When the girls came out of hiding, Jason asked, "Anyone want to go for a swim with Aunt Suz?"

All three of the girls shouted in unison, "I do!"

James was curious. "You going swimming, too, Uncle Jason?"

"We'll see."

Ester, looking a bit worried, put in, "You must-a done something awful bad, Miss Suzanne! Pa only carries us like that when we're in bad trouble."

"Jason! Put me down. Their little minds are impressionable! Think about what you're teaching them."

Jason turned to Ester who was trying her best to keep up with his long-legged strides. He winked at the wide-eyed girl and said, "Aunt Suzanne needs to learn that if she's going to play with fire, she could get burned! A nice dip in the creek should cure her, don't you think?"

"Jason!" Suzanne declared, as she slapped his back. "You're confusing the poor girl."

"You shoulda know'd better than to play with fire, Miss Suz!" Ester said.

James put in. "Uncle Jason's right, ya know. Pa says the man's always right."

She muttered to Jason, not wanting to expose the children to her dogmatic opinion, "No they're not, Jason Michaels! I'm of the opinion that if you weren't exposed to my brothers and their antics, you wouldn't have even considered throwing me in the creek!"

"How do you know? It's the creek or mucking stalls, you choose."

"Ha! Ha! Aren't you the funny guy?"

Gerty, hearing a commotion, was coming toward them. "Doctor Michaels! What on earth?"

Jason turned toward Gerty, exposing his drenched hair and face. "Trust me, Gerty, she's earned herself a cool dip and then some. We'll be back in a while."

Gerty's hand came to her mouth, giggling as she watched them leave. Their playfulness gave her hope that something could be stirring, and was she ever glad.

Jason put her down after Suzanne promised that she would hold his hand the rest of the way to the creek. "The children are so excited. Do you know if they can swim, Suzanne?"

"No, but we'll keep them close. It hasn't rained for a few days, so the current shouldn't be too strong." For a while they walked along in silence until Suzanne took a moment to really look at the children. "Jason, how do they manage to get so dirty?"

"They've been playing hard. And besides, a little dirt never hurt anyone."

"A little? Maybe you should look again."

As he did, his head swayed back and forth. "Do you still have that bar of soap stashed by the creek?"

She grinned. "Yes. If we can keep them in the house the rest of the day, we might even be able to skip baths tonight."

"Sounds like a plan."

The children lit up when they heard the water and James asked, "Can we run ahead, Uncle Jason?"

"Sure! But stay out of the water until we get there." They were a ways down the path when Carolyn tripped and started to cry. Jason scooped her up in his arms and brushed her off. Although her pantalets were torn, she was otherwise unscathed. "You'll be fine, Honey. Be careful, okay?" He kissed her rosy cheek and put her back down.

Suzanne and the girls were standing in their shifts at the water's edge, sticking their toes in, and James was already swimming when Jason came up behind Suzanne, gripped her hand, and pulled her into the water. Knowing she deserved whatever she got, she didn't fight the man with the devilish smirk. In truth, she had a little trick of her own to pull on him. When Jason yanked on her hand and sent her sailing into deeper water, she never let go, so a slight jerk was all it took to throw him off balance.

She stated the obvious when he came up, "Why, Doc, you're all wet!"

As his eyes narrowed in on her again, she suspected trouble and swam toward James. The water was colder than she anticipated, but she really didn't mind. Caring for this many children took a great deal of effort, and while she enjoyed them thoroughly, she welcomed the cool reprieve.

At home, the Huron had a tendency to chill her to the bone, but that had never stopped her from swimming. She'd gone back time and again—sometimes willingly, and other times as a penalty for her crimes.

While Suzanne's father was living, if he wasn't around to deal with her antics, her brothers would either throw her in the river or torture her with tickles. With three older brothers hovering, she didn't get away with much. Even so, swimming had always been a family favorite during the summer months.

Suzanne could see that Ester and James were good swimmers, but the twins hadn't even attempted to wade into the water. If she didn't get them in, Jason would have to haul water for bathing, and she didn't want that.

While Suzanne went for the bar of soap, Jason picked up Carolina and Carolyn and started walking toward their other siblings. If only getting them wet had been so easy. They were terrified of the water and screamed every time he took the slightest dip.

"Girls, you have nothing to be afraid of," Jason reassured them, but they weren't buying it.

James, being the matter of fact child, looked up at Jason and informed him, "Best to just get it over with. They scream no matter if the water's cold or not. Pa just douses them quick-like."

That seemed so cruel to Jason, but James was right. Washing them slowly didn't help. If anything, they yelled louder. By the time the girls were clean and standing back on the bank, the two adults were not only worn out, their ears were ringing from all the screaming.

Suzanne helped Ester wash and then saw to her own needs, before handing Jason the soap and saying, "I'm heading back with the girls. They're all shivering."

"That's fine. We won't be long."

As the girls neared the clearing, the glow from the setting sun was dissipating. They had been playing in the water longer than she thought. Suzanne was fretting over Gerty having to hold supper, when the girls noticed a raccoon and begged her to stop. How could she resist? He was standing on his hindquarters cleaning his tiny face. Needless to say, they were enthralled with the bushy-tailed bandit.

Had she been paying attention to the trail when they started to move again, Suzanne would have noticed the wolf coming their way. Most likely he only wanted a drink of water, but outside of a miracle, a confrontation would be unavoidable. Firming up her grip on her walking stick, she pushed the girls behind her and told Ester to fetch Jason.

If only the twins hadn't screamed when they saw the beast. The girls were quick to obey, but their shrieks set the wolf off. The hair on his spine was standing on end, and his fangs were exposed—every last one of them.

Long ago Jesse told her to stand her ground when stumbling upon a wolf. Showing fear would only make a wolf come after her. What she wouldn't give to have Jesse standing beside her right now!

Suzanne's courage was renewed as she heard Jason running up the trail. The way he leapt into the air, stomped his feet, and hollered like a mad man took her totally by storm, but it worked. The wolf high-tailed out of there.

Had Jason's antics not tickled her so, she might have sobbed with relief. Instead, she laughed so hard, tears came to her eyes anyway.

"Wasn't *that* funny, Suz!"

"Was, too! You didn't see your face, Jason. I don't think I've ever seen you so intense."

"Well, your legs were shaking so much, I figured I'd better do something!"

She wrapped her arms around him and gave him a great big hug before peering up and saying, "Don't get me wrong. I'm grateful, but I'll probably be laughing about your expression for days."

"Laugh all you want! I'm just glad you and the girls are unharmed."

She did not doubt that he meant every word. Sweet laughter did keep bubbling up throughout the duration of the week, but it was not only about Jason's antics. Suzanne had much to be joyful about, and so did the other adults in the Michaels' household.

Little ones have a way of brightening the lives of those around them. While parenting four children held many challenges for them, Jason, Suzanne, and Gerty's hearts would forever be changed because the Thompson children had come to stay in the Michaels' home.

Daisytales

He Loves Me!

Chapter Twenty-four

Love Is a Risk

"HOW ARE YOU, TRAVIS?" Suzanne asked the small boy as she came out of the meetinghouse.

"Doing fine, Miss Suzanne."

The service at Crandall's barn was over, and although ready to be on her way, Travis had other ideas. He reached for her hand and pulled her over to where his father stood. "Pa, look, I found her for ya. Don't she look perdy?"

Ray smiled at his son before he met Suzanne's curious look. "Would you mind if we walked with you for a spell? I'm in a bit of a quandary about a private matter. I'm hoping you'll take pity on a desperate man and offer a bit of feminine advice."

"I will, if I can," Suzanne said, glancing back to see if Jason was looking. She was hoping a bit of competition would do him some good and gladly accepted the arm Ray offered. As they strolled along the worn path, she said, "I had plans to go into town to check on Hattie. Would you mind heading that way?"

"Not at all."

Doctor Michaels watched the entire exchange unfold, disconcerted by what he saw. The way Suzanne hung on the man's arm, laughing and carrying on as if they were the best of friends, one would think ... recognizing the wave of jealousy passing through him, he pushed that thought out of his mind and headed into the Crandall home. Suzanne had been invited to share the meal with them, too, but she offered her regrets. Hattie was expecting her.

Suzanne seemed to be distancing herself from Jason of late, making excuses every time he asked her to do something with him. As of yet, they hadn't even gone on their picnic. Oh, he could force the issue, but wondered if that would be wise. Although he did want her around, he had no wish to make her feel bound to the house—bound to him. He relished his own freedom to come and go. Surely she needed her freedom as well..

Although Jason longed to expose his changing heart, the time had not presented itself. Perhaps that was just an excuse. Exposing his heart would put him in a vulnerable place with her. Was it worth the risk?

"Has your assistant found a new friend, Doc?" Ralf Crandall asked, as they headed toward the parlor.

"I've been wondering the same thing."

Ralf, noting the flash of concern in his friend's eyes, said, "If I'm reading you right, you'd best stake your claim before someone else does. Truth is, there has been talk."

Jason's brow furrowed. "About what?"

"It's nothing to get too concerned about yet, Doc. I'm not one to put much stock in gossip, but you are my friend. I'd rather tell you what folks are saying than chance your name being pulled through the mud."

"I can appreciate your honesty, so tell me ... what are they saying?"

"They understand why Suzanne did what she did, and they're willing to forgive her. But that's not the problem."

"Then, what is?"

Jason scowled, "You thought she was a man. Others have their doubts with you being a doctor and all. Having her living under your roof, even with Gerty there ... it's not a good thing. Now she's traipsing off with Ray. God only knows what they'll have to say about that!"

Jason, letting this news sink in, walked toward the small window and stared out.

Ralf gave Jason a few moments before asking if they could pray about it together.

"I'd appreciate that, Ralf. Suzanne has been placed in my care. I don't have a choice here—not if I want to keep her out of jail."

"If you don't want to tell me, I'll understand, but I've been watching you. I recognize the signs. You're in love with her, aren't you?"

Jason couldn't believe his ears. "Am I really that transparent?"

"To me."

"To you and her older brother. I spoke with Jesse about this while I was in Ypsilanti."

"What did he say?"

"He has no problem with me courting her—even marrying her if she's in agreement—but I haven't had the chance to make my feelings known to Suzanne. She's been distancing herself lately, and, well, I've been hesitant."

Ralf grinned. "Women are funny, Jason. As much as we might like them to, they can't read our minds. Even if they could, they still need to hear us say how we feel about them. Even after all these years, Celia still lights up when I tell her how much I love her and why."

Jason's hands went up in frustration. "Every time I try to talk to her she escapes me."

Ralf grinned, but seeing how this was troubling Jason, he offered, "So often God's blessings are at our fingertips, but we allow our fears and insecurities to keep us from them. If you love her, go after her. Don't give her an option. Insist that she hear you out."

Jason chuckled softly. "I ache to tell her ... at the same time ..."

"You feel vulnerable."

Jason eyes met his friend's. "Extremely."

"I've been in your shoes. Love is a risk, but it's one that is so worth taking."

"I'm sure you're right."

The two men joined hands, bowed their heads, and Ralf prayed that God would lead Jason in the days ahead. By the time Jason opened his eyes, he knew what he had to do.

"Ralf, will your family mind if I don't stay? I should speak with Suzanne before I lose my nerve."

"God go with you, Jason. But rest assured, I'm going to hold you accountable. If I don't hear from you by tomorrow, I'm coming by your place."

Jason sent him a sly grin. "Thanks, Ralf. I could use a friend who's willing to hold me to my word."

"Then you're in the right place. Go ... get out of here before I have to do any explaining."

※ ※ ※

After tying his horse to the post in front of Hattie's, the beat of Jason's heart increased with every step he took. Knowing Ralf intended to hold him accountable changed everything. There would be no backing out now. Jason half-expected Suzanne to answer the door, but instead it was Hattie.

"Hello there, Doctor Michaels. Come on in."

Jason followed her, but his mind was elsewhere.

"What brings you by?"

"Actually ... I was looking for Suzanne. She said the two of you were having dinner together. Did she show up yet?"

Hattie took Jason by the hand and was leading him toward the kitchen before she answered him, "I was beginning to think my memory was playing tricks on me. Does at times, ya know!" She pointed to the table. "I made all this food thinking she was coming. Any chance you're hungry?"

Jason wasn't sure if he should leave and try to find Suzanne or just wait. Although he would prefer to see her now, he didn't want Hattie to think anything was a miss. After all, Suzanne would arrive sooner or later. Something must have come up. Besides, he reminded himself, *anxious for nothing!*

"Everything smells wonderful, Hattie. Truth is, I'm starving. Sure you don't mind me imposing?"

She swatted at the air. "You know better than to even ask. You're family, Doc. Thought you knew that."

"You're something else. So tell me, what can I do to help?"

"As soon as I pour the coffee, you can say the blessing. Everything's already on the table."

Jason did say grace. He remembered filling his plate; even remembered taking a few bites. But as hard as he tried to be sociable, it was difficult to keep his mind from wandering. He'd been contemplating what he would say to Suzanne, if and when she arrived, but nothing was clear.

Hattie seemed sluggish. More than likely all her efforts wore her out, so Jason suggested, "Hattie, go ahead and take a nap. I can clean up and put the food away."

She offered an endearing smile. "I am tired. You sure you don't mind?"

"Not at all. If Suzanne doesn't come by the time I'm through, I'll go looking for her."

"Probably a good idea." Hattie sent him a playful wink. "While you're at it, tell her, Jason!"

Surprised by her comment he asked, "Tell her what?"

She swatted at the air as she ambled toward her room. "Jason Michaels ... you know full well what you need to tell her .... Get to it young man, or I'll do it for you."

"Hattie!"

Hattie only shook her head and disappeared inside her room.

Jason finished cleaning the kitchen and sat down to read for a while, but nothing he read made sense. After glancing up at the mantel clock several times, he finally set the book aside and went to look for the woman now consuming his thoughts.

He asked around town. No one had seen her until he passed by the livery and saw Glen, the owner's son. He said that when she dropped Buck off, Travis and Ray were with her. Unfortunately, she didn't mention where she was going from there.

Bill Chefan called out as he headed back to Hattie's. "Hey, Doc! Emmaline's been trying to track you down. Ester had a mishap. She might have broken her finger."

"I'll grab my bag at Hattie's place and head right over. Thanks for letting me know, Bill."

"My pleasure!"

The hour was late when Jason made his way home. Although his new niece fretted over the splint he had to put on her finger, she relaxed as the medication took effect. He had a hunch that with the pain subsiding, Ester enjoyed being the center of attention for a change. However, he was not surprised when she drifted off to sleep before he could say his farewells.

It pleased Jason to see how nicely his sister was fitting in with her ready-made family. Seeing them so happy made him long all the more for a family of his own.

Although exhausted, Jason hoped Suzanne would still be awake. He needed to talk to her. Regrettably, that was not the case. All was silent when he entered the house. Apparently, Gerty had gone to bed early as well. Perhaps it was for the best. He'd like to be fresh when he and Suzanne had this conversation. Taking the lantern, he headed down to the creek. A cool swim would relax him. He desperately needed to sleep.

Jason stood at the counter in his kitchen scribbling out a note as he rubbed his sleep-filled eyes.

Suzanne,

    Bill Chefan came by to get me. Stephanie, his oldest daughter, is running a high fever, and her breathing is labored.

    As soon as you eat breakfast, please come and relieve me.

~~Kind Regards,~~

~~Affectionately,~~

Love,

"Oh brother!" Jason exclaimed as he crumpled the note and threw it into the stove. *Why am I doing this? She's still my assistant in spite of the fact that she's not a man. Why am I giving her special treatment?*

Jason grinned as he climbed the stairs and knocked quietly on her door. By hook or by crook, he was going to find a way to spend time with this woman.

When there was no answer, he knocked again a bit louder. He had no wish to wake Gerty, but he was determined to take Suzanne along. No doubt about it, he'd been letting her do her own thing for too long.

He hated to invade her privacy, but she left him no choice. He opened the door only to find her room empty! His mind reeled. *Where could she be?*

Knowing his patient needed tending, he laid his frustrations aside and rode to the Chefans. Sharon was waiting for him at the door and led him up the stairs to their daughter's room.

"How long has she been struggling to breathe, Sharon?'

"She started coughing just after she went to bed. I wondered if something was wrong, but she was sleeping when I came in to check."

"The doll and stuffed teddy bear she's sleeping with—are they new?"

Wondering at the odd question, Sharon admitted, "The bear was a gift from a friend for her birthday. Stephanie turned seven yesterday."

"So this was the first night she slept with it?"

"Yes."

Bill, sitting beside his daughter asked, "What are you thinking, Doc?"

"More than likely the bear triggered her breathing condition."

Bill took the toy out of his daughter's arms and handed it to Sharon. "Get rid of this!"

"No," Jason said, "that's not necessary. After we get her lungs settled down, immerse the bear in a pot of boiling water. Once it dries completely, you can give it back to her. Her lungs are just more sensitive than most. If you get rid of the bear, she'll think her friend's gift is what made her sick. It's true to a degree, but I'm sure you don't want her thinking that."

"Suppose not," Bill agreed.

Sharon, fidgeting with the blanket to be sure her daughter was covered, asked, "Is there anything we can do for her now?"

Jason nodded and turned to his friend. "Bill, can you set some pots of water over to boil? We'll need all the hot water we can get." As soon as he left the room, he had Sharon collect the things he would need to enclose Stephanie in a smaller area. He hoped a good steam bath would help relax the child's lungs. Only time would tell.

Seven hours passed before Jason went for his horse at the livery.

Noticing that Suzanne's horse was still in the stall, he asked, "Glen, did Suzanne ever pick up Buck yesterday?"

"No, Sir. Suspected she would, but as you can see, he's here."

"Keep Flash a while longer, will ya?"

Glen nodded. "Be glad to!"

Jason strode toward Hattie's house, leapt up the back steps, and didn't even knock before entering Hattie's home. A surprised Suzanne sat at the table drinking a cup of tea in her unmentionables.

"Doc!" she exclaimed, somewhat annoyed.

A grin erupted on Jason's face, but he did turn around. "I've seen you in less than that, My Dear. Go ... get yourself dressed. You're going home where you belong!"

She didn't care for his dictatorial tone, but she wasn't about to confront him while she had so little on. She went for her robe and returned in seconds. "I've made plans for the day, Jason. I can't go home yet. Besides ..." she said, hesitating a bit too long, "I've decided I kind of like living here in town. I'm sure if I asked her, Hattie would let me move in."

He shook his head in denial. "Not going to happen, Suzanne."

"Why not?"

Jason moved toward her, turned her to face the bedroom, and gave her a slight shove. "Get a move on. I've had a long night with a sick patient. I required your assistance and you weren't in your bed. You have obligations that are not being met. I aim to see that change."

"I told you where I would be."

"You said nothing about being away for the night, and where were you when I came looking for you yesterday? Hattie spent hours preparing a delicious meal that you never showed up for. I'm not sure what has gotten into you, Suzanne, but some things are going to change."

She could see that he was not going to back down, but she had to stand up for herself. "Hattie and I discussed it, Jason. She understood my late arrival."

He pointed toward the room. "Get dressed. We can discuss this on the way home."

"But what about my plans?"

"With whom?"

Her gaze lowered. "That's none of your business."

"Oh, but that's where you're wrong, Suzanne. Everything about you is my business. You're my assistant, remember? Unless, of course, you would prefer to go back to Detroit?"

Her wide eyes met his. "You said you wouldn't do that."

"If I remember correctly, you haven't been keeping up your end of the bargain. Leave your friend a note. It's more than you've been doing for me."

"Fine!" she exclaimed as she stormed into her room and shut the door. She was mad enough to slam it, but she wouldn't chance waking Hattie. Her dear friend usually slept till noon, and in her frail state, she needed all the rest she could get.

Instead, she sat down at the secretary and penned a note to

her friend and his son. Suzanne about jumped out of her skin when Jason knocked firmly on the door.

"I'm going for the horses. Be waiting on the porch when I return."

"Fine!" she stated as she crossed her legs, her foot swinging tenaciously in irritation.

Jason, hearing her remark, wasn't angry. In truth, he blamed himself for the way she had been distancing herself.

Searching for a calm before the storm, he whispered a prayer as he turned to leave: "I'm beginning to see that the things Ralf told me are true, Lord. Guide me in the days ahead. Help me to find a balance where Suzanne is concerned. Being her caregiver and yet wanting to share my life with her is an awkward combination. I've not held her accountable like I should. I can see now that my lackadaisical attitude is doing more harm than good. Help me to do what is right in Your sight. Love is a risk, Lord, but Your Word says that it is the greatest gift we can offer.

Jason, hearing the smithy speak, was drawn from his prayerful state.

"You must be doing some real soul searching, Doc."

Jason grinned. "You might say that. Can you saddle up both our horses, Glen?"

"Sure thing! I take it you found Suzanne?" Glen tapped the nails into the hoof of the horse he was shoeing before leading Jason back to their stalls.

"I did!"

"Will she be back before the day is spent?"

"No ..."

Confused, Glen asked as he saddled the horses, "So ... I don't need to hold her stall like she asked me to?"

Curious, Jason took a seat on the feed barrel. "What did Suzanne want you to do?"

"She's paid up for the month. Said she'd be living in town from now on."

She did, did she? "In that case, don't bother giving her a refund, just credit the funds to our account."

Glen probed him for more details, but Jason remained silent. He would not belittle Suzanne, but he was thankful to be leaving the livery with a better feel for what he would be up against. She was not only planning to take flight again, in her mind she was already gone!

Hmm! Jason thought, *Love is a risk, but it's one I am ready and willing to take, Lord!*

He Loves Me!

Chapter Twenty-five

Kindness

*J*ASON SECURED SUZANNE'S SATCHEL on the back of her horse and offered her a hand up.

"I can handle this alone, Jason ...."

He nodded, gave her Buck's reins, and went for his own mount. Although he wondered if he should mention her foul disposition, he did not.

They were down the road a piece, when Jason opted for nonchalance and broke into the awkward silence. "How was Hattie?"

Suzanne met his gaze, her eyes narrowing in on him. "How would I know? You wouldn't let me stay long enough to find out."

His mouth curved up. Her sharp response amused him. "I was referring to last night."

In her testy mood, she could not accept his kind reply. "Fine!" she declared, just before she took off at a full gallop. She never stopped until she reached *his* place.

Jason continued at the same pace. He understood she would

need time to adjust. He found her horse tied to the post in front of the house when he arrived, but the special treatment, just because she was a woman, had come to an end. Jason left Buck there and went to bed down Flash. As always, Gerty greeted him kindly as he entered the house.

"How are you, Doctor Michaels?"

"Exhausted. Stephanie was ill during the night, but she's doing much better now. I'll need to get some rest." Jason walked toward the parlor. Finding it empty, he asked, "Did Suzanne head upstairs?"

"A few minutes ago. Is she upset about something? She didn't say a word."

Jason winked. "You might say that. Try to be patient with her, Gerty. We have some things we have to work out."

"I understand."

"It could get worse before it gets better. Are you willing to ride out the storm?"

Gerty took Jason's bag from him and said, "I'll be praying, Doctor Michaels, but I'm not going anywhere."

"Good!"

Jason went to the stairs and called up, fully expecting an adverse reaction. "Suzanne, put your brother's jeans on and come down. I'll leave you a list of things I need you to do while I get some rest."

She stuck her head around the corner, her face housing a dreadful scowl. "My brother said I can't wear them for a year!"

"Today's an exception. Besides, as long as you are under my care, you will do as I say. Jesse would agree."

"Fine!"

"Suzanne ..."

She knew she was in the wrong for allowing her temper to flare up, but he didn't have to be so—so pushy! A pang of conscience cooled her flaming tongue, and she forced herself to respond calmly, "I'll be down in a few minutes, Jason.

"Hi, Gerty," Suzanne said in greeting as she rounded the corner a half hour later. "I'm sorry I was so rude before. It's just, well, I have no excuse. I let my temper get the best of me and I took it out on you. I really am sorry."

Gerty's arms opened wide and Suzanne graciously accepted the offered hug.

"Sometimes I don't know why my friends put up with me, never mind the Lord."

Gerty's hand came up to tuck Suzanne's stray wisps behind her ears and offered, "Loving God doesn't mean we're models of perfection, Suzanne."

"I know. I'm thankful He shows me when I'm wrong, but sometimes I wonder if I'll ever get better at walking this walk."

Gerty pulled a slip of paper out of her apron pocket. "There's nothing we can do to earn our way, Honey. His grace is sufficient. Stay in the Word. Look to God—He will guide you."

"That's partly my problem. When I get busy with other things, I tend to forget how important it is to spend time alone with the Lord."

Gerty's tender glance warmed her heart. "Only you can change that. We make time for those who are important to us."

Suzanne's head dipped. "I know. Did Jason go off to bed?"

"He's down at the creek." Gerty held out a piece of paper and said, "Jason told me to give this to you."

Suzanne reluctantly took it from her hand, turned and walked out the front door, fully expecting it to be a long list of grueling chores. The cool breeze made her shiver as she sat down on the top step, gathered her unbound hair in her hand, and began to read. Unprepared for his insightful words, her heart swelled with untapped emotions.

Suzanne,

You're planning to take flight again, my friend, but there's no need. God has you here for a reason. Trust me, I have learned the hard way that we are safest when we remain under the shadow of His wing. You will find refuge for your troubled soul in only one place: His Word.

See to your horse's needs, and then find a quiet place to begin anew. All you will need is your Bible, your pencil, and, of course, your journal. Take notes, My Sweet, for we will be going over your studies in our devotions tonight ... and by the way, I will expect you to lead.

If I know you, your mind is all in a dither. Try not to panic! David will get you off to a good start. His sixty-third Psalm is amazing.

God, thou art my God; early will I seek thee: my soul thirsteth for thee, my flesh longeth for thee in a dry and thirsty land, where no water is; to see thy power and thy glory, so as I have seen thee in the sanctuary. Because thy loving kindness is better than life, my lips shall praise thee. Thus will I bless thee while I live: I will lift up my hands in thy name. My soul shall be satisfied as with marrow and fatness; and my mouth shall praise thee with joyful lips: when I remember thee upon my bed, and meditate on thee in the night watches. Because thou hast been my help, therefore in the shadow of thy wings will I rejoice. My soul followeth hard after thee: thy right hand upholdeth me. But those that seek my soul, to destroy it, shall go into the lower parts of the earth. They shall fall by the sword: they shall be a portion for foxes. But the king shall rejoice in God; every one that sweareth by him shall glory: but the mouth of them that speak lies shall be stopped.

When you finish, I'm sure Gerty could use a bit of help in the garden. She's trying to harvest the rest of the vegetables before the first frost.

In case you're wondering, I asked you to wear the jeans as a reminder of God's intervention in your life. Although it's good for us to remember, we are wise to learn from our mistakes. We can run, but we can never hide from the Lord. He loves you, Suzanne. You know He does. Don't run from Him—run to Him! He is waiting with open arms.

Until I wake,

Know that you are loved,

Your friend, your brother in Christ, and ....

Jason

He wants me to lead? I am loved? What is the "and ..." supposed to stand for? I thought he would be angry with me,

*Lord, but this—this is too much! Does the man plan to punish me
with kindness? A week's worth of chores is what I deserve—at
the very least. I know how wrong I've been, Lord.*

Finding no hope for her runaway thoughts, and knowing
Jason would expect her to come through no matter how kind his
words, she buttoned her sweater, numbly untied Buck's reins,
and led him to the barn.

It was the strangest—most wonderfully peaceful morning
she'd had in far too long ....

From the position of the sun, she realized that the noon hour
had come and gone. No wonder her stomach was gnawing on her
backbone. She headed into the kitchen to find something to tide
her over till supper and was not surprised to find Gerty sitting in
her rocker stringing beans, as she hummed her favorite hymn. "I
was hoping to touch base with Jason. Have you seen him, Gerty?"

"He left for town about an hour ago. He didn't anticipate
being gone long."

"All right. I need to eat something and head down to the
creek for a bath. As long as Jason doesn't need me for something
else when I get back, I'd be glad to pick the rest of the vegetables
in the garden."

Gerty smiled. "That would be nice. We have peppers and
tomatoes that should to come in. With the way that wind has
been blowing this morning, old man winter's sure to be on his
way."

Suzanne sliced a thin piece of ham, folded it inside a piece of
bread, and took a seat at the table. "Could be ... thankfully the sun
is out. The air is still reasonably warm."

"Hopefully, it will last. As long as we don't get rain, I'd like to have the rest of the vegetables on drying racks tomorrow."

Suzanne finished her sandwich and went to the counter. Inspecting the leftover sticky buns, she added the gooiest one to her plate. She then poured a cup of tea and reclaimed her seat at the table. Licking her lips in anticipation of the first bite of cinnamon delight, she savored every one that followed.

She enjoyed her bath immensely. As she came up from the creek, she looked up and saw Jason coming toward her. His stern look told her she was about to be scolded, but she wasn't sure why. Her gaze lowered. When she tried to run past him, he caught her arm and spun her around to face him.

"How am I supposed to protect your reputation if you're running around in your unmentionables, Suzanne?"

She scowled, prepared to defend her actions with every fiber of her being. "There's nothing wrong with my attire. The Somers women have been swimming in their shifts for years."

"I'm sure that's true, but you should dress before you come back home. No sense giving tongues more to wag about."

"Fine!"

"Suzanne ... I had hoped you'd be in a better mood after spending a morning alone with the Lord."

"I am ... I was ..." *What is wrong with me, Lord?* "Why must you irritate me so, Jason Michaels?" She sent him the oddest look.

He chuckled as he shook his head. She looked so young ... but that scowl! "Let me assure you, I don't do it intentionally."

That's good to know!

Uncomfortable with her present attire, he said, "Go ahead and get dressed. I need to speak with you."

Her soft blue eyes met his. "Should I bring my Bible

and journal?"

"No ... not yet."

Suzanne ran in the back door, up the stairs to her room, and slipped her dress over her head. Brushing quickly through her hair, she descended the stairs. As hard as she tried to calm the stirring within her spirit, nothing helped. She could only hope Jason wouldn't notice. Determined to find out what was on his mind, she joined him in the parlor. There was something in his big blue eyes that tweaked her curiosity even more ....

Taking a seat, she smoothed the folds of her worn skirt and looked directly at him. "Is something wrong?"

Jason's eyes never left hers. "I saw Ray in town today." Several silent seconds ticked by. "Interesting fellow ...."

"Very ..." she countered with a serene tone that belied the stirrings within. "What was he up to?"

"Plenty!"

"Oh?"

"Yes ... as it turns out, he was on his way to the Crandall's to drop off his son."

She shrugged. "That's nothing out of the ordinary. He enjoys playing with the Crandall children."

Jason grinned surreptitiously. "I'm sure he does, but this time will be different. The Crandalls will be keeping him for about a week. Ray's on his way to Detroit."

"Hmm ... did he say why?" *Couldn't pay me to go back there.*

Jason tried not to smile, but he couldn't quite pull it off.

"Jason Michaels, if I didn't know better, I'd swear you have a tale to tell."

"No, Ma'am! No tale, only facts .... Looking smug, he

announced, "Ray placed an ad in several papers a while back ...."
He paused for far too long.

"Jason, what are you getting at? The ad ... what was
it for?"

Holding her gaze he said, "A bride ...."

"Good! 'Bout time he got that son of his a mama. Did you
know that man proposes to me every time I see him? Truth is,
I'm plum tired of it."

He was so confused. "But I thought ...?"

"Thought what?"

"Well, you know ... that you were encouraging him.
What else?"

She shook her head, gleaming in the light of his quandary.
"Nope ... just using him!"

As if he wasn't confused enough already. "Using him?"

"Yes, Sir! And Ray was more than happy to oblige. A good
actor, wouldn't you say?"

His fingers ran haphazardly through his blonde hair. "Why?
To what end, Suzanne?"

She shook her head. "It's a good thing you're not one of those
doctors who try to understand what makes folks tick."

Now he was irritated. "Suzanne, answer me!"

"To get your attention, Jason .... What else?"

Realization dawned. "You little tease ... you were trying to
make me jealous!"

"Did it work?" Suzanne could see the dickens in his narrowed
eyes and decided now would be as good a time as any to take her
leave. She bolted out the back door and was heading towards the
barn when she heard him.

He was following fast in her footsteps, bellowing out in frustration, "Suzanne! If you're going to run off every time I try to talk to you, I'll never get around to asking you what I've wanted to for months."

She stopped dead in her tracks and slowly turned around, her eyes never leaving him as he closed the distance between them. The wind whistled through the trees. One of the horses whinnied. The cow mooed, and the cat meowed, but nothing distracted her. Jason had earned her undivided attention.

What she saw in his eyes frightened her—just a tad. "I really am sorry, Jason. Perhaps the games were not necessary, but a girl likes to be sought after. I was beginning to think you didn't care. Well, not in the way I wanted you to anyway. You weren't taking the hints I kept dropping."

He wrapped his arms around her, drawing her close. "Is this better?"

Timidity washed over her. She blushed. "A little."

His tone was soft, inviting. "Now that I've captured you, my timid dove, what do you suppose I should do with you?"

Her mind reeled—her stomach churned. She had dreamed of this moment—this day for so long. Now that he was ready to move forward, she ...

Did he read her wrong? He could only assume he had because the second his head dipped down to claim a kiss, she squirmed. He loosened his hold. "Suzanne, what is it?"

She took two backward steps to distance herself. She could hardly breathe, never mind think coherently.

"Where are you going, Suzanne? I thought ...?"

"I don't know. Oh, Jason. This is happening awfully fast.

Besides, Jesse told me ... well, you know ...."

His brow furrowed. "I'm not sure I do. Remember, Suzanne, my emotions are just as unsettled as yours. I've never done this before."

Her gaze lowered. He was right about her emotions, but how could she tell him this? She had to try. "My kisses ... they should be saved for ... for my husband."

Reaching out, he lifted her chin, her soft blue eyes sparkling in the light of day. "I see ... and I agree with Jesse wholeheartedly."

"You do?"

"Absolutely!"

"I'm afraid, Jason."

"Of what?"

"If you ask me what I think you intend to, I may never know the joy of spending my life with you."

He was so befuddled. "Why?"

Jason would think her childish if she were to tell him why—perhaps only in a fanciful sort of way, but childish nonetheless. She set her uncertainties aside, knowing that if she couldn't be herself with him, this would never work. "Because, having you near makes my heart take flight. What if ...?" How could she put it into words?

The light dancing in his sky blue gaze exposed a tenderness that was awakening new feelings in her. While she welcomed them, she wasn't too sure what to do with them. Not knowing where they would lead left her uncertain.

Jason slid his arms about her again. When that was not enough, his long fingers ran ever so slowly down her soft cheek. His nose brushed tenderly against hers. "I would find you,

Suzanne. You see, I'm convinced that we belong together."

"But, Jason, you don't understand."

"I would find you, My Love."

My love? Does that mean ... ?

When he drew her close, she was too stunned to move. The kindness emanating from his wonderful smile took her breath away. *He does love me!* This time when his head lowered to claim her sweet lips, she did not pull away but surrendered willingly to his tenderness.

Chapter Twenty-six

Denying Self

"SO DOES THIS MEAN your answer is yes?"

Her eyes fluttered as she spun on her heel and moved away from the smiling man before her. "No, it does not!"

Chuckling, he captured her hand and swung her back around to face him. There was no question in his mind; the woman was taunting him. When she rolled her eyes, he had all he could do not to laugh out loud. "Correct me if I'm wrong, but I could have sworn you were saving your kisses for your husband. You surrendered willingly, Suzanne."

She toyed with several strands of her long brown hair, twirling it around her finger and rubbing it across her upper lip as she contemplated what she should say. She opted for boldness. "And I would surrender again and again. Your kisses are amazing, Jason, but you've forgotten a few details."

"Oh?"

"You haven't asked me anything, so how can I answer you? Besides, I would not and could not even consider such things without my brother's permission."

"That's just it! Jesse has already given his permission. Of course, we'd have to be sure the preacher is in town before we could marry."

She was taken aback—bordering on irritated. "You spoke with Jesse without speaking to me first?"

"Well, yes. I know I was getting the cart before the horse, Suzanne, but we live so far away. I couldn't chance waiting. Besides, I had to know if he would allow me to court you."

"Court me?"

"Yes. Truth is, he knew I was in love with you and called me on it."

Suzanne giggled, noticing the odd expression on Jason's face. "If it's any consolation, I could never get away with anything as a child. My dad and Jesse could both read me like a book."

He winked as he took a daring step toward her. "That's not hard to believe. When Jesse and I talked, he said that until I exposed my heart to you, all I had was a wing and a prayer."

"He was right, you know."

"All too well. Suzanne, I'm sorry. I should have told you before now. I'm in love with you! Haven't you noticed? I've not exactly been myself of late."

All she heard was, "In love ... with you. *He loves me?* This was all happening too fast—way too fast.

Jason, sensing her unrest, tried to explain, "Since the first day I visited with you at Hattie's, I've been a lost man. Unfortunately, I was too intimidated to tell you."

Her brow knitted together. "Intimidated? You?" She knew it was true when he turned a nice shade of red.

"You've been sending me mixed signals, Suzanne. At times I thought you cared, but there were those perplexing moments."

"Well, I thought you were in love with Emmaline. Then she married John and you've still been putting me on hold. Quite frankly I've been annoyed with you."

Sweet laughter bubbled up. "I know ... I don't blame you."

Her eyes slid shut as she tried to take it all in. The soft brush of his silky lips against hers brought them face-to-face in a hopeful embrace.

"So will you?" His big blue eyes were silently imploring ....

She had dreamed of hearing the words, so she pressed him, "You're asking for an answer to a question you haven't asked. Really, Jason, you shouldn't be so evasive. I can't read your mind, you know."

His eyes glistened as his fingers weaved their way into her long tresses. Without a word, he hushed her ramblings with one delectable kiss after another. By the time he released her, she would have agreed to *almost* anything.

"Will you marry me, Suz?"

"Hmm ... maybe you should kiss me again. A girl needs to be sure about what she's getting herself into. Marriage is a huge commitment, you know."

"I'll kiss you all night, if you'll just say yes!"

Her eyes widened on his bold statement. "You will not, Jason Michaels. At least not until we are properly wed!"

His playful wink set her slightly on edge. "I know for a fact that the preacher is here until tomorrow."

"Jason!" she berated. How could he even suggest such a thing? It was nothing short of preposterous!

At first the notion sounded a bit crazy to him as well, but now ...? "No telling when he'll be back, Suzanne." Jason grinned mischievously.

"You're serious?"

He nodded. "What do you say? Should we fetch the preacher, go to the Thompson's and marry right now?"

She liked the idea ... but were they rushing things? "What will others think, Jason?"

"That we love each other and saw no need to wait." When she offered no response, he went on, "I didn't tell you before now because I didn't want you worrying. Last Sunday, Ralf made mention of rumors that are circulating."

"What? Let me guess. The good doctor has a single woman living under his roof, and it doesn't look good." Recalling what happened to her sister several years back settled everything. Besides, she had every intention of marrying this man. Perhaps not this soon—even so, her heart was steadfast. She loved him.

"If we marry today, we would be spared the indignity of the gossips coming to us and trying to force the issue."

"And I'd be joined for life to the woman I adore."

Her impish smile gave him hope. "I would love to be your wife, Jason, no matter if we marry tonight or months from now. But you should know, the idea of beating the gossips at their own game would thrill my soul."

"Mine, too!"

Her slender finger came to her mouth. "Tonight, you say?"

"Yes! Feeling feisty, are you, My Sweet?"

"Me? You're the one who suggested tonight. You seem so sure of yourself."

He grinned. "I've been praying about asking you for some time now. My commitment to you is unwavering, Suzanne. I'll wait if that's what you want, but I have no doubts. I want you for my wife."

She slid her arms all the way around his waist, melting into his sturdy frame. Her relief knew no bounds. As far as she was concerned, she was exactly where she belonged.

Jason gladly returned her embrace, savoring the moment—hoping—praying that at any second she would expose her heart.

"I love you, too, Jason. I tried to deny myself, but I've been miserable. It feels so different now that I know your heart. I want to say yes, but ...."

"Then what is holding you back?"

"Are you sure I'm the wife you want? Nothing has changed. I still faint at the sight of blood."

"Not all the time, and, besides, my patients love you. You're amazing with children, Suzanne, and I'd love to have several."

"Several?" She giggled softly, wondering what her brothers would say if she showed up at Christmas with a baby already on the way. Her smile deepened recalling how much her family loved this man. "And you think I can make you happy?"

"Happiness is a choice. Marriage is a step in faith. And there's only one way to find out what God has in store for us, My Love. Marry me!"

She hadn't planned to do anything like this without her family around her. Who would give her away? "I suppose John could give me away," she softly murmured more to herself than him. This was all too surreal. *Am I ready for this kind of commitment, Lord? A blood covenant should be entered into reverently.* But the thought had no more entered her mind when she realized the extent of her devotion to this man.

"I will!" When he didn't respond, she added, "I'll marry you, Jason Michaels!"

He stared into the depth of her soft blues. "You'll be my wife?" His smile went from ear to ear as he swept her off her feet and swung her around. When he slowed, the tenderness of his kiss was but a foretaste of what was to come.

"Be honest with me, Suzanne. Your family isn't here. I'll understand if you want to wait."

She shook her head. "The only thing I've ever been more sure of is my need for the Lord. He is changing me and gave my life purpose, Jason, but I believe our union is part of His plan. My family wouldn't want us to wait. They adore you."

"You're sure?"

Suzanne, knowing a moment of boldness, stood on her toes and kissed him soundly. Running her slender fingers through his blond hair, she met his tender gaze. "Now are you convinced?"

"Completely!"

"Good! Should we tell Gerty first?"

He nodded and held out his hand.

Her eyes glistened as her fingers laced through his. He was going to be hers. After months of confusion and uncertainty, her mind and heart were finally at rest. She was about to be joined for life to the man who not only rescued her from the right hand of the law, he had been instrumental in leading her back to Christ. How could she be anything less than overjoyed?

Although elated with their news, Gerty insisted on a few changes in their plans. Jason was sent to get the preacher and the Crandalls, while Gerty and Suzanne went off to see if Hattie felt up to attending their wedding at the Thompson's.

Suzanne could hardly contain her excitement. Gerty had no sooner brought the team to a halt in front of Hattie's than Suzanne jumped down. Forgetting her manners, she was opening Hattie's front door before she remembered that she was not alone and turned back to her friend. "Gerty ... I'm sorry."

Her hand swished at the air, "Go on ahead. I know you're excited, Honey. Besides, you should let her know you have a tag-a-long before I come barging in."

"Oh! You could be right."

Suzanne found Hattie slumped over in her rocker, napping as usual. She kneeled down beside her friend and patted her hand. "Hattie ..."

The elderly woman opened her eyes and smiled. "I was hoping you'd be coming by, Sweet Pea. Please tell me you settled things with Jason? He was angry the other morning when he came for you, wasn't he?"

"Yes, but we've talked. He's better now. In fact, he finally got around to telling me how he feels about me."

Hattie's fingers came to her lips. "Well, it's about time. Were you surprised to find out?"

"Find what out?" Suzanne was curious as to what she would say.

"That he's in love with you, Sweet Pea, what else?"

"How could I have been so blind, Hattie? He said he's been in love with me for some time. He just didn't know how to tell me."

Hattie leaned towards Suzanne. "And now that he has?"

"I'm relieved, of course. I convinced myself that he was in

love with Emmaline, and now, well, he asked me to marry him."

Hattie's mouth dropped open. "Well I'll be! He must have taken me at my word."

"What do you mean?"

"I told him if he didn't get around to asking you soon, I'd ask you for him."

Suzanne giggled. It wouldn't have surprised her a bit if Hattie had. "So tell me, do you feel up to coming over to the Thompson's for a while? Jason's going to meet us there with the preacher."

Hattie wondered if she misunderstood. "Right now?"

"Well, yes, Hattie. If you don't come now, you'll miss our wedding."

Leaning forward, she whispered, as if the walls had ears, "Did I miss the fire? What's the rush? Ain't nothing been going on that needs confessing is there?"

Suzanne could see why she might wonder. "No, Hattie. But if you're concerned and you know us, imagine what others might be thinking. Since we love each other and intend to marry anyway, we decided it was best not to wait."

Hattie's brow knitted together. "Truth is, I've heard a few tales that got my dander up. I set the dear ones straight the second the words flew out, but it would just tickle me pink to see you put an end to their falderal."

Suzanne grinned. "You don't miss a thing, do you, Hattie?"

"Not if ..." Hattie's words trailed off when she took in Suzanne's attire. "Oh, Honey! No girl of mine is going to be married in such disarray!" Hattie stood and insisted on Suzanne following her.

But Suzanne suddenly remembered that Gerty was waiting

on the porch, so she went to let her in.

Hattie said her how-do-you-dos, and then they followed her into her room. Lifting the lid on the carved chest at the foot of her bed, Hattie pulled out package after package of things she had been collecting and slung them on the bed.

"Hattie," Suzanne inquired, "what is all this?"

"It's a good thing I like to plan ahead. That day you ran off to Ypsilanti, Jason told me everything. I suspected you'd come around and say yes sooner or later, so I started shopping out of those catalogues at the country store. I had all that extra room in the chest after Emmaline made use of the other wedding dress."

Suzanne, still in shock, said, "Looks to me like you did more than a little shopping."

"I couldn't resist. Besides, I can't think of anyone I'd rather spend money on."

For a long moment Suzanne just stood there in awe.

Hattie was quick to bring her back to her senses. "If you don't get started opening, we'll be late to your wedding!"

Suzanne was more than happy to oblige. The way Hattie and Gerty doted on her as she put on layer after layer of lacy garments, made her feel so special. It saddened her to know that her own mother couldn't share in these moments, but there would be other special times for them to share.

For now she was determined to think only happy thoughts. She had much to be thankful for. These two dear ladies had touched her life in many ways. Hattie and Gerty went on and on about how lovely she looked as they put the finishing touches on her hair.

However, it was the expression on Jason's face when Suzanne

walked into the Thompson's parlor that made her heart sing. She noticed everything about Doctor Jason Michaels. The way the light danced in his deep blue eyes—the length of his fingers as they raked slowly through his soft blonde hair—and the strength of his frame as he stood in his dark jeans, with a freshly pressed shirt and a black coatee. He looked so handsome, she could not look away. Then there was the gentle curve of his mouth as he claimed her hand and leaned to kiss her warm veiled cheek.

Jason was thankful Emmaline had insisted on his wearing his Sunday best. His bride was a vision in white satin and lace that had been tucked and frilled, accenting her womanly curves in all the right places. Suzanne's lovely face, though veiled, exposed a contentment that could not be denied. His heart filled with joy. More than anything, he adored the woman inside the lovely garments and promised before God and man to love her for the rest of his life.

When the preacher finally said with a smile, "Jason, you may kiss your bride," Jason lifted her veil, drew her close, and was in no hurry to release the woman who willingly surrendered to his tenderness. If only the enchantment could have gone on and on. A firm knock at the door interrupted their splendor.

John went to see who it was.

Suzanne's heart sank as she listened to the frantic man outside. She clung to her new husband.

Jason's warm hand cupped her cheek. "You heard him, Suzanne. His wife is having a baby and she's in distress. I hate having to leave you on our wedding night, but I really have no choice. You knew what you were getting yourself into, My Sweet."

"I suppose ...." He being the only doctor in the area, was at a disadvantage, but she would have to get used to it.

Jason pulled Suzanne into his arms and kissed her soundly again. "You stay and visit with everyone. I'll send for you if I need you."

"Are you sure?"

"Completely!"

Her coy expression made him chuckle. "I'll miss you, Husband."

He leaned close, kissed her soft neck and whispered in her ear, "Not nearly as much as I'll miss you. Keep *our* bed warm, will you?"

Her eyes widened. "Jason," she softly murmured as she glanced around to be sure no one was listening. "I'll just sleep in my own room ...."

His eyes narrowed in on her. "No you will not. You're my wife now. Besides, I'm giving your room to Gerty. She'll enjoy having the upstairs to herself. She can turn your old room into her sewing area or whatever else suits her."

Suzanne teased, "For a man who only asked me to marry him today, you sure do have things well planned."

"I've had too much time on my hands. I'd better go. You and Gerty head home before it gets too dark."

She rolled her eyes.

He latched on to her arms and drew her close. "Be good, Young Lady!"

She blushed. "I'd really rather not, but you are my husband now, so I'll try to comply."

He shook his head, grinning as he kissed her and turned to leave. Although difficult to walk out the door, he felt certain she understood. God's call on his life had to come before all else ... even his lovely bride.

Chapter Twenty-seven

Turbulent Days and Nights

"*J*ASON!" Suzanne bellowed as she sat up in bed. She scanned the room, but nothing was amiss. *Thank God! It was only a nightmare.* Wiping the moisture from her eyes, she lit the lamp on the end table beside the bed.

Her dream had been so real—so terrifying she could not stop trembling. Jason was on his way home to her—the bear—she couldn't reach him—it was too late!

Suzanne shuddered, needing to put the gruesome details out of her mind. Besides, giving place to the enemy's lies would only bind her. *Fear is the absence of faith, isn't it, Lord?*

Though tired, she could no longer remain in bed. Wrapping the extra afghan around her shoulders, she wandered through the rest of the lower level. Finding all in order, she peered out the window, praying for her husband and the woman who must still be laboring to deliver her child. *Why didn't I go with him?*

Suzanne, while she longed to have Jason home with her on their wedding night, felt relieved to a degree. Was God giving her the time she needed to consider the changes that would take place in her life, now that she was his wife?

Not only was there the physical side of marriage that she knew little about, they had never discussed their expectations of one another.

She knew so much, yet so little about him. Although he tended to be straightforward in his profession and in his relationship with the Lord; but with her, not so much. Mostly she found him kind beyond measure, playful, loving, and when necessary he could be unwavering. Would she be the wife he needed and longed for? She had no way of knowing for sure, but she prayed it would be so. *Forgive me, Lord. I know I'm worrying, and it's all for nothing. Thank you for bringing us together. Be my guide and comfort in the days ahead. Thank you that Your perfect love casts out fear.*

Thinking she could use a cup of tea, Suzanne picked up the kettle and moved toward the back door. Although reluctant to go out into the night, she was determined to move past her fears. Peering out, she saw no critters lurking, so she went to the barrel and filled the kettle half way. She turned, gazing in wonder at the velvety expanse. A fair portion of moon hung in the sky, and the stars—a bazillion of them—sprinkled the darkness. *You simply thought of everything, didn't You, Lord? Your Word says that you knew me before I was formed in my mother's womb. My mind can hardly fathom such things, but then, faith is the substance of things hoped for, the evidence of things not seen.*

Before her conception, God knew she would be standing out here alone, mesmerized by His handiwork on the very night of her wedding. *If only Jason could be here with me. Be with my husband, Lord. Keep us safe in the shelter of Your arms. Bless our union, and may the life we share bring glory and honor to You.*

A sense of peace washed over Suzanne as she reentered the house. She set the kettle back on the cold stove, deciding she didn't need that tea after all. Instead, she went back to bed. She would need her rest—especially if her new husband came home to claim her as his own.

When morning came without a word from Jason, Suzanne shared her concerns with Gerty, but she kept herself busy with the drying vegetables.

However, when dinner had come and gone with still no sign of him, she decided to do a little probing. Surely, someone would know where the man who had come for her husband lived. John had said that he didn't recognize the scruffy farmer, but that was nothing out of the ordinary. Unless folks had children in school, they mostly kept to themselves.

Suzanne ran up to her room. The air had cooled considerably, so she added a few layers and pulled her warm sweater on as well. She found Gerty tidying her room and interrupted her. "Gerty, I'm heading out to see if I can figure out where Jason is."

Gerty shook her head. "Oh, Honey, do you think it's wise to go out in this?" Gerty moved to the window and glanced out. "Those clouds are awfully dark. A bad storm must be on the way."

"I'll be fine. Buck doesn't seem to mind bad weather. If Jason comes back, tell him I've gone to the Crandall's. I'm hoping Noel or Ralf will know where he is. If I'm not coming back, I'll try to get word to you. Don't worry about supper. We'll just have sandwiches or something easy."

Reluctant to let her go, Gerty said, "Be careful, Honey. I'll be praying."

Suzanne appreciated Gerty's concern, but something wasn't right. She could feel it in her spirit. Her husband needed her. She hugged Gerty and headed for the door. Stepping down off the porch, Suzanne shivered as the biting wind caught her unawares. Thinking she'd better grab a warmer coat, she went back into the house.

Gerty's look was hopeful. "Did you change your mind?"

Suzanne smiled tenderly as she reached out and squeezed Gerty's hand. "No. It's colder than I thought it would be. I need my warmer coat." Seeing Jason's coat on the rack, she took it along as well. When she found him, he would need the added warmth.

Noel was in the barn and came out into the yard when he heard a rider come in. He couldn't imagine who would risk coming out with a storm brewing. "Suzanne! What were you thinking?" Noel reached for Buck's reins and led him into the barn. "You're either desperate or crazy. Which is it?"

"A little of both. Jason is still missing, Noel. I came by to see if you or your dad knows the man who came for him yesterday."

"I've seen him around ... drunk mostly. He's hardly worth a hill of beans, but his wife's a pretty thing. Can't imagine why she'd bother taking up with the likes of him."

Suzanne's brow furrowed. "It's not like you to be so judgmental, Noel. Folks who drown themselves in a bottle usually have something hurtful they're trying to forget."

Unremorseful, he said, "So I've been told."

"You and I know Christ can help them, but they don't. They're blinded by the pain of their past."

Noel, having heard enough, sneered. "Jasper has a choice, just like I do. If you ask me, he's shirking his responsibility."

"You're right. I had a choice, too, Noel. I could have been honest with Jason from the start, but I allowed my fears to hold me to that lie. All of us are going to make bad choices. It's what we learn from them that makes the difference."

"I suppose ...."

"Jason keeps reminding me that God's concerned with the condition of our heart. Pray for the man that God will open his eyes. Who knows, maybe you and I can somehow make a difference in his life."

Noel, taken aback by her persistence, grinned. "You've been spending too much time with that man you married. He's rubbing off on you."

"It's God's Word that is changing me, but you're right; fellowshipping with Jason and other believers has strengthened my faith."

Noel nodded. "You go on in and talk to my parents. I'll take care of Buck."

It was apparent to her that Noel was done talking. "Leave his saddle on. I'll be heading right back out."

He shook his head. "Pa won't let you leave with this storm brewing. Jason would agree ...."

She frowned. "Then I won't ask him. I'll just go into town and ask around. I have to find him. Something isn't right!"

Noel was younger than she, but he was bigger and housed a will set in granite. When she reached for Buck's reins, he would not release them. He simply turned and walked the other way.

She stomped her foot in protest. "Fine! Be that way! I'll go talk to your pa."

He snapped right back, "Go ahead. He'll set you straight!"

Maybe she was acting like a child ... perhaps it was dangerous to be out in this weather, but she had no choice. She had to make Ralf Crandall understand that.

Suzanne ran up the front steps and knocked harder than she intended. She could hear the children scuffling inside and Ralf demanding that they go to their rooms. Had she frightened them? She saw Celia peek out the front window, just before her husband opened the door.

"Suzanne," Ralf greeted in his normal stoic manner with a nod, and then stepped aside so she could enter. Is something troubling you, Mrs. Michaels? Where is your husband? To be quite honest, I'm surprised he'd allow you out with this storm brewing."

She, feeling doubly scolded and about three feet tall, glanced at Celia before looking back to Ralf. The concern on both of their faces was well noted. "I am sorry if I've upset you, Mr. and Mrs. Crandall. That was not my intent. I've come because I'm concerned about Jason. He hasn't been home yet. I was wondering if you know where the man who came for him last night lives?"

Ralf led her into the study, and suggested, "Celia, I'm sure our guest could use a cup of tea."

"Yes, Dear."

But Suzanne was quick to interrupt. "Celia, I appreciate the offer, but it's not necessary. I won't be staying."

Ralf sent his wife a knowing glance. "Celia, please see to the tea."

Suzanne was all too aware of what Ralf was doing. He wanted his wife out of the room so he could speak with her alone, and that made her more than a smidgen nervous. Feeling smaller by the moment, she took the seat Ralf offered and waited. She often wondered if the man had been in the military or if he was possibly an English Lord. Whatever he was, this man had an air about him that commanded respect—obedience was more like it.

Ralf retrieved his pipe from the mantel, emptied it, added more tobacco, and lit it.

After several puffs, he took a seat. For a long moment he only stared at the young woman sitting across from him who had become a family friend.

As hard as she tried not to, she couldn't help squirming under his watchful eye, suddenly thankful he was not her father— and that he was on the other side of the room. The smell of tobacco had a tendency to make her nauseous, and his pipe was no exception. *No matter,* she thought, *if things go as planned, I'll be out of here in no time.*

Clearing his throat, Ralf began, "I do know where the Jones' cabin is located, Suzanne, but I'd hold myself personally responsible if something were to happen to you. I can't in good conscience allow you to go back out in this storm."

His genuine concern warmed her heart. But it did not dissuade her. "I assure you, Mr. Crandall, I am quite capab ..." her words trailed off.

He was shaking his head and mouthing the word, no. "Be that as it may, in your husband's absence, I'm going to insist on your staying here until this storm has passed."

"But I can't ...." *He has no right!* Although she was sorely tempted to get up and walk out, how could she defy him? Footsteps coming their way, diverted her attention.

Noel strutted into the room, his gaze riveted on his father, "Do I need to lock her in the storage room, or have you convinced the daring young bride to stay put?"

Her eyes widened. "You wouldn't let him, would you, Mr. Crandall?" Suzanne asked, completely unsure of what his response would be.

Ralf's brow rose in question. "I assure you, Suzanne, I would prefer not to, but desperate times often call for desperate measures. Your safety is my first concern. I'm sure you would find the spare room on the second level much more comfortable."

"But haven't you been listening? My husband is missing. I need to find him, Mr. Crandall."

His mouth curved up ever so slightly. *Young love truly is blind.* "Noel and I will take you to him as soon as the storm passes."

Had his tone been patronizing instead of kind, she would not have even considered conceding. A quick peek at Noel told her he was quite pleased with himself, but she refused to let him get to her. He was still sore with her for not being a man. In truth, she didn't blame him. They had both lost a confidant when she exposed the lie she'd been living.

Suzanne, feeling awkward and out of place, left the men and went to join Celia in the kitchen. She was busy kneading bread. "Hi, Celia."

"Suzanne. Will you be staying the night?"

"Yes ..."she droned. "That husband of yours is holding me captive until the storm passes."

Celia smiled in the light of her disgruntled words. "He can be persuasive, can't he?"

"I'm not sure that's what I'd call it."

Celia, having no wish to add to her frustration, changed the subject. "The tea is ready if you'd like some, Suzanne. I'd sit with you, but I really need to get supper started."

Thinking it best to keep herself busy, Suzanne asked, "Can I help with anything?"

"You could start a batch of cookies for me."

Suzanne moved closer to her friend and chanced a question, "Are you sure you don't want to tell me where the Jones' cabin is?"

Surprise registered on her round face. "Suzanne, are you trying to get me in trouble? Remember, I have to live with the General."

Suzanne giggled when Celia shuttered in mock fear.

"Trust me, Honey, it would not be wise for you or me to defy him."

Unsure, she asked, "Do you really think he would lock me in the storage room?"

Celia's head tilted. In fact, she was about to speak when Noel came around the corner and answered Suzanne's question for her.

"Without a second thought!"

Suzanne turned to him and glared. "Go away, Noel. This is a private conversation."

He sat down at the table and crossed his arms. "My house. I can stay if I please. Besides, my father thinks we'd be wise to keep an eye on you."

Now she was really annoyed. In fact, she turned, walked out of the house, and headed toward the outhouse. At least there she wouldn't have to look at his haughty smirk.

When she came out, she saw Noel glaring at her from where he stood just inside the barn, but she ignored him and went in the back door, thankful she and Celia would be alone.

"You'll have to forgive my son's behavior, Suzanne. Ralf will have a talk with him."

Suzanne could appreciate her words, but ... "To be honest, I might be better off if you just left it alone. He's still sore at me for not being a man."

"That may be, but there is no excuse for his rudeness."

Suzanne's head lowered as she contemplated what she could say without exposing Noel's confidence. "He told me things ... private things he wouldn't have told a woman."

"I see ...."

"Makes things a bit awkward."

Celia nodded. "I won't say anything to his father, if you'll promise to tell me if he gets out of hand."

"I will. Thanks for understanding."

Celia showed Suzanne the cookie recipe, and the two women had the meal underway in no time at all. Before Suzanne knew it, she was lying in a bed upstairs listening to the storm outside. She kept praying that it would settle so she could be on her way, but it was not to be.

The turbulent days and nights since her marriage were beginning to catch up with her. She drifted off to sleep, waking the next morning to giggling children.

Rachael stood next to Suzanne's bed holding her baby sister Shayla, and Danielle stood quietly alongside them.

Rachael was the first to speak, "Good morning, Miss Suzanne.

Do you feel more rested? Pa said he'd take you to the Jones' cabin as soon as you've had your breakfast."

Suzanne sat up and stretched. "What time is it?

"Close to noon ... you must-ta been plum worn out."

"Oh, no!" In a bit of a panic, Suzanne chased the children out of the room, threw on her riding clothes, and pulled her disheveled hair back away from her face. She didn't have a brush, but it would have to do. Jason had seen her look worse. Suzanne gave no thought to her rumbling stomach as she descended the broad staircase.

The smell of that retched pipe led her right to her host. He was in the parlor, relaxing with an open book in his hands. When he did not acknowledge her presence she cringed. Unwilling to let him bully her today, she cleared her throat. Commanding presence or not, she was going out to look for her husband. If he would not tell her the location of the Jones' cabin, she'd find someone who would.

"Mr. Crandall, I'm sorry if I kept you waiting. I'm ready "

He grinned and shook his head. "First things first, Suzanne. Your breakfast is on the back of the stove."

"But I'm really not hungry. I'd rather go."

Ralf's head continued to shake. His face held a look that told her he would not take no for an answer.

She sighed in frustration. *Here we go again!*

Ralf pointed to the kitchen. "Go eat, Suzanne. No telling how long it'll be before your next meal, and I won't have you passing out from hunger. I'll be ready soon. I just have one more thing to read."

Read? Does he not understand the urgency here? My

husband could be in trouble. I need ... Suzanne groaned as she turned and went to the kitchen, determined to eat a few nibbles—just to pacify her host. But all that changed when she lifted the lid covering her food. Celia was a wonderful cook, and the aroma made her stomach growl unmercifully. With her plate in hand, she took a seat at the table and ate every bite. The tea Celia had left in the pot was sweetened to perfection. In fact, Suzanne was working on her third cup when Ralf walked into the room.

"Did you get enough, Mrs. Michaels?"

"Plenty!" She swallowed the last of her tea and carried her dishes to the washboard. Although she hated to leave them for Celia, Ralf insisted.

"Noel has our horses saddled; we should be on our way."

The heavy rains from the storm made traveling arduous along the mud-soaked path leading to the Jones' cabin. Often they were forced to ride deeper into the woods. Although the temperatures had cooled considerably, the change was not enough to rid the forest of pesky insects—insects that showed no mercy.

The mosquitoes were the worst. They came in swarms. Closing her eyes to shut them out did little to keep them from sampling her flesh. They buzzed incessantly in her head, demanding their presence be heard. She covered her face when she could stand it no more, but it was too late. As if the turbulent days and nights had not been enough to deal with, the red bumps from the numerous bites on Suzanne's tender flesh began to itch profusely. Wondering what her husband would think of his lovely bride now brought on a case of the giggles.

Chapter Twenty-eight

A Time of Waiting

"THAT'S FAR ENOUGH!" Jasper Jones declared as the three riders neared his small cabin. "Ain't nothin fer you here, so get!"

Jasper had apparently been drinking heavily. While this came as no surprise, Ralf did not understand why he would demand that they leave. Something wasn't right. Opting for nonchalance, Ralf asked, "Jasper, are you a papa yet?"

Jasper spewed his chaw off to the side and took a long swig from the bottle in his hand—his eyes still riveted on them.

Were it not for the long gun pointing in their direction, Ralf might have ignored his antics and proceeded to dismount. "Jasper, I'm not sure if you remember me or not? My name is Ralf Crandall." He pointed at the other riders, "This is my oldest son Noel, and the woman is Doctor Michael's new wife Suzanne. She's worried about her husband and rightly so. She hasn't seen him since they were wed. We came by to check on Doc and your wife. Can we come on ahead?"

349

"Wife's gone ...."

His tone was so matter of fact, Ralf asked, "But you said your wife was having a baby. Isn't that why you came for Doc?"

"True enough ... now get along."

"Be glad to, Jasper, as soon as we talk to Jason."

Jasper stood so fast that the chair he had been sitting in fell back against the cabin wall. Though unstable, his gun was still pointed at Ralf. "Go on now ... said more-an I shoulda ...."

Suzanne's mouth dropped open. "Jasper, please! I need to speak with my husband."

For a split second his eyes met hers. However, his greedy look silenced her right off.

Ralf, afraid she might try something desperate, reached for Buck's reins and led her back the way they had come.

"Ralf!" she insisted. "What are you doing? We can't just leave. You know as well as I do he's hiding something."

They were out of earshot before Ralf sternly avowed, "I'm all to aware of what is going on here, Suzanne, but this is now a legal matter. I'm going for the sheriff."

Ralf turned to his son and said, "Noel, I need you to escort Mrs. Michaels home or back to our place. The choice is yours, Suzanne, but I'll expect you to abide by my wishes, and let the sheriff handle this. I'm not about to chance you getting shot. Besides, I saw the seductive way he was eyeing you. The man's not thinking clearly."

On impulse, a shudder caught her unawares. Ralf was right. Be that as it may, she couldn't just walk away knowing her husband might be hurt or worse!

If only her brothers were here. They would know what to

do. She considered going for John, but decided that would not be wise. If he got hurt, who would do his farming for him? And besides, her nieces and nephew had already lost their mother. The thought of them losing their father, too, was unthinkable. No, best to not even tell John that Jason was missing. If worse came to worst, she could go for him later.

"What have you decided, Suzanne?"

Hearing Ralf's voice, she glanced up at him. "I'll wait at home. Will you send a messenger when you hear something?"

"Do I have your word that you'll stay put?"

An elder in their church, the man's concern was only for her safety and she had done nothing but balk at his leadership since she asked for his help. "I'm sorry I've been giving you such a hard time, Mr. Crandall. If you'll tell me that you won't relent until my husband is found, I'll do whatever you ask."

Noel's mouth dropped open. He could hardly believe his ears. The change in her was astounding.

Ralf grinned at Suzanne. "I should think you already know that answer, but if it will put your mind at ease, you have my word."

"Thanks. Gerty and I will be praying."

"I appreciate knowing that. I'll get word to you as soon as I know anything."

Suzanne had been watching Noel. His expression was one of disbelief. Could her influence over him be stronger than she thought? For a while Suzanne and Noel rode in silence, both pensive.

"Noel?"

"Hmm?"

Her eyes glassed over as she turned to her friend. "I really am sorry for giving you and your father such a hard time yesterday. I asked for his help, and then I wasn't willing to accept what he had to say. Out here alone, I could have gotten myself into another big mess."

"You don't need to apologize to me, Suzanne."

"Yes, I do. When I'm in the wrong, it may take me a while to see things clearly, but I'm willing to admit that I am. Besides, I miss our friendship. I hate the tension that hangs between us because of what I've done. Any chance you'd be willing to forgive me and start again from here?"

"I suppose. If you'll forgive me?"

Her brow furrowed. "For what?"

He rolled his eyes. "You know as well as I do how obnoxious I've been."

She lowered her head and then peered up. "Can't say as I blame you. I did lie to you ... and, I do know about the crush you have on Cynthia ... and how could I ever forget what you did the last time we went fishing ...."

He glared fiercely. "If that ever leaks out, I'll know where it came from."

Her hand came up to forestall his threats. "Not to worry. Your secret is safe; besides, who would believe me if I did tell?"

"Suzanne!"

Her hand came up again. "I won't tell, Noel."

"Good!"

They were riding up to the house when Suzanne asked again just to be sure, "You'll keep me posted, won't you?"

"Even if we don't hear anything, I'll come by tomorrow."

"Thanks. You're a good friend, Noel. I hope that never changes."

Noel grinned mischievously, reined his horse around, and was gone before she could say another word.

Suzanne led Buck into the barn and proceeded to get him settled. As she did, she prayed for her husband and the men that would be out looking for him. Although she would try her level best to be strong, she could feel her resolve crumbling against the weight of all that had transpired. As hard as she tried to ward them off, tears filled her eyes and spilled down her cheeks. *Lord, please let Jason be all right!*

For a time, Suzanne closed her eyes and thought about her wedding day. She had been thrilled when they decided to marry without delay. Knowing she would not have time to make herself look special for her groom had saddened her heart, but she soon found out that Hattie had planned ahead. The wonderful treasures Hattie had purchased, believing she and Jason would someday marry, were a perfect fit. Her show of affection had brought so much joy to Suzanne's heart. And as always, Hattie reveled in Suzanne's delight. When Jason saw her walk into the room, he was mesmerized. She would never forget his tender expression as he took her hand in his. He made her feel so treasured—so loved.

Their celebration afterwards was wonderful as well, but her groom had been stolen away too soon. It just wasn't right.

If Suzanne didn't get a handle on her spiraling emotions, she would end up doing something crazy. *Lord, thank you for Your protection over Jason. Help me to rest in You.*

After putting her horse in his stall, Suzanne headed toward the house. Gerty must have heard her ride in because she came toward her in the yard and greeted her with a great big hug.

"I'm sorry I couldn't get word to you. The storm."

Gerty moved back up onto the porch, held the front door open and followed Suzanne into the kitchen. They sat next to each other at the table. "Where did you stay for the night, Suzanne?"

"At the Crandall's," she droned. "You know what Ralf's like. He wouldn't let me leave."

"I'm just glad you're safe. That was quite a storm."

Suzanne fought against the tears threatening to escape, but there was something about this woman. She could relax in her presence, let down her guard, and just be herself. "Gerty, I'm sorry. I told myself I was done crying."

"Honey, what's wrong? Is Doc all right?"

"I don't know. I'm afraid something terrible has happened. When Ralf and Noel took me by the Jones' farm, Jasper was drunk ... he said he didn't have a wife anymore."

"What?"

"That was all we could get out of him. He wouldn't tell us anything about Jason. And then he forced us to leave at gunpoint."

For a moment Gerty just squeezed Suzanne's hand, desiring only to ease her concerns. "I'm sure Ralf will do everything he can to find Jason."

"I know he will; it's just so unsettling. Ralf is going for the sheriff. I wanted to go, too, but you know how men are. If they still thought I was Zanne, they would have ..."

"Suzanne Michaels!" Gerty scolded, not allowing her to finish. "You're bound to be tempted to fall back into your old ways, but you need to resist, girl."

"I know ...." Suzanne, realizing how foolish she must sound, tried to ease Gerty's mind. "Jason ... he's been telling me ..." she wiped her tears with the back of her hand.

"What has he been telling you, Honey?"

In an attempt to get a handle on her emotions, Suzanne stood and walked to the window. "Jason has been saying that although the temptation to follow my own path is strong and often shorter or easier, God's way is always best.'"

Gerty nodded. "He's a wise man. Keep telling yourself that, Suzanne."

"Don't look so worried. I'm glad everyone knows who I am ... it's just, well, you know ...." Suzanne's lower lip came out in a little girl pout. "Men don't think twice about putting themselves in sticky situations, but the minute a woman tries to do something brave, she's looked down on and sent to the safety of her home." Suzanne giggled softly. "I guess I did sort of get myself into a bunch of trouble when I was pretending to be a man, didn't I?"

"Yes, you did, so don't you even think about doing anything foolish. Promise? Please listen to your husband, Honey. God's way is always best."

"I know. I keep wondering if I should go for my brothers. They would know what to do." Suzanne glanced at her friend, trying to predict what her response would be.

Gerty, understanding Suzanne's reasons for wanting her brothers close, calmly said, "Jason is your husband now. God would want you to honor his wishes, so ask yourself what Jason would want you to do. If you don't know, talk to the Lord about it."

"I'll give them till tomorrow night. If there is no news by then, I'll catch the stage to Ypsilanti."

Her young friend wasn't thinking clearly, and while Gerty

understood Suzanne's desperation, she had to say, "I'd do some praying about that first, Suzanne."

Slow me down, Lord. If this is a test, I surely would like to get this right. "Will you keep a prayer vigil with me until he's found, Gerty?"

Absolutely."

Suzanne nodded, filled the kettle, and put it on the stove. "Are you getting hungry?"

"A little."

Suzanne secured her apron and moved toward the back door, thinking, *No time like the present to get started praying.*

Remembering that she had forgotten to tell Gerty where she was going, she stopped and glanced back at her friend. "Gerty, I need to spend some time alone with the Lord, or I'll never get my head set on straight. While I pray, I thought I'd see if the birds left any apples on the tree by the garden. Doesn't an apple pie sound good?"

Gerty nodded. "Wonderful. Anything in particular you want for supper?"

"I'll let you choose. If you don't mind fixing the meal, I'll make the dessert."

"Sounds like a plan."

Suzanne smiled at her friend. "Guess my mind's a bit scattered. I put the kettle on. Would you mind making a pot of tea when it boils?—I'll have some when I return."

"Not at all."

The next few hours passed in quiet communion while the women went about their duties. Being still before the Lord did not come easy for Suzanne, but she was determined to do just that. Fretting about Jasper's wicked schemes would do her no good. Worry was a sin. God was still God no matter what evil Jasper had planned, and she needed to trust Him. If the man lost his wife in childbirth, he had to be hurting, so she prayed for him, as well. She knew better than anyone how grief could cloud one's view.

After a filling supper, Suzanne picked up her needle and thread and set the sleeves into the new dress she and Gerty were making Ester for her birthday. She loved the soft green of the fabric, and the pattern Gerty had designed was darling. Thoughcoming together nicely, Suzanne's restlessness made it impossible to press on. Gerty had almost finished crocheting the lacy trim they were planning to add when Suzanne stood and went to the front door, glancing back as she said, "I'll be back in a little while, Gerty. I'm going out to sit on the porch. Just need some fresh air."

Suzanne stepped out onto the porch and wrapped her shawl tightly around her shoulders. The cool breeze, while she found it invigorating, told her winter was creeping in. Before long, puffy clouds of white snow would cover the last remnants of autumn's vibrant shades. In truth, Suzanne could hardly wait. She loved the winter months. Winter had always been a time of renewal in the Somers' household. A time to sit back, relax and enjoy the fellowship of those around her.

She couldn't help but wonder how much her life would change when her husband finally came home. There were so many things she and Jason hadn't discussed. Their future plans were a mystery to her. He mentioned his plan to take over for Doctor Taylor some day, but she hadn't asked him how long they would remain in Saline. Right now, all that paled in the light of their present circumstances.

Taking a seat on the swing, she listened to the sounds of night as she swayed back and forth, but there wasn't much to be heard. The crickets and frogs had settled into their winter havens weeks ago. While the wind whistled through the trees and the creaking of the swing in motion distracted her to a degree, the one thing she wanted to hear more than anything was her husband's voice. Unfortunately, that was not to be—for now anyway.

No one had come by with news, and while she longed to see her husband, she wasn't going anywhere. God heard her prayers. She would wait on Him. "I entrust him to You Jesus." Speaking the words out loud brought peace to her soul.

Being out in the fresh air had a way of clearing her mind like nothing else could. It also made her sleepy. When she reentered the house and found Gerty in the parlor, they held hands and prayed together before calling it a night.

Chapter Twenty-nine

Shadow of Death

"MR. CRANDALL, WHAT DO YOU MEAN the sheriff is gone?" Suzanne could not believe her ears. Ralf and Noel had stopped by the Michaels' farm. They were now sitting in the parlor with her awaiting tea.

"I'm sorry, Suzanne, I wish I could tell you otherwise, but the sheriff is often called out for other duties."

She started to cry. Four days had passed since her husband's disappearance, and still there was no word of his whereabouts. She was trying to be reasonable. It wasn't easy. "Do you know when he'll be back?"

"No one knows for sure. Another epidemic of cholera hit Detroit. He was ordered to set up roadblocks to try and contain the disease. Cholera spreads like wildfire. It could wipe out a village as small as Saline in no time at all, you know that, Suzanne. Precautions are a necessity."

"I know ...." Suzanne's thoughts went to her family, but she couldn't give place to her fears. Not now. She needed to keep her wits about her. "Mr. Crandall, I mean no disrespect, but I can't just sit at home and do nothing. Something isn't right."

"I'm well aware of your concern. I feel the same urgency. I sent a man to Ann Arbor to see if Kane is able to help us out."

Suzanne, though surprised by this news, was pleased. "Henry's a good man. A few years back my sister was taken from her home by force. He was able to bring the perpetrators to justice."

Suzanne, feeling a sudden chill, went to stoke the fire. "If for some reason he doesn't show ... I've been contemplating some other ideas."

Ralf braced himself. "Like what, Suzanne?"

She reclaimed her seat and for a long moment only stared at him, wondering what he would say. "We both know Jasper has taken a shine to me, Mr. Crandall. I know it would be risky, but what if I were to go in and try luring him away from the cabin? Could give you and the other men a chance to search his place."

It took every ounce of restraint he could muster not to berate her for even considering such a thought. Understanding her duress, he lowered his head and merely said, "I'll keep it in mind, but I don't want to put you in a vulnerable spot unless it becomes absolutely necessary."

Suzanne sighed. She had suspected as much.

"I met with the men in the community yesterday, and they're willing to do whatever they can to help. We have men watching the cabin at all times."

Her brow knitted together. "Have they noticed anything suspicious?"

Ralf nodded. "There was a bit of a skirmish inside the cabin, but when the men came close, Jasper fired at them."

"So ... was someone else in there, or was he just fumbling around in one of his drunken stupors?"

Ralf held her gaze. "I have no way of knowing."

Disappointment washed over her.

Ralf, sitting next to her on the settee, reached for her hand and held it tight.

Suzanne could appreciate his desire to reassure her, but she was too close to tears. In an attempt to ward them off, she stood and walked to the window. For a time she just stared out. When she finally glanced back at Ralf, she asked, "Are you going to tell me about the plan you've come up with?"

His head swung once in denial. "You're going to have to trust me."

"Mr. Crandall, if he isn't found by tomorrow, I'm going for my brothers. I can't just sit and do nothing anymore. My husband's life could be at stake."

Ralf did not doubt that she meant every word, but neither was he prepared to tell her all that was being done on her husband's behalf. "Give me two more days. Bill and I have gone to great lengths to put this plan into actions. If Jason is hurt, he'll need you. You know more about doctoring than the rest of the folks in this village."

She hadn't thought about that. "I appreciate your efforts, really I do ...."

Ralf's heart went out to her. The tears standing in her eyes were too much for him. He moved toward her and offered a fatherly hug.

"I'm sorry, Mr. Crandall. I'm not normally like this. It's just ..."

"You don't need to explain, Suzanne."

"I have to keep myself busy, so I'll head over to Hattie's and do a bit of cleaning. If you need me ..."

"I'll find you."

Ralf went on his way, and Noel had gone to the barn to saddle her horse. Suzanne stepped out on to the porch. As much as she wanted to take matters into her own hands, she needed to trust the Lord in this.

Noel met her in the yard and handed Buck's reins to her. "Hang in there, Suzanne. Before you know it your husband will be home and you'll begin your new life together."

Suzanne hugged her friend. "Thanks, Noel. I hope you're right."

"Suzanne ... wake up sleepy head." A strong male voice was calling her from her slumberous state. He sounded familiar, but it couldn't be him! Thinking she had to be dreaming, she forced her eyes to open. "Jesse?"

"Yes, Suzanne, it's me. Henry and Jared are here, too. Do you think you can show us where Jasper's cabin is?"

"Oh!" she said, as a irrepressible stretch caught her unawares. Scooting off the bed, she hugged her brother. A quick glance at the window told her morning had not come yet. No wonder she was still tired. "Jesse, the men in town have put some kind of plan into action. Maybe we should check with Mr. Crandall before we do anything."

"Get dressed, Suzanne. I'll go saddle your horse. We can talk on the way."

Suzanne ran upstairs. After throwing on a skirt and blouse, she went to the kitchen, scribbled out a note for Gerty, grabbed her jacket, and hurried out the front door.

"Hi, Suzanne," Henry said on a nod. "Sorry to hear about your troubles. Hopefully, we can get to the bottom of this soon."

"I appreciate your coming. My husband's life could depend on it."

Jared was moving towards her, and Jesse was leading her horse out of the barn when both brothers stopped in their tracks and stared. They had heard what she said to Henry.

Jesse was the first to ask, "Did I hear you right?"

She grinned halfheartedly. "Jason and I were married just before he disappeared."

Jesse wrapped his arms around her and squeezed her tight. "This is good news!"

Jared came up, pulled her out of Jesse's arms, and offered his congratulations as well. "You two were meant for each other, Suz. I'm just glad you finally figured it out."

Tears welled in her eyes. "Just pray, Jared."

"He's in the Lord's hands. We need to trust Him."

She spoke her thoughts, "So was Daddy, and look what happened to him."

Jesse swung her up on her horse. "God's will, not ours, Sis. He knows best. If you and Jason are meant to share this life together, you will. Your love and trust in God can't be based on what you think He should do. What God wants to know is will you love Him no matter how this turns out? I don't mean to sound heartless, but you need to think this through, Sis."

She shook her head. "I don't have to, Jesse. I already know the answer. I'll love the Lord no matter what."

He nodded and mounted Shadow. "That's my girl!"

Time passed in a fog. The message Henry had gotten from Crandall told them to meet on the trail leading to the cabin. They were about a hundred yards from the cabin when they saw Ralf standing behind a tree.

The men introduced themselves. Ralf thanked Suzanne for bringing them and then told her she was to go back to the Crandall's with Noel and wait.

Jesse noted his sister's shock and pulled her off to the side. He attempted to soften the blow. "Suzanne, I'll come for you the minute this is over. You'll be no good to anyone if you get hurt."

"I'll stay back here, Jesse. I won't move until you tell me it's safe, but please don't make me go."

He wanted to tell her no, but her eyes filled with unshed tears. "Noel, will you stay with her?"

"Sure." Noel led her to a nearby tree. Tying their horses to a branch, they took a seat on a fallen log.

Suzanne listened intently to the men's whispers, but everything was obscure. Surely an hour or two had passed before she heard a skirmish near the cabin. She went to stand up, hoping to get a closer look, but Noel grabbed her arm and pulled her back down.

"You made your brother a promise, Suzanne Michaels."

The sound of her new name being spoken made her forget what she was about to say. Gunshots resounded in the air and ricocheted off trees. She couldn't move, for fear of missing something—a sound—a voice. *Oh, God, please let everyone be all right.*

Time seemed to stand still while she and Noel waited for news. When Jesse finally showed up, the grim look on his face did not bode well.

Fear sliced through Suzanne with a vengeance. "Jesse, what is it?"

"Noel, will you take my sister home?"

She leapt to her feet before he could grab her, declaring, "I'm not going anywhere, Jesse Somers. Not until I see my husband!"

"I'm sorry, Suzanne ...."

What are you saying? "I have to talk to him, Jesse ...."

"I'm sorry, Honey ... I wish I could tell you differently, but Jason didn't make it ...."

"Nooo!" she screamed amidst heart wrenching sobs.

Jesse wrapped her securely in his arms, but she found no comfort there.

Minutes passed before she calmed enough to say, "I have to see him." Jesse shook his head, but she wasn't about to take no for an answer. "Take me to him. I have every right. He's my husband."

Jesse, realizing that she was not going to leave, held her close to steady her faltering frame as they walked, sheltering her eyes the best he could from the scene in the yard.

She peered up at her brother when they passed Jasper who was lying on the ground face down. "Is he dead?"

"Yes ... it was him or us, Suzanne."

She wondered if Jason would still be alive if they had shot Jasper the first day, but she couldn't allow her mind to go there.

As they entered the house, she gagged from the putrid smell

of decaying flesh. Jasper's wife still lay on her bed where she had apparently died giving birth.

The shadow of death was a foreboding presence in the small cabin. Like a haunting scene from a dime novel, the aura was thick—stagnating. Needing to get out of here as soon as possible, she peered up at her brother. "Where is Jason, Jesse?"

"He's in the cold cellar. If you'll wait here, Noel and I can bring him up."

She shook her head. "I need to go to him myself. Can you light the lantern?" She could feel her resolve wavering as she moved down the steps into the cool air. The tears standing in her eyes clouded her vision, but she could make out Jason's still form. He was lying against the wall where he had apparently been huddling to keep warm. *Oh, Lord, why him? All he ever wanted to do is help people.*

She nearly kicked a bucket of water over when she moved toward him. Partially eaten apple cores were scattered around and a package of milk powder had been left open. *At least he didn't go hungry.* An old quilt was tucked securely in his arms. She wondered why he wasn't using it to cover himself, until she approached and saw faint movement coming from within. Her wary heart raced as she unraveled the blanket. "Jesse, come quick!"

"What is it?"

"A baby girl. She's weak, but she's alive." Suzanne wasn't sure how, but her husband had apparently been feeding her. There were drippings of dried milk on her skin.

"Give her to me, Suzanne."

Although reluctant, she relinquished the delicate infant to

her brother. As she turned back to her husband, an onrush of tears blinded her. She wiped them away and reached to hold Jason's beard-stubbled face in her trembling hands. *Always the physician, My Love—even to the bitter end.*

Lord, You know best, but will I ever understand why? We haven't even had a chance to begin our life together ....

Her thoughts came to a sudden halt when she realized, while her husband's skin was chilled, she could feel warmth from within. Her hopeful heart beat at a murderous pace as her fingers slid along his neck.

Jesse's deep voice startled her. "Suzanne. You need to come. This baby needs nourishment. The men and I will bring Jason back to the house."

"Jesse, give Noel the baby and help me lay Jason down."

His sister's frantic words made him wish he had stuck to his guns and not allowed her to come near the cabin. *Lord, please help her to accept what she cannot change.* Jesse did turn to Noel, who was waiting on the steps. He reached out and took the baby from Jesse, who then went to his sister and took a firm hold on her arm. "We need to go, Suzanne. I know it's hard, but your husband is no longer here, he's with the Lord."

She looked up at Jesse and grinned. "Not yet, he's not!"

Thrown for a whirl, Jesse asked, "What are you talking about? Henry checked him. He has no pulse."

"His pulse is weak, but he is alive."

"Praise be!" Jesse released his sister's arm and did as she asked. There wasn't much room in the cramped storage room, but he was able to stretch Jason out enough for Suzanne to get a better look at him.

Suzanne turned to her young friend and said, "Noel, take the baby upstairs. Look around for some dry blankets to wrap her in. You know what she's going to need. Gather everything you can find. Jesse, will you bring some of the men down here? We should take Jason out as soon as possible. I'm not sure if you'll find one in the barn or not, but we're going to need a wagon to transport him."

Jesse left the cold cellar with a renewed sense of hope. Jason was not out of the dark by any means, but he was alive. To see the way his sister took charge, doing what needed to be done, told him much.

While Jesse was gone, Suzanne examined Jason. He had a severe gash on the back of his head. The wound was serious, but otherwise he appeared to be fine. Taking him back to Ann Arbor would be risky, but she saw no other way. He and the baby should be under a real physician's care, and Doctor Taylor was the only other one she knew.

Jared drove the wagon back to their house, and Suzanne rode in the buckboard with Jason, his wounded head resting on her lap. She stroked his face, hoping and praying that her touch would waken him, but it did not. The moment they stopped in front of their cabin, Suzanne fluffed the blanket she had taken from the small cabin and rested her husband's head on it.

As Jared helped Suzanne from the buckboard with the sleeping infant in her arms, she cast her wary eyes back on Jason's still form. "There's a covered wagon behind the barn. We should take it in case it rains. I have a large tick we can lay him on. That should soften the bumpy trail a little. I'll need several blankets if I'm going to keep him and the baby warm." Looking at her brother in a daze, she continued, "I'll pack a few things, and have Gerty try feeding the baby some milk powder before we leave. Hopefully the milk will hold her."

"Bring the extra milk powder along just in case. Jesse should be here at any time, Suzanne. He can help me get Jason settled in the other wagon. I'll stay with him. You go ahead and get things ready to leave."

"I'll throw the tick out on the porch, Jared, and see what I can rustle up food-wise."

Jared's hand went to his rumbling stomach. "Didn't want to be a bother, but I am starving."

Suzanne grinned weakly, "You're always hungry, Jar ...."

They had been traveling for hours before Suzanne convinced herself to lie down beside her husband. There was nothing more she could do for him, and she was exhausted. Snuggling close, she placed the contented little dolly between them, hoping to keep her warm while they slept.

Darkness had settled over the land, and the sounds of night became a warm presence. Familiar passages came alive in her heart and mind as she conversed with the Lord.

The shadow of death was all around the Jones' cabin today. I could feel it, Lord, but I was not afraid. I know you were with me. You protected my husband and this innocent child, in spite of evil intent. Continue to be with them. May Your healing hands reach down and touch them both. I don't know the extent of my husband's injury, Lord, but You do. I come against the spirit of death that tried to take him from me. Thank you that no weapon formed against us shall prosper. Thank you for my brother's gentle reminder, Your will not mine. Thank You for anointing our heads with oil. My cup is running over, Lord. May Your goodness and mercy follow us all the days of our life.

As Suzanne kissed the wee babe now resting between them, her heart filled with so much love. *She'll never know her own mother, Lord. My heart aches for her, but I have to trust that You know best. I'm not sure what my husband will say, but I would love to raise this little dolly as our own. In the midst of her parents' deaths, you brought joy into this world. Joy, hmm, Lord, what about that name? Too weary to contemplate it further, she drifted off.*

Chapter Thirty

Hope and a Future

"SUZANNE," Jared whispered, having no desire to wake the small infant in her arms. "We're home."

Confused, Suzanne scanned her shadowed surroundings, asking as she scooted out of the wagon, "I thought we were going to Ann Arbor?"

"Jesse took the turn-off a while back with Henry. He'll fetch Doc. We just thought you and the baby would be more comfortable here while you're waiting for your husband to recover."

"I suppose you're right."

Jared touched the sleeping baby's soft cheek and smiled. "Take her into the house, Suzanne. Mom will help you get a bed ready for Jason. I'll stay with him."

"Thanks for all you've done, Jared. I'm sure you're worn out."

"Nothing a good long sleep won't cure."

Suzanne entered the front door without knocking. Calling up the stairs, a sleepy Louise and Joe traipsed down, taken aback when they saw the infant in her arms.

Louise was quick to ask, "Whose baby, Suzanne?"

"I'm hoping Jason will want to raise her as our own. Her mother died in childbirth, and her father ... well, he died, too."

Louise came and took a closer look. "She's so sweet. Does she have a name?"

"I'd like to call her Joy." Suzanne shrugged. "Depends on what Jason says."

Joe had to ask, "Don't take me wrong, Suz, but aren't you getting the cart before the horse? Last I heard it's best to get married before starting a family."

For a split second, her eyes glistened as she met his curious look. "Already done, Joe. Jason and I were married before all this happened."

Reluctantly, Joe asked, "Is Jason all right?"

"I'm not sure. He's still unconscious. Do you mind helping Jared carry him in?"

Jayne, having overheard their conversation entered the parlor, Josiah following. "Another son, and possibly a granddaughter, too ...?" Jayne took Joy from Suzanne's arms and kissed her soft cheek. "Oh, Honey, she's so precious."

"You might not think so when she starts squalling. I've been giving her milk powder, but she needs something more nourishing. Any chance you still have that nanny goat?"

Josiah spoke up, "She's as ornery as ever, Suzanne, but she has milk to spare. I have some in the cold cellar from this morning."

Suzanne turned to her sister and asked, "Louise, would you be a dear and put some in a pan to boil?" Suzanne then reached for her stepfather's hand. "Papa, Jesse went for Doc and Jared's outside with Jason. He has a bad head injury—hasn't been conscious since we found him."

Josiah turned to his wife. "What room do you want him in?"

"Ours. We can move upstairs until Jason's back on his feet."

Jayne told Suzanne where the clean linens were and went to the kitchen with her small charge. The blankets surrounding Joy were damp, and that just wouldn't do. While Louise put the milk over to boil, Jayne found the things she would need to make the baby more comfortable.

Jason moaned when her brothers carried him into the room, and although he didn't open his eyes, Suzanne was thankful for this small sign of life. She didn't like knowing he was in pain, but knowing he could feel pain was a good thing. Now, if he would just wake up ....

Josiah helped Suzanne get Jason all cleaned up and into a nightshirt before he left the room. Not knowing how long it had been since he'd had anything to drink, she drizzled small amounts of water into his mouth. She had been sitting with him for some time when her mother poked her head in the bedroom.

"Suzanne, I thought I'd start a pot of soup. Any special request?"

Thoughtful, Suzanne's eyes fell on her husband. "I don't know how long it's been since Jason has had anything nourishing. I should start giving him broth. How about chicken vegetable?"

"Sounds good, Honey. I made tea and muffins. I'd be glad to sit with Jason while you eat."

Suzanne was hungry, but couldn't leave him. She wanted to be with him when he woke up. "Would you mind bringing me some food in here?"

Jayne, understanding her daughter's desire to be with her

husband, smiled tenderly, pleased to see how much Suzanne had come to love this man.

I was so upset when she took off the way she did, Lord, but look at her now. Our prayers have been answered. Jason took her under his wing and in the process led her back to You. You used Jason to encourage her, but only You could change her heart. Thank You, Lord.

"Honey, I'll bring a tray in right away."

Jayne was about to close the door when Suzanne asked, "Do you need my help with Joy?"

"No, Honey. Louise is quite taken with her. She'd be heart broken if you stole her away so soon."

Suzanne, though yearning to hold Joy, too, smiled halfheartedly. "Then let Louise enjoy her. Jason needs me right now."

Several hours came and went before Doc finally knocked on the bedroom door. Suzanne hugged the elderly man who had become so dear to her entire family.

"Jesse told me that you and Jason were married before all this happened, Suzanne."

She nodded. "He was called away right after the ceremony, and ..." tears filled her eyes as she added, "Henry thought he was dead, Doc. His pulse was weak, but it's stronger now. He was chilled to the bone when we found him in the root cellar."

"Has he been moving around at all?"

She shook her head. "He moaned when the boys carried him into the room, but that's about it."

Doc's brow furrowed. "Have you tried talking to him?"

Somewhat confused, she met the good doctor's gaze. "I didn't really think about it."

He nodded. "Always helpful to let a loved one hear your voice, Honey. Could be the one thing that draws him out of this coma."

Suzanne nodded, watching closely as Doc checked her husband over.

"Suzanne, come here and help me. I need to get a better look at the back of his head."

Jason moaned again as they rolled him on his side, but he did not wake up. She hated seeing him like this. He had been her source of comfort and strength, rescuing her when calamity came knocking at her door. If only she could have done the same for him. Why did she listen to Mr. Crandall? She should have taken Jasper by force. He was dead anyway.

"If I had gone after him like I wanted to instead of waiting on the men, Jason wouldn't be in this condition."

Doc stopped what he was doing and scowled at her. She was distraught about her husband's condition, he understood but her view was twisted. "Suzanne, think about what you're saying. Vigilante justice is not justice at all. You should know that better than anyone. If I remember correctly, Jesse told me you were arrested in Detroit and charged with a crime you did not commit."

She could not hold his gaze. "That's true, but this was different. We knew Jasper was holding Jason hostage."

He stood to his full height and reached for her chin, bring her reluctant gaze to his. "So, you saw Jason in the cabin?"

She didn't know what he was getting at. "Well, no, but the men heard a skirmish. They knew someone was in there with Jasper."

"Then tell me, Suzanne. What would you have done

differently? Would you have shot Jasper in cold blood on an assumption?"

Her head lowered. "I see what you're saying, but he's dead anyway, Doc. I wish I understood why they waited is all."

Jason moaned, drawing their immediate attention.

"Jason!" Suzanne called out, her heart hopeful. Unfortunately, he did not respond.

Doc checked his patient's vitals and then tried to wake him with a damp cloth. When he still remained unresponsive, Doctor Taylor looked up at Suzanne and continued with their conversation. "They did what they thought was right at the time. Tell me, Suzanne, how would your husband feel if you ended up hanging for saving his life? You would have if you took matters into your own hands and shot Jasper on a hunch."

The answer came from a craggy voice that was barely audible, "Horrible!"

Stunned, she darted around the bed, kneeled beside her husband and gently caressed his face. Her eyes glistened with unshed tears.

Jason's lips worked awkwardly as he forced out, "You didn't ..."

Speechless, she shook her head, and lifted Jason's hand to her cheek.

Doc answered for her, "This is quite the assistant you've trained, Jason. She didn't do anything wrong. We were just discussing what could have happened if she had taken matters into her own hands and tried to rescue you on her own."

Weak, Jason managed to caress her cheek. "My bride."

Suzanne said, "You've been through quite an ordeal."

When Jason's hand went to his throat, she reached for her

cup of sweet tea on the table. Doc helped her lift him so he could take a sip. After he had his fill, she asked, "Jason, we found the wound on the back of your head. Are you hurt anywhere else?"

"Not that I know of ...." Concern suddenly etched Jason's brow. He glanced down at his arms and then looked around the room.

"Baby Joy is fine. Louise has her."

"Joy?"

She looked up at Doctor Taylor and smiled. "I had time to do some thinking on the way here."

Jason peered up at his colleague and winked. "Should I be worried?"

His playfulness was a good sign, but she didn't see it as such. "Don't tease me, Jason."

"Then tell me, My Love. What were you thinking?"

"Out of all the sadness surrounding her parents' deaths, Joy came into this world. This probably isn't a good time to ask, but I really would like to raise her as our own."

His smile was tender.

She could see that he was fading, but she held her breath, hoping he would respond before sleep claimed him.

"We can't get our hearts set on it, Suzanne. We don't know if she has kin."

Suzanne had a response, but she held her tongue. It was not her place to judge others by Joy's father's actions.

"I was hoping you would love her. I'm not sure I could part with her if she has no one. She and I have been through so much together."

"What about her name?"

"Joy ... a wonderful name. I'll only agree to name her Joy if her middle name is Suzanne."

She beamed. "I'd like that."

Jason glanced at his elderly friend. "What do you think, Doc. Will you start an inquiry to see if we can adopt her legally?"

"I'll see what we can do, but you need to rest right now and get yourself feeling better. Do you need something for pain?"

"No ... I'll be fine."

"Then I'll leave you two alone. He should sleep, Suzanne, so just a few minutes," Doc said, closing the door behind him.

She never took her eyes off Jason's face, smiling as his eyes drooped.

When he insisted on her coming close for a kiss, she ignored the odd sensation in her stomach and did as she was told. Thankfully, he was too sleepy to offer much more—his breath about gagged her! In the seconds that followed, she thanked the Lord for His goodness as Jason drifted off.

Suzanne, feeling much more at ease, joined her family for the noon meal. She checked in on her husband often, feeding him small amounts of broth throughout the day, but as she suspected, he could barely stay awake.

It was morning before Jason's mind cleared enough to realize that he had just spent the night with his bride. Lying on his side, he stared at her sleeping form for the longest time. *She's my wife now, Lord! Thank you for all You've brought us through.*

Unable to resist any longer, he ran his finger's through her silky lengths. Her arms rose suddenly above her head, and she offered an exaggerated stretch before she turned, curled on her side, facing him. Her soft blue eyes never opened until his lips brushed tenderly against hers.

She smiled affectionately. "Good morning, Husband."

He, on the other hand, frowned. "Some Husband I've turned out to be. Now that were finally together, I can't stay awake long enough to claim you as my own."

Her face heated. She would have turned away, but her husband's arms were drawing her closer. She had no idea what he was thinking, so she squirmed in his hold. "Jason, you can't ... I won't ...."

"You won't what? You're my wife, Suzanne. There's nothing wrong with my wanting to hold you."

Inwardly, she sighed. "As long as that's all you have in mind, Doctor Michaels. You have a head injury, and you need to heal before ... well, you know."

He kissed her forehead, enjoying her flustered state a smidgen too much. "Suzanne, if you can't even speak of intimacy, how ..."

Her fingers came to his mouth. "You're not being fair. You're a doctor. I expect you to be more at ease talking about such things. If you keep this up, though, I'm going to think you enjoy making me blush."

He chuckled softly. "Perhaps I do?"

"Then perhaps I should have one of my brothers take care of you until you decide to be good."

His head swayed from side to side. "That won't be necessary. You see, I'll be joining my new family for breakfast."

Her mouth dropped open. "No you will not!"

He nodded in contradiction of her declaration. "I need a bath, and if I don't do something about my wicked breath, my bride will refuse to kiss me again—and that will never do, because I have plans to kiss you long into the night, My Sweet."

The man was incorrigible! She took a firmer approach. "Am I going to have to fetch, Doctor Taylor? He'll see that you mend your ways, Young Man!"

His long fingers trailing slowly down the side of her face not only silenced her, they earned him her undivided attention. "You forget too easily that I know what to watch for. I won't push myself."

"But Joy needs ..."

"A father who will love her, and if we can adopt her, she will also want siblings to play with some day."

Suzanne buried her face in his chest, refusing to allow him to take in her deepening flush—he would only tease her. "Will you at least promise to take things slow?" When he offered no response, she reluctantly peered up.

"I promise to take things slow ...."

"All right. Letting you out of this bed goes against my better judgment, but if you'll let go of me, I can help you sit up?"

Jason made it as far as the outhouse, and although he was flagging when they reentered the house, he washed his hands in the basin and took the last seat at the table.

Suzanne's family welcomed him, and Louise, who was still snuggling her small charge, surrendered Joy to her sister. Suzanne was quite pleased. Jason lit up when he saw how much stronger Joy was.

Glancing at his new family around the table, Jason grinned. "I'm sure Suzanne told you that she is now my wife."

Jayne was the first to respond, "We couldn't be happier, Jason. You're certainly a welcome addition to our family."

Everyone around the table agreed.

"I'm sure you're wondering about Joy, so I'll tell you. When I arrived at the cabin, her mother was barely alive. I have no way of knowing how long she had been laboring. She was delirious—unaware of my presence for the most part. Joy was born just before her mother took her last breath. When I told Joy's father that his wife had died in childbirth, he didn't handle it well. He put a gun to my head and locked me in the cold cellar, but he was so drunk he didn't even notice the bundle in my arms. He kept bringing me water, so I'm not convinced he wanted me dead. But when I tried to break out, he panicked and clobbered me over the head. At first I was dizzy, but I was still able to feed the baby. My head ached, so I bundled her up and rested my head against the cool wall. That was how Suzanne found me."

Josiah wanted him to know, "We've been praying for you for days, Jason. I can't tell you how glad we are to see you on your feet again."

Confused, he asked, "For days? But ... how did you know something was wrong?" Jason glanced at his wife, looking for answers.

"Crandall sent for Henry, who asked Jesse and Jared to come along. The three of them were part of the group that stormed the cabin the day you were rescued. At first Henry thought you were dead. In truth, I'm not surprised. Your pulse was faint when I checked it myself, but it was still there."

"I'm curious, Suzanne, what made you check it again?"

Tears filled her eyes, recalling that heart-wrenching moment. "I was trying to say goodbye—holding your face in my hands—when it dawned on me that even though your skin was cool, there was warmth in your body."

With the palm of his hands, Jason dried the tears falling down her face. "So you have been listening."

"Of course! A girl never knows when her husband's life could depend on her knowing a thing or two."

"I'm certainly glad someone figured it out. The thought of being buried alive doesn't sit well."

Suzanne shuddered at the thought.

Josiah, thinking the conversation could use some help, suggested they join hands in prayer.

Before she bowed her head, Suzanne glanced around the table at her family members, her husband, and then as her eyes fell on the precious baby in her arms, she whispered her thanks. Not only was she home again, but she was also amazed by all that had transpired in the last few months. Her whole outlook on life had changed. Although running from God and family had been her intent, God had something entirely different in mind. She had been miserable until she surrendered her life to Christ. No longer did she doubt His great love for her. God's plan was to prosper her and not to harm her—to give her hope and a future. And she was so very glad.

Chapter Thirty-one

Surrender

THE HIGH WINDS RIPPLED the moving waters of the Huron, sweeping dry leaves from the tree limbs into the air. Like snowflakes that would soon take their place, a colorful array continued to fall to the ground in great abandon, as Suzanne and Jason walked hand in hand along the muddied banks. Autumn's vibrant display was spectacular as always.

Being near the water brought to the fore so many wonderful childhood memories—memories she hoped to someday share with their children, should God allow. Suzanne loved being in Ypsilanti. Spending time with her loved ones was a gift she treasured. Everyone seemed pleased to learn of her recent marriage. Her family adored Jason, and Joy, who never lacked for loving arms to hold her, was already woven into their hearts. Perhaps Suzanne's motives were selfish, but she couldn't help praying that no one would contest Joy's adoption.

Over the last few days Suzanne had noticed a growing unrest in Jason. Although reluctant to ask, she had a feeling he was ready to head back to Saline. Was she wrong to pray that he would want to stay? Perhaps it was a far-fetched dream that would never come to pass. Fortunately, she had come to terms with this very thing several days back. Wherever her husband decided to put down roots, she would be with him.

Jason's recovery had been slower than he hoped, but Suzanne, so thankful to have him back in her life, didn't mind at all. Sleeping in his arms and his wonderful kisses were enough. His physical condition had forced him to take things slowly, and to her that was a good thing. She loved having the time to really get to know him.

Noting his wife's pensive state, Jason slid his arm around her waist and drew her close. "Anything I should know?"

She smiled up at him. "I was wondering the same thing about you. You've had something on your mind for several days now, Jason. I've been hoping you would tell me what it is."

"I needed time to pray. Maybe I should have discussed this with you days ago, but I've been torn."

As their steps slowed, she turned her inquisitive gaze on him. "About what?"

He stared at the woman he loved, contemplating his next words—and the effect they could have on their marriage. "You're going to be heartbroken if I say it's time to head back to Saline, aren't you?" His hidden struggle shone in his deep blue eyes.

Suzanne, needing to hold him, slid her arms around his waist, and for a long moment she stopped walking and just held on tight. "I'm your wife, Jason. My home is with you, wherever that is."

While Jason could appreciate her willingness to accept his

decision, the tears standing in her eyes told him much about her inward turmoil. "I'm not saying I can give you the desire of your heart, Suzanne, but if I could, where would you want to live?"

She shook her head. "I think you should tell me what you want first."

His brow furrowed, fully aware of her intentions. "Why, so you can just agree? Honey, I hate to do this to you, but I'm going to have to insist. I really want to know where your heart is on this."

Unable to hold his gaze, she turned away, the cool breeze blowing her hair across her face.

When he gathered her silky lengths in his hand, she gently stated, "I can't tell you, Jason."

He understood her uncertainty, but he had to know. Capturing her hand, he turned her back to face him. It did little good. Her stormy gaze lowered, and she was unwilling to yield.

"Honey, please look at me." When she didn't readily respond, he added, "How is this marriage going to work if you won't obey me?"

"I want to Jason ... I'm just afraid ...."

He, needing to be sure she would not flee, wrapped his arms securely around her. "Of what?"

"That you'll want to be one place and me another. Not exactly a good way to start a marriage is it?"

He nodded. "Good point, but I still want you to tell me."

She had an idea. "You could write your answer here in the sand," she pointed to another spot a few feet away, adding, "and I could go over there. Then both of us would be exposing our thoughts at the same time."

The deviant look in her eyes did not go unnoticed. "Can I trust you to be honest?"

Her face sobered.

"Can I?"

Suzanne smiled as her father's words ran through her mind. "A good marriage must be founded on trust."

"I couldn't agree more."

"I overheard a conversation my father had with Elizabeth on the subject." Thoughtfully, she admitted, "The sound of his voice is fading from my memory, but at times I can hear him loud and clear." Giggling softly, she added, "I'm not sure what Lizzy was up to that day, but he was quite adamant."

"I wish I could have known him."

Suzanne's features brightened. "You would have liked him, Jason. I know he would approve of our union."

"I'm glad."

"Considering all the ways I've deceived you in the past, your trust is something I'll have to earn."

Her insightfulness surprised him. "I wish I could tell you otherwise, Suzanne, but you're right."

"I know. In this you can trust me."

Jason kissed her tenderly, as if to seal her promise. He then bent down to pick up a couple of sticks and handed her one. They held each other's gaze for the longest moment before proceeding as planned.

In the worst way she wanted to write what she thought he would like to hear, but knowing how hard it was to live with a lie, she kept her word. It was even harder than she thought it would be to consider trading places with him. When Jason moved toward her, she stood frozen in place. As childish as her actions would have been, she wanted to kick the sand. Instead, she held her breath as his eyes fell on her words.

He read them aloud. "You are home to me, Jason, but if I could choose, I would want to live here in Ypsilanti."

When he didn't seem moved, she released the breath she'd been holding.

Jason's features were unreadable when he motioned for her to go and see what he had written. When she didn't budge, he reached for her hand. "Thank you for telling me, Suz."

Curious, she asked, "Do I want to know what you wrote?"

His head tilted. "That depends. I'm willing to discuss this and pray about it some more, but in the end, will you accept my decision no matter what it is?"

We're going back. Although quick tears filled her eyes she didn't hesitate before answering. "God will lead me through you, Jason—I don't doubt that."

"Then I hope that means you're going to spend our lifetime praying for me."

"I will. Is there something you haven't told me?"

Noting her confusion, his fingers ran down her soft cheek. "I would never do it intentionally, Suzanne, but I can almost guarantee I'm going to fail you from time to time."

She grinned, relieved by his honesty. Drying her remaining tears with the hanky she had up her sleeve, she said, "That goes both ways. Only God is capable of perfection." Assuming she already knew her husband's answer, she started to move away, but Jason's question stopped her.

"Suzanne, don't you want to see what I wrote?"

She shook her head, "No need. I'll pack as soon as you feel up to traveling."

He stared at her nonplused. Her tone was saddened, yet her willingness to yield so easily not only surprised him, it also brought him much comfort. At the same time, he couldn't let her go on thinking ... Jason latched onto her arm and steered her toward his answer.

Suzanne was baffled by what she read. "But I thought ... you said ... Doctor Jason Michaels, were you testing me?"

He grinned playfully. "Yes, Ma'am! I'm afraid I was."

Her lower lip came out in a youthful pout.

When he could stand it no more, Jason gathered her in his arms. "Knowing you're with me no matter what, means the world to me, Suz. It's just that some things take time. Trust is one of those things."

Sin's consequences, she silently acknowledged ... thank you, Lord, that Your blood covers it all. Help me to put my past behind me and honor You and my husband in the days ahead.

Suzanne stood on her toes and kissed him soundly. "I love you, Jason—for better or worse. I'm not the same girl who ran away from all that was good in her life. God is changing me. In so many ways He has used you to help me. Old things are passed away. I'm still in process, but He's making me new." When he didn't readily respond she added, "I'm done running, Jason. You're stuck with me, so get used to it." Since she had been holding his gaze, she knew the moment his eyes lit with pleasure.

"I'm so glad." Jason, knowing that their plans could not be set in stone, said as they were moving back toward the house,

"Don't say anything to your family until after we meet with Doctor Taylor, Suzanne."

"Okay. Can I ask why?"

Hearing concern in her tone, he reached out, his knuckles softly grazing her cheek. "I'm not real sure how he'll feel about me being this far out of town. I'd like to live close to your family, but we have others to consider."

Although unsettled by his words, she nodded in acceptance. If God wanted them in Ypsilanti, He would work out the details— all of them. "What about Saline? Are you wanting to go back until they can find a replacement?"

Jason shrugged. "I'm not strong enough to travel that far yet, but when I am, we should go back, if for no other reason than to say goodbye to our friends and my sister's young family."

Suzanne twirled several strands of her long brown hair around her finger and rubbed it along her upper lip.

Jason noticed and smiled tenderly. She only did this whenever she was unsure or contemplative. In truth he understood her uncertainties; he had some of his own. He had come to love and depend on many in Saline. Leaving them would not be easy but at the same time, God seemed to be filling his heart and mind with a new vision. Whenever he prayed, he had a calm assurance. Doors were closing in his heart, but new ones were opening. He fully intended to follow God's lead.

"I know you're right. It's just that I've never been very good with goodbyes."

"Letting go of our past is never easy, but it is necessary if we're ever going to move forward in what God has for us."

She smiled up at him as the full impact of Jason's call—and now hers as his wife and assistant, came to rest on her like a warm and welcoming cloak. "Body and soul: God can use the knowledge He has given us to heal this earthly body, but without considering the whole man, we'll miss our true calling."

He chuckled softly, pleased that she finally understood. "Think about it, Suzanne. Christ was wounded for our transgressions; he was bruised for our iniquities; he bore all of our sorrows; and it was by his stripes we are healed. God gives me wisdom to help heal the physical body, but without considering the whole man, we miss the most important part of God's call on our life."

"To follow His example: love as he did, and live a life that will glorify Him. Without pointing others to the healer of our soul, it is all for nothing."

"Our life is not our own. In surrendering our life to Christ, we find it and so much more."

"Suzanne, are you ready?" Jason asked as he came in the back door.

Tentatively, her soft blue eyes met his. "Where are we going, Jason? I really don't like leaving Joy behind."

"We've been over this. I need time alone with my wife—time for us to enjoy each other as God intended. Louise and your mother were thrilled when I asked them to keep her. She will be fine."

"Do you promise we'll only be gone for three days?"

He grinned. "I promise."

Her brow knitted together, thinking three days without their sweet baby Joy seemed like an eternity to her. Even so, she agreed with Jason. With their rough beginning, they still had doors that needed to be opened. "I'll just be a minute."

Suzanne ran up the steps to capture Joy's precious little face one more time before she took her leave. As she suspected, the baby was sleeping soundly, unaware of the love that swelled within Suzanne's heart for her. Blowing a kiss, Suzanne turned back toward the stairs. She had kept her husband waiting long enough.

Jason offered her a hand up into the covered buggy he borrowed from Doctor Taylor. Settling the blanket around their legs, he grinned as her soft blue gaze, filled with excitement, met his.

Kissing his cheek, she latched onto his arm and gave it a squeeze. They were well on their way before she summoned the courage to ask for the third time, "Now are you going to tell me where we're going?"

"Nope!"

"Fine!" she declared and then turned away. She knew he hated that word, but she'd been waiting for days. The suspense was killing her.

When he pulled the buggy to a halt, she took a quick peek. His pointer finger was motioning for her to come near, but she shook her head, unwilling to submit to his silent order.

He folded his arms and sat back in the seat. "I'm in no hurry, Suzanne."

"Fine ..." she softly murmured as she slid next to him on the bench.

Though humbly spoken, the word was still spoken, and it grated on his nerves. "New rule!"

Her brow furrowed as she met his stern look. He had her attention, but he wasn't speaking, so she asked, "What?"

He patted his leg. "Come on you."

She giggled. "Jason, don't be silly!" He had that look in his eyes that made her stomach flutter, so how could she comply?

"If you insist on using that word, I insist on being compensated for the way it annoys me."

"Fine!" A second too late her hand came to her mouth.

Jason's raised brow put her even more on edge. "Three! Care to say it a few more times? Truth is, I don't mind a bit."

"Perhaps I should find out the penalty for my crime before I get carried away."

This time when he patted his leg, she took her place on his lap.

She could feel the heat traveling up her neck. "Jason, we're out in the middle of nowhere. What would a stranger think of the new doctor if he happened upon us?"

"He would think I enjoy kissing my wife."

"Kissing ... Jason Michaels, we're not ki ..."

Moments had passed ... several, in fact, before she dreamily inquired. "The new rule ... you never said what is it, Jason?"

He grinned mischievously. "Since your temper is usually flaring when you use that word, I'll expect you to come willingly and compensate me."

Thoughtfully she ran her slender fingers through his golden hair, scowling just a tad. "I might not always feel like kissing you when I'm angry, Jason."

He stole another kiss. "Then don't use the word."

She tried to get up, but he would not release her. "Fine!" she declared and her hand came to her mouth. How could she have let it escaped again?

A soft chuckle followed.

She, knowing what he would expect, refused to look his way.

"Temper! Temper!" Jason tauntingly intoned as he gathered her to him. The cool breeze held the promise of rain, and all that remained of the golden sun was hidden behind a clouded expanse, but neither husband nor wife were in any hurry to be on their way. Reluctantly, Jason released his bride, picked up the reins, and urged Buck into a steady gait.

Perhaps her husband was trying to beat the storm—or something else that spurred him on. His intense look gave nothing away. Although she still didn't know where he was heading, she no longer cared. Just knowing they would be alone and together for the next three days filled her heart with joy. *Joy!* Suzanne closed her eyes and could almost see her sweet face, but she said nothing to Jason about the direction of her thoughts. Instead she latched on to her husband's arm and was swept away by the memories of all that had brought them together.

Jason was heading down the lane to the Woods' home before Suzanne finally asked, "We're going to visit with Grandpa and Grandma?"

He shook his head. "They're visiting friends and offered us their home while they're away."

Suzanne couldn't have been more pleased. "Now I know why Mom and Louise insisted on sending so much food."

Jason pulled the team to a halt in front of the cabin. "They didn't want you to have to do anything today, and neither did I."

Her twinkling eyes glistened with mischief as he helped her alight from the buggy. "Nothing at all, My Husband?"

He lifted her easily into his arms and murmured as he carried her across the threshold of their temporary home, "Nothing but surrendering to one another, My Love."

"Fine! Well, you know what I mean, Jason. That's fine with me."

Jason took the first seat he came to and was about to insist on being compensated when she distracted him quite thoroughly. He was perfectly content with her altered plan ....

Chapter Thirty-Two

What We Stand To Gain

"NO!" SUZANNE PROCLAIMED as tears flooded her eyes.

"Honey, I'm struggling with this, too. I love Joy as if she were my own, but the sheriff will be by to claim her if we don't take her ourselves."

Jason could see that Suzanne was ready to collapse from the weight of his words. He understood. In his desire to comfort her, his arms opened wide, and she surrendered to his warm embrace. She sobbed uncontrollably when he lifted her in his arms, sat in one of the chairs by the fire, and just held her.

The damp wood he had added to the burning embers only minutes ago crackled and popped as he stared into the flames that grew hotter and hotter. Finding no solace for his runaway thoughts, his eyes slid shut as he spoke softly to the Lord.

"Father, Your Word says that in all we do, we are to honor You. For a while you entrusted this precious little one to our care. She has touched our lives in such a special way, and for that, we thank You. The time we've had to love on her has been a gift we will always treasure. Although we don't understand why she's being taken from us now, we need to trust You, even in this. Protect Joy and keep her safe in Your loving arms. Help us, Lord, to find our rest in You, the Source of all comfort."

Suzanne calmed, but she still had unanswered questions. "Why did they wait so long to come for her, Jason?"

"Ralf found a scrap of paper in the cabin that said Jasper was leaving all of his earthly possessions to his brother James. He had to come all the way from Chicago."

She drew in a shuddering breath. "Did Ralf tell James she's been with us for over a month? Did he tell him that we love her?"

Jason dried her damp eyes as she peered up at him. He understood her heart was breaking. His was, too.

They had been back in Saline for over a week now. There had been no news from Chicago, so they assumed the adoption papers they filed would go through uncontested. Now their life was being turned upside down again.

"Would you like me to take her alone?"

She shook her head. "I need to see for myself that this man will love her, Jason."

"Just so you remember that we are not his judge and jury. He is her uncle, Suzanne. He has every right to raise her."

"I know."

"I'll go saddle our horses while you gather her things."

She moved numbly around the house, wondering as she did if the ache in her heart would ever ease.

Jason slipped soundlessly in the back door and for a while just stood there, listening to his wife whispering words of love to

Joy as she bundled her up for the cool ride. When his eyes filled with unshed tears, he grabbed the bags off the table and headed back out.

Suzanne, hearing the back door, ambled out with her precious bundle snuggled close in her arms. Jason took Joy from Suzanne's arms so that she could mount. After kissing Joy's soft pink nose, Jason met his wife's gaze as he handed Joy back to her. Neither said a word. They dared not. As hard as it would be to let her go, they would have to find a way to accept this and go on. For now the somber couple moved slowly down the path. As they rode up to the Jones' cabin, everything appeared different. The yard was neat and tidy, the porch had been swept, a new water barrel sat on one side of the door, and a pile of wood had been stacked neatly on the other.

Jason tied his horse to the post and was taking the baby from Suzanne when a tall gentleman stepped out onto the porch to greet them. Jason waited for his wife to dismount before joining the man on the porch.

"You must be the doctor Ralf told me about. I'm James Jones, Jasper's older brother."

Suzanne took Joy from Jason's arms as he said, "I'm Doctor Jason Michaels, and this is my wife, Suzanne."

"I can't thank you enough for taking care of the wee one until I could arrive." He dipped his head toward the bundle in Suzanne's arms and grinned as he asked, "Mind if I take a peek?"

Reluctantly, Suzanne opened the blanket and tucked Joy in the crook of his arm. "We've been calling her Joy."

Jason put in, "We were planning to raise her as our own until ... well, as Suzanne said, we've been calling her Joy Suzanne."

"That's a fine name." James took Joy from Suzanne and snuggled her close. "I can see why you called her Joy. She's a pretty little thing. Much smaller than I expected, I suppose."

"She's just a little over one month old now."

James turned back toward the door, mesmerized by the small wonder in his arms.

Suzanne and Jason were about to question him when he faced them and asked, "I hope you can stay and sit a spell. Haven't ever cared for a little-un. Might need some directions."

Jason and Suzanne shared a concerned glance before Jason went to collect the baby's things.

Suzanne could clearly see that Jasper's brother was harmless enough, but she did wonder if the man had a clue as to what he was getting himself into. As she followed him into the house, she stopped just inside the door and glanced around, stunned by the changes he had made in the interior of the cabin as well. She was impressed.

Noting her surprise, James admitted, "I've been busy. Things were in disarray when I arrived. No place for a wee one to grow up, if you know what I mean."

"I do."

"If you don't mind holding Joy for me, I'll pour the coffee."

Suzanne reached for Joy, more than happy to oblige. "So tell me, Mr. Jones. Are you planning to stay and farm the land?"

He nodded as he filled three cups. "I worked in an artesian shop in Chicago as an apprentice."

"Making furniture?" Suzanne asked.

"Yes. The man who taught me his trade was very gifted. In

the off-season I'll be building furniture until I can get enough business going to support us."

She'd like to ask how he planned to do that with a little one to tend, but Jason was coming in the door, and he might think her prying.

James looked up at Jason and said, "I hope you're better, Doc. Heard my brother took you hostage and clobbered you a good one. Terrible thing when a man takes to the bottle. Jasper wasn't always a bad sort. Never was the same after he caught his wife cheating on him."

Suzanne and Jason looked at each other and then back to James. This was definitely news to them.

Jason said, "Knowing won't bring them back, but it certainly eases my mind."

"About what, Doc?"

"You."

James grinned and went for the milk and sugar. "I can appreciate your concern for Joy, but let me assure you, my brother and I were as different as night and day. She won't lack for love and attention, I can promise you that. Truth is, I adore children. I've been so busy learning my new skills, I haven't had time to do much courting, but I do hope to marry someday."

"I'm glad to hear you say that you love children, James."

Suzanne would have offered to lend him a helping hand if he ever needed her, but knowing they would be moving back to the Ypsilanti area within a month kept her from doing so. After filling James in on how to care for his niece, Jason reached for Suzanne's hand and they said their farewells.

Although tears spilled down her cheeks as they rode away,

the heavy weight of losing Joy had lifted, if only to a degree.

Suzanne stuck her head in the back door and called out, "Jason, I'm heading in to town. Do you need anything?"

He came around the corner. "Wait up. I'll ride with you."

She shook her head. "I've got several stops to make. Truth is, I'm in a hurry."

Concern swept over him. Since the morning they had taken Joy to her uncle, she'd been spending most of her days away from home. At first he had thought she was trying to keep herself so busy she wouldn't have time to think about her loss. But there were other things going on that concerned him: she was barely eating her meals, and more times than not, she would drift off during their evening studies. That wasn't like her. He didn't think she was ill because come morning, she was always raring to go again. He was, however, beginning to wonder if she were up to something. Earlier that morning he had saddled his horse and left him in his stall. Jason was determined to find out what his lovely young wife was up to.

He watched her ride away, waiting until she rounded the bend before he ran to the barn for his horse and followed her tracks. He was hot on her trail until she rode straight though town. Bill Chefan had come out of his store to greet him, and by the time Jason turned back to follow her, she was gone.

Jason needed to find her, but he didn't think it wise to ask folks questions. They might think ... he chased those thoughts out of his head and rode back home. After wearing himself out working in the barn, he grabbed the buckets and began hauling water. They could both use a warm bath tonight, and he might as well get his out of the way.

Jason was relaxing on the porch when he saw her ride in. Opting for nonchalance, he headed her way. "Did you have a good day, Suzanne?"

She dismounted, kissed him fiercely, and smiled as she said, "I had a wonderful day! How about you?"

"Intriguing ..."

"Oh?"

He wrapped his arms around her and stared into the depths of her soft blue eyes. "I have your bath ready. I'll see to Buck and be in soon to start dinner while you have a good soak."

She kissed him again, but as she let go of his shirt, her eyes twinkling with glee. "Thanks, Jason. Did anyone ever tell you that you'd make a fine wife?"

He playfully swatted her backside. "Get in there, you sassy thing, before I change my mind and douse you in the cold creek."

She giggled as she ran off to do his bidding.

Jason, though tempted to ask her for more details about her day, thought better of it. Tomorrow he would attempt to follow her again.

After almost losing her on the third day, he smiled when he reached the far side of town and caught a glimpse of her blue dress as she veered off and took the small path into the woods. She had been moving for quite a stretch before she dismounted and tied Buck's reins to a tree. Grabbing the satchel she had tied to the back of her horse, she stepped into the trees. They were out in the middle of nowhere. He didn't think she would leave without her horse, so he waited patiently in the shadows.

When she returned, something akin to fury swept over him. The little stink! He could hardly believe his eyes. *Why, she's up to her old tricks again!* She was fully clothed in her manly garb ....

Confusion swept over him. *I thought ... I thought Jesse confiscated those clothes .... Apparently not!*

Her hair was slicked back, tucked inside her shirt, and she had even taken the time to change into her brother's bluchers. As much as he wanted to confront her on the spot, he held himself in check. He would find out what she was up to before he did anything rash.

Jason stayed just out of sight. She must have heard something because she kept looking back. Either that or her guilty conscience played havoc with her mind.

The only cabin up the path she took belonged to James Jones. It wasn't hard to figure out that her detour from reality had something to do with the small bundle they had lost. His fury swiftly dissipated, but in its place was a grave concern for his wife's state of mind. When she hobbled Buck before she reached the cabin and walked in, he waited for a while and then did the same. He was able to get close enough to hear parts of her conversation with a bedraggled looking James.

"Boy, am I glad to see you!"

"I know you told me not to come back until tomorrow, but I thought I'd stop and see how your night went. From the looks of you, I'd say she didn't sleep much."

Jason's concerns mounted when James pulled his wife into the house, but he relaxed when he said, "She's all yours." The door had no sooner closed, when it reopened and James said,

"I'm going to get some sleep in the barn where it's quiet! If you need to leave before I wake up, just come get me."

"I'll be fine, Mr. Jones. You just go ahead and get your rest. You'll need it to make it through the night."

James walked away, admitting, "How well I know."

Realizing that his wife was not in harm's way, Jason turned around and headed back home. As tempting as it was to show up at the door, he decided that this confrontation should happen in their home, not here. Fortunately, Gerty was staying at her son's house awaiting the arrival of her newest grandchild.

"Hi, Suzanne," Jason said as he came in the back door. His wife was standing at the cook stove, frying the chicken he had butchered earlier. While she returned his verbal greeting, she did not look at him. After removing his bluchers, he sidled up behind her, slid his arms around her waist, and kissed her soft cheek.

Tears were standing in her eyes when she craned her neck around to kiss him.

"Suzanne, Honey, what's wrong?"

"Just having an emotional moment. I'll be fine." Unable to hold his tender gaze, she turned away and flipped the chicken.

Jason, unwilling to be put off, pushed the pan off the heat and turned her to face him. "Go and wash your hands, Suzanne. We need to talk."

"It's nothing, Jason—really!"

"Be that as it may, we still have things to discuss." Ignoring the puzzled expression on her face, he reached for two cups, filled them with tea, and carried them into the parlor.

Had he needed her help with a patient and couldn't find her? She hated having secrets between them. His disappointment in her would be great, but she had decided to tell him everything. Without trust, their marriage would crumble, and she didn't want that. Unfortunately, knowing what she needed to do did nothing to make facing him any easier. In fact, she dreaded it.

"Suzanne! Are you coming?"

Hearing her husband's call, she pulled her hanky out of her sleeve, dried her tears, blew her nose, and said, "Coming ...."

Had Jason not been watching her closely as she entered the room, he might have missed seeing that the bluchers she normally wore with her manly garb were still on her feet. And if he wasn't mistaken, she still had her jeans on! Bracing himself, he refused to give in to the overwhelming desire to laugh out loud. That would never do. He had to make her see that her deceptive ways could not go on. In this, he would not back down.

Jason's firm stance crumbled the second she fell into his lap and gave way to heart-wrenching sobs. As hard as she tried telling him what was wrong, he couldn't understand a word she said. "Honey, it couldn't be all that bad."

Apparently, it was. Minutes passed before she drew in a shuddering breath and began to calm.

Jason reached in his pocket for his clean hanky and placed it in her hand. Rubbing her back, he waited. He had never seen her this upset.

"Jason ..." she said, but she did not look up.

"Hmm?"

"I've done something ... I mean, I've been doing something ...."

When the silence trailed on, he tried to help her along. "Does this have anything to do with Joy?"

Suzanne's eyes met his. "Well, yes. But how would you know that?"

"What I know is irrelevant. You go ahead. Finish what you were about to say."

"You're not going to like it."

He was trying hard to be patient. "Just tell me."

Seconds ticked by before she summoned the courage to go on, "James Jones had a notice up at the store for part-time help."

"And?"

She blew her nose again. "When I showed up at the house, he was desperate to get some sleep, so he hired me on the spot. I know I should have talked to you about it first, but I didn't think you would let me, so I didn't ask. I'm sorry Jason! Maybe you can turn your back on her, but I had to see for myself that Joy was being cared for."

"Is she?"

Jason didn't sound angry, so she chanced a quick peek. "Yes, but that's not the worst of it."

"Oh?"

"I don't know when he had the time, but he met a young widow with a small child of her own. She's from the other side of town. They're getting married—today!"

Jason shook his head. "Sounds to me like God brought two people together who need each other. Don't you think that's a good thing, Suzanne?"

"Maybe ..."

"I would think you'd be happy for them."

"But he was so close to giving her back to us ... he even said as much."

"So we could raise her?"

"Yes. Isn't that what you want?"

Jason fingered the blond highlights in her long brown hair as he said, "Honey, you're hurting right now. All you can see is your loss, but you need to set all that aside for a minute and think this through. If you and I had children, and heaven forbid we were to die, wouldn't you want family to raise our children if they could?"

"I suppose ...."

"God's will is not always ours. When we reach out to others, it can never be about what we stand to gain. If we love as unto the Lord, we'll leave the outcome in His hands. Sounds to me like you've been trying to manipulate things to lean in our favor."

She hadn't thought of it that way. "I suppose I have."

Jason's hand covered her flat stomach. "If you'd quit falling asleep the minute your head hits the pillow, maybe someday ..."

A warm flush crept up her neck. "I'm sorry. I've been so busy watching out for Joy, I've lost sight of all that God has given me."

"And what is that?"

Her hand slid over his evening shadow. "A husband who loves me."

"More than life itself."

She snuggled closer to him, accepting the many kisses he offered.

"I want to have children of our own some day, Jason, but I'm in no hurry. To be honest, I like the idea of having you all to myself for a while."

Jason grinned. "I kind of like that idea, too. Since we're sharing our thoughts, I believe you have another confession to make, don't you ... Zanne?"

Her brow furrowed. "Zanne? Suppose I did leave that one small detail out."

"Yes, Ma'am, you did."

Her brow furrowed. "I'm curious, how did you know?"

"I followed you ...."

"You did?"

"And ..." He flipped her dress up, exposing her jeans and bluchers.

"Oh!"

"Oh, nothing! Those clothes seem to get you in all kinds of trouble. Do I need to burn them, Suzanne?"

"No ..."

"Are your Zanne days over?"

"Maybe ..."

His brow furrowed. "There's no maybe about it! You're either putting you're old ways behind you, or you're not!"

She grinned mischievously. "Amy tells me Shakespeare would have been proud to have me on his stage."

"That may be, but this little performance is going to cost you, Mrs. Michaels!"

"It is, is it?"

"Yes, Ma'am! Sin's consequences, you know."

Her blue eyes twinkled with glee. "And I'm thinking you have a specific penalty in mind?"

"Absolutely, My Dear." The room grew quiet when he drew her close, offering only a small sampling. "And, you can finish making amends after dinner. I'm starving!"

"Fine!"

"Suzanne Michaels!"

She leapt off his lap and giggled as she took off running ....

The heart-wrenching goodbyes to be said to friends and family after service weighed heavy on Suzanne as she sat next to her husband on the wooden bench Sunday morning. She held tightly to Jason's arm and for a long moment allowed her eyes to scan the room. Hattie smiled when Suzanne met her tender gaze. Oh, how she would miss her! Emmaline had promised to take good care of her. As much as Suzanne would rather see to the task herself, knowing how much Hattie loved having the Thompson children about her brought Suzanne a measure of relief. As her eyes continued on, she noted Celia's gentleness with her young daughter. She would miss the Crandall family. While she was thankful Jason did not house Ralf's stern countenance, she had come to respect and love the man as a father figure, in spite of his commanding nature. Suzanne couldn't allow herself to dwell on the Thompson family for long, or she would never make it though the service without bursting into tears. They had become so close. Her newest nieces and nephew were treasures—every one of them. Why did leaving loved ones have to be so hard? Perhaps, they could plan to come for an extended visit some time.

Mr. Crandall stood to lead the small gathering of worshipers in song. While she found his deep baritone voice a soothing presence, she could not join in just yet. Standing close to Jason offered a measure of comfort; still, her impending loss made it difficult to sing. Every time she tried, tears would catch in her throat, and the words would not flow freely.

Lord, why do I struggle so with goodbyes? First, it was

Daddy. Looking back, I can see so clearly that You had a plan. Yes, we all miss him, but his suffering is over. Josiah ... he's such a wonderful addition to our lives. Thank You, Lord, for helping me to see that. Mama needed him most, but so do we.

Suzanne watched James Jones with his new ready-made family. He looked so happy. His new son was content in his arms, and his new wife Carrie was obviously a gem. The way she doted on Joy warmed Suzanne deep within. *Thank You, Lord, for giving her parents who will love her as their own. Forgive me for trying to take matters into my own hands. You had a plan there, too, didn't You, Lord. You sure didn't need any help from me. I can see now that Your way is best. I will miss her, but knowing she is loved eases the pain of losing her.*

Jason put his hand over hers and gave it a squeeze. Although she suspected he knew she was struggling, she could not bring herself to meet his gaze. If she did, she would start to cry and never stop.

In truth, she hoped the message would be uplifting. She surely could use a good jolt of something positive—a bit of levity—anything that would distract her from this downcast mood.

Suzanne would have given much to avoid this day altogether, but she could see so clearly that God had things for her to learn in every experience. With that realization at the forefront of her mind, she might as well learn what she needed to and get it over with. Otherwise, God might allow her to go through it over and over again until she did.

Jason would remind her often that God isn't concerned with our comfort; He is, however, concerned with the condition of our heart. She, knowing this to be true, allowed her to see her Heavenly Father in a different light.

Daisytales

He Loves Me!

Chapter Thirty-three

Whatever It Takes

*I*T WAS LATE when Jason pulled the team into the Somers' barn. Glancing back at his sleeping wife, he couldn't help smiling. Suzanne appeared so young and innocent all curled up in the buckboard amongst their belongings. While he tended the horses, he let her sleep. But, when he finished and tried to lift her in his arms, she stirred.

Her eyes were still puffy, reminding him of all the tears she had shed over leaving their friends and family in Saline. "Jason, where are ..." her words trailed off when she recognized her surroundings. "We're home?" She sat up straight, but an irrepressible yawn followed, contorting her slender frame.

Jason caressed her soft cheek. "Are you all right?"

Nodding, she admitted, "I'm sure I look awful, but I really am fine. Oh, Jason, can you believe we're finally here?"

He scanned the barn, taking in the surroundings that would be home to them for years to come. Looking back at his wife, her blue eyes glistened in the lantern light as he helped her to her feet and drew her close. "It wasn't easy leaving everyone, but I'm so glad to be here."

"Do you mean it?"

He nodded, "Absolutely! I'm looking forward to putting down roots in Ypsilanti. Could be a while before our house is ready to move into ... do you mind?"

She snuggled close against him. "As long as we're together, I am home, Jason."

He sighed as his knuckles ran slowly down her face, before lifting her chin and claiming her lips in a tender wave of passion. "Have I told you lately how much I love you?"

She peered up. "A time or two, but I love you, too, and I'll never grow weary of hearing it."

"That goes both ways. We'd best head in. Unlike you, I've had no sleep. I'm about dead on my feet."

Suzanne reached for Jason's hand and eagerly pulled him along. Everyone would be sleeping right now, but she had every intention of getting her rest and being up early so they could greet her family together.

❦ ❦ ❦

"Well, well, well ... would you look who finally decided to grace us with her presence!" Jared teased as Suzanne meandered into the kitchen.

She accepted the hug he offered, admitting, "I've missed you, Jared." She reached up and ruffled his overgrown hair. "Good thing I'm here. Looks like you could use a haircut!"

He chuckled. "I could at that." Jared glanced at Jason and

asked, "Has she told you about the first haircut she gave me?"

When Jason shook his head, Jared winked at his sister. "Be thankful she learned on me instead of you. Took me months to look normal again, but my sweet tooth was good and filled!"

Jason was wondering what sweets had to do with a haircut, but a single glance at his wife's red face told him he should question her when they were alone.

Suzanne chided, "You'd better be nice, Jared Somers."

"Always! Welcome home, Sis."

Suzanne glanced around the table. Her family and Jason were already eating their noon meal. Had she really slept through breakfast? Feeling a tad bit guilty, she went on only half-apologetically, "I really did plan to be up early, but you know how it is."

"Whatever you say, Sis!" Joe offered as he stood and pulled her into his arms.

Suzanne made her way around the room and hugged everyone else before taking a seat between her husband and Louise.

Jason cupped her chin and stole a kiss before asking, "Do you feel better?"

"Yes ... just hungry." Catching her mother's eye, Suzanne asked, "Are there any leftovers from breakfast?"

Jayne pointed to the stove, "I hid some things for you under a lid on the warmer."

"Thanks!" she said as she stood and retrieved her meal. After snatching the jam jar off the pantry shelf, she reclaimed her seat and prayed silently. She could hardly wait to take a bite of her mother's luscious biscuits. No one could make them quite like she could.

Josiah and Jayne shared a knowing glance before he said, "Suzanne, Jason told us about Joy's uncle coming for her. I know you had your heart set on raising her. We're sorry for your loss."

Suzanne reached for her husband's hand, her eyes glassing over. "God had a different plan. I'm just thankful she's with folks who love her."

"We are too, Honey," Jayne reaffirmed.

Suzanne, needing a change of subject looked at Jared. "How are Jesse, Olivia, and the twins doing?"

"Jesse's holding his own, but Olivia's ornerier than ever. You know what she was like the last time she came close to delivering."

Suzanne's nose curled up. "Is she huge?"

Joe put in, "Depends on what you're comparing her with. She's not half as big as she was the first time, but she is rather lumpy."

Josiah offered. "She's had several false alarms, but she told me in no uncertain terms that she was not having this baby until the new doctor and his assistant arrived."

Suzanne was sipping her tea and started choking when she laughed suddenly.

Jason handed her his napkin. "What's so funny?"

Louise spoke for her. "When Olivia had George and Maryse, Suzanne kept her distance. She tends to faint at the sight of blood."

Jason, avoiding his wife's gaze, whispered to the inhabitants of the room. "She gets a bit queasy talking about it, too!"

Suzanne playfully smacked his arm. "That's not true anymore, Jason Michaels. I did just fine with Tandy Parker, and you know it!"

Jason, suspecting he would get clobbered again, couldn't

resist adding, "Yeah, you kept your eyes riveted on the woman's face the entire time."

Suzanne tried to pinch his leg, but he caught her hand before she could and squeezed it tight.

Louise put in, "Suzanne, with all you've been through, I thought you would have learned to respect your elders by now."

The room at large burst into laughter.

Jason's eyebrows rose into his hairline and he wasted no time reaching around his wife to tickle his little sister. "Are you trying to say I robbed the cradle, Louise?"

"Quit, Jason! She is seven years younger than you, but I was only teasing."

"I know ... my wife is a wonderful assistant, even if I do give her a hard time. Truth is, we make a good team."

"Well, we're glad to hear it!" Jayne affirmed.

Louise began clearing the food off the table, and Suzanne was gathering the dirty dishes when a rider came into the yard. Josiah reached for his cane, stood, and went to open the door.

Although Suzanne wondered how long it would be before he could walk without pain etched on his face, there were no guarantees. Josiah was not one to complain. When she asked him about it a few weeks back, he had reminded her that a bum leg was better than the alternative. She didn't have to ask what he meant, she knew. He would have died if she hadn't come along when she did.

"Henry, it's good to see you. What brings you so far out of town?"

"Wish I could say it was just a social call. Jack Bemis came by my office looking for Doc Taylor; his father is hurt bad. Did

Suzanne and the young doctor arrive?"

"They rode in late last night." Josiah opened the door so Henry could come in. "Where is Doc Taylor?"

"He and his wife had a family emergency in Chicago."

"Hope it's nothing serious."

"Couldn't say."

Overhearing parts of the conversation, Jason glanced at his wife before standing to welcome their new friend. "Who's hurt, Sheriff?"

"Mr. Bemis, a rancher on the other side of Ann Arbor. His son said he fell from a ladder and he's in a bad way. One of the bones in his leg came clean through his skin."

While Suzanne ran upstairs to get Jason's bag, Jared went to the barn to saddle their horses.

Henry and Jason were standing in the yard when Jared moved toward them with two horses. Curious, Henry asked, "Are you coming along?"

Jared shuddered. "No. Jason and Suzanne can manage just fine without any help from me."

Troubled by his admission, Henry turned away, contemplating what he should say on the matter. "I know what Bemis is like. He probably won't let Suzanne in the house, never mind tend him."

Jason scowled. Why a man in such a desperate state would choose to hold fast to his pride was beyond him! He needed Suzanne if he was going to be able to set the bone properly. The truth of the matter was, she had more experience and knowledge about setting bones than he. He didn't agree with Bemis' way of thinking, but he would have to try and honor his wishes.

When Suzanne came out of the house ready to go, Jason tucked her arm in his and took her aside for a private moment. "Honey, from what Henry has been telling me, Mr. Bemis won't let you help me anyway. You might as well stay here."

Her mouth dropped open to speak, but recalling what Mr. Bemis was like the last time she ran into him in town, she opted to keep her comment to herself. She simply kissed Jason goodbye and said, "I'll be praying for both of you."

"I know you will, Honey, and I appreciate it."

Suzanne went back into the house, helped her mother with clean up, and was hanging her apron from the hook when Jesse came in the back door and pulled her into the pantry. Confused, she asked, "What are you doing?"

"Something I never thought I would."

Now she was really curious.

Jesse cleared his throat and said rather sheepishly, "I need you to run upstairs and put on your manly garb."

Suzanne stared at him for the space of several seconds before bursting into laughter. "Funny, Jesse!" He had to be testing her. She turned to walk away, but he reached for her arm and stopped her. "I'm serious!"

Her arms spread apart in disbelief. "You told me I couldn't wear them for a year ... but I didn't listen and paid a hefty price for my deception. No thanks! I've learned my lesson. I choose God's way, so quit fooling around."

He reached for her chin and brought her gaze back to his. "Suzanne, a man's life could be at stake. I agree with you, but I don't have time to argue. Your husband stopped by my house on his way out. He couldn't elaborate because Henry was right there."

"What did he say?"

"He told me to go for Zanne, and bring him to the Bemis ranch just in case."

"In case what? Henry doesn't think he'll let me near him."

"As a woman, no. I'm sure Jason won't lie to him, but I think he's hoping he won't ask questions when he sees you in that get up."

"It's still deception, Jesse. God will never honor it."

"I know ... I hate it, but Jason ..."

Sensing her brother's duress, Suzanne simply said, "I know what you're thinking. Jason is my husband and I need to honor him. I agree. I would do almost anything for him, but not this. I have to remember whom I serve. I promised God that my days of deceiving others were over. Obedience to Him has to come first. Jason will understand. He's the one who showed me in Scripture how important this is." When Jesse only stared, she added, "God can make a way where there is no way, I've seen Him do it over and over again."

"Then we'll pray to that end."

She hugged her brother. "I can leave right now if you're ready."

"Good. Grab your warmer coat in case the temperatures drop. We'd best hurry."

Suzanne nodded in acquiescence, but she couldn't resist grumbling as she moved away. "Just when I finally come to grips with the folly of my ways ... you two try to mess with my mind!"

Chuckling, Jesse ran back to the barn and saddled their mounts, well aware that what he and Jason had asked Suzanne to do was wrong. While saving the life of a stubborn man was at the forefront of their minds, Suzanne was right. The end never justifies the means.

Suzanne and Jesse rode hard until they reached the wooded trail that led into the Bemis ranch. Jesse wasn't saying much, but she understood. They had cleared the long row of pines before Jesse interrupted her thoughts.

"The house is around the next bend." Jesse preferred to go in alone, but he refused to leave his sister on this desolate trail. "Mr. Bemis is getting up in years. Time has a way of mellowing folks out so I'm hoping he'll be more agreeable than he used to be."

"Don't worry, Jesse. God will work it out."

He smiled and shook his head. "You're something else. Dad would be proud of the woman you've become. Truth of the matter is, I am, too."

Her eyes met his. "I'll bet you weren't saying that a few months back."

His gentle smile warmed her heart. "Then, you were only thinking of yourself."

"I'm so glad God got my attention ...."

"Me, too! Suzanne, wait here for just a minute." Tying his horse to the post, he stepped up onto the porch and knocked at the door. Jesse was about to give up and just let himself in when one of the hired hands finally opened the door.

"We're busy! What do you want?"

So much for the welcome mat being laid out! The man's dreadful intolerance told Jesse he'd best get to the point and quick. "I'm Jesse Somers, the doctor's brother-in-law. I need to speak to him."

Although reluctant, the man let him in as Tom was coming out of the back room.

"We're in here, Jesse. Come on back."

Jesse was pleasantly surprised to see Tom sober. His father would need him. As Jesse entered the injured man's room, it didn't take him long to figure out that Jason was doing the best he could to make Mr. Bemis comfortable, but the man was obviously in a great deal of pain. When Jason noticed his presence, he looked relieved.

Leading Jesse out of the room, Jason whispered, "I need to speak with you alone." When they neared the parlor he asked, "Did you bring her?"

"Yes. She's outside on Star, but she came as a woman." He sighed deeply, and Jesse wondered if something had changed.

"I've been praying about this. I won't start my practice having to deceive anyone. If Bemis wants my help, he'll accept that my wife is going to be at my side."

"I'm glad to hear it," Jesse admitted, grinning as he added, "You do know she's never going to let us live this down?"

Jason chuckled softly. "I'm sure I'll still be hearing about it when I'm ninety."

"Could be ...."

"There's really no need for you to stay if you have other things to do."

Jesse opened the front door and was walking out with Jason when he said, "I have to pick up a few things in town. I'll come back by before I leave the area, just in case Suzanne wants to head home."

Jason was tying Star's reins to the post when he called out to Jesse who was moving away. "I appreciate your bringing her."

"Not a problem. I just wouldn't leave her alone with Tom

and Jack."

"Jesse!" Suzanne protested.

"*Jesse* nothing; you know better than anyone not to let down your guard with them."

Knowing her brother was right, she let it drop.

"See you in a few hours."

Jason wrapped his arms around his wife and stole a kiss before filling her in. "Our patient is in a great deal of pain. I gave him some laudanum. It should be taking effect, but either way, this isn't going to be easy."

She nodded. "What made him change his mind about me?"

"He hasn't, but I have. It wouldn't be right to try and deceive him. Besides, that's no way to begin our practice."

A single eyebrow rose. "Our practice?"

He tweaked her nose. "Yes, ours. We're a team, Suzanne. I've been praying about this since I spoke to Jesse. I was wrong to ask you to come as a man. It won't happen again."

"You were thinking of your patient, but the end doesn't justify the means, does it, Jason?"

"Not when deception is involved."

She peered up at him, her soft blue gaze full of mischief. "But you, My Dear Husband, will pay dearly for even suggesting it!"

"I figured as much ... we'd best get in there."

Her hand came to her mouth to dispel soft giggles. "You'd better hope he's asleep. You forget, Jason, I know this man. I mean no disrespect, but he's about as pigheaded as they come."

With a tilt of his head, he sent her a playful wink as he opened the door. "Oh, I don't know ... I'm quite fond of a certain woman who can dig in her heels when she's of a mind to."

"Jason Michaels! Well, I never ...."

His hand came out to swat his young wife, but he changed his mind when he caught movement out of the corner of his eye. Jack was coming out of the back room.

"Who is our lovely guest, Jason?"

Jason's arm slid around her waist. "I thought you knew each other. This is my wife, Suzanne."

It took Jack a moment to recognize her. "Your wife? Little Suzanne Somers is married?"

Jason pulled her closer, uncomfortable with the way Jack gawked at her. "Suzanne Michaels, Jack. She's no longer a Somers."

"I see ...."

Somewhat annoyed with his invasive look, Suzanne said with sarcasm oozing from her tone, "Yes, Jack! Even spunky little girls grow up!"

Jack grinned. *The years may have altered her looks, but her plucky disposition remained strong.* "Tom said you were a looker, but who would have thought you were already ... well ..." Unprepared to comment further with her husband standing so close, Jack glanced back at Jason. "Do you think the medication is working?" Without pausing, he turned back to Suzanne. "Make yourself at home, Suzanne. There's a pot of coffee on the stove. And if you get bored, feel free to start dinner. I butchered a ..."

Jason interceded, "Jack, Suzanne is not only my wife, she is my assistant. I need her to help me set your father's leg."

His features hardened. "You're wasting your time even trying, Jason. He's not going to let her near him."

With a slight tilt of his head, Jason stated. "Then he'll lose his leg because I can't set it without her help."

Jack, stunned by the young doctor's bluntness, his mouth dropped open. He looked back and forth between Suzanne and her husband, but neither of them wavered in their determination.

Suzanne, noting Jack's mounting irritation, reached out and touched his arm. "I know what your father is like, Jack. Years have passed, but my love for him has not waned. Will you at least let me try to speak with him?"

He stared at her for the space of several seconds. "You're welcome to try. I sure don't want to see him lose his leg."

Suzanne said nothing more as she whispered a prayer and moved cautiously into their patient's room. They had God's answer when they found him sleeping. She and Jason got right to work.

Three days had passed before the elderly man opened his eyes. When he did, he found the most exquisite young woman asleep in the chair next to his bed. Had he not recognized his surroundings, he might have thought she was an angel. For a time he just lay there studying her face, trying to determine who she really was and why she would be here in his room.

When his son ambled into the room, he met Tom's gaze and asked, "Did you finally find yourself a wife who'd put up with your indiscretions?"

Tom offered a wry grin. "Wishful thinking, Pa. Ain't a woman alive who'd put up with the likes of me."

His father shrugged. "There was a time she might have."

Jason was leaning back in a chair at the back of the room, resting his eyes. When he overheard their conversation, he stood and came toward them saying, "She's already taken, Mr. Bemis.

I'm Doctor Jason Michaels, and the sleeping beauty in your chair is my wife. Thanks to her expertise, you might just walk again."

A single brow rose as he said with disdain, "A woman with doctoring skills?"

Jason quickly to added, "And a heart of gold."

"A woman's place is in the home. If you're wise, you'll set her straight before it's too late."

"When we do start a family, she could want to be home. For now, she has been taking exceptional care of you. Although she hasn't mentioned why, you hold a special place in my wife's heart." Jason reached for the glass beside the bed, offering his patient a few sips.

Mr. Bemis then looked at his son. "Do I know her, Tom? She looks familiar."

Tom was about to speak when Suzanne opened her eyes and answered the elderly man, "Yes, Mr. Bemis, you do know me. I'm George and Jayne's second daughter, Suzanne."

He scowled miserably. "Why you're the little ..."

Her face lit with pleasure as she finished his sentence for him, "... Spitfire, who used to find a way to make you smile, even when you were determined to be a grouch."

His hand slid over his thick beard. "Well, if that don't beat all! Little Susie Somers. And look at you now! You've grown into a lovely young woman." He glanced at Jason. "You take good care of this one, Doc. She's a gem, she is!"

"I'll agree with you there."

"My Mary adored her."

For the first time in years, Suzanne could have sworn she

saw Mr. Bemis smile. And for a passing moment, she was a little girl again, tugging on his pant leg, begging him to hold her so that she could touch his soft, fluffy beard. She had almost forgotten how much she adored him—how much she enjoyed making him laugh. To see what he had allowed himself to become tore at her heart. It was as if the gentle man she had come to love had died with Mary, and in his place was a bitter old man who refused to release his grief.

Suzanne suddenly and painfully became aware of the person she could have become if she had allowed her father's death to destroy her. Bitterness could eat away at a person's heart leaving him or her cold and unfeeling—affecting not only the individual but also those around them.

Her father would have been heartbroken if she had allowed that to happen. *Will it ever cease to amaze me how much Your presence in my life has altered my path, Lord?*

She understood Mr. Bemis' struggle. Accepting what she could not change was not easy, but in her weakness God showed Himself strong.

Tears flooded Suzanne's eyes as she watched Mr. Bemis drift off again.

Lord, she prayed, open his eyes. Bitterness has kept him bound for far too long. Whatever it takes, Lord, reveal Yourself to him like You did me. Help him to release his grief and begin anew.

He Loves Me!

Chapter Thirty-four

Fruit That Remains

AS SUZANNE STOOD at the worktable, attempting to put a dent in the huge stack of breakfast dishes waiting to be washed, she gazed out the window in wonder. So much had transpired since she left Ypsilanti at the beginning of summer. In many ways she was not the same girl. Coming to know God had changed her view on everything. His love broke through her tough barriers. She would always look back on this journey with a mixture of trepidation, heartache, and joy, but she had no regrets. How could she? Not only had she come to know the peace that passes all understanding, her rescuer had become her cherished husband! So much had taken place to bring her to this place of undeniable contentment.

As frightful as it was to be thrown into jail for a crime I did not commit, I can see so clearly why it happened. You were trying to get my attention, weren't you, Lord? Now I see so many things that should have given me a clear view of

You while I was growing up, but I was blind to all of them. I heard Your Word spoken on numerous occasions. Until I saw the affect my sin was having on others and myself, I could not receive the life and love You were offering. Thank you for the godly influence Jason has had on me. You used him to help me see the error of my way.

Had I not been thrown into jail, I would be in New York with Amy instead of being married to Jason. My greatest nightmare became one of my greatest blessings. Thank you, Lord. What a travesty it would have been to miss out on all that our union will bring!

The days of summer had marked a vast change in her life here in Ypsilanti. With the coming of each new season, more changes would occur, but she was no longer afraid to face them. With God, she knew all things were possible. Her anxious soul had finally found rest.

Autumn was quickly coming to a close. While it saddened her to see the colorful leaves turning an earthen brown and giving way to winter's dismal presence, she looked forward to all that the new season would bring. Winter, a time of rest and revitalizing, was necessary. All too soon, spring would be here, and the cycle of life would begin anew.

Suzanne's eyes lit with pleasure when her husband smiled up at her as he passed the window. Her heart still leapt at the sight of him, and, oh, how she prayed it would always be so. When Jason stuck his head in the back door, she teased, "What have you been up to all morning, Mister?"

"Much!"

She looked into his sparkling eyes, and noting his

pleasure, she knew something was up.

"Suzanne, grab your sweater. Jesse showed me the perfect spot for our new home. I'm hoping you'll agree."

Her insides were all in a whirl, as she turned to meet her mother's gaze. The dishes were almost done, but Suzanne hated to leave when she had promised to help. "Do you mind?"

Jayne shooed her away with her floured hands. "Go ahead, Suzanne. I've been tending things without you for this long, another day won't make a difference."

"As long as you're sure ...?"

Jayne's expression told a story all its own. "I am quite sure." Jayne watched Suzanne take her sweater off the hook, put it on, and secure the buttons before she asked, "Do me a favor will you? Stop by and ask Olivia if they'll come for supper. I saw Kaleb earlier, and they're all coming."

"I'd be glad to."

Jayne peered out the window as her daughter walked out the door. She couldn't resist spying on the newlyweds. Suzanne, hardly containing her elation, flounced down the back steps, stood on her toes to kiss her husband, and then reached for his hand. Jayne adored her children, and seeing them with mates who loved them made her heart sing.

After covering the dough so it could rise, she washed her hands in the sudsy water and headed toward her room for her sweater. Apples were plentiful this fall and Josiah had mentioned that he had a hankering for pie. She had an inkling the rest of her family would agree. Although the cold cellar was filled to the brim with the succulent fruit, she picked up her basket and headed toward the trees. The apples that remained were sure to be good and sweet.

❀ ❀ ❀

"Where are you taking me, Jason?" Suzanne questioned.

Although his wife's elation was more than apparent, he gave nothing away. Jesse was coming toward them, so Jason said, "Why don't you ask your brother?"

Suzanne's cheerfulness spilled forth as she ran into Jesse's open arms and hugged him tightly.

"I take it you're glad to see me, Sis?" His eyes twinkled as he reached up and caressed her face.

"I'm always glad to see you, Jesse. Why would you ever doubt it?"

He winked playfully. "Oh, I don't know. I can recall a few times you weren't so very happy to see me!"

She purposefully bumped into him. "Be nice. Those days are passed. I'm not a little girl who needs her brother to set her on the straight and narrow. I'm a grown woman with a husband who loves me and wants to build me a house. So tell me, where is this perfect setting?"

His sheepish grin only added to her excitement. "Come on. I'll show you, but you and Jason will have to promise to be good neighbors, or I'll rescind my offer to let you live so close."

"Close? What are you saying?"

"You'll have to wait to find out!"

Suzanne's curiosity peeked, but when she glanced back

at her husband, he, like Jesse, gave nothing more away.

Jesse had to make a quick stop off at his house. After greeting Olivia, Suzanne and Jason stooped down and tried to coax their niece and nephew to come to them. In their reluctance, they held fast to their mother's legs.

George was the first to let go. He giggled as he ran to Jason, who swung him up and whirled him around. Maryse, a bit more hesitant, peered up at her mother with uncertainty.

Olivia cupped her little chin and warned, "You'd best give Aunt Suz some of your girly germs, or she is going to tickle you until you do, Maryse!"

That was all she needed to hear. Tittering, the little dolly ran to Suzanne. After hugging her tightly, she grazed Suzanne's cheek with a sweet kiss.

Instantly, Suzanne's eyes glassed over. Maryse was so precious, and thinking about her living nearby filled her with joy. "Maryse, would you and George like to go for a walk with us?"

George was quick to respond, "Yep ... Papa say so!"

Suzanne took a gander at her husband. It was no secret that the children called their grandfather Papa, and since he was not present, nor had he been all morning, her mind began putting pieces of the puzzle together.

"What else did Papa tell you, Maryse?"

The child was about to speak when Jesse sent her a stern look. "Maryse ... we don't tell surprises, remember?"

Her lower lip came out. "Member ...."

Suzanne tickled her sides, saying, "It's okay, Honey. Daddy isn't mad at you. He just knows how hard it is for the

Somers girls to keep a secret."

To prove her point, Jesse came and kissed his daughter's cheek. Her tender heart never ceased to amaze him. George though a good boy for the most part, he had a stubborn streak a mile long. Maryse, on the other hand, sought to please him. He could only hope that she would never change.

Sensing a set up, Suzanne's blue-eyed gaze met Jesse's as she tauntingly added, "Daddy has something he wants to show me ... and I have a sneaking suspicion he and Uncle Jason have something they're not telling me."

Jason, needing to alter his wife's intent, met his sister-in-law's watchful gaze. "So tell me, Olivia, how are you?"

Willing to play along, Olivia's hand splayed across her stomach. "Other than running out of room, I'm feeling fine, but I am getting anxious to see this little one."

Jason nodded. "Doesn't look like you'll have long to wait."

"Since you two are here, tonight would suit me just fine. I'm tired of being fat!"

Anxious to get everyone moving, Jesse reached for his wife's hand. "Come on, Liv. You're welcome to waddle along with us. Who knows, the walk might do you some good."

She swatted his arm. "What are you saying, Mister Smarty Pants?"

Jesse kissed her cheek. "Now don't read more into it than there is. You know I love you just the way you are."

Olivia, realizing that her children were hanging on their every word, swallowed the retort hanging on the tip of her tongue and simply kissed her husband instead.

Jason, while he enjoyed their lighthearted bantering, had no intention of missing Suzanne's reaction to their surprise.

However, Suzanne was so busy talking to Jesse when they entered the clearing, it took her a moment to realize that Josiah, Jared, Kaleb, and Joe were stepping off the front porch of a good-sized cabin—a cabin that was not there the last time she was in Ypsilanti. Suzanne's gaze immediately fell back on her husband, but Josiah's words brought her baffled look to him. "Well, what do you think?"

"Think?" Suzanne managed. When she noticed that her brothers and father-in-law all wore the same odd expression, she recalled what the family had done for Kaleb and Elizabeth and wondered ...

When she didn't respond, Josiah asked, "What do you think of the setting, Suzanne? Will it do?"

Suzanne finally found her tongue. "Are you saying ..." she paused long enough to spin around and look at Jesse, "is the house ours? Did you guys ..?"

He nodded. "We've been very busy since you two left."

They all knew the moment the lights went completely on, because Suzanne squealed out loud. When her heart finally stopped fluttering, she turned to her husband. "Jason, did you know?"

"Absolutely! They even let me help with a few of the finishing touches. Could take me a lifetime to pay them back for all they've done, but I certainly appreciate all their hard work."

Noting the glint in her husband's eye, she prodded, "And ..."

He leaned closer and spoke for her ears alone, "And I like the idea of having you all to myself."

Suzanne offered no verbal response, but her cheeks turned a nice shade of cherry. Hoping no one would notice, she led the way toward the house.

Josiah said, as they moved up onto the porch, "We figured you two would be so busy taking care of this growing family and the neighbors who have already gotten wind of there being a doctor in Ypsilanti, that you wouldn't have time to build a home, so we did it for you. We couldn't allow anything to keep you from putting down roots, now could we?"

Suzanne laughed with glee when Jason released George's little fingers, took Maryse from her arms, and set Maryse on the ground before swinging Suzanne up into his arms so he could carry her across the threshold of their new home.

Jason held Suzanne closely in their new parlor and kissed her tenderly. When he spoke, he only had eyes for her, but his heartfelt words were meant for all to hear, "It's our prayer that the roots we put down will not only be intertwined with all of yours, they will run so deep that George Somers' godly legacy will be passed down from generation to generation."

Quick tears filled Suzanne's eyes. It was so important to her that her father's legacy not be forgotten. How did Jason know? Glancing at Jesse, she wondered if he had said something to him, but then she realized it really didn't matter.

A peaceful reverence filled the room when Josiah added, "Fruit that remains."

Joe asked, "That's the passage from John, isn't it, Pa?"

"Yes, Son .... I can't tell you how much I thought about that verse when I was interviewing potential husbands for my Olivia. And look at all that God has done since then. Because I took the time to seek wisdom from God, instead of caving in to my fears and letting my circumstances destroy me, God has blessed me far beyond what I could have asked for or imagined."

Jesse was curious, "Pa, do you know the verse by heart?"

"Oh, yes! *Ye have not chosen me, but I have chosen you, and ordained you, that ye should go and bring forth fruit, and that your fruit should remain: that whatsoever ye shall ask of the Father in my name, he may give it you.*"

Suzanne, seeing tears in her pa's eyes, wrapped her arms around him and hugged him tightly. When she tried to tell him again how sorry she was for shunning him at first, his hand came gently to her mouth.

"Without the struggles in this life, Suzanne, how will we ever know the joy of victory?"

"I suppose ...."

Jason pulled her back into his arms and held her close. "I suppose! Is that all you have to say, Mrs. Michaels?"

Knowing where this conversation was going, she leaned over and whispered in his ear, "Can we talk about this later ... when we're alone, Jason?"

He nodded, and the tour began ....

Suzanne and Jason were relaxing by the hearth in their new home, skimming over their journals and discussing their latest entries, when she heard something outside. The same noise distracted her from their studies a second time, so she asked, "Did you hear that, Jason?"

When he only nodded, unmoved, she stood and moved cautiously toward the window. The wind was whipping through the trees; the limbs were swishing frantically about; bats were swooping looking for food; but nothing else seemedout of the ordinary.

Jason, stood and joined her at the window, trying to reassure her, "More than likely, it's just a raccoon or a possum."

"Perhaps!" she admitted, but she wasn't convinced.

Taking a closer look, Jason pointed up the way. "Your culprits are right over there, Suzanne." He chuckled softly. The Somers' tomcat had just pounced on one of the females, who screeched in protest and took off running.

Jason cupped her chin and brought her gaze back to his. "Come and sit with me, Suz." When she didn't readily respond, he added, "The creatures of the night are merely taunting you, Honey, keeping you from enjoying this wonderful blessing. Our family went out of their way to build us this beautiful home. We're finally alone. Maybe that old tomcat has the right idea. Snuggling with my wife sounds nice."

Her tentative gaze met his. While his adoring look did appeal, she was not readily drawn in. After a few more starry-eyed scans of the yard, she set her discomfiture aside and complied.

Leaving her journal and Bible where they lay on the table, Jason reclaimed his seat, and she curled up in his lap, sighing deeply. There was no place on earth she'd rather be than in his soothing embrace, finding comfort in the sound of his voice as he read his notes aloud.

"In understanding the battles of life, the right perspective is what brings victory." He was flipping through his Bible looking for the next passage.

For a time, she was lost in her own ruminations as she stared into the burning embers. "It's so true, Jason. When my mother told me she was going to remarry, I was sickened by the thought. I couldn't see what Josiah would bring to this family. All I could see is what her marriage would do to my father's memory. Losing him was horrible enough. I refused to stand by and watch another man try to take his place. That's why I left home in the first place."

Her words were so filled with sorrow.

Needing to be closer, he rested his forehead on hers. "Your resentment and pain clouded the way you viewed your circumstances. All of us have been there at one time or another, Honey."

Peering into his face filled with love brought tears to her eyes. "But I wasn't just running from my family, Jason, I was running from God."

His expression held not the slightest measure of judgment. "You didn't have a chance. God loves you too much to ever let you go. And besides, your family was holding you up before the Lord. So was I, after you were put in my care."

"I should have known. Looking back, I can see so clearly how God used you, Jason. Being arrested on false charges frustrated and terrified me. I was glad to be out of that jail, but the thought of having to spend a year with a strange man did nothing to ease my mind."

Jason was not surprised by her admission. "Did our discussion in the sheriff's office help?"

"No! If anything it made me feel trapped. Amy's religion I could handle. You, on the other hand, are a living example of faith. It's a part of who you are. I left home to get away from God. Then you insisted on me going to church, taking notes, and studying the Scriptures. It was like you were issuing me another jail sentence!"

He chuckled softly. "I learned that trick from an expert."

Her brow furrowed. "Who?"

"My father did the same thing to me when I told him I didn't believe in God the way he did anymore. God's Word does have a way of changing hearts, doesn't it?"

"Fruit that remains .... I take it your father was a man of God like mine."

Jason's eyes glassed over in remembrance as he met her tender gaze. "That he was."

"If I hadn't been arrested, I wouldn't have you in my life. So how can I regret the trials I went through to bring us to where we are?"

"God had a plan, didn't He, Suz?" She peered up at him, and for a time they were swept away by a gentle wave of passion.

As Suzanne caressed his evening shadow, concern etched her lovely face. "So tell me, Jason, what are we going to tell our children when they ask us how we met?"

His deep hearty laugh sent her dander to flaking. "It's not that funny, Jason ...."

As hard as he tried to hold it in, another small chuckle escaped. "I'm sorry, Honey. I wish I could tell you otherwise, but it is funny!"

"But, Jason," she whined, "what are we going to tell them?"

Sounding all too much like the doctor he was, Jason opted for honesty, "We have time to think about it. As it stands right now though, I'm hoping they won't ask."

"Fine!" she declared as she leapt off his lap and moved just out of reach.

"Suzanne Michaels ..." he gently admonished.

With a roll of her eyes, she tauntingly mocked, "What, Jason Michaels?"

He patted his leg, fully expecting her to come and pay the penalty for her crime.

She might be stepping out on a limb, but she could not comply. Suddenly her insides were all in a flutter. While contemplating her next words, she had, in fact, opened her mouth to speak when he spoke instead. "You know, Suz, for a woman who usually runs when she gets herself into a tight spot, you're living on the edge tonight."

"True ... but *a heart takes flight* for many different reasons, Jason." The twinkle in her soft blue eyes did not go undetected.

"Care to elaborate?"

"I'll admit I do tend to flee when I get scared—or when I'm uncertain about what I'm facing—or even when I'm annoyed with my husband."

"That is true, but you're forgetting where the victory lies." His tempestuous blue eyes held a flicker of light. He was not angry, just determined to claim his due. His words only confirmed her suspicions. "You have a debt to pay, My Dear, and I'm waiting."

Timidity washed over her. "So ... are you saying the victory lies in my willingness to yield?"

"Only when we're willing to surrender all, My Love, will we truly be one as God intended."

"Hmm ... all, you say?" she thoughtfully reiterated as her finger came to her mouth.

"To the Lord and to each other, Suzanne." Jason's heart overturned with love for his wife as she gazed longingly at him. When the distance separating them became too much, he stood and gathered her to him. "So, what do you say, Mrs. Michaels?"

She smiled and kissed the tip of his nose before finding his lips and sampling their sweetness. "Surrendering to the man I love sounds wonderful to me, Doctor Michaels."

Without an ounce of reserve, Jason swept her off her feet and spun slowly around. Perhaps it was the gentleness of their touch, the warmth in their eyes, or their passionate kisses that came one right after the other, but in this they were in one accord. By surrendering all, they found love and so much more ....

Epilogue

August 1834

*S*UZANNE AWOKE ABRUPTLY. Someone was banging on the door. "Jason!" she called out above the din. When he offered no response, she nudged him.

"Hmm ..." he said, and then only rolled over, so she shook him.

"The door, Jason. Someone is at the door!"

"Who is it?"

She started to giggle. "Jason! How am I supposed to know? I'm not going to the door in my unmentionables in the middle of the night."

"All right," he droned, as he pulled himself out of bed.

Lighting the lamp, he stuck his feet into his slippers and went to the door. He was not surprised to find Jesse on the other side.

Without so much as an apology for waking him, Jesse announced, "It's time, Doc!"

Jesse's words did the trick. Jason was suddenly wide-awake. "How far apart are her pains?"

"They're practically on top of each other!"

Hearing distress in her brother's voice, Suzanne secured her robe and came out of their room.

"Suzanne," Jason said as he slid his feet into his bluchers, "put your boots on while I grab my bag. The baby is coming quickly."

The three of them ran all the way. It was a good thing they did, because Maryse and George were on the bed with Olivia, sobbing. They were too young to understand their mother's painful condition. Although Olivia tried her best to comfort them, her pains were coming fast and furious.

"Suzanne," Jason suggested, "maybe you should take the children upstairs and tell them stories."

"That's fine." Suzanne met Olivia's gaze as Jesse peeled the children off their mother and handed them to his sister. "We'll be praying, Olivia."

Suzanne didn't wait for an answer; another contraction hit, and she needed to get the children out of earshot.

"Mama ..." they cried, as they left the room reaching out for her. But hurting children were Suzanne's specialty. She had them settled before they reached the stairs. While climbing up to their room, she asked, "So, my little darlings, which story is it going to be tonight?"

George's brow furrowed, and he was quick to set her straight. "Me's not dar-in, Aun Suz. Me's George ...."

She bounced him just a bit. "I know you're George, silly, and your sister is Maryse, but you will always be my little darlings!"

"No me not!" George firmly avowed.

"Well ... if you're going to be such a stick in the mud, I suppose I'll have to call you George and Maryse."

When he appeared satisfied, she got them settled in their bed and asked, "So ... tell me George and Maryse, after we pray for Mama, what is it going to be? Shall I tell you the story of Slimy Salamander and Slippery Frog? Or ..."

They both giggled, and their heads bobbed up and down. There was no need for Suzanne to come up with another title to tempt them.

After praying for their mother and new brother or sister, the story began to unfold before them. In fact, George and Maryse had been searching the muddied edge of the pond for several minutes with Auntie Suzanne before they happened upon their two new friends.

Maryse was the first to spy Slimy Salamander wallowing in the mud. Slimy Salamander immediately accepted Maryse's offer to go off on an adventure with them. And, lo and behold, it was only seconds later when George found Slippery Frog hopping merrily in circles on the bank. Slippery Frog was so busy making frog prints in the mud that he never saw Georges approach and jumped straight up in the air when George asked, "Want to go splor-in, Swippery Frog?"

The five of them had been on quite an adventure before they called it a day. George, Maryse, and their new friends Slimy Salamander and Slippery Frog were growing very sleepy. When they placed their imaginary new friends on a floating lily pad, Slimy Salamander and Slippery Frog immediately laid their weary heads down, said their farewells, and drifted out onto the pond.

George and Maryse snuggled into their quilts and closed their eyes while Suzanne lulled them off to sleep with several lullabies.

Suzanne stayed with the children for a while longer to be sure they would not awaken. Their angelic little faces brought tears to her eyes. They were so precious, and she was so thankful to have the opportunity to play an active part in their little lives.

Suzanne made her way back downstairs and bustled into the bedroom just as Jason was handing Jesse and Olivia their new baby girl. The joy that filled their faces was a sight to behold!

In so many ways, Jesse had been a wonderful father to her. To be here as God added to their family was a gift she would treasure.

Impulsively, her hand splayed across her own stomach. She had been reading everything she could find in Jason's medical books about this miraculous event, trying to gain a clearer understanding so that she could help other women who were laboring. But suddenly, she was curious. How would she feel if and when her time came? Although she was in no hurry, she couldn't help but wonder.

After helping Olivia get cleaned up and settled, she looked down at her niece and tears flooded her eyes. "She's so beautiful ... and look at all that dark hair—just like her papa."

Olivia met her husband's tender gaze. "She is beautiful, isn't she, Jesse?"

"Just like her mama." Jesse admitted.

Olivia beamed in the light of his comment, but she couldn't resist teasing him, "Your opinion is biased."

"True, but my opinion is the only one that matters on the subject. So tell me, Liv, are we in agreement on her name?"

Her mouth curved up. "Yes ..."

Suzanne couldn't stand the suspense. "Are you going to tell us?"

Jesse's eyes lit with pleasure. "Jayne Ruth ..."

A bit surprised, Suzanne confirmed, "After Mom and Kaleb's Mom?"

"Yes ... we got to thinking about how our families came to know each other. I'm sure you've heard Ruth's story."

"Mom was telling me ... hard to believe, isn't it?"

"I'll agree with you there. Ruth, out of desperation, started going to a meeting where Dad just happened to be preaching. She and Mom became friends right off. One thing led to another and eventually our families were inseparable. Jayne Ruth may not be poetic, but to us it's a perfect name for our daughter."

Jason wanted to hear more, but his patients were drifting off. He and Suzanne needed to leave them alone so they could rest.

"Jesse, we'll be back in a few hours to play with the children and make breakfast. Come for me if you have any concerns."

Jesse followed them to the door. "I will. Thanks again for all you've done."

Jason spoke for both of them. "It was our pleasure."

As they headed home, Jason wrapped his arm around his shivering wife. The air was cool and while the sun had not risen above the puffy clouds, a faint wedge of moon guided them along the wooded path.

"Does it ever cease to amaze you how meticulous God is, Jason?"

"No ... just look at little Jayne. She is beautiful, isn't she?"

"Yes ... God's Word says that He knew her before she was ever formed in her mother's womb ...."

Jason pressed his lips to her forehead. His wife's mind was always filled with wonder. "Tomorrow I'd like to hear the rest of the story about Ruth."

"All right .... Jason, do you think God knew before she was born how much Ruth would suffer before her husband found Christ?"

"He knows all things, Suzanne. We live in a fallen world. Although God has promised to be with us no matter what we face, we must take the first step and call out to Him. Unfortunately, we take matters into our own hands, and things happen along our journey that God has nothing to do with. Have you noticed that He often uses our trials to get our attention—or to teach us something?"

"Like He did with me in that jail cell ...."

"We both had much at stake that day. Every time I hold you I'm reminded of how close I came to denying Amy's request. Had I not been willing to listen to that still small voice and take you on, I would have missed my greatest blessing, Suzanne."

When her soft blue eyes met his, Jason could no longer restrain his desire to hug her. He drew her close for an amazing kiss, but when that was not enough, he swept her off her feet. "You've told me on several occasions, My Love, that *a heart takes flight* for many reasons. At this moment mine is flapping quite wildly!"

She giggled softly. "You're not alone. Kiss me one more time the way you just did, and I'm sure mine will be flying."

"Just one more?"

Her slender fingers slid into his flaxen hair. "One after another, My Love, and our hearts will soar as one ...."

He Loves Me!

The Michigan Chronicles

Donna's signature series, *The Michigan Chronicles*, is fiction at its best, with purpose.

As one reader tells us:

> *"Donna Rhine has a gift for writing stories that entertain and warm your heart, while teaching moral and Biblical principles. Her works may be fictional, but she has a real relationship with the Lord, as evidenced in every book she writes."*
>
> K. MacDonald

Book 1

A Decision of the Heart

He said her heart was a gift that only she could give ... *Could she?*

Not just a moving story of faith rising above suffering, slander, and life's circumstances, it's about a tender love that begins with a decision -

A Decision of the Heart

www.amazon.com/dp/0615455336
6x9 Paperback: 478 pages
Kindle Book

The Michigan Chronicles

Book 2

A Heart of Joy

When her impending loss plunges her into an uncertain future, her faith will be tested as never before ....

A moving saga of overcoming faith, it's also a heatwarming romance filled with adventure that ultimately leads to:
A Heart of Joy!

www.amazon.com/dp/0615466060
6x9 Paperback: 450 pages
Kindle Book

Book 3

A Heart Takes Flight

Will exposing the truth send her back to jail or into the arms of love?

A life changing story of God's abounding Grace and love's powerful influence - filled with intrigue, romance, and so much more ....

www.amazon.com/dp/0615486665
6x9 Paperback: 464 pages

The Michigan Chronicles

Book 4

A Heart Set Free

Her trials led to surrender. Could they also lead to her greatest blessings?

An an intriguing love story that evokes the heart's greatest passions, exposing the degradation of abuse in the light of God's Word — the power of God's redeeming love.

www.amazon.com/dp/0692021906
6x9 Paperback: 411 pages

Quick Note from Donna,

Thank you for all your continued support.

If this book has blessed you please let me know. Your comments and insights are both encouraging and enlightening. So often your input comes at a much needed time.

My hope and prayer is that my books have helped you get a little closer to the awsome God we serve.

My email: **donna@daisytales.com**

Other Works by Donna Rhine

In addition to Donna's popular series, *The Michigan Chronicles,* she has co-authored other books. Some of these titles include:

- *Still Dancing* - Gabriel Ford's autobiography shares the inspirational details of her life as a way of encouraging others yo move beyond their struggles and know that anything is possible.

- *Silent Tears, Loud Victory* - This heart wrenching story of one little girl's survival of abuse and her jourrney to become a woman of God. Edith Eddins reminds us that with God in our hearts, not only can we overcome horrific tragedy, we can forgive even the most deplorable sin and shine in the world as an example of His all-encompassing love.

You can find these and other works by Donna Rhine on Amazon.com by typing her name (Donna Rhine) in the search bar. Additional titles are in development, soon to be released.

Armoury House Publishing

Armoury House Publishing is dedicated to equipping of the saints through the printed word and other electronic media. Our mission is to draw all people one step closer in their personal relationship with Jesus Christ

Other Titles published by Armoury House Publishing:

Old Paths Series by John Charles Ryle

JC Ryle's conversational style of writing is easy to grasp and understand. Deep enough for the oldest of saints to find healthy portions of meat but lean enough to feed the new born Christian.

INSPIRATION of the Bible

How was the Bible written? Where did it come from ... Heaven? or of man? To what extent is God's word really God's Word? What do we mean when we say the Bible is inspired by God? How do the answers to these questions impact the way we live?

www.amazon.com/dp/1497476283
5x8 Paperback: 64 pages

OUR HOPE - The 5 Marks of a Good Hope

How do you distinguish a good hope from a mistaken hope that ultimately ends in a lie? Bishop Ryle gives us five characteristics of a good hope to follow.

www.amazon.com/dp/1499229798
5x8 Paperback: 48 pages

Old Paths Series (continued)

PERSEVERANCE

One of the most misunderstood topics of God's Word.

www.amazon.com/dp/1497590728
5x8 Paperback: 87 pages

KNOWING GOD THE HOLY GHOST

What place has God the Holy Ghost in your religion? What do you know of His office, His work, His indwelling, His fellowship, and His power?

www.amazon.com/dp/1499317018
5x8 Paperback: 76 pages

ALIVE OR DEAD?

By far one of JC Ryle's best talks. A topic deserving our full attention. What does God say?

This is a great read for every Christian. A good book to pass on to those who are searching for an answer to life's biggest question, are you among the living, or among the dead?

www.amazon.com/dp/1497554136
5x8 Paperback: 54 pages

C.H. Spurgeon Works

Plain Advise For Plain People

The wit and wisdom of one of the greatest men of the 19th century. Formerly published as "John Ploughman's Talk."

Spurgeon spans the denominational lines. His focus being that *"good wisdom is that which will turn out to be wise in the end; seek it, friends, and seek it at the hands of the wisest of all teachers, the Lord Jesus."*

John Ploughman

www.amazon.com/dp/1796309044
6x9 Paperback: 165 pages

These and other Armoury House Publishing books are available on Amazon.com and other on-line book distributors.

Thank you.

Armoury House Publishing
P.O. Box 60
Carleton, MI 48117   USA

No god is like you, O Lord.
No one can do what you do.

Psalm 86:8
GOD'S WORD Translation